GW00319761

About the author

Shadleigh T. Brown is a South African born writer and a long-time resident of London's renowned East End. His in-depth, first-hand knowledge of the city, and its underworld culture, allows him to immerse the reader in stories set against the backdrop of one of the world's great capitals.

Shadleigh T. Brown

The Sins of the Fathers

Vanguard Press

VANGUARD PAPERBACK

© Copyright 2023
Shadleigh T. Brown

The right of Shadleigh T. Brown to be identified as author of
this work has been asserted by him in accordance with the
Copyright, Designs and Patents Act 1988.

A CIP catalogue record for this title is
available from the British Library.

ISBN 978-1-80016-691-2

This is a work of fiction. Names, characters, businesses, places, events and incidents are
either the products of the author's imagination or used in a fictitious manner. Any
resemblance to actual persons, living or dead, or actual events is purely coincidental.

Vanguard Press is an imprint of
Pegasus Elliot Mackenzie Publishers Ltd.
www.pegasuspublishers.com

First Published in 2023

Vanguard Press
Sheraton House Castle Park
Cambridge England

Printed & Bound in Great Britain

The Lord is of great mercy, forgiving iniquity and transgression, and by no means clearing the guilty, visiting the iniquity of the fathers upon the sons.

Num. 14.

PROLOGUE

The monster sat silently in the darkness. The quiet was disturbed by the drone of an occasional passing car or by the distant voices of jubilant pedestrians making their way home after a night out. Lockdown had ended. He swayed gently as if a slow song played in his head. Reaching back slightly, he ran his hand along the young girl's body, feeling her torn and broken flesh through the thin latex glove. He breathed in deeply through his nostrils, held his breath for a second and then exhaled. The air in the room was infused with the odour of blood and death. He remained sitting on the edge of the bed savouring the atmosphere. A ticking clock marked the seconds. He was not unaware of the brutality of his actions. The world would see them as abhorrent. Yet the blame was not his to bear. Eventually he stood and reached down to find the switch for the side lamp. The bright bulb lit the room. His lips curled when his gaze found the girl's father hanging from the wall like a grotesque display of gothic art. The man's lifeless eyes were still fixed on the bed where his daughter lay.

He rolled his wrist and looked at the illuminated dials on the otherwise black timepiece. Dawn was approaching. It would soon be time to retreat into the shadows. He had one more task to complete. He lifted a compact black backpack from the floor. Unzipping a side pouch, he removed a small, clear plastic packet and held it to the light.

It had been effortless to access the detective's house to harvest the samples needed. The house had been poorly secured and had not been cleaned in some time. Amongst the debris of a human life there had been many remnants of what had once formed part of a body – discards that contained a genetic code, the blueprint that instructed Mother Nature in the construction of a particular individual. He reached into the packet and carefully removed a fine strand of hair. Turing back to the bed, he lifted the girl effortlessly with one hand and carefully placed the hair beneath her right shoulder. He lay her lifeless body back on the bed, then extracted another single hair and placed it on her bruised and bloodied neck.

After years of preparation, of patiently waiting, the time had come. He was the weapon that could finally be unleashed. The sword that would strike them down. The instrument of her vengeance. He knew that she would never find peace until he was done. The wounds that disfigured her gentle soul would never heal. Their pain would be the remedy to cure her. Their blood, and the blood of those they loved, would wash the darkness from her and leave her whole and pure again.

CHAPTER ONE
Killing Time

Detective Chief Inspector Frank Palmer stepped through the white awning that had been erected at the front of the house onto the wet pavement. He stripped off the disposable white coverall and the damp shoe covers and handed them to the sullen-faced officer guarding the entrance. The light mist amplified the blue and red lights rotating on the roofs of several vehicles that were parked along the barricaded road. The street was lined on one side with terraced houses and on the other by semi-detached dwellings. Beyond the residences the open expanse of Victoria Park was visible. Despite the rain and the constant, "move along, folks, there is nothing to see here", of half a dozen uniformed officers, a crowd, absent of any social distancing, had gathered along the police cordons. Their curious faces were covered by masks of varying design. The new normal.

The onlookers whispered among themselves in muted tones. They knew that something terrible had happened. They speculated as to what horror the Barkers' housekeeper had discovered at number forty-seven. The street was usually quiet. It traversed a secure neighbourhood that consisted mostly of restored Victorian properties. The rapid gentrification of many areas in East London had created pockets of exclusive housing that seemed a world apart from the council estates which had once dominated many of the city's working class areas. Situated along the northern end of Victoria Park, the area had become affluent. The typically yellow brick properties, unaffordable to most, now housed investment bankers, share traders and other City elite.

Palmer stood in the road outside the Mobile Command Centre and let the cool air wash over him. The scene inside the house had been as gruesome as any he had seen in his many years on the force. It had been made worse by the fact that he had known the victims. The detective was aware that these murders would be the catalyst for a tsunami of violence that would engulf the city's underworld.

The world had changed. Not in the slow incremental way that was the product of time passing, but rapid change. The pandemic had required an immediate modification to human behaviour. Things taken for granted had quickly become unlawful. The simple acts of visiting a neighbour or travelling long distance. The sight of people in masks had become mundane. An invisible enemy had been haunting the world's population. It had destroyed economies and families, with equal vigour. The tide seemed to be turning. Metropolises such as London were slowly waking from a year's slumber.

The detective removed his mask and rubbed his hands over his face, trying to dispel the lingering hangover that clouded his thoughts. Billy Barker had been a villain, renowned for his love of expensive cars, designer suits and armed robbery. What remained of him now was a bloodied mess hanging by six-inch nails from his bedroom wall. His murder, while brutal, was nominal when compared to what his twelve-year-old daughter had suffered. Her broken body lay across her parents' blood-soaked bed like a discarded rag. Beside the bed laid the body of her mother, her face fixed in a cold lifeless stare. Evidence of the terror that she had felt before she had been mercifully dispatched by a single gunshot. While the walls, floor and even the ceiling of the master bedroom were stained with red streaks, pools of congealing blood, and fragments of flesh, every other room in the lavishly refurbished Victorian home had been left in an immaculate state. Billy's wife had had taste, supported by a boundless stream of cash that needed spending.

DCI Frank Palmer had known Billy Barker for almost forty years. Although he had been a career criminal, he had not been prone to needless violence. He could hold his own and had been a skilled boxer. He had been feared. Not in his own right, but because he had been the younger and only brother of Jack Barker or, as he was more often referred to, Big Jack. Big Jack Barker was a ruthless villain who had worked his way through the ranks of the London underworld, annihilating anyone and anything that had stood in his way, until he had become the wealthiest and most feared criminal in the city. Unlike his now late brother, Jack Barker revelled in violence.

Frank Palmer had grown up with the Barker brothers on the tough streets of London's East End. They had come from dirt-poor working class families, with fathers who had drunk too much, worked too little, and used their fists too often. Their common experiences of maltreatment and neglect had forged a bond between them as young boys, as they had tried to make sense of the world around them. Beneath the surface they knew that the men that they had become would always be tainted by their past. Nature versus nurture was a flawed debate. A person's nature was often the result of their nurturing, or lack thereof.

'Frank?' Patrick Casey's voice startled Palmer. 'Are you okay, mate? You look like shit,' the grey-haired pathologist opined in his usual direct manner. He looked genuinely concerned by the chief inspector's appearance.

Palmer was a tall man with a broad, handsome face. At forty-seven he still had an athletic, muscular physique, the result of countless hours spent in a boxing gym. But time, which had so far been kind to him, appeared to be having a change of heart. His dark hair was flecked with grey. The lines of age had begun to show around his eyes. There was the slightest hint of a bulge beginning to show around his midsection. In the dull morning light, his face looked pale and drawn. He had left his coat in his car and his suit jacket did little to keep the rain at bay. He stood with his hands dug deep into his pockets.

'I've had better mornings,' he answered, grimly. 'I remember when this area was all working class,' he added absently, raising his head.

Casey nodded.

'Yeah, this city has certainly changed in my time,' he responded. Neither man was in the mood for small talk.

They stood side-by-side in silence, until Palmer asked the pathologist, 'You done inside?' Casey nodded. The past year of the medical examiner's life had been consumed by death. He had been at the sharp end of the pandemic. Despite that, Palmer could see the effect that the scene inside the house had had on him.

'Just about,' he answered. 'We'll be moving the bodies out in a while. We're just finishing up and waiting for the CSM to give us the okay,' Casey explained, removing his wire rimmed glasses and rubbing his eyes with a thumb and forefinger. The strain of his work was etched onto his weathered face. His life, like so many medical professionals, had been choked by the pandemic. Death and suffering on such a scale had taken a heavy toll.

Although Casey was older, he and Palmer had formed a friendship of sorts over the years. A relationship based largely on their work and their mutual appreciation of a good single malt whiskey. Everyone in their respective professions found some way to protect themselves from the constant onslaught of violence, death, and decay. Some drank, some had religion, but eventually the strain of their work wore everyone down. It got under their skin and into their souls and slowly wore away their faith in humanity. Very few crime scenes penetrated the armoured skin of the most hardened investigators. The scene inside the Barker house had been one of those that had pierced the shell. They were living in extraordinary times. So many lives had been disrupted by the new plague. The lockdowns had reduced Palmer's workload, but for Casey it had been the opposite. Palmer felt for the man.

'You knew them, didn't you?' Casey asked, though he already knew the answer. Palmer's association with the Barker brothers was common knowledge. Unlike many, Casey never had an opinion on the matter either way.

Palmer nodded. He had not had an opportunity to speak properly with the pathologist inside the house. It was the first time that the men had seen each other in months. They had engaged in the usual, "*how have you been*", exchange, as Palmer had carefully moved around the crime scene. Their usual banter had been quelled by the horror around them.

Now after a brief silence, Palmer asked, 'What have you got for me, Pat?'

Casey raised his heels and rocked on the balls of his feet. It was an old habit. Those who knew him well knew that it signified that he was carefully focusing his thoughts. The light spring rain began to fall harder, but neither man seemed to notice. Casey's sparse wet hair clung to his furrowed forehead like a creeper vine. The pathologist was still dressed in a white coverall that doubled well as a raincoat. Palmer welcomed the refreshing feel of the rain on his face.

'Well, someone made a right fucking mess in there,' Casey replied when ready, stating the obvious. The language was out of character for

Casey. Palmer ignored it. He remained silent waiting for the pathologist to continue. The pressure in his chest grew, as if an invisible foot were pushing down on it. To their left cameras flashed as a press officer briefed the media. An angry resident was complaining loudly about access to his parking.

'The wife was killed first, clean, a single gunshot, small calibre, to the left temple at close range, killed her instantly. My guess is a .22.' Casey formed a gun with the fingers of his right hand and placed the hand against his head to demonstrate the action.

'I'd put her time of death at some time yesterday evening, between six and eight p.m. Because the heating was turned way up in the room it is difficult to give a more accurate timing.' His voice was even, void of emotion. Palmer wondered whether the killer had turned the heat up purposely. A shiver ran through him as he recalled the overwhelming stench in the room. His face hardened.

'The husband was nailed to the wall, two heavy nails in each arm,' Casey continued. He used his hands to indicate the position of the wounds on Billy Barker's arms. The image of Barker's bloodied body hanging from the wall like a macabre crucifix flashed in Palmer's mind. It was clear that the attacker had left the scene in a way that would shock anyone unfortunate enough to witness it. The horror had been staged, but the positioning of Billy Barker's body had also been for practical purposes. He had been forced to be a ringside spectator to the cruelty that his daughter had suffered.

'His eyelids were removed, both upper and lower. I suspect that he would have to have been sedated before that was done, but we will know more when we get the toxicology reports back from the lab. His carotid artery was severed sometime later. My guess is two to three hours after the initial injuries were sustained. What appears to be the letter P was carved into his chest, post-mortem.' Palmer's mind was racing, trying to reconstruct the events as Casey spoke.

'The daughter…' the pathologist started, stalled and then began again, coughing to clear his throat. Palmer noted a slight, almost imperceptible waver in the pathologist's voice.

'The daughter sustained multiple injuries. Most appear to have been ante-mortem.' He breathed in heavily, then continued, turning to look directly at the detective.

'This was no frenzied attack, Frank,' he explained. 'Whoever did this was cold hearted and deliberate, they knew exactly what they were doing, a real fucking pro. This was no exercise in minimalism, this kind of brutality takes a special kind of skill set.'

Palmer nodded. The two men stood in silence again, in the brisk, gusting wind. Palmer pulled his hands from his pockets and laced his fingers.

'Do you think that you can narrow down the time of the deaths?' he asked. His voice diffused. His accent heavier than usual. To Palmer it seemed like the entire world was trapped in a nightmare from which it was struggling to wake. The coronavirus pandemic had torn across the planet like viral tornado, leaving unprecedented devastation in its path. World governments seemed powerless to stop the spread. People were getting vaccinated, but there was lingering doubt about the true efficacy of the vaccines. There was also the ever-present threat that a new variant would arise that the current array of vaccines could not deal with. It would be back to square one.

'… midnight and two this morning, definitely no earlier,' Casey was saying. 'But judging by the clotting around the husband's head wounds, I'd say closer to midnight.'

Palmer nodded slowly, resisting asking Casey to repeat what his wandering mind had caused him to miss. It would no doubt be in the pathologist's report. When he had finished Palmer said, 'We need to prioritise this one, Doc.' The pathologist shot Palmer a glance that implied that the prioritisation of the case was a given. Casey had already been made aware that the autopsies were to be fast tracked. The sound of the morning traffic was getting louder. The city was getting into its daily stride. The road closure would cause several to arrive late to work, but that would not deter the team dealing with the scene. The rain had stopped, the crowds had grown larger, with little social distancing evident. Palmer could hear more complaints from pedestrians being told to turn back and find an alternate route through the area. Although the city was paused at step three restrictions, it was quickly returning to normal. A new kind of normal.

Palmer thanked Casey, disregarding the look of trepidation on the pathologist's face. He looked back briefly at the facade of the Barker house, then turned and walked slowly along the street. He pushed through the police cordon, ignoring the frantic calls of several reporters. The detective sat in the unmarked Ford Mondeo. The engine was idling. The windscreen wipers were slapping slowly across the glass. His dark, penetrating eyes narrowed. His wet hair was pushed back on his head. A deep frown creased his forehead. He had the sensation of sinking back into his seat. He looked at the screen of his phone and scrolled through his contacts. He quickly found the number he was looking for. His eyes remained fixed on the illuminated screen. His breathing quickened. He pressed the green icon and slowly lifted the phone to his ear. It was answered silently on the fifth ring.

'Jack?' Palmer probed, unsure who had answered the call. He heard movement. 'Jack,' Palmer asked again, more harshly than he had intended.

'It's Rita, who's this?' The high-pitched voice of Jack Barker's mistress was unmistakable.

'Rita, it's Frank Palmer. Is Jack with you?' Palmer questioned.

Rita hesitated. Knowing who Palmer was, she seemed unsure how to answer.

'Rita, it's fucking important that I speak to Jack, so if he's there, put him on the bloody phone now!' Palmer said forcefully.

Rita scolded him for his language, then reluctantly told the agitated detective that Jack was still asleep. It took another minute for the detective to persuade the uncertain woman that it was in Jack's best, and immediate, interests that he be woken. Palmer heard muffled sounds before he caught the unmistakable voice of an incensed Jack Barker growling in the background. The big man finally barked down the phone.

'Who the fuck is this?' he snarled, adding, 'This had better be good,' before Palmer had a chance to reply.

'Jack, it's Frank,' Palmer replied. He had to pause and steady himself before he could continue. He had hoped that Barker would have already been made aware of his brother's demise. It was immediately clear to Palmer that he had not been notified. The detective knew that others on Barker's firm would have received the news about Billy by now. None would have been brave enough to break the news to Jack. Jack Barker had a reputation for shooting the messenger. Sometimes literally. Palmer doubted that Jack had ever been given worse news.

Barker was silent as Palmer spoke, but his breathing became steadily more ragged and audible. When Palmer finished, Barker simply said, 'I'll see you at the yard in an hour.' He was not asking.

Palmer tossed the phone onto the passenger seat and wiped his hands across his face again.

'I don't need this!' he bellowed and slammed his hands onto the steering wheel. He was so close to getting out, getting away from it all – from the force, from Jack Barker, from a life that had become so twisted and distorted that most days he could not tell up from down – and now this. Frank Palmer had passed through depression years before. He had come out of the other side of it disillusioned and alienated from the world around him. He had wanted things to improve. He wanted to be a better version of himself, but he was plagued by the intuitive knowledge that he never would be.

Jack Barker sat on the edge of the bed enveloped in anger. It clouded his mind to the point where no rational thought was possible. There was only the numbing state of fury so powerful that it rendered the gangster immobile. His courtesan had known well enough to leave him alone. She had spoken gently to him once a flurry of calls had verified what Frank Palmer had told him. Then his eyes had darkened and Rita had known to stop talking.

She had seen Jack enraged before. Despite all of his success and his wealth, he was still perpetually angry at the world. The mood that she had watched grip him was unlike any she had seen before. It had terrified her. She had made the only possible decision: leave the man to his thoughts. Now he sat motionless. His head was tilted slightly downward, his fingers were dug into the thick muscles above his knees. Inside he felt as if he was shaking violently, which belied his calm exterior. In his eyes there was movement. There were storm clouds forming.

Frank Palmer's mind fixed briefly on the image of Lucy Barker. He thought of his own daughter. She was one of the few things that still made life worth living. Thinking of her calmed him slightly. He breathed in deeply, compelling his mind to focus. When he had first got the call, he had assumed that the victims had been misidentified. Until he had personally laid eyes on the carnage in the house, he had not believed it to be true. He pulled out from the parking not bothering to look first to see if the road was clear. It was not. A loud blast from a car horn jolted him. He lowered his window, put his hand out as a half-hearted gesture of apology and pulled out in front of the car. Whatever had happened to Billy must be linked to his brother. Palmer was sure of that. Jack Barker was a force of nature. A destructive force that was a magnet to bedlam.

'The super is looking for you, guv, she wants you in her office as soon as possible,' the polite mask wearing officer at the front desk informed Palmer as he entered the station. He grunted in reply. He was not ready for the barrage of questions that he was about to confront. He crossed the tiled lobby and felt that every eye in the station was fixed on him. Most were. As usual, a handwritten sign fixed askew to the lift door informed all that would use it that it was out of commission. He climbed the stairs to the second floor. The stairwell was rich with the familiar scent of pine-scented disinfectant. He stopped along the corridor to catch his breath and straighten his appearance before ignoring the superintendent's PA and knocking on the door to Jane Fletcher's office.

A gruff, 'Come in,' echoed in the reception and Palmer pushed open the heavy wooden door.

The superintendent looked sombre. It was her default appearance. Her considerable frame filled the space behind her paper-strewn oak desk. The immaculately presented DCI Young, head of the local CID unit, sat in one of two leather seats facing the senior officer. His fingers were knitted together, resting on his lap. Photographs and awards decorated the off-white walls. Like most of the ageing grade II listed building, the office, although neat, was long overdue a fresh coat of paint. An antique cabinet, on which was perched a long-dead potted fern, guarded the wall to the right.

The station commander was house-proud, but the combination of rising crime rates and more than a decade of austerity policies had left the force understaffed and ill-equipped to achieve the results expected of it. Superintendent Fletcher had little time to concern herself with the diminishing state of the old brick building that housed the station. Most of the surrounding area had evolved from rundown council estates and endless rows of ageing terraced houses, into lavishly refurbished homes, the price of which no police officer could ever afford. There was little doubt that the same fate would soon befall the station building, as the city continued its precipitous expansion eastwards.

Since 2008, the country's police services had paid a heavy price for the greed of investment bankers. Years of budget cuts and stagnant wages had reduced the number of serving officers, and the infrastructure needed to support them. As the first signs of a real recovery had begun to show, the country had voted to leave the European Union. It had been another setback. As the dreaded Brexit deadline had approached, a virus had escaped China and had begun tearing across the globe. The pandemic had been devastating for the people and the economy. The recovery for cities like London would be long and hard.

The two officers eyed Palmer as he entered.

'Ma'am.' He nodded to the heavily built, red-haired woman behind the desk. He took a seat next to DCI Young before being invited to.

Although Palmer and his Major Investigation Team were housed at the station, their direct chain of command did not include the station commander. They were guests in her house, as she often had cause to remind Palmer. The unwelcome visit to her office was a courtesy. The murders had happened on her patch. Her officers would undoubtedly be involved in dealing with the fallout, but the investigation would be under the jurisdiction of the Homicide and Major Crime Command.

Palmer was smart enough to know that he would need the station commander's assistance in the coming days. He glanced across at DCI Young. Despite his name, he appeared older than his years. It was an illusion he seemed to promulgate purposely. Young had been one of the first officers at the Barker scene. When Parker had arrived at the house, Young had been exiting the Barker residence looking as grey and ashen as the sky above. An uneasy pause followed before the superintendent said, 'Thank you for making the time, Frank, I can imagine that you have your hands full.' Palmer nodded but remained silent. The senior officer coughed to clear her throat and then asked, 'So, what precisely is the situation, Frank?' Fletcher was aware of Palmer's connection to Jack Barker, past and present. She had been the station commander for eight long years. During that time Palmer's involvement with the London underworld had been an issue on more than one occasion.

"The situation is that the young daughter, of the only brother, of a very, very nasty man was savaged while he, the brother, due to having no fucking eyelids, had been forced to watch. Now that same very nasty man is going to take your little piece of heaven and turn it into a scene from your worst fucking nightmare," Palmer thought, but did not share.

It was palpable that the normally unflappable superintendent was not her usual contained self. The same was true of her lapdog, DCI Young. In different circumstances their noticeable discomfort would have amused Palmer, but now it did more to heighten his own anxiety. The foot on his chest pressed harder. Palmer's shoulders sagged as he began to brief the senior officer with the limited information that he had available. When he had finished, he sat waiting for the predictable questions. DCI Young interjected before the superintendent managed a word.

'What are we looking at here, Frank, contract killings, a rival firm?'

Palmer shrugged and shook his head slowly.

'I'm not sure,' he answered truthfully. 'We'll know more once scenes-of-crime are done and we get the autopsy reports, but at this stage we can't rule anything out.'

It was the superintendent who asked the pertinent question.

'What do you think Jack Barker's response is going to be?' she tested, her Scottish heritage evident in her accent. Palmer had anticipated the question and the way it would be delivered. As if he would have a deep insight into Barker's conduct. He gave the superintendent the same answer that he had given Young.

'I'm not sure, ma'am.'

This time his answer was not entirely true. He knew that Barker would react quickly and violently, as he always did. Whom he would target was uncertain, but he would send out a message, and send it quickly and with as much force as possible. Palmer knew that every member of Barker's firm would be swarming toward the Silver Town

21

scrap yard where he held court. Orders would be given. The bloodletting would begin. There was no preventing it.

'We need to try to keep this situation under control or we're going to have a lot more bodies turning up,' Young declared with little conviction.

The DCI's rise through the ranks of the London Metropolitan Police had been swift. His career had been driven by the influence of his father-in-law, a Tory MP, who was not secretive with his opinion that his daughter had married beneath her. Having grudgingly accepted that his daughter would not revise her choice of husband, he had set about using his connections to ensure that Young would reach a position in the force that would ensure that the proper status and standing of his family was maintained. Young was not an entirely useless detective but dealing with the likes of Jack Barker and the inevitable bloodbath he was about to orchestrate was beyond him. He was not a brave man. He was thankful that he would be on the sidelines of the investigation.

Looking at the superintendent but addressing Palmer, Young said, 'We will give you all of the assistance that we can with this one, Frank. I believe that SCD East will be sending additional resources to assist. Everyone will be aware of the potential explosiveness of the situation, so we can expect a lot of interference from up on high.' Young paused, and then added, 'We would like to be kept updated, in the loop, Frank.' Palmer could not resist a smile. Young was a master at weaving his way past anything that may impact negatively on him. He sounded involved, but he would not be within a hundred yards of this investigation. After a further five minutes reviewing what they knew, which was nothing concrete, bar the fact that three people had been murdered, Palmer gladly recognised his cue to leave.

As he stood, Superintendent Fletcher added, in a suitably solemn tone, 'We will need to issue a brief statement to the press.' Palmer smiled. In most other circumstances DCI Young would have leapt at the opportunity to get in front of the cameras. Palmer guessed correctly that Young would not volunteer today. Nodding, he reached for the door handle. The last thing he wanted was to deal with a bunch of vultures. The more blood, the more vultures; the press room would be crowded.

As the door clicked shut behind Palmer, Young looked across at his senior officer.

'I don't think this is going to end well, ma'am,' he said smiling sardonically. 'This could finally spell the end for Palmer,' he added.

'I agree Tom. I have a feeling this thing is going to get very nasty, so let us be sure to keep enough distance between us and the DCI or this could spell the end for all of us.'

Young smirked. He had no doubt that Palmer would one day stumble and be unable to pull himself back up. Perhaps that day had come. He disliked the DCI. He had made several unsuccessful attempts to have Palmer and his unit relocated. He was fearful that simply being in the proximity of the tainted officer might somehow tarnish his reputation. But it was difficult to argue with Palmer's record. It was the one reason that he still had a job on the force. He solved more cases than most. This was due in part to information he regularly received from his underworld contacts. There were always villains who wanted to deal with their adversaries the easy way, by sending them down for a long stretch. Nonetheless, despite his shortcomings – most would argue that they were many – Frank Palmer was a brilliant detective.

'I don't think there is any question that this will end badly, guv,' Young repeated with a resigned sigh.

His commanding office managed a weak smile. Unlike the occasionally naïve Young, she knew all too well that the coming storm would leave no one in its path unscathed. Whatever Palmer's inadequacies, she knew that he was their only slim hope of keeping Jack Barker restrained.

The news of Billy Barker's murder spread across the city. Many who heard the news, knew what it portended. A looming shadow of fear stalked even the bravest amongst them. London was a city that had thrived on corruption for centuries. There had always been two worlds, which existed together in the ever expanding metropolis. Even in times when class had been the racism of the day, the aristocracy and the common folk had found neutral ground in the underworld. Drugs, women, gambling, smuggling, theft, murder. These were the pillars upon which the hidden realm had been constructed.

In the modern day, corruption still thrived. Men with power and money could buy anything. Greed and lust had fuelled the criminal world and driven it to new heights. Globalisation had added oxygen, accelerating the growth of illegal enterprises. Jack Barker had revelled in the darkness. His ruthlessness knew little comparison. His road to the top of the underworld had been paved with the bodies of broken men and women. He saw the outside world as the pretentious place, where people hid their true natures in order to go about their lives within the bounds of the laws of man. Among them were few that ever showed their true nature to those around them. Not even to their nearest and dearest. People had natural desires. They yearned to be their real selves, to release the nature within them that society forbade.

Jack knew people. He saw humanity for what it was. Immoral, perverse. Men sinned and then quickly sought redemption, then sinned again. Iniquity was, for the majority of mankind, the default setting.

Barker was on full alert. The large imposing metal gate that protected the entrance to the scrap yard was shut and guarded. From behind the wheel of his car, Palmer could hear the incessant barking of the pack of vicious, flea-bitten hounds that Jack Barker kept guarding the stacks of rusting metal at night. He liked to call them "the hounds of the Barkerville". He laughed whenever he said it. Amused or not, those around him at the time all laughed too. A hinged door in the gate opened. The short, stocky figure of Harry Black stepped through it. He approached Palmer cautiously.

Black was an overconfident and psychopathically violent young villain, who had already had several run-ins with Palmer. Black had killed a man at age fifteen. He had served seven years for it. Palmer knew that Barker saw potential in the thug. That guaranteed that by thirty, Black would either be dead, serving a life sentence, or he would be part of the small group of villains for whom crime actually paid. Palmer saw far less in him than Barker did. He would give good odds that Black's outcome would be one of the former.

Black sauntered up to Palmer's car.

'Detective Chief Inspector, always nice to see you.' Even in the dull winter light, the thick scar that ran across the right cheek of Black's pit-bull face was vivid and grotesque. Vines of ink covered the right side of his neck.

'Put a fucking sock in it, Harry, before I get out of this motor and put my boot in that big mouth of yours. Now open the gate like a good little boy, eh,' Palmer snarled.

Harry raised the middle finger of his right hand to Palmer and disappeared back through the door. A few seconds later the main gate began to slide open, and Palmer drove into the yard. Stacks of cars in various states of decay lined the concrete road leading to the single storey flat-roofed building that housed Jack Barker's offices. Behind the building a large crane was depositing a load of tangled metal onto an enormous pile of rusting scrap. Several cars that were obviously not ready to be laid to rest in the yard, were parked outside the office building. Barker's army was gathering.

Palmer parked and headed for the office. The sound of Barker's raised voice stirred a familiar feeling in him. He was a big man. Although not easily frightened, since the day he had first met Jack Barker, in the schoolyard of St Elizabeth primary school in Bethnal Green, something about Barker had unsettled him. Quashing the feeling, Palmer walked into the large reception room, the domain of Barker's frigid and devoted secretary. The door slammed shut behind him. There was a momentary silence as he scanned the familiar faces of the men seated on the expensive leather chairs. Despite the location, Barker's offices were lavishly and tastefully decorated. The reception seemed more fitting of a corporate bank than an East London scrap yard. All eyes in the room fixed on the detective.

The anxiety and belligerence in the air was tangible. Only Norris Jones, a fixture at Jack Barker's side, nodded a greeting. Palmer recognised all the men. There was not one amongst them that was not a killer.

Jack Barker's voice shattered the brief silence, booming through the double timber doors separating his office from the reception area. His secretary looked up over her rimless glasses and said, 'Go through, Mr Palmer, he is expecting you.' She had the terse, abrupt tone of a headmistress. The woman's age was difficult to tell. Although neatly dressed, her large breasts were evident beneath her blouse, her cleavage proudly vaunted. Palmer felt obliged to obey. In all the years that he had known her, he had exchanged less than a dozen words with the stern woman.

The detective reached for the door handle, his eyes closing for a second before he pushed through. Barker was standing in front of his desk, looking down at the anxious figures of Paul Burrows and Tommy MacFarlane. The powerfully built Burrows was a born and bred Essex boy who had served with distinction in the SAS before returning to civilian life. For the past ten years he had headed up Barker's security. MacFarlane, seated beside the ex-soldier, matched Burrows in size. He was the son of an Irish builder who, until injury had prevented him, was heading for a world boxing title. MacFarlane oversaw the collection of debts outstanding to Barker's firm.

The gangster ignored Palmer's entrance for a moment, finishing his business with the two men facing him first.

'If they go into hiding, smoke them out. I want to see everyone on that list, Paul, no fucking exceptions.' Barker finally looked up at Palmer and motioned with his head toward the door. It was a signal for Burrows and Macfarlane to leave. They obliged willingly, having borne the brunt of Barker's rage for almost half an hour.

Barker straightened and walked behind his desk. His office was vast. Like the reception area, it was tastefully and expensively decorated, bordering on ostentatious. The walls were covered with solid oak panelling and expensive, original oil paintings. Although Barker had little formal education, he had an eye for the finer things in life. It was well known in the London underworld that he could readily and accurately appraise the value and authenticity of almost any work of art. He had made a great deal of money over the years by fencing stolen works. Standing across the room from Palmer, Barker was an imposing figure – as tall as Palmer but with a more muscular physique. His greying hair was cropped in a military style. The scars and lines on his face enhanced his rugged, dangerous look. Faded tattoos covered the top of his hands, adding to his threatening appearance. They were a testament to his troubled youth. He wore them like a badge of honour. Now, his face was icy. As always, Barker was impeccably dressed in perfect fitting, expensive clothing. His dark blue suit jacket was hung over the back of his leather armchair. The top buttons of his shirt were unbuttoned, exposing his thick, muscular neck.

Palmer approached cautiously as the big man removed a cigar from the box on his desk, clipped it, and lit the end. Plumes of tobacco smoke hung in the air. He motioned for the detective to sit. Palmer obeyed. Barker drew on the cigar, still standing, looking across the desk at Palmer, and exhaled a large cloud of smoke. He was an old school gangster. He said nothing and Palmer's apprehension grew. Eventually, Barker spread his arms wide and asked, 'What is going on, Frank?'

The question was rhetorical. Jack Barker had an extensive network of high-ranking Met officers, either on his payroll or protecting the release of sensitive information that the gangster had acquired regarding their personal lives. He knew more about what happened on the streets of London than the millions of rats that called the city home. Barker had been fully briefed about his brother's murder and the fact that there seemed to be little evidence by which to identify the perpetrator. He was also aware that Frank Palmer would remain as the senior investigating officer on the case. It was a decision that he had influenced.

Now he paced like a caged predator. There were no niceties today, no "How are you, Frank?" Palmer sensed Barker was fighting to keep control. His face was more red than usual, his eyes darting.

'What are your thoughts here, Frank, I need something?' he growled. The impatience of his words was noted. Barker's voice was deep and rough. It was the result of a crushing blow to the throat that he had received in a particularly nasty street fight many years before. His opponent that day had been a six-foot-four Jamaican drug dealer named Winston Green. Winston had put up a good fight, but in the end, he had been blinded in one eye and he still walked with a cane.

'We have no idea at this stage, Jack, unless Billy had trouble with someone we don't know about. There's not much to go on right now, but we…' Palmer spoke calmly, trying to keep his voice steady. Barker erupted. He moved quickly around the desk and was in Palmer's face, his nose an inch away from the startled detective's cheek.

'They killed my brother!' he yelled with such fury that the veins bulged from his neck and forehead. His eyes visibly darkened, and his face turned red, as drops of spittle flecked Palmer's cheek.

'They nailed him to the fucking wall,' Barker raged, one hand still clutching the cigar, and gesticulated wildly as he shouted,

'The wall, in his own bedroom, and mutilated his little girl while he watched, Frank!' He paused, momentarily relieved by opportunity to vent his anger. His heart was racing, anger numbed his mind.

'I need to know who, Frank, I need to know why.' His voice cracked from the strain, his breath secreted a scent of stale liquor and tobacco. 'Who would do this, who?'

His hand slammed down on the corner of his desk as he pulled back from Palmer. The detective's eyes were unable to hide his fear. Barker turned away, wiping tears from his eyes. He lifted a hand to cover his face.

He turned back slowly to face Palmer, the blood draining away, his normal colour slowly returning.

'I want to know everything you know, Frank, when you know it. I want to be informed, Chief Inspector,' Barker ordered. 'Are we clear?' He stared at Palmer, who fought to regain his composure. The detective nodded.

'Jack,' he said, clearing his throat before continuing, 'we'll find out who did this, but if you go tearing the city apart it's not going to help.' Palmer looked pleadingly at Barker. 'Give me a few days, Jack, please, just a few days. I'll let you know everything we find out; you have my word.'

Barker returned to his seat and collapsed into it. In all the years Palmer had known him, he had never seen Jack Barker look the way he did just then. Like the victim of a demonic possession.

'Frankie, you go and do what you need to do, and I'll do what I need to do,' he said calmly.

Palmer knew that there was no point arguing. He had tried to avert the coming storm. However futile, he had made the attempt. He stood to leave, then turned and looked back at Barker.

'I'm sorry Jack, about Billy,' he said with discernible sincerity. 'He was a good man; he was a mate,' the detective continued. 'We will find whoever did this, we'll find whoever's responsible, and we will make them pay.'

Their eyes locked for a moment, unblinking. Palmer had known Barker for many years, but the man he was looking at now was a stranger. A cold chill ran down his spine. He dropped his eyes, turned, and left the office. Barker stared vacantly at the door. His mind was anesthetised, frozen.

There was no doubting that he was a sociopath. The gangster freely acknowledged that he was. He was damaged goods. A man moulded in his youth by endless beatings, humiliations, and violent assaults, mostly at the hands of his father. It was something that he and Palmer shared. It was what had drawn them together many years before. Both had too often arrived at school with bruised and broken bodies. They had retaliated against their fathers by beating other children. Children who had happy lives and homes with loving parents. The brutality of Barker's father had left many bodily scars, but they had healed in time. It was the unseen injuries that could never be healed. No matter what he achieved, all the wealth and power that he amassed, it had never enough to vanquish the demons that haunted him. He could keep them at bay for periods of time, but, like an active volcano, the anger and rage were always there, festering beneath the surface, waiting to erupt.

Billy had been different. Jack had protected him from his father, which had usually resulted in him being subjected to extended beatings. Billy was the only person that he had ever genuinely loved. He had cared for his mother, but her weakness had disgusted him. He could never forgive that she not done more to protect her children. To protect him. After Lucy was born, Jack had believed for the first time that there was some hope for them. He had made the decision to get Billy out of the life. He wanted to buy him a legit business, to let him have a proper life, to let his children have a proper life. He should have known better. The joy of life that so many took for granted was not for them. It was not for their kind. They were cursed. Tainted forever by the sins of their father. Barker was angry at the world that seemed to unrelentingly conspire against him. That fury fuelled the rage that he felt for losing his brother.

"If the world wanted it that way, then so be it," he thought.

Jack Barker closed his eyes. From deep within a rage like none he had ever experienced consumed him. His head fell back. He opened his mouth and roared.

CHAPTER TWO
The Fading Light

Palmer was shaken. He needed a drink. His mind was racing, unable to focus. Thoughts bombarded his mind, too many at once to control. He could usually see trouble coming. He knew how to insulate himself from it. He was a survivor in the primal sense. The shock of what he had witnessed was beginning to set in. It was amplified by the fear of what was to come. A screeching sound startled him. His foot instinctively lifted off the accelerator and slammed down on the brake pedal.

'What is your fucking game, you muppet!' an irate cab driver yelled, leaning out of his cab window to wave an angry fist at Palmer. It dawned on the detective that he had jumped a red light and was stopped halfway across the intersection, having narrowly avoided a collision.

He ignored the further insults hurled by the cab driver and continued his way west along the A13. To his left the towering structures of Canary Wharf reached high into the Dockland's sky. The impressive estate that had once been the symbol of success and prosperity now stood as a shameful reminder of the greed that had plunged the entire planet into financial chaos. Since 2008 the recovery had been slow. It seemed that just as the city had been regaining its feet, the coronavirus had struck. The only good thing to come out of it was that it had put a stop to the endless talk about Brexit. Britain's exit from the European Union had come and gone with little fanfare. People had a new focus. One that had made everyone take stock. It had been sobering. Many feared that it was still far from over. The pandemic had laid bare the many flaws in social structures around the world. Only time would tell if it had been enough to evoke any real change.

Palmer's thoughts soon returned to Billy Barker. He had been shocked by the murders. Billy had been a villain, no argument, but he had been well liked – a genuine, old school outlaw. He had an influence over his brother that kept Jack under some measure of control. Billy had been someone that people could talk to. He had been a peacemaker, a problem solver. He had been his brother's right hand, his consigliere. Without Billy, his brother would be unrestrained. Palmer cursed loudly and gripped the steering wheel until his knuckles turned white.

He had known for some time that he had to get away, far away. He was holding onto his job by the thinnest of threads. The sword of Damocles, or in his case, the sword of the Directorate of Professional Standards (DPS), was hanging precariously over him. He had appeared in front of the DPS, five times in the previous four years, answering a torrent of questions about his relationship with various known villains. The DPS, formerly the Complaints Investigation Bureau, were responsible for policing the police. They still had nothing concrete to charge Palmer with, but he knew that it was only a matter of time. Time that he had no intention of giving them. That bastard, DCI Penfold, a DPS bloodhound and long time adversary, was on his case. Penfold was determined to bury him under enough evidence to prevent his usual serpentine slither from the claws of justice. Palmer's frequent visits to the DPS also put a tacit strain on his relationship with his colleagues. Not that he was concerned about them. Not anymore.

He had not set out to be a bad copper. He had fought to put his old life behind him. The life forced on him at a young age by circumstance and poor lineage. He had been away from London for a long while, in self-imposed exile. He had returned to the city with good intentions, but without the self-restraint to match those objectives. Eventually he had been dragged back into the murky underworld. The dark twisted world that existed in the shadows just beneath the realm of normal, everyday society.

In truth he had allowed himself to be drawn back into the realm where his old friend, Jack Barker, had flourished. Palmer was a man of vices, which made the underworld difficult to resist. Once Barker had had him back in his clutches there had been no letting go. The gangster had felt betrayed when Palmer had joined the police force. It was a personal betrayal that he had never forgiven, even now. There was no denying that Palmer had benefited financially from his association with Barker and his firm. He had tried for years to break the ties, but it had proved futile. Palmer had finally decided. He had to get out. It was the same decision he made years before when he had left East London and had relocated to Belfast, his mother's home town. He had gone to Northern Ireland without any clear intention other than to escape his life in London. His uncle, a hard-line Unionist, had been a member of the Royal Ulster Constabulary.

After a series of events that Palmer could scarcely recall, he had followed in his uncle's footsteps and joined the force. His toughness and his willingness to look the other way when his colleagues engaged in questionable conduct, had made him a ready fit. It had been the time of "the troubles", a dark period in the history of Northern Ireland. Murder had been a way of life. The young Palmer had soon established himself. He had enlisted with the controversial Headquarters Mobile Support Unit in 1996 and had later been selected to join a Murder Squad in the notorious C Division.

By the time that the RUC had been rebranded as the Police Service of Northern Ireland, under the terms of the Good Friday Agreement, Palmer had achieved the rank of detective inspector. His career had plateaued. Although never accused of any offence, his name had been inextricably linked to a hard-line UVF faction with ties to the RUC. He had remained with the Northern Ireland force until early 2006, when he had requested a transfer to London. He had joined the London Metropolitan Police shortly after. Before his return, Palmer had been aware of the Barkers' ascendance to the pinnacle of London's underworld. He had managed to convince himself that his friendship with Jack Barker would not be an issue. That false reasoning had quickly been challenged.

Now heading into Whitechapel, the detective still fought to gain control over the torrent of thoughts that filled his head past capacity. He had stopped en route at a pub in Limehouse. The single malt had done little to calm him. He entered the narrow maze of streets that ran behind the mix of aged and modern hospital buildings. The older buildings dated back to the eighteenth century. Several of the modern buildings had only recently been completed. The architectural fusion of aged yellow brick and ultra-modern glass and aluminium was an abomination. Palmer parked in the first vacant spot he found, ignoring the clearly displayed disabled parking sign. He looked up at the bright blue wall of glass in front of him. It did little to cool his anxiety. He listlessly stepped from the car and headed toward an older part of the hospital. As he walked, he fixed a black mask over his face. It was an action that had seemed unfamiliar a year ago, but now had become a routine part of life.

Palmer hated morgues. The smell of government-standard disinfectant vaguely disguised the lingering scent of death. He walked along a narrow corridor. The lime green walls had been freshly painted. They were decorated in places with posters and signs, many of which were COVID 19 related. Mask Up. Sanitise. Social Distance. Get Vaccinated. The floor was green vinyl, polished to a high gloss. The deteriorating state of the National Health Service had left many of the capital's hospitals in a substandard condition, where superbugs like MRSA had killed as many people as any disease. The Royal London Hospital had deteriorated more than most, because directly adjacent to it they had been finalising the construction of its modern replacement. Now the completed new and the refurbished old had been reintegrated. Irrespective of the architecture, it was a monumental improvement.

Detective Inspector Jill Mullins waited along the corridor. She was young, intelligent and ambitious. Mullins was the only detective on his team for whom Palmer had any real regard. When the astute detective had first been assigned to Palmer's MIT squad, she had instinctively assumed that it had been the curves of her body that had caught his attention. In time she had come to realise that Palmer had recognised her potential as a detective and had intuitively guessed her sexual orientation. A mutual understanding had developed between the two investigators. Like Palmer, Mullins was an outsider: a black lesbian officer in the Metropolitan Police Service. She was loyal to herself. Palmer liked that about her. You always knew where you stood with someone who did not see any wrong in looking out for number one first. Jill Mullins knew how to use every asset that she had. She was tall, five foot eleven. She had an athletic body that could readily have sustained a modelling career. She was pretty, more so than beautiful. To her, her piercing green eyes were her second best feature. Her first was her intellect. She had ambition. Unlike many who did, she had the intellect to achieve it. She had recently completed a Master's degree in criminology and had been tipped for great things. Even as Palmer's possible successor.

Mullins respected Palmer. She enjoyed his dark sense of humour and his often bizarre and unshakeable beliefs. She was also aware that the DCI was not likely to be around for much longer. She worked hard to avoid being lost in his shadow. He was an officer whose connection to known criminals was common knowledge. He was, by all accounts, already living his ninth life with the Met. She recognised that despite his vices, Frank Palmer was an exceptional detective. Mullins knew that she could benefit from his knowledge and experience, while ensuring that she did not get dragged across his event horizon. She would also be ready to step into his position, when the inevitable occurred.

'Afternoon, guv,' she called as he approached, her face partly hidden behind a blue medical mask. Palmer instinctively checked his watch. It had just passed three p.m. Palmer noted that Mullins had dressed for the cameras. He had briefed her on his way to meet Barker. *Following various lines of enquiry, cannot release details, ongoing investigation, public are asked to come forward with any information.* Mullins excelled in front of the press.

'They're getting started on the girl,' she informed Palmer, indicating to the door opposite to where she was standing. Her rushed tone inferring that Palmer was late. Palmer nodded absently. He knew that what he was about to experience would probably haunt him for the rest of his life. Another wound to an already desiccated spirit. The detective opened the door and stepped into the large open room, lingering for a moment at the threshold, then stretching his arm back to hold the door open for Mullins. The smell of formaldehyde, disinfectant and body fluids assaulted their senses as they entered the not surprisingly, green-walled room. Stainless-steel shelves and benches lined the walls. Four polished steel tables filled the centre of the room.

On one table, a distinctly human form was evident beneath a white sheet. On another table lay the body of Billy Barker. Palmer barely recognised him. His head had been clean shaven. A large Y now covered his abdomen. It was formed from the dark thread of rough sutures. In the centre of his chest, Palmer could clearly see the letter P carved deep into the flesh. Bulging eyes, now cloudy, stared endlessly at the ceiling, until an orderly mercifully pulled a fresh sheet over them. On the third table lay what remained of Lucy Barker. She had been small for her age. The almost unimaginable brutality of her death was immediately evident. Palmer felt his eyes begin to water. His stomach tightened. He remembered the first time that he had seen Billy Barker proudly pushing his newborn daughter along the Bethnal Green Road, his beaming wife beside him.

'Frank, still your miserable old self I see.' Dr Michael Crawford, the home office pathologist, greeted Palmer.

'I guess so,' Palmer replied dejectedly.

Crawford sensed that Palmer was in no mood for their usual macabre verbal exchanges. The humour of death. He could understand why. In all his years as a pathologist, Lucy Barker's death would rate as one of the most horrifying that he had ever had the displeasure of examining. A request from the highest office had been made for Crawford to drop everything and to work on examining what remained of the Barker family. Palmer was not surprised. Crawford was commonly acknowledged to be the city's best pathologist. He often had an international audience attend his lectures and his academic writings were widely used at medical schools.

'Just finished off with Mr Barker,' he advised in his usual polished accent. Crawford looked like an academic. He had an air of hyper-intelligence about him. Palmer had seen Crawford on various television shows over the past year, discussing the pandemic. He was exceptionally eloquent and highly respected. He and Palmer exchanged a few more pleasantries and Palmer introduced DI Mullins. Crawford had looked over the top of his glasses at her and nodded his approval. Intelligence could sense intelligence. An assistant busied herself organising the tools and medical devices that Crawford would be using.

When all was ready, the pathologist pulled a microphone, suspended from the ceiling, into position and prepared to examine the young girl's body. He raised his eyebrows toward Palmer to indicate that he was ready to begin. Palmer's gaze met his and both managed a grimace.

'The subject is female, Caucasian, twelve years old,' Crawford began, moving to the young girl's feet.

Apart from the toxicology reports, which would take a further day to complete, the thorough autopsy of Lucy Barker was completed in a little under two hours. The pathologist was sure that the tests on Lucy Barker's blood would reveal that some form of chemical, perhaps an amphetamine, had been used to keep her conscious throughout the ordeal. A fact that would make the overall understanding of her final hours even more horrific. She had had a total of one hundred and twelve separate injuries, including broken bones, burns and lacerations. The wounds had been the result of the perpetrator's use of a variety of torture implements and techniques. The killer was, as Michael Crawford had stated during the autopsy, "a real scholar of the art". The pathologist had been unable to determine an actual cause of death. No injury by itself had been life threatening. Shock, he had hypothesised, had been the most likely cause of her ultimate demise.

Billy Barker's physical injuries, the pathologist had informed Palmer and Mullins, had been nowhere near as appalling as his daughter's. The neatness and precision with which his eyelids had been removed meant that he had almost certainly been unconscious at the time. The assailant had cleaned and treated his wounds to ensure that the blood flow would not blur his vision. Unable to close his eyes, he had been forced to stare helplessly as his daughter had been savaged. It had not been lost on anyone that what Billy had endured watching his daughter die in that way would have been more torturous than his physical injuries. He had eventually died from exsanguination after the killer had severed his carotid artery. His assailant had then carved the letter P onto his chest. It seemed certain that the inscribing had been carried out after his demise.

Palmer was glad to be out of the morgue and into the fresh air again, or air as fresh as a major metropolis offered. The skies had cleared, and the falling sun lit the buildings around him. He drove back to the station numb, fighting back his emotions. He forced himself to think clearly, methodically. He went over the likely series of events that had led to Billy Barker's death. His wife had likely returned home first. The killer, or killers, had been in the house already, or had been let in. Perhaps someone she knew? Palmer made a mental note. That would explain the lack of a forced entry. She had been taken to her bedroom and had been executed, clinically, quickly. Then the killer had waited until Lucy had

36

arrived home. She had been dropped off by Janet Alden, the mother of a friend, shortly before six p.m. Lucy had been subdued on entering the house. Then the attacker/s had waited for Billy to arrive home. Billy had been seen leaving a local pub around seven thirty. Somehow, he had been incapacitated when he had arrived home. He had then been crucified on his bedroom wall. Lucy had been tortured and killed. Shortly after her death, Billy had been dispatched. Palmer felt ill.

Billy Barker had been popular. Even in dealings with other underworld figures, he had a reputation for being fair. He did not use unnecessary violence. Like many villains, he utilised brutality as a working tool rather than for any personal gratification. Like his brother, Billy had been a big man, a good fighter. He could handle himself. He would not have been easy to subdue. Palmer was certain that the killings had not been random. The attacker must have been aware of Billy's identity. Moreover, who his brother was. The killings likely had more to do with Jack Barker than with his brother. Was someone sending Jack a message? What did the letter P represent? An initial seemed most likely, but it could mean anything. Whatever the meaning, whatever the message, Palmer was certain that it was essential to determining the motive for the murders.

He used the rear entrance into the station to avoid any unwelcome encounters. He did not want any distractions. He climbed the emergency stairs and arrived at his office unhindered. The detective stood for a moment with his back pressed against the closed door. Reaching into his pocket, he withdrew a strip of pink tablets. He popped one out and threw it into his mouth. Xanax, the brain vitamin of the modern man. It was his third of the day. He fell slowly into his chair and looked at the file that had been placed on his desk. Mullins, efficient as ever. After leaving the scene, he had asked her to have Billy Barker's name run through the National Crime Agency's database. He wanted the case files for every case that Billy's name had been associated with, directly or indirectly over the past five years. There were many. A summary of the results had been printed and neatly filed. Palmer thumbed through the pages. He favoured tangible documents rather that staring at a screen. The answer had to be amongst papers somewhere.

The vast storage shed smelled of carbon monoxide and burnt oil. Along one side stood neatly stacked metal bins filled with salvaged copper, aluminium, and other non-ferrous metals. A large sliding door was partially opened on one side of the structure. The old dock was visible through the gap, beyond which the River Thames covered most of what could be seen. Toward the centre of the run down building two orange forklift trucks stood silently in the dim light. Rain fell through the roof and created pools on the pitted floor. A third forklift idled near the rear of the shed. Jack Barker strode toward it. Despite wearing handmade Italian leather boots, he made no effort to avoid the puddles. He was transformed from his earlier dishevelled state. The villain had made a fortune buying up old industrial buildings in East London. He had received credible information that London would win the bid to host the 2012 Olympics well before it had become public knowledge. He had embarked on a campaign to own as much of the land earmarked for the games as he could. Although some way from Stratford, the building he walked through now had been purchased as part of a package of East London properties. The man that Barker had bought the properties from had been reluctant to sell. He had died in a horrific accident and his son had quickly decided to sell the properties at a reduced price.

Jack was dressed in an immaculately fitting black suit over a black cotton shirt. He had the appearance of someone without a care in the world. He walked slowly with his usual menacing gait. He could see that the forks of the machine were raised high on the mast, several metres above the ground. Something was hanging from them. The fumes from the diesel engine became stronger. As he neared, he recognised Paul Joss. His suspended form was illuminated by the forklift's lights. He was hanging by a chain secured to his feet, his blonde hair inches from the oil-stained concrete floor. His face was bright red. Harry Black and Tommy Macfarlane stood beside him, talking casually.

When he reached the suspended man, Barker looked down at him, his hands sunk deep into the trouser pockets of his Savile Row suit. Black and Macfarlane stopped talking and stood silently, waiting for Barker to speak. Both men feared and revered their boss. Either would give their life for him, without question. They were fully aware that, despite his appearance, their boss' mood was dark and unpredictable. In these circumstances silence and obedience were the best and only options. Barker ignored his soldiers and focused on the dangling captive.

'Hello, Paul,' Barker greeted. Then asked politely, 'Have you got something to tell me then?' The sound of Barker's voice startled some pigeons from their perches. Their flapping wings echoed in the high roof above.

Joss wriggled. His body swayed on the chains securing his feet to the forks above him. He tried to lift his head to take the pressure off his chest, but his energy was drained. He mumbled incoherently and bubbles of spittle formed on his lips and ran down across his cheeks. He had been hanging upside down for almost an hour. The burst blood vessels in his eyes were evidence of how much the experience had strained his overweight, heavily tattooed body. Barker looked up at Black and nodded slightly. The young thug smiled and reached across to pull a lever next to the forklift's steering wheel. At first Joss began to lift higher. Harry Black apologised sarcastically,

'Sorry, Paul mate, wrong way.' He pushed the lever in the opposite direction. Joss sank slowly to the floor until only his legs remained suspended. Blood trickled from the deep ridges the chains had cut into his ankles. The redness drained from his face. Joss stared up at Barker with venomous eyes.

Paul Joss was from North London. He was young and fearless. The trafficker had accumulated a lot of wealth in a short space of time by getting into bed with Jamaican and Nigerian drug dealers. He had a reputation for violence. Through the network that he had established, he had been landing almost fifty kilos of high-grade cocaine every week. His newfound wealth and status had quickly gone to his head. It had made him reckless. He had thought that he had enough muscle and money to take on anyone. A month earlier, he and Billy Barker had exchanged words in a West End nightclub. The altercation had ended with nothing more than threats of violence being hurled. Billy Barker had mentioned the incident to his brother. Jack had marked the man's card but had taken no action.

'So, Paul, have you got something to tell me?' Barker asked again. Now the lingering fury was more notable.

'Fuck you, Barker!' Joss spat. Flecks of spittle and blood landed on Barker's shoes. Barker almost admired the younger man's courage.

'Do you think that provoking me is the best way for you to go in this situation, Paul?' Barker asked, looking down at the defenceless man. He sounded calmer again.

'Is that the smart choice, son?' he questioned before launching his foot into Joss' side without warning and with immense force. There was a sickening crack. The captive villain cried out in pain. The animosity drained from his eyes. For the first time, he seemed to realise that he was in real trouble.

'Let us try this again, Paul. You know they say that confession is good for the soul, don't they,' Barker urged, making the sign of a cross on his chest. 'It will be good for your health too, son,' he added in a low menacing tone and drove his boot into Joss' side again. 'What have you got to tell me?' he asked again, the calmness fading as quickly as his quarry's courage.

Paul Joss squirmed, banging his head against the unrelenting concrete.

'I fucking swear I don't know what you want!' he called out, his voice trembling.

'Did you boys hear that?' Barker asked, addressing Black and McFarlane. 'He doesn't know what I want,' he taunted. 'He's got some bottle hasn't he?'

Barker dropped to his knees making no effort to protect his clothing from the filthy surface. He leaned over until his face was inches from Joss'. He clasped the drug dealer's face with an iron-grip right hand.

'What did you do to my brother?' he hissed.

Joss' eyes opened wide, terrified. The fearlessness was replaced by a foreboding look. A look of defeat and resignation that no matter what, his fate was sealed.

'I... I... don't know nothing, Jack, honest, I don't know nothing,' he began to plead.

Barker looked down at the pathetic man who had dared to think he could challenge him. The fear in his eyes told him that what he was saying was true. Such a worthless prick would never have dared to kill his brother.

'All's the fucking pity for you then,' Barker spat.

He stood and brushed the dirt from his knees, then slapped his hands together.

'This is a new suit, mate,' he said looking down at Joss. He shook his head in mock disappointment. Then raised his eyes and looked at Black. His eager young protégé reached over to the forklift's controls again. This time the steel forks lowered immediately. Paul Joss screamed as the hydraulic force crushed his legs and then his chest. A gurgled whisper escaped as the life was crushed from him. The three men stood in silence watching the red froth bubble from the dead man's mouth.

Eventually Black asked, 'Who next boss?'

CHAPTER THREE
Fear is the Price

'Guv, it's good to see you,' DI Mike Williams said insincerely. He had knocked, then opened the door and walked into Palmer's office before the detective had had time to respond. He and the three officers accompanying him had arrived at the station after visiting the scene at Billy Barker's house. Palmer had been expecting them. Williams had been disconsolate when the order had come from the Serious Crime Directorate that he and two of his MIT colleagues were to report to Palmer. Even so, when he had learned that the order had come directly from Chief Superintendent Sloane, the head of the Operational Command Unit, the promotion-conscious Williams had known better than to question the decision. He had known Palmer for several years, but they had never directly worked together. Williams was six years younger than the DCI. Like Mullins, he was on the up. He was tipped for promotion and would then head his own Major Investigation Team. He was uncompromisingly by the book. His entire demeanour was rigid. He had the appearance of a store mannequin.

Alongside DI Williams stood DS Galloway. Palmer knew Galloway by reputation only. Bitch was the term most often used to describe her. Now, seeing her for the first time, he disliked her instantly. She had eighties style big hair. Palmer detested big hair. The dyed-red explosion invaded the space around her. That she was opinionated was as obvious as her hair was offensive. The sight of Detective Sergeant Dylan Porter, behind the intrusive hair, was altogether more welcome. Palmer knew the talented young detective well. He liked the aggressive and tenacious Manchurian. Porter had served under Palmer when Palmer had headed a local CID unit. Porter had a broad, pleasant face. His amiable facade had proven to be a great benefit in his work. People found the detective nonthreatening, easy to talk to. Hovering just inside the office door, beside Porter, was Jason Bright.

Bright was a broad-shouldered detective sergeant with the Serious and Organised Crime Group. He had been drafted into the investigation team because one of the victims had been involved in profoundly serious and very organised crime. Bright was aware of Palmer's reputation and of his suspected involvement with several leading gangland figures. He nodded as Williams introduced him. His hostility was poorly disguised.

Palmer could sense that none of the four detectives crowding his office, were overtly pleased to have made the journey to the borough. Palmer's reputation preceded him. He got results, that could not be argued. It was how he got those results that his peers had an opinion about. He did not care for their opinions. Palmer knew better than anyone how grave the situation was. He understood the mayhem that Jack Barker was about to unleash on the city. He was aware that the officers standing before him did not fully comprehend the extent of the savagery that was, likely, already being metered out. There was one way to temper Barker. Find the person or persons responsible for the carnage at his brother's house. That was all that he needed from the investigators stood before him.

The incident room was crowded when Palmer arrived. He had issued DI Mullins instructions to have his team and the four assigned officers who had been selected to assist in the investigation, assembled in the incident room. He has also requested that DCI Young provide a team of uniforms to assist the investigation team. Young had offered two. Palmer walked to the front of the room ignoring those present. He stared at the large whiteboard on which photographs of each of the three victims had been fixed. The start of a murder board. Even in the era of technology, homicide investigators used the tested investigation technique. Anxiety was giving way to anger. After a moment, Palmer turned and studied the room. The two rooms normally designated for use as specialised incident rooms had been deemed too small to meet the team's requirements. Hence the larger room. Its size was representative of the scale and nature of the investigation. The decor was bland. The furniture consisted mostly of non-matching desks, tables and chairs that had accumulated in the station over many years. A corridor ran adjacent to the rear wall of the room. The upper part of the wall was formed from glass panels. It was a design which did not allow the occupants protection from wandering eyes.

'Miller,' Palmer called. The young, uniformed officer sprang up and walked over to where the senior officer stood. Palmer pointed to the glass panels. 'I want those blinds kept down so that we don't look like animals in a fucking zoo.'

The officer nodded vigorously and asked, 'You want it done now, guv?'

'Yes, Miller,' Palmer growled, shaking his head. 'Now.'

Palmer waited impatiently as the uniformed officer nervously fought the tangled ropes that controlled the blinds. When finally, he had managed to drop them, Palmer barked, 'Right, quiet down!' bringing immediate silence to the room. No matter what people thought of Frank Palmer, he was the kind of man that it was wise to pay attention to.

Nine officers formed the task force. Closest to him was DI Mullins. Next to her sat DS Mark Campbell and DC Trevor Watts, both eager young detectives of the new variety. College educated and designer dressed. Campbell's father had been an assistant chief constable with the Kent County Constabulary until his untimely death six months earlier. His passing had deeply affected his son. Mark Campbell had grown up in the shadow of his domineering father. Since his death, Campbell had become more focused. He appeared to have a constant air of unrelenting determination about him. Watts, on the other hand, was easy going. He was tall, dark and handsome in the traditional sense. His physical appearance gave him confidence. In truth, despite his partner's newfound resolve, Watts was a better detective than Campbell. The two men were friends. Despite their differences they had forged a strong partnership. They had joined Palmer's Major Investigation Team a month apart and had since cemented their places on the team. Behind them sat constables Claire Hunter and Paul Miller, who had been drafted in from an already short-staffed uniform relieve, despite their sergeant's protests. Whether with supercilious intent or by a simple choice of seating, the four supporting officers sent by the SCD were separated from the rest of the team by a misshapen row of empty desks.

The atmosphere in the room was tense. It was manifestly strained. Every officer that worked in London knew of Jack Barker. Although Big Jack kept himself from the limelight, his name had become synonyms with crime in the city. Most officers had never had any reason to engage with Barker. He kept a solid arm's length between himself and his criminal dealings. It was known that Barker had connections in the highest places. He was an untouchable figure. For most of the officers in the room, this would be the first time that they would be involved directly with the highest echelons of the London underworld. It worried the officers for good reason.

Palmer began by introducing each officer in turn. He had already worked out a framework for the investigation. He had mentally allocated a task for each member of the team. He began by recounting the morning's events. He started at the beginning with the nine-nine-nine call received from the Barkers' housekeeper at 7.02 a.m.. All except for the uniformed officers had been to the scene. Only Palmer had seen the bedroom before the bodies had been removed.

When he had finished reviewing what little new information had been ascertained from the autopsies, he outlined the initial lines of enquiry. Although nothing could be ruled out, Palmer was certain the murders had something to do with Billy Barker's criminal activities. Or, more likely, the activities of his brother. They had not been the victims of an indiscriminate attacker.

Palmer instructed DS Porter to team up with Campbell and Watts. The trio were to scrutinise Billy Barker's movements during the past month. They would interview anyone that he had been in touch with. The initial P was relevant to the case. The letter carved into Billy Barker's chest had to be significant. It was the only real clue that their suspect had left. Palmer advised the investigators to be mindful of that. He asked Mullins to share the file that they had received from the NCA with the three detectives.

'Whoever killed in this manner could not be doing so for the first time.' Palmer apprised his audience. 'This was practiced, precise, so there must be history here that we can uncover.'

45

DI Williams and DS Galloway would chase the forensics. Once scenes-of-crime had completed their fingertip search for evidence at the Barker house they were to go over it again. Every inch.

'Get the sequence of events right,' Palmer insisted. It was important that they know exactly what had occurred in that house and when it had occurred. They needed to collate an accurate timeline. They were also to interview the Barkers' neighbours.

'I don't care if uniform have interviewed them ten times already,' he insisted. 'Somebody must have seen or heard something, speak to them again.'

Bright and Miller would send out enquires and check the national crime database to see whether any murders with a similar MO had been reported anywhere else in the country or abroad. They would engage with the NCA, and search VICLAS, the Violent Crime Linkage Analysis System. Perhaps the MO of the murders was the signature of some criminal organisation. The IT department had already installed a bank of computers in the room. Claire Hunter was charged with monitoring the newly installed phonelines and collating all the information received.

Palmer's voice became louder and more insistent as the briefing progressed. Right or wrong, he was the senior investigating officer. His orders would be followed, to the letter. Despite the brutality of the murders, it was obvious that they had been meticulously planned and executed. Palmer doubted there would be much physical evidence, but no one killed three people without being seen or without leaving some trace. They were not hunting a phantom. Lastly, Palmer informed the team that he and DI Mullins would make another trip to see Jack Barker the following morning. The tension in the room heightened at the mention of the gangster's name.

It was late when Palmer dismissed the task force. Once they had filed out of the room, he turned and fixed his eyes on the board. The ringing startled him. He retrieved the handset from his pocket. The name Jack was displayed on the screen. The conversation was short. In the background the detective could hear the unmistakable resonances of a boxing gym. The birr of skipping ropes, the thud of leather beating leather. Palmer guessed correctly that Barker was visiting his East

46

London club. The gangster seemed more in control. It was unsettling. There were no updates, no new information.

The station was quiet when he eventually left. The nightshift was out prowling the empty streets. Palmer knew that it would be wise to go home and get some much-needed rest. It had been the longest day that he could remember. He would need all the energy that he could muster, and more, in the coming days. He trudged across the wet parking lot, fishing in his pocket for his keys as he walked. In the dull lit interior of the car, he squinted at his watch as he pressed the ignition button. As it often did, wisdom failed him. He decided on a quick drink at The Crown and Anchor before heading home.

He was glad to see that the pub was not busy when he arrived. The post-lockdown surge had abated after a few weeks. He walked to the bar and pulled a tall stool away from the counter. It was a traditional pub, many years past needing extensive renovation. It had been reconstructed in the late nineteen fifties, having been bombed out during the Blitz. Much of it looked exactly as it had when it had reopened.

'All right there, Frank,' a man to his left said, looking across at the detective.

'All right, Hal,' Palmer responded, nodding a greeting to the retired cab driver. He quickly turned his attention back to the bar before the man could strike up a conversation.

'Frank, get you the usual?' Mary, the gregarious barmaid, asked Palmer. She had already poured the large scotch and was adding the slightest dash of soda. Palmer smiled and nodded. The pretty young girl placed the drink in front of him and took the twenty-pound note the detective had left on the bar, whispering,

'I'm supposed to ask whether you sanitised.' Palmer raised his hands in a waving motion.

'So, what's the craic then, Frank?' Mary asked, returning to place his change on the bar top. 'You working that business with Billy?' Palmer looked into the girl's eyes. She could tell he was in no mood to talk about it. She smiled and left him in peace. The peace did not last long.

'Well, Detective Chief Inspector,' a sultry voice said behind Palmer. It's nice to see you.'

He turned slowly, recognising Sharon Collins' voice. Sharon was the errant sister of Clifford Collins, a notoriously unskilled blagger whom Palmer had sent down for a ten stretch. Sharon was a twenty-eight-year-old unwed mother of three. She despised her brother, for reasons that Palmer had never sought to question. The young woman was pretty in a worn, sluttish way. She had long blonde hair and large breasts that were never restrained by a bra. She and Palmer had developed an easy friendship to the disgust of everyone who knew her bank-robbing brother. It was a friendship predicated on casual, deviant sex and the mutual appreciation of class A narcotics. Sharon pulled a stool across the floor until it was almost touching Palmer's. She was not one for social distancing.

'So, you got any gear then?' she asked softly.

Palmer said nothing. He turned to face the bar. Staring at the rack of bottles opposite, he lifted his glass and drained its contents.

'Not tonight,' he eventually replied.

Sharon was not a girl easily rejected.

'Ah, come on, Frankie, just a taste, eh,' she pressed in a teasing voice. 'You know I'll make it worth your while.' She moved closer, leaned over his shoulder, and whispered, 'You can use the belt, Frankie.'

Palmer smirked, recognising that the growing craving in his gut would overcome any resistance that he had to offer. He slowly placed the glass on the counter and said, 'Let's go.'

A nagging cramp woke the detective early. As usual he had fallen asleep sitting in his worn leather recliner. The television was still on. He listened to Sky News for a while before opening his eyes. More bad news, another COVID variant was sweeping across the country. This time it had originated in India. The Delta variant they were calling it. It looked as if the great summer re-opening would be placed on hold again. The weather was getting warmer, more rain to come. It was seven a.m., back to the headlines. The story about the brutal slaying of an East London family forced Palmer's reluctant eyes open. He wearily surveyed the unkempt room to reassure himself that he was in his own house. On air, a reporter stood outside the Barker residence, relaying what was known about the shocking events that had occurred within its nondescript walls. Without turning his head, Palmer pawed the overloaded side table until his snaking hand located the remote control. He pointed it at the television set and pressed the red button.

He lifted himself off the chair gingerly, groaning as he did so. Once standing, he steadied himself and stumbled toward the bathroom. In the passage he tripped over discarded clothing. He needed to call his cleaner and get her in to decontaminate the entire house. His agent was bringing someone to see the place tomorrow. He needed the house sold, but buyers in the property market were almost an extinct species. He had dropped his price twice and still had no firm taker. Time was running out. The icy water made him jump as he turned the shower facet. He took a deep breath and forced himself under the cold spray.

A half hour later the detective stood looking into the full-length mirror in his bedroom. As was typical, he was dressed in a dark grey, single-breasted suit with a white shirt and a tie. He owned four suits, all the same colour and same cut. It made the mundane task of selecting his daily attire easier. The only variable was choosing which tie to wear. He had whittled it down to two options. He nodded at his reflection. He looked good for forty-seven, considering his many vices. He had few wrinkles and a full head of hair, albeit his hair was thinning and was flecked with an ever-increasing amount of grey. He looked younger than his age, except for the perpetual dark rings beneath his eyes that gave him a slightly haunted look. He lifted his hand and slipped on a pair of Wayfarers. The improvement to his appearance was instant.

He took a drink of milk from a two-day-old carton and left the house. His phone rang before he got to his car. It was DI Mullins.

'Morning, guv,' she said, sounding bright and alert. Her news was anything but bright.

'I'm afraid it's not a good one. We've got three bodies in the hospital, all sustained heavy beatings, all known faces. One had a hand amputated.' Mullins stopped to catch her breath. 'No one's talking, guv, no one saw anything, all are giving the same line, they were attacked by unknown assailants.'

Palmer was not surprised. There was never a reason good enough to justify grassing on your fellow villains, even if they had landed you in a hospital. Jack Barker's backlash had begun. Palmer knew that only the

49

survivors would have made it to a hospital. Those who had not survived the night would be in steel cages on the deck of a trawler, headed for an eternity in the depths of the English Channel.

'I'll meet you at the station,' Palmer advised, opening his car door. He sat for a minute before starting the engine. He had to find a way to rein in Barker. The man had to see reason, but it was not going to be easy. His mind clearer, the detective headed for the station. En route he made a call to an angry bookie that he already owed more than ten grand. He ignored the man's disgruntled bickering and placed a bet on Germany to win. The sky still hung low over the city and a fine summer rain fell. The traffic was still lighter than it had been pre-COVID. He almost missed the morning gridlock. He listened to the eight a.m. news headlines. As expected, the main story remained the murders of Billy and his family.

The detective could still make no sense of Billy Barker's murder. The crimes were precise, deliberate. There was meaning to the selection of the victims and the manner in which they had been executed. Palmer knew that much. It was an unwritten, but unbreakable canon in the British underworld that family were off limits, especially children. If someone were trying to send Jack a message, there was little point if the sender could not be identified. Palmer knew that Jack Barker was deeply unpopular. He was feared and that was enough. The villain did not want or need friendship or love. Nevertheless, there would have to be good reason for someone to strike at the gangster in such a ruthless manner. Whoever had done so would have to be either very brave or very stupid. Palmer was certain that the monster they were hunting was not stupid.

When he arrived at the station, the incident room was deserted except for PC Hunter, seated in front of a curved twenty-four-inch screen, and a stranger who stood at the front of the room studying the photographs of Billy Barker and his family fixed on the murder wall. Hunter was on a call. An array of IT equipment had been installed in the room. It looked more functional than it had the previous day.

'Can I help you?' Palmer asked approaching the unknown woman. The annoyance in his voice was undisguised.

The stranger turned to face Palmer. She was smartly dressed in a light grey suit, about thirtyish, Palmer guessed. Her face was attractive, but stern. Her athletic build was evident even fully clothed. The woman's straight blonde hair hung neatly to her shoulders. Her blue eyes had a disarming quality about them. She had the air of a woman who was used to getting what she wanted. She held Palmer's gaze without flinching.

'These murders were personal, Chief Inspector,' she said in reply, walking toward Palmer and stopping a few feet from him. 'I believe that you are correct on two points, detective,' the visitor continued, looking up at the detective, and raising a hand with two fingers extended,

'Firstly, this was certainly not a random attack,' the woman declared, then paused. Palmer remained silent, notably unimpressed. The stranger ignored his reticence. 'Secondly, whoever committed these crimes must have killed before; this could not have been their first foray into this level of violence.'

Palmer disregarded what the visitor had said, and instead asked, 'I'm sorry, but who the bloody hell are you?' His tone made his displeasure clear.

The stranger smiled.

'I apologise,' she responded extending her hand. 'I should have introduced myself first, Doctor Tara Moore. I am a forensic psychologist and criminal profiler with the National Crime Agency. I was asked to come in to assist you with a profile of your suspect.' Palmer did not take her hand immediately, partly because of his frustration and partly because it was no longer something that people did. When it became uncomfortable, he shook her hand hurriedly. He had the sudden urge to sanitise after.

'I know right', the psychologist said. 'To shake or not to shake has become one of the biggest questions of the day.' It was Palmer's turn to smile.

'Who knows how to behave nowadays?' he replied rhetorically.

"Tara Moore," Palmer thought. He had certainly never heard of her. He had a niece called Tara, miserable girl, fifteen years old, and already twenty pounds overweight. After an awkward pause Palmer asked, 'Who exactly requested your assistance, Doctor?' He sounded more detracting than he had intended.

'Chief Superintendent Sloane, I believe,' the psychologist answered, meeting his stare again. 'Do I assume from your reaction that you are averse to my being here, Chief Inspector?' A slight grin formed as she spoke.

A smart arse, Palmer thought, just what I need to start my day.

'Most people will tell you Doctor Moore that you should assume little of me,' Palmer replied. He hesitated, not sure whether he was still annoyed. He continued, realising that he was.

'I am fully aware of the benefits that your sort can bring to an investigation,' Palmer advised. 'I just prefer to make the decisions regarding my cases and not to have them made for me.' Her eyes gave little away. Palmer turned to the photograph of Billy Barker.

'Now that you are here, however,' he said tapping the board. 'I would be glad for any help and insight that you can give.' He looked directly at the profiler, nodded and turned to leave.

He found DI Mullins in the canteen and hustled her out to the car park, cup of coffee in hand. He let Mullins drive and dialled a number on his phone as she waited for the station's automatic gate to open.

'Guv, its Palmer,' he said when the senior officer answered.

'Frank, what can I do for you?'

'Do you know a Doctor Tara Moore?' Palmer asked, his tone abrupt.

'Yes, she is a criminal profiler, comes highly recommended,' the man answered. 'She has been working with the NCA for the past year, before that she trained with the FBI at Quantico, so she should know what she's doing.' There was a brief pause, then the speaker added, 'We can use all the help we can get.'

Palmer knew that it was the right choice to bring in a criminal profiler but having one thrust into his investigation without notification angered him. He had a suspicion that she had probably been sent to assess him as much as to offer any profile of their suspect. *Paranoia – get a grip, Frank.*

'I'm sure she'll be a great help, guv,' Palmer responded. 'However, it would look better for me if I knew what was going on in my own investigation.' Palmer restrained himself from raising his voice.

There was a brief silence before the senior officer replied, 'Point taken, Frank.' The call was disconnected.

'Problem, guv?' Mullins enquired. Palmer shook his head.

They went through the usual routine at the entrance to Barker's yard. This time it was Bill Harris on gate duty. He was certainly a step up from Harry Black. It showed that Barker was taking his security more seriously. Palmer was sure that Barker would have slept at the yard – his command centre. He knew that a good deal of blood would have been spilled there overnight.

Barker's secretary immediately directed the detective go through to the gangster office, while Mullins waited in the reception area under the icy gaze of two enormous minders. Both men had obvious tell-tale bulges beneath their jackets. The detective refused a seat and stood uneasily, shifting on her feet, as Palmer disappeared into the adjacent office.

The air was permeated with the smell of stale cigars and air freshener, a futile attempt by Barker's secretary to rid the room of its suffocating aromas.

'What have you got for me, Frank?' Barker asked at once. He sat unmoving, slumped behind his desk. He looked rough. Palmer guessed correctly that he had had a busy night. An excessive intake of cocaine had caused the villain's nose to swell and redden. Barker could do without any narcotics induced paranoia, Palmer thought.

'I was hoping that you had something for *me*, Jack,' Palmer replied.

Barker sniggered.

'Something for you, Frank?' His head rolled. His eyes were wide, bloodshot and unblinking.

'Something for you?' he repeated. 'No, Frank, I've got nothing for you.' He leaned forward and stood. He was shaky on his feet. Palmer noticed large patches of what looked like dried blood on his otherwise black shirt.

'I'll tell you what, Frank, why don't you sit here,' he gestured toward his ornate leather chair. 'And I'll go back to the fucking nick and go and be the copper, huh?' He walked around the desk unsteadily. 'My brother is dead, my niece was butchered like some animal, while he watched, and you,' he pointed at Palmer, 'are asking if I have anything for you!' Barker laughed. He rubbed his hands over his face.

'I've got a good team working on this, Jack,' Palmer pressed. 'We'll find who did it. But if you can give me anything, it'll help us both.'

Barker laughed louder, but without any humour.

'Fuck me, Frankie, I don't even know who you are any more,' Barker said derisively. 'Listen to you; you sound like just another filth.'

Palmer realised that it was a mistake to have come to see the villain. The man was beyond reasoning. Still, he tried again, saying firmly, 'Jack, I've got three bodies in the hospital and another two on the missing list. If I must run around sorting out that bollocks, I haven't got the time to find out what the happened to Billy.' He waited for Barker's incensed response. It didn't come.

Barker looked at the detective, unimpressed by his outburst. He was no fool. He knew that his reaction to his brother's murder had not been in his best interests. He had sent out a message, loud and clear. It was time to rein in the pack and to see what word came off the street. He needed Palmer too. Even in his drug and alcohol induced haze, he knew that. He turned and walked behind his desk, collapsed into his chair, and sighed deeply.

'I've got nothing, Frank,' he said evenly. 'I can't figure it, but I'm not finished yet.'

Palmer kept his eyes on Barker, looking for any sign that he was being untruthful.

'Just give me some time, Jack, without any distractions,' Palmer pleaded.

Barker nodded slowly and closed his eyes. Palmer took it as a signal to leave. He walked out of the office and past Mullins without saying a word. She turned and followed him to the car. Above, the sky was clearing. The scrap yard's normal functions had been halted. A huge steel claw hung idle from the monstrous crane. Below was an enormous pile of metal, mostly stripped from old cars.

It had gone as well as could have been expected. He may have bought them a little time. He knew that Barker would need rest. His message had been delivered with a sledgehammer. He would take a brief pause to assess the response. Not long. Patience was not in Jack's arsenal of attributes. Palmer cursed under his breath, shaking his head. Mullins glanced across at him but said nothing. They had to find out who murdered Billy and his family, and they had to find out soon. Palmer had liked Billy Barker, but over the years he had come to despise his brother for the hold that he had over him, the control that he had over his life. Control he refused to relinquish.

DI Williams knew Roddy McBride well. He was a lowlife nobody who lived on the periphery of the London underworld. He was a small time crook and a big-time drug addict. Despite his low standing among credible villains, he had often been a source of reliable and useful information. Mostly because people did not see him. It enabled him to get close without being noticed. He had been a registered informant for years, although as his drug habit had worsened, so had the reliability of his information. Grassing was still how he earned the money that paid for the crack cocaine that had become the centre of his existence. He still made it his business to know other people's comings and goings.

Williams watched as McBride walked along the busy street, stopping every few metres to look down at the ground in the hope that he would find something of value. A habit shared by most addicts. The detective's eyes tracked him through the throng of bargain hunters crowding around the market stalls. They made the pavement almost impassable. He waited until McBride turned into a side alley before instructing Galloway to stop the car. Williams climbed out quickly and darted after his target, grabbing McBride's shoulder from behind. The destitute-looking man squealed and spun around to look at Williams. His eyes were wide with fright. A filthy mask covered the lower part of his face. He looked a bedraggled sight.

'Roddy, how are you?' the big detective asked, smiling.

'Ah, fek, I've done nothing! What do you want with me?' the man wailed.

McBride was near the end of a downward spiral. Williams knew it would not be long before he was discovered face down in a dirty alley, like the one he now stood shaking in.

'Settle down, Roddy, I just want a word,' Williams said calmly. 'You forgetting who pays your fucking way, son?' He added in a more menacing voice. McBride stopped struggling and looked around nervously. Williams loosened his grip.

'Now then, Roddy, what have you heard about Billy Barker?' he asked.

The detective's imposing physique towered over the broken addict, who paled at hearing the name spoken. He quickly offered, 'Billy Barker, no guv, I don't know nuffing about that. That is some messed up dangerous business, not even you want to get involved in that, no way.' McBride bounced on his feet as he spoke, his eyes darting, avoiding contact with the detective's.

'Nobody has said a word, Roddy?' Williams pushed. 'You must have heard something; there must be talk on the street, eh?' McBride looked down and shook his head.

'There's no talk, honest; no one wants to know nuffing about it,' the informant muttered. 'Big Jack is going fucking mental.' He looked back up toward the high street and then toward the dark end of the alley. 'Everyone's keeping their heads down, no one's saying anyfing.'

Williams stared at the decrepit figure. McBride finally looked up at him. 'Well, you keep those ears of yours open. If you hear anything, you contact me.'

McBride shrugged. Williams kept staring until Roddy confirmed, 'Okay, okay, if I hear anything I'll let you know, but believe me, you want to get yourself off this one, guv. This is the Prince of Darkness come up from down there.' He pointed to the ground. 'There'll be hell before all of this is over.' Williams had never seen the snitch so frightened. He released his grip and McBride turned and continued hurriedly into the dim light of the alley. Williams watched him go. An unnerving feeling engulfed him. He knew that McBride was right.

When he fell back into the passenger seat of the unmarked car, Galloway asked, 'Anything?'

'He is scared, like everyone else,' Williams replied. His eyes betrayed his own apprehension. Bad things were coming.

CHAPTER FOUR
The Road to Hell

PC Hunter was arched over her colleague, focused intently on the screen sat on the desk before him. It was not in her nature to recognise personal boundaries. She ignored them without ill intent or any undue insinuation. She was a people's person. Her proclivity to engage with others physically had often been misinterpreted. Men tended to wrongly construe any unsolicited corporeal contact. DS Bright did not. His finger indicated the text that he wanted Hunter to read. There was a sense of excitement between the two officers that had nothing to do with their proximity one another. Claire Hunter was a sharp, attentive and intuitive police officer. She had been on the force for a short enough time to still possess unrelenting motivation and enthusiasm for the job.

'What do you have?' Palmer asked, sensing her excitement as he and Mullins entered the incident room.

'It may be nothing, or it may be something, guv,' DS Bright answered cryptically. He had been directing Hunter as they had executed a deep dive on Billy Barker. Her IT skills were well above par, which had made his job easier.

'Do you remember that case about two years ago, guv,' Hunter interjected. 'A young girl was killed in a hit and run, not far from here, along the Roman Road?'

Palmer shook his head. He could hardly remember what crimes had been committed last week, let alone two years ago. Noting his ignorance, Hunter continued. 'Well, sir, the car that killed the young girl – Patty Smith her name was – it was a stolen vehicle.' A faint recollection crept into Palmer's head. 'It was later found that it had been used in an armed robbery on the same day of the accident,' Hunter finished.

Bam. The recall rocked Palmer like a sucker punch.

"Fuck," he thought. Why hadn't they thought of this before?

There was no need for Hunter to continue. Palmer's eye narrowed.

'Billy Barker was one of the men put in the frame for it,' he voiced in a half whisper as if talking to himself. Palmer clicked his fingers, to spur his memory.

'The father lost it, threatened to find whoever was responsible and to make them pay.' An impatient Mullins looked on, still in the dark.

'I remember the scene he caused at the front desk,' Palmer added. *Could it be that easy?* he thought. *P. P is for Patty.*

'That's right, guv,' Bright confirmed. 'But there is more. We know that the father had Billy Barker's name as a possible suspect for the hit and run. We confirmed that with the family liaison officer.'

The room fell silent for a moment before Palmer began filling Mullins in on the details. In hindsight it seemed improbable that this has not been flagged earlier.

'Do we know where he is now, the father?' Palmer asked.

'We're trying to trace him, guv, but he moved lodgings six months ago. The wife left him; he was hard on the drink by all accounts. No one has seen or heard from him since,' Bright answered. Caught up in the moment of perhaps having made headway in solving the horrific murders, his animosity toward Palmer had momentarily thawed. It went unnoticed by Palmer.

'Keep searching,' he instructed. 'We have to find him.' The senior detective paused and looked directly at Bright, then shifted his gaze to Hunter. 'And keep this to yourselves,' he ordered firmly. 'No one finds out about this. No one.' His pointed finger was meant to reinforce the gravity of his message.

Before leaving the room, he asked, 'Have either of you seen that shrink?' Bright and Hunter shook their heads in unison. Palmer turned to Mullins and said, 'Find her and get her to my office, let's see what she thinks of our Mr Smith.'

Palmer sipped a too hot coffee as he read the case file. He was already feeling lighter. It made sense, it all added up. Bryan Smith had been a normal man. He had had a young wife, an eight-year-old daughter, and a five-year-old son. He had owned his own business installing heating systems and by all accounts had done well by it. That was until one wet

April day. His daughter, Patty, had been making her way home, after visiting a friend. The teenage girl has been traversing a pedestrian crossing on the Roman Road when a speeding car had struck her. The driver had ignored the crossing, hit her, and continued without stopping.

Her injuries had been horrific, but she had been a fighter. It had taken Patty Smith three days to die. Her father had never left her side during that time. The police had attempted to trace the driver. The car had later been found burnt out on an abandoned lot in Romford. It had been reported stolen two days before the accident. The investigators discovered that the vehicle was being used as a getaway car at the time that it had struck Patty Smith. Despite having several suspects – the chief one being Billy Barker – the police had never arrested anyone in connection with the accident. Her father's patience had deteriorated as rapidly as his mental health, when the police had failed to make an arrest. Bryan Smith had pledged to hunt down the people responsible. He was a viable suspect in Billy Barker's murder, considering the anger that the killer had directed toward the villain and his daughter.

A knock on the door startled Palmer. He looked up and saw a silhouette behind the frosted glass. 'Yes,' he called.

'I believe you were looking for me, Chief Inspector?' Dr Moore asked as she opened the door.

'Yes, please come in,' Palmer invited. 'Take a seat.'

The psychologist complied and waited for Palmer to speak. She was impeccably dressed in a dark blue business suit. Every strand of her blonde hair was perfectly placed. Her minimalist make-up was flawless. She sat patiently looking across the desk at Palmer, who was lost in the documents that he was reading. After a while she asked,

'Was there anything specific that you wanted or were you simply looking for the company Detective?'

Palmer looked up and smiled.

'I'm sorry, Doctor,' he apologised uncharacteristically. 'I won't be a minute,' he assured, half raising his empty hand without raising his eyes. He finished reading the page he was holding and then placed back it into a folder on his otherwise barren desk. He turned his full attention to the woman seated in front of him. He gave the psychologist a brief account of the Patty Smith case. Palmer did not detect any reaction when he finally asked her what she thought of the father as a possible suspect in the Barker murders. The profiler sat stoic, giving nothing away. Then after a brief silence she responded.

'He does fit some of the initial profile that I've prepared, but certainly not all of it. He is missing what I believe to be an essential attribute.' She paused and leaned forward.

'It is unlikely that the person we're looking for killed for the first time when he entered Billy Barker's residence,' the profiler offered. 'Our man has killed before, this was not his first foray into violence.' Her eyes met Palmer's. Pushing back in her seat, the psychologist confirmed, 'It is certain that we are dealing with a man here. The level of violence, and particularly the level of violence used against the girl, makes it improbable that a woman was involved.' Palmer nodded. He had already reached the same conclusion. The psychologist continued.

'I consider that it is more likely that the crimes were those of a single perpetrator. There is a strong element of intimacy in the killings; I don't think that would be the case with multiple suspects.' Palmer pursed his lips but remained silent until the psychologist finally added, 'In my opinion this was the work of a single, highly organised and calculated individual.'

Palmer nodded. His agreement was tentative, but it did make sense. The murders of Billy and his family, while brutal, were precise and well executed – not the work of an amateur or a crazed attacker. The question was, could Bryan Smith have gained the necessary experience somewhere in the months since his disappearance, or could he have hired someone to do the job for him? That kind of talent cost money, real money.

They did not have to wait long to find out. DC Hunter burst into the office without knocking as Palmer and the psychologist sat discussing Smith.

'Sorry, guv, but I think we've found him,' the uniformed officer said excitedly. 'In a doss house in Basingstoke. Inland Revenue have him listed at the address there as of last month.'

Palmer was unable to resist a smile. You could always trust the taxman to find you. You could be sure that even Osama Bin Laden had been getting tax bills until his untimely demise.

The traffic was thinner than usual, but it was still enough to make the journey across the city painstaking. Bright was at the wheel, across from Palmer. Mullins and psychologist shared the back seat. The vehicle's usually concealed lights were flashing, and its piercing siren assisted in parting the traffic. The fifty-mile journey took ninety minutes. Basingstoke was a large town situated to the west of London. It was the kind of working class town that had been economically ravaged by the pandemic. As they approached the town centre, they rendezvoused with a contingent of Hampshire Constabulary Investigations officers and two Joint Operations Armed Response Vehicles. A search warrant had been arranged and in good time. Palmer held an impromptu briefing with the waiting officers. The armed units looked competent, the investigators less so. When he had finished, they set off at high speed in convey, to the east of the town, in search of their target.

'It's not far, guv,' a young local detective had informed Palmer before he had hurriedly made his way to a waiting car that had then led the way, followed closely by the luminously marked armed response vehicles. In the spring weather Basingstoke lost some of its cheerless appearance. The streets were busy. Masked people busied themselves with getting back to the new normal. The lodge house where Bryan Smith was reportedly staying was in a quiet, indigent area. As they neared the location, they killed the lights and sirens. There was no use forewarning their suspect. If he ran, they may lose him in the densely populated residential streets. They weaved their way along narrow roads until the lead vehicle came to a sudden stop. The two-armed response units followed suit. The trained officers, wearing bulletproof vests, sprang from the vehicles with skilled efficiency. Within ninety seconds they had surrounded the house on all sides and had breached the front door.

'Armed police!' the black-clad officers screamed as they entered the ramshackle house. The house was old and poorly maintained. Paint peeled from its walls and damaged gutters hung awkwardly from the edges of a moss-covered slate roof.

A few minutes later, the commander stepped from the house with the arrogant, cocksure strut typical of most armed response officers and announced, 'All secure, guv, three men detained in the house, all IC one males.'

Palmer nodded, thanked the man, and walked toward the house. The interior reeked of stale tobacco and beer, reminiscent of an old English pub. In the front room, three men were lying on their stomachs on a worn and stained carpet. Their hands had been secured behind their backs with disposable restraints. The room was filthy. A thick layer of dust covered most surfaces. The furniture was old and tattered. Overflowing ashtrays and cans of cheap lager filled the centre table and the two small side tables, which guarded either side of a tattered three-seater sofa. The only sound in the house, apart from the whimpering of one of the men on the floor, came from an old television set, on top of which a makeshift antenna was precariously perched.

Palmer looked at the photograph in his hand and then down at the men. The smell of urine assaulted his nostrils and he grimaced. He pointed to two of the men and said, 'Take them outside for now, but keep them close. I'll want a word with them before I leave.'

He lifted the third man off the floor and pushed him hard into a faded armchair.

'Mr Bryan Smith?' he asked. The man nodded weakly. The red spider veins on his swollen face and his bloodshot eyes revealed his alcohol addiction.

'I am Detective Chief Inspector Frank Palmer. I need to ask you a few questions to assist us with our enquires into a very serious matter.' Smith was unmoved. He remained silent.

'You will need to come with us Mr Smith,' Palmer advised him.

The detective nodded to a uniformed officer who led Smith away.

'Okay,' Palmer ordered. 'I want this place turned over from top to bottom, especially Smith's room.' Having seen Smith and taken in the surroundings, the detective knew that Smith was unlikely to have had anything to do with their case. That was not to say that the case did not involve his daughter. Palmer's face was pensive. An inner voice had cautioned him that it could not be that straightforward. Doctor Moore looked across at the detective guessing at his thoughts. Their eyes locked for an instant, but Palmer said nothing.

The interview room was silent. Bryan Smith sat in one of four chairs, staring straight ahead at the blank, beige wall. Beside him the masked duty solicitor paged through a folder. Palmer looked at the suspect from behind the mirrored glass in the adjacent room. Tara Moore stood beside him. The drive back to London had been sullen. There had been the hope that they would discover that Bryan Smith had added six stone of muscle and had spent years training in the dark arts of an assassin. Or perhaps that he had achieved financial success that would allow him to have hired someone with those deadly talents. What they were looking at was a far cry from either.

'Right,' Palmer said after a while. 'Shall we go and have a chat with our Mr Smith then?'

They walked into the interview room, startling Smith. He turned quickly to look at Palmer.

'You again,' he hissed and then turned back to face the wall.

'That's right, Mr Smith,' Palmer said as he took a seat, placing two large envelopes on the table as he did. He could smell the odour of sweat, stale tobacco and something else. Fear, he could smell fear on the man.

'And this,' the detective introduced, indicating to the psychologist, 'is Dr Moore. She's a forensic psychologist; she'll be sitting in on the interview.'

The young duty solicitor looked up and nodded his approval.

Dr Moore took a seat next to Palmer and said caringly, 'Good day, Mr Smith, how are you feeling?'

Smith stared at her with bitter eyes.

'Oh, I'm just peachy, thank you very much for asking,' he answered sarcastically.

'Right then,' Palmer said, ignoring Smith's tone. He unwrapped a new tape cassette and inserted it into a recorder seated on the table. He pressed the red record button.

'Let's get started. The time is eight fifteen p.m., Thursday the twenty-ninth of July twenty-one. I'm commencing with the interview of Mr Bryan Smith. Present are Mr Bryan Smith, solicitor Allan Walton, Detective Chief Inspector Frank Palmer, and Dr Tara Moore.' He turned to look at the uniformed officer standing motionless in the corner of the room and added, 'And Constable Neil Blake.'

Palmer paused and beat his thumbs on the interview table, his eyes firmly fixed on Smith. The man's clothes were old and dirty. It had clearly been a while since he had concerned himself with his personal appearance. He had the familiar look of the destitute. His hair was greasy. His fingernails were overgrown and black.

'Mr Smith,' Palmer said, looking directly into Smith's soulless eyes. 'Can you tell us where you were on Tuesday night between six p.m. and six a.m.? That's Tuesday just past, Bryan.'

'Well, that's not Tuesday then, that's Tuesday and Wednesday,' Smith said mockingly, correcting Palmer.

The detective smiled and nodded.

'Right you are then, Mr Smith,' he replied politely. 'So Tuesday evening, Wednesday morning, where were you?'

'I was at home,' Smith replied, 'in my room.'

'Alone?' Palmer asked.

'No, with Angelina Jolie,' Smith spurted with false bravado, then quickly added, 'Yes alone.'

'Can anyone vouch for you being there?' Palmer asked.

'I don't know, you'll have to ask them,' Smith answered.

'Them?' Palmer queried.

'The others that live in the house,' Smith replied, shaking his head.

'Ah, okay,' Palmer nodded. 'But can you remember whether you spoke to anyone between those times? Did anyone come into your room? Did you go to the kitchen, the toilet and bump into someone?' Palmer asked, continuing in an even, friendly tone.

'I don't know, I can't remember. Maybe, I don't know,' Smith answered.

Palmer hesitated before asking another question. He thought carefully, his eyes never straying from Smith, who was becoming unnerved by the detective's unwavering stare. His head dropped lower and lower.

'Have you ever been to the Victoria Park area, Mr Smith?' Palmer asked.

Smith looked up. 'Of course I have,' he replied. 'I lived around that area for years.'

'Have you been there recently?' Palmer asked.

'No,' Smith confirmed. 'I haven't been home for a while.'

'Any reason why?' Palmer queried.

Smith gave him a steely stare and then looked down again. He didn't answer the question.

'Is it because of what happened to your daughter?' Palmer pressed.

Smith stiffened visibly but remained silent.

'Your daughter was killed in a hit and run accident in April, two years ago,' Palmer stated, withdrawing a black and white photograph from a manila envelope. He placed the photograph of Patty Smith on the table. Smith fought to keep his eyes averted from the picture. He could not stop himself from looking. He sucked in his breath sharply and touched the photograph gently.

'Do you know who Billy Barker is?' Palmer asked.

Smith was silent. He did not seem to hear the question. His mind was suddenly ringing with the pain that he had spent years trying to deaden with volumes of cheap alcohol. Palmer repeated the question. Smith heard it the second time.

'Yes, I know who Billy Barker is,' he responded. 'He killed my little girl.'

'Allegedly Mr Smith, Mr Barker was never charged or even questioned regarding your daughter's accident,' Palmer corrected, then asked, 'Are you aware, Mr Smith, that Billy Barker and his family were murdered in their home near Victoria Park on Tuesday evening?'

Smith laughed. It was the crazed laugh of a barely sane individual. Palmer did not interrupt him. He waited patiently. Smith's solicitor seemed unnerved by his client's actions. He reached over to touch his shoulder, but withdrew his hand quickly, not wanting to contaminate himself with his client's filth.

'You think I killed them?' Smith asked incredulously when he had stopped laughing. His head juddered as he spoke. 'I would've loved to have killed him, Detective, I would've loved to have seen him suffer, but I was too much of a coward,' Smith revealed. Then he added, 'I knew he was killed. It's been in every newspaper.'

'Do you have any idea who killed Billy Barker and his family?' the detective asked.

Smith shook his head and answered,

'No, but if I did, I'd buy him a drink, a large one.' He let out another deranged laugh.

The detective removed a second photograph and placed it on the table in front of Smith. It showed Lucy Barker lying on a stainless-steel autopsy table.

'You'd buy the man who did this a drink?' he questioned, tapping the photograph forcefully. Smith was silenced instantly. He turned his head away, his face greying. The room went quiet.

Palmer thought for a while and then removed a book from the large envelope on the table.

'Is this your book?' he asked, showing Smith the hardback that scenes-of-crime had removed from his room. It was an SAS combat handbook.

Smith sniggered.

'Yes, it's mine,' he answered.

'Planning on joining the SAS?' Palmer asked.

Smith smiled and shook his head, all the time keeping his eyes away from the table.

'You can never be too careful,' he replied.

Palmer reached into the envelope again and withdrew a plastic bag containing a military style combat knife with a sharp, four-inch blade.

'Is this your knife, Bryan?' the detective probed, tapping the through-tang on the table. Smith looked at the knife but said nothing.

'Done any carving with it lately?' Palmer asked. He repeated the question, but Smith still refused to answer. For the benefit of the tape recording, Palmer said, 'I am showing Mr Smith a combat knife, which was recovered from his residence in Basingstoke. Mr Smith refuses to answer the question. Mr Smith, I understand your anger toward Billy Barker, although it was never proven that he had any involvement in your daughter's death,' Palmer said while removing three more photographs from the envelope.

'But his daughter did not deserve this.' He spread the three colour photographs out on the table. Smith still refused to look down at the images, until Palmer shouted, 'Look at them!'

Smith jumped.

The detective fixed his eyes on Smith until his head slowly turned downward. When he saw the pictures, it seemed to take a few seconds for his brain to make sense of them. He inhaled deeply, his eyes widening.

'Jesus, God,' he uttered.

'No,' Palmer said. 'This was not the work of any god; this was the work of a man, a fucking monster. Now, I am going to ask you again, do you know who killed Billy Barker and his family?'

Smith's solicitor interjected.

'Detective, we are starting to stray into the arena of intimidation,' the man said. His superior accent riled Palmer.

'You have asked, and my client has answered. These horrific images will not change his response,' the solicitor stated.

Smith's bravado was gone. He looked at his solicitor and shook his head. His eyes returned to linger on the photographs.

'I don't know, I swear to God, I don't know who killed them,' the dejected man said. Palmer knew that it was the truth. It was the last question Palmer asked. He terminated the interview, ejected the tape, and he and Dr Moore left the interview room.

As they headed down the corridor toward Palmer's office, he asked, 'So what do you think, Doctor?'

She answered him with a question.

'Did you notice how his hands shake?'

Palmer nodded.

CHAPTER FIVE
Fresh Blood

The Mirror, Friday

Gangland Erupts After COVID 19 Calm

A wave of gang-related violence has erupted across the city. This latest violence is believed to be in retaliation for the brutal killing of Billy Barker, brother of renowned gangland figure, Jack Barker. A police source confirmed that they are bracing themselves for more violence but they are confident of an arrest in the Barker slayings soon. A man is believed to be helping the police with their enquiries.

Years of experience told Palmer that Bryan Smith was guilty of nothing more than being unable to come to terms with his daughter's death. He was a broken man trying to escape the pain and heartbreak that controlled his tortured existence. Tara Moore also doubted Smith's capacity to commit such brutal and calculated murders. The only good news that Palmer had was that Jack Barker seemed to have reined in his firm. No more wounded had turned up in local hospitals. There had been no newly reported disappearances. Palmer knew it was only a lull. This was not the end. If they did not identify a suspect soon, the violence would start again.

A symphony of raised voices fought to be heard in the incident room. The noise level only dropped slightly as Palmer entered the room.

Tara Moore sat alone at a desk at the front of the room. Her eyes were fixed intently on the screen of the tablet in her hand. Palmer's head throbbed. Single malt still wept from his pores.

'Okay, that's enough!' he shouted. The room quietened except for Bright and Miller, who continued a heated exchange.

'I said that's enough,' Palmer growled. The two officers complied.

Miller turned to face the front of the room, and Palmer asked, 'What's going on, would you like to share with the rest of the class, Miller?'

Miller reddened but remained silent.

'Well?' Palmer urged.

'It's nothing, guv,' he insisted.

'So then, where are we today?' Palmer asked loudly, not expecting an answer. He continued before any was offered.

'We're going to hold on to Bryan Smith for the time being,' he continued, scanning the room as he spoke. 'We are not discounting the possibility that these murders may have some connection to Smith's daughter's death, but he's not looking good for this, so we're back to where we started, which is…' He raised his eyebrows and gestured with his hands that he expected an answer. None was forthcoming.

'Nowhere,' he barked, fighting to keep his voice even. The strain of the past forty-eight hours and the unwelcome effects of a bottle of scotch were telling. The room sat silent.

'Most of you,' Palmer continued, digging his hands into his pockets, 'have met Doctor Tara Moore by now. She's a criminal profiler, and,' he paused, removed one hand and wagged his index finger at his audience, 'she is hopefully going to give us some insights that might help us, because God knows we need help.'

The detective looked across at the profiler and nodded. She stood and walked to the front of the room tapping the screen of her tablet. The psychologist wore a pair of black trousers and a perfectly fitting blue cashmere top. Palmer looked at her appreciatively, and a little too obviously. She blushed almost imperceptibly, pushed her hair behind her ear with one hand, and coughed to clear her throat.

'It seems that two assumptions have been made about this case,' the psychologist began, without any introduction, looking up from her screen to ensure that she had the room's attention. A few heads nodded, most looked at her unmoved.

'The first assumption is that we're dealing with a single suspect. The second is that the murders are somehow related to the criminal activities of either Billy Barker or his brother, Jack Barker.'

'Or both,' a voice added.

The profiler ignored the interjection, turned to face the screen mounted adjacent to the whiteboard. She tapped the tablet in her hand and a photograph of Billy Barker appeared on the sixty-five-inch screen. The villain was nailed to his bedroom wall, his dead eyes bulging from their sockets. The image was horrendous. It got the reaction she had expected. Turning to face her audience, she said, 'I do not believe the evidence fits with both assumptions. We are, I believe, dealing with a single killer.' She paused, glancing back at the screen.

'But, we are dealing with an individual who had a deeply personal motive for committing these crimes. These murders were symbolic and specific,' she tendered. The image changed. It was a closer shot of Billy Barker from a different angle. His exposed, dead eyes appeared demonic.

'These murders had profound meaning to whoever committed them.' The profiler turned her head to glance at the screen then turned back to face the investigators seated before her.

'It is likely that these murders were driven by revenge.' It was a working theory that most of the detectives agreed with,

'However,' the profiler paused to ensure that she had her audience's attention. 'Not revenge for an underworld transgression, this was not...' She stopped, to think of the correct wording. 'Business related,' the psychologist added. Turing to face the screen again, she continued while pointing to the image to Billy Barker.

'This was personal, it was passionate.'

'Revenge for what, then?' Jason Bright asked with obvious scepticism in his voice. His work with organised crime had introduced him to the worst that humanity had to offer. He did not think that such barbaric killings were beyond the work of some gangland psycho. There were many of them available for hire.

'Well,' the psychologist began to reply, tapping her screen. The two images of Billy Barker appeared side-by-side. 'What do these pictures tell us?'

'That we're dealing with a sick fuck!' Dylan Porter blurted out.

There were a few sniggers. Dr Moore smiled.

'Perhaps,' she agreed. 'But what else do they tell us?' The question was rhetorical. She continued before anyone attempted an answer.

'They tell us that our killer's anger was directed toward the father, but the father's pain, his punishment, came from witnessing his daughter's suffering.' She pointed to the screen again, explaining further. 'The killer wanted us to experience the horror of the scene, it is a reflection of what he experienced, and also that someone close to him suffered.'

'So our killer was taking revenge for something Billy Barker did to someone else, someone close to him?' Jill Mullins proffered. The profiler shot her index finger toward the detective.

'That's correct, but I think that the crime scene, and the ritualistic nature of the killings, tells us more.' The psychologist looked directly at Mullins as she spoke.

'The crimes were representative of a past event, an event involving Billy Barker and a third party.'

It was obvious that the profiler was losing her audience, but she continued.

'These crimes were a direct result of a past event.' The faces of most of her audience remained impassive. Tara Moore pointed back at the screen. 'This was retribution for something particular; it was the consequence of a distinctive incident.' Tara Moore paused again to gauge whether the investigators were able to understand her opinion. The blank stares indicated that most were not.

'Our man is taking revenge not only for a third party or parties, that Billy Barker wronged, but also for his own suffering that resulted from that event.' A few of the detectives nodded, they were beginning to comprehend the profiler's assessment. Doctor Moore was relieved.

'His suffering was the direct result of whatever Billy Barker did, or what the killer perceived him to have done, to someone close to him.'

'Well, that fits Bryan Smith like a fucking glove,' DS Bright interposed. Some heads nodded.

'Or his missus,' a voice theorised.

Palmer had already considered that possibility. It was, according to Tara Moore, unlikely that Sheila Smith was involved in the killings, though not impossible.

'That's why we're not finished looking at the Smiths yet,' Palmer confirmed.

The profiler waited for the room to quieten down before she continued, her voice remained even and professional.

'Our killer meticulously planned these killings, he fantasised about them, went over every detail again and again. I believe what he gained from the murders was gratification and release. He could only achieve that gratification by killing these specific victims in these specific ways, fulfilling an elaborate fantasy most likely developed over an extensive period.'

The profiler looked down at the screen in her hand.

'Physically, our suspect is male, white, late twenties to early thirties. He will have a history of violence. He has almost certainly killed before.'

'Why do you think the wife was killed so cleanly and the daughter was tortured?' Mullins asked.

'That is a good question, Detective. I have considered that point,' Dr Moore informed truthfully.

'I think that it indicates again that the killer was concerned only with the father and the child. The mother was killed simply because she was there; that's why she was dispatched quickly and cleanly – she played no part in his fantasy, so she was of no interest to him.'

Mullins nodded. It was the same conclusion that she had drawn. Palmer shook his head. He wanted to hear it all again.

The van stopped outside the house. The driver pulled up the handbrake and turned to the passenger.

'Let's do it!' he said and opened the door. He got out and opened the sliding panel, which accessed the rear of the van. It had ferried many passengers in the past days, some of whom had made return journeys neatly parcelled in black bin liners. The driver let the side panel close but made sure the lock did not engage. It made it easier to get their target into the back in a hurry. The two men headed to the front door of the house. The taller, neatly dressed man rang the bell. Beside him the younger, the muscled, heavily tattooed man turned and eyed the street. The North London neighbourhood was quiet. It was the kind of place where people minded their own business. A young boy clutching a smart phone answered the door.

''Ello, mate,' the neatly dressed driver said, looking down.

'Is your mum home?' The boy looked up and then turned and ran off into the house without saying a word. He left the door slightly ajar. A few minutes later a pale, dark-haired woman in an apron appeared in the small entrance hall.

'Hello,' she greeted as she approached the door. 'Can I help you?'

'Are you Sheila Smith?' the taller man asked pleasantly.

The woman nodded, sensing too late that something was wrong. The man swung his fist. The heavy blow landed on the woman's jaw. She dropped to the ground, unconscious. Behind her, her young son stared silently, shaking, moisture darkening his trousers. The men quickly lifted their target and hauled her to the waiting van. A minute later they were making their way through the traffic back to the yard.

Jack Barker was alone with the woman in the Blood Pit. The subterranean chamber had been constructed from two twenty-foot sea containers that had been buried several metres below the ground and protected by a foot of steel-reinforced concrete. The chamber was accessed via a hatch that had been strategically concealed between rusting metal carcasses at the rear of Jack Barker's scrap yard. A door allowed access from one container to the other. The space had been constructed with the objective of striking fear into the hearts of his adversaries. Many knew of the chamber's existence. They had heard the rumours of the depraved torture that occurred within the confines of the steel walls. It had been designed to serve as a deterrent. It worked.

The woman was still unconscious, sitting tied to the steel chair that was bolted to the floor of the container. The walls and roof of the chamber had been painted with products that made the surfaces easy to clean. As a further measure, to minimise the potential for any evidence to remain, the walls were lined with plastic sheeting. The floor was covered in linoleum. It had been installed to allow water to drain easily into a sump, which then allowed the liquid and any fragments it contained to be sanitised and disposed of.

Sheila Smith's head was tilted to one side. Red spittle ran down her swollen face. Barker circled her, like a hyena around a dying gazelle. The only sound came from the whirring of the small fan sucking air into the chamber. Barker picked up the bucket of icy water that had been placed

73

in the room and threw it over the woman. She woke, startled, struggling against her restraints. 'Whaa, whaa, what's happening?' she asked in a startled, panicked voice. Barker said nothing. He was standing behind her. He slapped the back of her head and the woman cried out.

'Oh, my God, oh my God.'

Barker leaned toward the woman and snarled.

'Your God is not here, bitch, he is nowhere near here.' He reached into his pocket and removed a small vial. He unscrewed the cap and poured a heap of white powder onto the top of his fist. He snorted it, repeated the action, and returned the vial his pocket. He walked slowly around to face the woman, wiping flecks of powder from his nose.

She looked up at him, terrified. She recognised him instantly.

'What's going on?' she pleaded.

Barker's hand lashed out and the woman's head flew backward. In an instant he lurched forward and grabbed her hair, pulling it back viciously.

'Now,' the gangster said, his face close to his terrified prey. 'I want to know who did it.'

Sheila Smith shook her head furiously, trying to clear it her mind. As the shock eased slightly, she began to make sense of what was happening. She had read in the paper about Billy Barker's murder. She had read it and smiled. She had said a prayer and had thanked God for taking the life of the evil man she blamed for her daughter's death. She had been sorry to read that his wife and daughter had died too, but that was what happened to evil men. They dragged the innocent into their dark world and the innocent suffered for their sins.

'I had nothing to do with that,' she said, shaking her head. 'I had nothing to do with that.' She looked from side to side, trying to understand where she was.

Barker looked down at her. The villain had been informed that Bryan Smith was assisting the police with their enquires. He did not believe that the man was capable of his brother's murder, but he could not ignore the possibly that his family had somehow been involved. It was not impossible that his brother had been killed as revenge for the death of Patty Smith. Nothing else seemed to make sense. Barker remembered the incident well. He knew that his brother had been driving the vehicle that had killed the young girl. He knew that because he had set the job up; it had been a good score. The girl's death was an accident. It was an accident and Billy had felt remorse for it. Jack had seen it as collateral damage.

'Who killed my brother, Sheila?' Barker asked venomously. 'It wasn't that worthless piece of shit husband of yours, so who was it? Did you hire someone? Your old man has no money, but you have a few bob, so what… did you hire some talent to do it? Did you have someone kill my brother?'

The woman's sagging head shook slowly. She was staring at the pools of congealed blood on the floor of the container. Then Sheila Smith went still for a moment. She raised her head and looked up at Barker defiantly, burning hatred replaced the cold fear in her eyes.

'Your brother killed my little girl, he deserved to die,' she said in a wavering voice. Then spat, 'I hope he suffered good and proper, but me and mine 'ad nothing to do with killing him.'

'There's an urgent phone call for you, guv, line three. It is Sergeant Cummings over at Leyton nick,' a uniformed officer informed Palmer.

Palmer reached over and picked up the nearest phone.

'Palmer,' he barked.

'Frank, hello, mate, its Den, Den Cummings,' the caller said.

Palmer knew Cummings from the Met snooker club.

'Den, how've you been?' he asked.

'So-so, mate,' Cummings replied. 'Listen, I've got a young boy in here, says his mother was abducted from their home in Leytonstone. One of our lads think it may have something to do with this Barker business.'

'What's the boy's name?' Palmer asked.

'It's Smith, Bryan Smith.'

Palmer stiffened.

'All right Den,' he advised. 'Please keep him there. I'll send a car to get him.'

He slammed down the phone, then picked it up again quickly and dialled a number. He let the phone ring until an electronic voice asked him to leave a message. He hung up and dialled another number. It was engaged. He hung up and tried again. Barker's secretary answered on the second ring.

'Essex Scrap Metal,' she said in a singsong voice.

'Linda, its Frank Palmer. Is Jack there?'

'I am afraid not, Mr Palmer,' she answered. 'Mr Barker is out of the office at the moment.'

'Linda, it's important that you get a message to him. He needs to call me, do you understand? It's a matter of life or death,' Palmer insisted, trying but failing to sound composed.

Unmoved, Linda calmly replied, 'I'll tell Mr Barker you called.' And hung up.

Jack Barker picked up a cloth from the floor of the container and wiped his hands in a futile attempt to clean the blood. The woman was still seated in the chair, her head hanging at an impossible angle. Her battered face was unrecognisable. Barker opened the door to the adjoining room. The second room was fitted with a glass shower cubicle and change room. A clean shirt and complete suit hung neatly from hangers on a steel rack. Barker stripped off his clothes and stepped into the shower. He washed the crimson from his body, relaxing in the warm spray. His mind was anaesthetised. He dressed in the fresh set of clothes. When dressed he looked into the full-length mirror and admired his appearance. Then he climbed up the ladder and opened the hatch leading into a tangle of scrap metal that hid the entrance of the chamber. He absently dusted his trousers, and headed for his office, passing Harry Black on his way.

'Get rid of her and clean the pit,' he ordered without stopping.

Ignoring his secretary, he slammed the office door behind him and took a seat at his desk. He buried his head in his hands, fighting to clear the miasma that dulled his thinking. He had to get a grip. He was losing control. He took the vial of cocaine from his pocket and emptied the contents onto his desk. Using a credit card, he scraped the white powder into a line and fashioned a straw from a ten-pound note.

The woman had known nothing, he was sure of it, neither had any of the other recent visitors to the Blood Pit. So, what was going on? His brother had not been a random victim. He could not have been killed by chance, at the whim of some passing madman. Someone knew who had killed him, someone out there knew.

The big man relaxed back in his chair. Despite the rush of the almost pure cocaine, he somehow managed to fall into a fitful sleep. The buzzing of the intercom on his desk woke him.

'Mr Barker, Mr Palmer is here to see you,' his secretary informed him. As always, she refused to refer to Palmer by his rank. It was the third time that she had seen the detective in as many days.

Barker wiped his eyes and sat up straight. He took a moment to compose himself, then pressed the button on the intercom and said, 'Send him in.'

The door opened and Palmer entered. He walked over to Barker's desk and stood looking down at the red-eyed killer.

'Frank, take a seat,' Barker said.

'Where is she, Jack?' Palmer asked, ignoring the gangster's invitation.

'Where's who, Frank?' Barker answered, slurring his words.

'You know who I'm talking about Jack, Sheila Smith, Bryan Smith's wife, where is she?'

Barker shook his head and pursed his lips.

'How the fuck would I know that, Frank? Why would I know where she is? Did a little birdy tell you stories?' Barker's tone was mocking.

'Listen, Jack, known thugs disappearing is one thing. Right now, people are happy to look the other way for the sake of peace, but when civilians are abducted from their homes in front of their fucking children, that is another matter, Jack. Now, where is she!' Palmer asked forcefully, just shy of shouting.

It was not often that someone raised their voice when talking to Jack Barker. He let it slide. He was aware that he had made another mistake. His need for revenge was ravenous and insatiable. Palmer looked at him. Years of knowing the man told him the worst was true. Sheila Smith was dead.

'Fuck, fuck,' the detective cursed loudly and collapsed onto a chair in front of Barker's desk. The two men sat in silence until Palmer said, 'She had nothing to do with this, Jack.'

Barker raised his hands in a weak gesture of defence but said nothing.

'This has to stop,' Palmer urged, his voice mildly panicked. 'It's not helping Jack, it's not helping. We'll find whoever killed Billy but killing innocent people won't help.'

Barker looked up at Palmer, his eyes dark and narrowing.

'When I find who was responsible for Billy,' he spat, 'then people will stop dying.' Any regrets for his actions were gone, swept aside by his all-consuming anger. A cold sting ran down Palmer's back. When Palmer left Jack Barker sank back into his chair. His mood was black.

'Palmer, the cunt, who the fuck does he think he is?' His mind raced. 'You have to be smarter than this, Jack, Palmer's right. Fuck them all and fuck Palmer. They killed Billy. He's gone and he's not coming back, ever. But sitting in a prison cell for the next thirty years won't help to find them that did it.

'God grant me the foresight to know where I'm going, the hindsight to now where I've been and the insight to know when I have gone too far.' It was a saying that his mother had often spoken. His eyelids dropped and repeated it. Then he slowly opened his cold, trenchant eyes. There was no time for weakness.

Palmer answered his phone and held it to his ear, steering with one hand. It was Pat Casey, the pathologist. He informed Palmer that he had received the toxicology reports and the final autopsy reports.

'Hold a minute, Pat,' Palmer said before Casey began his summary of the information he had received. The detective fiddled with his phone, enabling the Bluetooth that connected his phone to his car. He wanted Mullins to hear what Casey had to say. It turned out to be less than he had hoped for. The scene-of-crime examiners had discovered little evidence. The only potential clue was a hair found on the girl that didn't belong to her or either of her parents.

The follicle was still intact so they would almost certainly be able to extract DNA. The lab was still working on it. Casey did not have to confirm that it had been made a top priority. Unlike the fantasy realm of television, extracting a DNA profile was not as simple as scanning an item with a high-tech gadget that provided an instant result. The hair could prove to be their first useful evidence. It was something.

Casey's hypothesis at the scene had been correct. Billy Barker had been drugged. In fact, his blood held a smorgasbord of chemicals. y-Hydroxybutyric acid, commonly known as GHB, cocaine and a large amount of amphetamine. They had also found Xylazine, an alpha-adrenergic tranquiliser commonly used to subdue animals, and ketamine. Casey surmised that the Xylazine-ketamine compound had been used to incapacitate Billy. How it had been administered was unclear. The y-Hydroxybutyric acid had likely been used to keep Billy Barker immobile but cognitive while he had been forced to witness his daughter's suffering. The cocaine had only been detected in trace amounts. It was likely self-administered by Barker before the attack. High levels of amphetamine had been found in his system, most probably used to keep him conscious.

They had also found high levels of amphetamine in the daughter's blood. The chemical had likely been administrated for the same purpose, to keep the young girl awake and alive for as long as possible during her ordeal. Just like Michael Crawford had said, the killer was a real scholar of the arts. Casey had never seen anything like it in all his years as a pathologist. He relayed that to Palmer. The drugs were relatively easy to come by, even the Xylazine. The Dark Web hosted many sites that sold the products. The difficulty was knowing how and in what dosage to administer them.

The killer had been conversant in the use of the various chemical compounds. The film industry had spawned the belief that rapid acting human tranquiliser darts had been covertly developed. There was some evidence that suggested that sedative compounds that included chemicals such as dimethyl sulfoxide had been developed to instantly incapacitate humans. They could not rule out the possibility that Billy Barker had been injected or even darted.

When Casey finished delivering his precis, Palmer felt obligated to ask questions. None came to mind. Instead, he dejectedly thanked the pathologist and glanced across at Mullins.

'What are we dealing with here?' he asked rhetorically.

When he arrived back at the station, Palmer found Dr Moore at home in his office. Crime scene photographs and medical reports were strewn across his desk. He startled the profiler as he entered.

'Chief Inspector, I apologise for the intrusion,' she expressed, standing as Palmer walked behind his desk. At least she had not taken his seat. He indicted for her to sit.

'I don't mind, Doctor, as long you find something in there that helps us solve this case,' he lied. He was annoyed by the intrusion. His house may be a mess, but at work Palmer's office was always immaculately kept – pathologically so. He liked it that way. Also, there was also a bottle of Smirnoff vodka in his desk drawer that he was eager to get his hands on.

'Anything new?' he asked.

'Well, the forensics reports, and the autopsy reports have come through. The scene was remarkably clean, as you suspected, and the extensive use of chemical agents in the murders has been confirmed.'

Palmer nodded.

'Yeah, Pat Casey just called me,' he replied, lifting a sheet of paper from the desk.

There was a knock on the door. Palmer looked up to see Paul Miller standing in the doorway.

'Come in,' Palmer said to the constable.

'Guv, we've checked all of Smith's family. His father is dead, cancer eight years ago; his mother died earlier this year, COVID 19. He has one brother in Australia and no other close relatives we can determine. Pretty much a similar story with his wife. Both parents dead, no siblings, no close relatives as far as we can tell.' Palmer nodded. Before he left, Miller added, 'I believe that the wife has been abducted, guv.'

Palmer nodded his head but ignored the comment.

'So, let's go back to Billy Barker. He must have done something damaging to someone; if not Patty Smith, then who? It must be there, dig deeper,' Palmer ordered.

Miller nodded and made to leave.

'Here,' Palmer said before he left, scratching through the papers on his desk. He found the sheet he was looking for and held it up for Miller.

'These are the chemicals likely used to floor Billy Barker.' Miller leaned forward and took the sheet from Palmer.

'The xylazine and ketamine may have been used in a tranquiliser compound.' Miller's expression was unsure.

'You mean like a dart gun, guv?' Miller questioned. It was not lost on Palmer that it sounded implausible.

'Or a syringe, Miller, he could have been injected,' Palmer replied to clarify. The junior officer left.

'What are we missing here, Doctor?' Palmer asked, shrugging his shoulders, when he was alone with the profiler. 'What kind of killer would have these capabilities?'

'I'm not sure, detective,' she replied. 'But I think that the answer is in here somewhere.' The profiler placed her hands on the mix of files in front of her.

The uniformed officer in the brightly marked patrol car recognised Tommy Macfarlane as soon as he emerged from the betting shop on the Mile End Road. The Glaswegian's heavy athletic frame filled a trademark dark green suit. Most officers in East London knew Macfarlane on sight. He was a known face, a nasty piece of work. The officer monitored the ex-boxer as he walked east. He stopped when he reached a late model silver Mercedes C63. The office waited until the gangster was in the car, before turning the patrol car around. As the Mercedes pulled into the traffic, the patrol car's lights and siren were activated.

A BOLO had been issued for Macfarlane in connection with the disappearance of Sheila Smith. The patrol officer expected Macfarlane to pull over. Experienced villains seldom ran from the police. They preferred to be questioned or detained and to allow their high-priced solicitors to get them released. Running created unnecessary nuisances. Macfarlane would throw "fucks" at the officers all the way to the station, but men like him had no fear of the police, or the filth, as they more commonly referred to them.

This time the Scotsman surprised them. Instead of pulling over, he accelerated. The engine of his high-performance car roared. The patrol car gave chase. The officer in the passenger seat called in the pursuit as they went after Macfarlane. He had driven many getaway cars and was a skilled driver. He swung hard right heading south toward the river. His reckless manoeuvre caused a crowded bus to swerve into oncoming traffic. He turned east, pushing the car to a hundred and twenty miles per hour. He narrowly avoided several startled pedestrians. His side mirror caught a cyclist, sending him crashing to the ground. He saw that the lights ahead were red. He swerved around the stopped vehicles in front of him and careened across the busy intersection. There was no way for the white Ford delivery van to avoid the collision. The sound of screeching tyres and crunching metal reverberated throughout the surrounding area. The force of the collision sent shattered glass flying in all directions. Stunned onlookers stared in dismay. Within seconds everything was still again. Macfarlane's car had struck the van on the driver's side door. The impact had sent the unsecured boxer crashing through the windshield and into the side of the van. The van's driver had been knocked sideways into the passenger side door, where he lay bloodied and still. The two pursuit officers raced to the mangled wreckage, stopping in the centre of the intersection. They hurriedly exited their vehicle and headed to the mangled wreckage. Macfarlane was clearly dead. One officer went to the van driver's aid. Experience told him that nothing could save the man. He died minutes later. The traffic quickly backed up in all four directions. Angry drivers hooted. Crowds of pedestrians, many with phones in hand, gathered to observe and film the aftereffects of the collision.

'This is a mess,' the driver of the patrol car said nervously to his partner. His colleague nodded his silent agreement as he surveyed the accident scene. One officer leaned into the window of the crushed Mercedes. Why had Macfarlane run, was there something in the car that he did not want them to find?

The officer moved around to the boot of the Mercedes. It was slightly buckled, but mostly intact. The lock still functioned. He depressed the silver button and forced the boot open.

'Jesus Christ!' the officer gasped, stepping back from the car. A stench emanated from the plastic-wrapped body.

'Little bloody wonder he ran,' his partner said, as he walked around to where the patrolman stood staring in the trunk.

'What!' Palmer asked, hoping that he had misheard Mullins. The detective repeated the facts. Palmer collapsed into his chair.

'Who gave the order to pick up Macfarlane?' he asked incredulously.

'DI Williams, guv. I thought he'd cleared it with you?' the anxious detective confirmed.

'The Smith kid picked Macfarlane out of a photo line-up; he was one of the men who abducted his mother,' Mullins explained, and included, 'DI instructed the BOLO to be issued.'

Palmer slammed the phone down. He was numb again. This was a nightmare that there was no waking from.

'Problem?' Dr Moore asked, looking up from the screen that she held in her hand.

'Big problem,' Palmer replied standing. He stormed out of his office, without offering any further explanation and went in search of Williams. He found him in the canteen.

'Excuse me, Sergeant,' he said to Galloway, who was seated opposite Williams,

'I need to speak with the DI.' Unable to disguise his anger, he grabbed the back of the detective's arm, lifted him from his seat, and marched him out of the canteen. All eyes followed them. Once they were in the corridor, Williams asked calmly, 'What is it, guv?'

'You gave the order for Tommy Macfarlane to be picked up without clearing it with me?' Palmer asked, forcing his voice to stay low.

'Ah,' Williams stuttered. Then went on, 'Well, we got a positive ID from the boy,' he clarified. 'Macfarlane abducted a woman from her home in broad daylight, guv, that is why I ordered the BOLO, we needed to speak with him.'

'Without notifying me first?' Palmer snarled. '*I* am heading this investigation, *me*. Are we fucking clear on that?' The detective slammed his hand against the wall.

Williams sighed, unmoved by Palmer's outburst,

'We're on the same team here, guv. I assumed that you would agree with the decision.'

Palmer laughed, wiping a hand across his face.

'Assumed?' his eyes bored into Williams. 'Macfarlane is dead.' His reaction showed that the detective was clearly unaware of Macfarlane's demise.

'Now,' Palmer continued, his finger poking at Williams' chest. 'We can *assume* more violence,' Palmer said. He started at the detective inspector and in a tone bordering on desperation, added effusively, 'You think that you know Jack Barker, but you don't.' Palmer stepped back slightly and continued in a more deliberate voice.

'Whatever idea is swimming in your limited imagination of how bad the situation can get, you're nowhere near comprehending,' Palmer lectured. He held Williams' gaze until the shorter man averted his eyes, then he turned walked away, his anger still burning.

'Chief Inspector,' Williams called after him, 'we cannot tolerate the killing of innocent people; we can't tolerate it.' His words sounded hollow and unconvincing. Palmer ignored him. He marched back to his office. His phone rang as he headed into the stairwell. He looked down at the illuminated screen before answering.

Palmer had known Jack Barker for long enough to have guessed what his reaction to Macfarlane's untimely death would be. Barker exploded when he heard the news.

'What was Tommy doing with that bitch's body in his fucking motor?' he bellowed at Harry Black. The young protégé swallowed nervously. A river of sweat ran down his back. Paul Burrows stood silently beside him in front of Barker's desk. Their boss had remained seated. Thankfully.

'I asked you a question, you bloody moron, are you deaf as well as dumb?' Barker roared.

'He, uh, he… well, the van is in for a clean, boss,' Black stuttered. 'Jamie is working on it now, lot of claret spilled in there, boss. When Tommy left, he said he was going to the Black School, so I asked if he could drop the meat there, to let Larney deal with it.'

'Did you clean her properly before you bagged her?' Burrows asked, his head turning to face the younger villain.

Hearing the question, Barker's eyes bored into Black. His DNA would be all over the body. He studied the henchman carefully.

'One hundred per cent,' he assured. 'Honest, boss, there'll be nothing on that bitch, she was scrubbed and sterilised, like we always do.' Harry Black was all too aware that given Barker's mood, a simple nod from his boss could end his life. He was a soldier, loyal to the end.

Barker's focus remained on Black as the office fell silent. Eventually he nodded and visibly relaxed. He knew that it was standard operating procedure for his boys to thoroughly clean each body that was shipped out of the yard for disposal. You never knew when you might get a capture. Even the best brief in London would find it difficult to explain a significant amount of DNA on a mutilated corpse.

Barker was frustrated. He knew that it was Macfarlane's own mistake that had cost him his life. The fool had been unnecessarily driving around with a body in the boot of his Mercedes. He had stopped at a betting shop for fuck's sake. Jack had liked Tommy. He had been a hard nut who had normally acted wisely. Most importantly, he had been loyal and honest. At least he had been honest in his dealings with Barker. That was what counted. The gangster's forehead creased. He looked up at Paul Burrows and then across to Harry Black. What was done was done. Barker did not do sentimentality.

'No more fuck-ups, do you understand me, Harry?' Barker stressed, pointing up at Black. The young man nodded vigorously, glad for the opportunity to hide his shaking.

'Now then, get the fuck out of here,' Barker ordered.

Palmer sat staring into a near empty glass. The drink rested on an old wooden table, one of four in the windowless basement room. The walls were decorated with outdated, nicotine-stained wallpaper. Framed prints depicting scenes from Victorian London added to the antiquated atmosphere of the space. Except for the scar-faced giant who guarded the door, the room was empty. The only sounds were the dull hum of the air conditioning unit and the muffled resonance of the music playing in the pub. The detective could never comprehend why many successful villains insisted on doing business from the ramshackle neighbourhoods they had worked so hard to escape. The truth was that you could take a villain off the streets, but you could never take the street out of a true villain.

Palmer had not been completely surprised to receive a call from Charles O'Connor. The innocuous-looking drug baron, known to most as Irish Charlie, had been unwittingly dragged into the Billy Barker saga. O'Connor's firm controlled much of Irish London, particularly the north-west suburbs that housed large Gaelic populations. Charlie had a long and amicable relationship with Jack Barker, but now his youngest son was in the hospital. His twenty-four-year-old nephew was on the missing list. Palmer was aware of a rift between Irish Charlie's nephew, Liam Flanagan, and the Barkers. Liam and Billy had done a piece of work together in Maidstone. When it came down to dividing up the spoils Billy had insisted that his brother Jack be paid an even cut, even though, by all accounts, Jack had had nothing to do with the job. Flanagan had gone to O'Connor to lodge a complaint. O'Connor had met with Jack Barker. After the meeting, Irish Charlie had convinced his reluctant nephew, Liam, to accept the split. The young firebrand had conceded, begrudgingly. Afterwards he had been vocal in his declaration that he would never to work with the Barkers again. The affair had been a storm in a teacup by gangland standards. The word was that Billy and young Liam had made up and had been planning another heist together. Now the Irishman had been on the missing list for two days. There was little doubt about his fate. His cousin was still laid up in West Middlesex hospital.

Charles O'Connor was an intelligent man who had been raised on the war-torn streets of Belfast. His father, a member of the Provisional IRA, had died at the hands of a British soldier when Charlie was sixteen. His mother had sent him to her brother in London to get him away from the troubles. At the time his uncle had owned a downmarket pub in north-west London, catering mainly to the Irish trade. Charlie had quickly settled in. He had liked London and had soon realised that there was easy money to be made in the city. He had started by selling eighths of hash to the punters in his uncle's pubs. Within five years he was turning over fifty grand a week selling hash, heroin and cocaine on the streets of north-west London. Aged sixty-eight, he was now one of the largest suppliers and distributors of cocaine and heroin in south-east England.

Charlie was not a man who feared other men, but he was a realist. Jack Barker had more money and more power than any other criminal in

London. He was also capable of doing the kind of things that few men, no matter how hard, were willing or able to do. Barker's nature had attracted a clan of sociopaths to his side. His people were loyal in the extreme. His firm was like a cult. Charlie knew all too well that Barker was mentally unstable, even at the times when he appeared sane. Still, he and Barker had made money together over the years. Barker's trucks ferried his illicit goods from mainland Europe to London and then distributed the product throughout the country. Heroin and cocaine were a lucrative business. O'Connor had made certain that Jack Barker shared in the spoils. In return Barker took care of any competitors who interfered with Charlie's business. Their relationship was symbiotic and mutually beneficial. Nonetheless Barker knew no boundaries. He had little respect for other people, even those who he worked and made money with. Many, Charlie included, agreed that this time he had gone too far.

O'Connor still owned several pubs, including the one that he had inherited from his uncle. Palmer sat in secluded room of one of those pubs, waiting for the Irishman to arrive. When he did, the blithe smuggler immediately ordered the giant watching the door to have Palmer's glass refreshed. Then he pulled out a chair opposite the detective and sat down heavily.

'Thanks for coming down, Frankie,' he said in an Irish accent that was still as thick as the day he first stepped off the ferry. He was an average height, heavyset man with thick tattooed forearms, and fingers like pork sausages. His red hair hinted at his fiery Irish temper, but he did not have the look of a violent man. He had the appearance of someone who knew things that no one else did. Despite his wealth, he dressed only slightly better than the construction workers who filled his pubs every afternoon. Palmer knew that it was purposeful. Expensive suits and flashy cars drew attention. Charlie did not like attention.

'What's this about, Charlie?' Palmer asked, sidestepping any small talk.

'I think you know what this is about, Frank,' O'Connor replied, staring straight at the detective.

Palmer had an uncomfortable familiarity with most serious criminals in London. Although he had run with the Barkers back in the day, he was still the filth. He was still an outsider. He and Irish Charlie shared a more open and cordial relationship, despite the fact that Palmer had once served with the RUC. Charlie was not a man of faith. He cared little for religion. He had seen the barbarity perpetuated by both sides in the name of the same God.

'Why don't you fill me in anyway, Charlie,' Palmer responded. A young, attractive barmaid with short blonde hair disturbed them momentarily as she entered the room and placed their drinks on the table. She mutely removed Palmer's empty glass. When she had left O'Connor looked idly around the room, absently turning his glass on the table.

'I still can't figure you out, Frank,' he began. 'After all these years, I still can't figure you out.'

Palmer lifted his freshly filled glass and took a long sip. He looked at O'Connor and said nothing.

'Okay, here's the craic,' the Irishman finally conceded, hunching forward. 'Let me be straight with you. Your man Jack is out of order; he's out of control. My son, my youngest… the little fekker is just off the tit… and my nephew, Frank. What am I going to do, nothing?' He spread his hands wide.

He breathed heavily as he drew back and rested his hand on his chest. Palmer knew that O'Connor had little or no regard for his nephew.

His youngest son had also drifted off on his own path. Still, they were his kin.

'And it's not just me who thinks that Jack is out of fekking order, Frank. Your Jack, he's pissed a lot of people off,' O'Connor finished, slamming his hand down on the rickety table.

Palmer nodded. It was more than he had expected to hear. It was seldom that anyone, even Charles O'Connor, spoke so openly about Jack Barker in such a subversive manner. Palmer shrugged.

'Jack is his own man Charlie, I have no sway over him, especially now.' Palmer tilted his glass and raised it to his lips. He took another sip. 'What do you expect me to do?' he asked weakly. 'God knows I've tried to reason with Jack, but this thing with Billy, it's really messed with his head.'

The room fell quiet except for the dampened noises filtering through from the pub. O'Connor drummed his fingers on the wooden table. Palmer detected a subtle change in his demeanour. The Irishman seemed suddenly hesitant, unsure. After a brief silence he leaned forward again. His heavy frame pushed against the table. In a low conspiratorial voice, he asked, 'Have you heard of a man named Roman Kobec?'

Palmer recognised the name. The man was Russian. He was suspected of involvement in various criminal activities. As with many Russians of questionable character, Kobec had legitimate business interests in London. His companies were undertaking numerous large-scale property developments in and around the city. He had conducted his business out of the public eye until 2020 when he had sought to furtively acquire Millwall Football Club. As far as Palmer was aware the man had never been accused or suspected of committing any offences in the United Kingdom. Allegations against him were just that. Despite being nothing more than hearsay, the negative speculation in the press had proved sufficient for the FA to block his takeover of the renowned London club.

'Roman Kobec, the Russian that tried to buy the Dockers?' Palmer questioned guardedly in response, looking directly at O'Connor. The Irishman nodded. The detective's forehead creased as he shifted, suddenly uncomfortable in his seat. The hair on the back of his neck raised. Charlie hesitated. He had reservations about confiding in Palmer. He knew that he would be taking a gamble, but he had reckoned that the detective was as concerned about Jack Barker as anyone. Barker controlled Palmer, used him. There was no longer a friendship or loyalty to their relationship. O'Connor and others were counting on that.

'Well,' Charlie started cautiously, studying Palmer intently as he spoke. 'Kobec is interested in acquiring certain business interests of Jack's.' Palmer's reaction was not difficult to interpret. As the detective digested what the Irishman had said, his eyes widened. He paled visibly. If anyone had overheard what O'Connor had said, they would both be as good as dead. More probably, they would be begging for death long before it came.

'Are you out of your fucking mind, Charlie?' Palmer hissed. 'You have some foreign cunt wanting to make a move on Jack, now, you have to be completely insane, mate,' Palmer snarled in a raspy whisper.

He was genuinely shocked. It was not at all what he had expected to hear from the Irishman. It caught him off guard. His reaction was, however, what O'Connor had expected. Charlie remained silent, allowing Palmer to vent.

'This is piss-poor timing, Charlie,' Palmer continued, nervously looking around the empty room as if somehow their conversation could be overheard. 'Now isn't the time to bring more trouble on yourself,' he hesitated, his mind rocked by a sudden realisation.

'Unless…' his voice trailed off, his eyes grew larger.

O'Connor raised a hand to stop him before he could continue.

'No, Frankie, don't even go there. Kobec had nothing to do with this Billy business, Billy was a mate; I was at his daughter's christening for fek's sake. Whoever did that was a wrong'n; Kobec had no hand in that.' O'Connor breathed in deeply, then leaned forward and added, 'If I thought for a second that he did, I would have put a fekking bullet in him myself and that's the god's honest truth.' Charlie touched the imaginary ends of a cross as he finished speaking. It was an unbreakable habit formed by a thousand slaps across his young head.

He was fighting to keep his composure, but his eyes betrayed him. He knew the risks and the consequences of his actions. Palmer sensed his nervousness and the slightest hint of fear. The detective felt certain that O'Connor believed what he was saying about Kobec's involvement in the Barker slayings. That was not to say that it was true, only that Charlie O'Connor believed it to be true.

'I don't see what Kobec has got to do with me,' Palmer whispered harshly. 'And why the hell would a man like him want to get involved in Jack's business?' Palmer questioned. He was becoming angry. It made little sense to him. He knew that O'Connor had placed him in a precarious position.

The Irishman had regained his composure and explained evenly, 'He'd like to meet with you, Frankie, he wants to explain his position personally.'

Palmer's head was spinning, bombarded by an avalanche of thoughts, each fighting to be heard. He remained still. His eyes again fixed on the liquid swirling in his glass. There was a long, unnerving silence. The detective was trying to grasp the situation. Was this a set up, some absurd test of loyalty initiated by Barker? As his thoughts settled, Palmer realised that it was unlikely that this was anything other than what

O'Connor had explained. In that case, Roman Kobec has inserted himself into the situation. No matter what Charlie believed that made him suspect number one to Palmer.

His eyes locked with the Irishman's until O'Connor eventually looked away. Then the detective asked, 'When?' O'Connor's relief was palpable.

'He'll be in contact with you,' he answered sighing heavily.

A tight knot had formed in the pit of Palmer's stomach. He drained his glass and stood to leave, wanting urgently to escape the suffocating room. He looked down at the seated O'Connor and said, 'You're playing a very dangerous game, Charlie. It could spell the end for both of us.'

O'Connor nodded. He knew the detective was right. He raised his glass and cited, 'May we get to heaven long before the devil knows we're dead, eh, Frankie.'

Palmer pulled a solid wooden stool away from the bar and slipped onto it. He felt as if he was losing control. The meeting with O'Connor had left him feeling vulnerable and exposed. He was involved now. If he did not tell Jack about the conversation with O'Connor, he would be implicated in any dealings with Kobec. If the gangland boss found out about any of it, a full scale war would erupt. He would be cannon fodder – first in the firing line. He ordered a large scotch on ice, sank it in one gulp, and shaking his glass he ordered another. After his fifth double his anxiety began to ebb. He left the pub.

It was raining again. He lifted the collar of his coat and crossed the street to where his car was illegally parked. As he fumbled in his pockets, searching for his keys, a voice startled him.

'Mr Palmer?'

Palmer swung around and saw two oversized, well-dressed men standing behind him on the pavement.

'What do you want?' Palmer snapped. He was instantly alert.

'Our boss wonders if you have small time to spare for him?' the smaller of the two men enquired politely. He tightened his lips, and added, 'He assures it is for your best interest, Detective.' He had a light, almost comical East European accent.

'Does he now?' Palmer replied. 'Well, you tell your boss, whoever he is, that I am not available.' The detective's eyes had narrowed. He had already scanned the man for weaknesses. He would need to strike the taller man first. He had a long neck, his Adam's apple was prominent and exposed.

'If he needs to speak with me, he can call at my office, like everyone else, and make a fucking appointment,' Palmer appended offensively. He knew that the "boss" that these goons were referring to must be Kobec.

The two men stood unmoving. Palmer's mind played out the attack. Hard right fist to the throat, kick to the groin, left elbow to the face. Instead of initiating the confrontation, Palmer sighed and asked, 'Where is this boss of yours?'

'He is just along the street, it will take not a minute,' the taller man replied, indicating the direction. By their appearance and manner, it was clear that the two were not low-level henchmen. Palmer nodded, signalling that he wanted the man to lead the way. They headed a short distance along the High Road and turned onto a side street, where a dark limousine stood idling. One of the men tapped on the rear passenger side window. Like a scene from an Ian Fleming spy novel, the window dropped slightly and then closed. The taller chaperone pulled the door opened.

'Good evening, Chief Inspector,' the sole passenger in the Bentley greeted when Palmer was seated opposite him. The spacious interior of the car was luxuriously finished. The rear of the vehicle had four seats, arranged with two plush white leather seats facing each other. The adjacent seats were separated by dark stained burr walnut veneer consoles. The console beside Roma Kobec held two lead crystal decanters and four matching glasses.

'A drink for you?' the Russian asked and confirming, 'Scotch, single malt on ice?'

Palmer nodded and his host poured a generous drink from the lead crystal decanter and handed it to the detective. He took a large sip. The quality of the whisky was instantly notable. It was well aged.

'Right then, I'm in no mood for games, so let's cut to the chase. What is it you want, Mr Kobec?' Palmer pushed.

'Yes, of course, Chief Inspector,' the man replied, taking no offence at Palmer's tone. 'As you are probably aware by now, my name is Roman Kobec, and progress Chief Inspector, is what I wish to discuss with you.'

Palmer was able to scrutinise the Russian in the cavernous interior. The man appeared younger than the detective had expected, although he was several years older than him. He was impeccably groomed, wearing an immaculate dark suit with a silk cravat that did not look dated on him.

'Times are changing. We are entering a new world, changed forever by greed and capitalism that,' Kobec said and raised his index finger, 'given the rope to run wild, has hanged itself and now lies bleeding in the halls of power of most western nations, gasping its last breath.' Kobec's voice was authoritative without being loud. It was obvious that he was an intelligent man.

'We need to change with the times, or we will be forgotten, living in the past, like dinosaurs,' Kobec declared.

Although accented, his English was perfect. His words made little sense to Palmer. The detective stared out of the window sipping his scotch. The Russian continued.

'I have many interests in your city, Chief Inspector. It is now my home. It is a place of many opportunities.'

He paused. Palmer turned to face him again. He did not look like a violent criminal. He had a calm, refined air about him. His face was handsome in a Mediterranean kind of way, his perfectly styled, pitch-black hair combed back on his head. His deep, cold and blue eyes revealed the real man, even in the dull light. His eyes radiated malevolence. The knot in Palmer's stomach tightened and narrow fingers of fear crept up his spine. This man could well be responsible for the murder of Billy Barker and his family.

'Your friend, Mr Jack Barker, he is having some problems and he is acting in an unprofessional manner,' Kobec stated calmly. His hands were used to support his words. His eyes were fixed on Palmer, reading his reactions, however slight.

'Jack has upset many people. People who want to do business, to make money. They do not want all of this bloodshed and violence, it is unnecessary, and it is problematic for everybody.' He spread his arms like a priest giving mass as he finished.

Palmer remained silent for a while, but eventually asked, 'What has this got to do with me?'

Kobec drew a deep breath and pursed his lips. He selected his words carefully.

'Well, Chief Inspector, let me be direct. I believe that Jack Barker has made his alliance with many of his associates untenable.' His hands flared,

'There is a need to have this situation attended to. I have the necessary,' he paused, 'attributes, let us say, to resolve this situation and to incorporate many of Mr Barker's interests with mine.'

The man raised his eyebrows, still looking directly at Palmer. The detective gave the very slightest of nods to indicate that he understood.

'You see, Chief Inspector, what needs to be avoided is yet more bloody conflict. Money drives men like us, not conflict; conflict is bad for business, it attracts unnecessary attention.'

Palmer gave another almost imperceptible nod. He could scarcely believe Kobec was being so open about his intentions. He was dubious about the man's intentions. It seemed absurd that a man of his stature would step away from his lavish comforts to cavort with the likes of Charlie O'Connor. It was obvious that there was more truth to the rumours of Roman Kobec's criminal enterprises than many believed. Despite his wealth and success, he was just another felon, albeit more of a Bond villain than simply a garden variety underworld figure.

'You know Jack Barker, you know his organisation, and you are a senior policeman,' Kobec sipped his drink. 'These are attributes that can be very helpful to me.' The Russian hesitated, gauging Palmer's reaction before appending, 'Of course, your services would not be without considerable reward.'

Palmer looked out of the car's window. The rain had stopped.

'Do you honestly think that Jack Barker is that easy a man to deal with?' he asked, turning back to look at Kobec. The man smiled. He had anticipated the question.

'Normally, I would say no, Chief Inspector,' he answered honestly. 'But this business with his brother, it has weakened him, and a clever predator can always sense a weakened prey.'

Palmer nodded and asked the most relevant question, staring directly into Kobec's eyes.

'And how much did you have to do with that business with his brother?'

Kobec pushed back into his seat. He raised his right index finger and moved it in a long arch to and fro.

'I can assure you, Chief Inspector, that I played no part in that. I am a businessman, not a madman, and that was the work of a madman.' The Russian was a difficult man to read.

'Well, I'm not sure that I want any part of this,' Palmer responded and drained his glass.

Kobec nodded and said evenly, 'I understand, Chief Inspector. I did not expect for you to make a hasty decision.' He hesitated and added, 'Think about what I have said, we will speak again.'

Palmer walked back to his car. He ignored the rain that was falling harder now. The limousine passed him as he tapped his pockets in search of his keys. He sat in the darkness thinking. However dangerous it was, what Kobec had said made sense. Palmer knew that Jack Barker had angered a lot of people. It had made him vulnerable. He also knew Barker well. He had witnessed first-hand the consequences of underestimating the psychopath. Roman Kobec's true objective still concerned the detective. His intuition told him that something was amiss. He could not dispel the lingering sense that such direct involvement by the Russian in a potential coup against Jack Barker seemed wrong.

Palmer needed information. He scrolled through his phone book and found Dylan Porter's number. Holding the phone to his ear he manoeuvred his car out of the parking space and onto the empty street. The call to Porter went unanswered. Roman Kobec had been very sure of himself, but however wealthy and powerful he was he would not find Jack Barker easily vanquished. If it turned out that Kobec was connected to Billy's murder, all the money in the world wouldn't protect him. Palmer sighed. He knew without doubt that things would get a lot worse before they got better.

He jumped when his phone rang. It was Porter.

'Dylan, you must be busy if you can't answer my calls,' Palmer said cynically, edginess evident in his voice. Porter was apologising when he was cut short.

'This conversation goes no further than us, are you clear,' Palmer informed the detective constable. Porter confirmed his understanding.

Palmer continued, asking, 'Tell me what you know about a man named Roman Kobec.'

There was silence on the other end of the phone. Porter knew the name, but he took a short while to place it.

'Kobec,' Porter eventually repeated. Then said, 'The Russian, he has money, real money, he has a reputation as a bit of a phantom, kind of a Keyser Söze, you know.'

Palmer didn't.

'He is heavily into property, as far as I know guv,' Porter continued. 'Wasn't much known about him until he tried to buy Millwall, then all those stories about him came out.' That was as much as Palmer knew.

'What else you know about him?' he asked.

Porter, hesitated, before replying, 'Not a lot, guv, other than what was in the papers.' Porter paused and then asked quickly, 'You think he's involved in our case?'

Palmer did not answer. Instead, he said in a low, staid tone, 'Listen carefully, Dylan, I want you to compile as much information about Kobec as possible. I want to know everything there is to know about him, but you need to be discreet, tell no one about this. I mean no one, do you understand?' Porter confirmed his understanding, but to reinforce the point Palmer added, 'If the wrong people get word of this, we'll be dealing with a fucking massacre.'.

Porter confirmed again that he grasped the seriousness of what his senior office was saying. Palmer cut the call. He knew Porter well enough to trust him. Despite Kobec's assurance that he had nothing to do with Billy Barker's death, Palmer was not convinced. He had seen in the Russian's eyes the same cruel, indurated mien as was in the eyes of men like Jack Barker.

The house was dark and still, infused with the soothing hum of electrical appliances. The alarm was hopelessly inadequate. He had disabled it effortlessly. He had been in the house before, to familiarise himself with its layout. Now he stood in the large entrance hall, allowing his eyes to adjust to the dark interior. When he felt ready, he cautiously made his way up the stairs. When he came to the first bedroom, he gently turned the doorknob. The door made a slight noise. He froze, waiting to be certain the sound had not disturbed anyone in the house. When he was sure it had not, he pushed the door open and stepped silently into the room.

The form of a man was evident beneath the covers of the sprawling double bed that filled much of the room. He approached, looked down at the sleeping figure, and, in one graceful, flowing movement, he extended his arm and depressed the trigger of the slender weapon held in his hand. The dart escaped with a quiet hiss, quickly finding its target. He turned and left the room.

In the next room a couple lay entwined on a bed. Light from an adjacent street lamp entered the room through a gap in the curtains. He raised his hand again and fired a single shot at each, this time using a different weapon. There was no quiet hiss, only the brief sound of metal against metal. A small red dot appeared on the foreheads of the unsuspecting victims. He fired again, another round into each.

Wasting no time, he turned and headed for the last room. There a young boy lay on a single bed, his small frame visible in the blue haze of the nightlight. Model aeroplanes hung from the ceiling. Toys filled the tall shelves lining one wall of the room. What a happy boy, what a happy life. He stood looking down at the sleeping figure, slowly removing the neatly fitting black rucksack from his back. He removed a glass bottle from the bag, opened it and poured a portion of its clear, acrid-smelling contents onto a small black kerchief, which he held tightly against the boy's face. His little body struggled for a moment and before falling still. He neatly folded the small cloth and placed it in a clear Ziplock bag, together with the glass bottle. He returned the contents to his pack before lifting the listless body from the bed and carrying the child into the adjacent room. He gently laid the boy on the bed, then pulled his lifeless parents onto the floor. He drew the curtains and switched on a side lamp. A dullish light filled the room. The surrounding area housed upper-middle class families. It was mostly semi-detached housing that had quadrupled in value in two decades. People had grown far more accustomed to being socially distanced their neighbours since COVID. They would not be disturbed.

He returned to the first room he had entered. Now less concerned about making a noise, he dragged the unconscious man from the bed and into the room where the family now lay quietly. He moved a small ornate dressing table and positioned the man against the wall where the table had stood. Retrieving his rucksack, he reached into the bag and withdrew a syringe. When he had finished injecting the man, he placed the used syringe in a side pocket of the bag. With the precise and rehearsed movements he withdrew a hammer and several long nails.

He lifted the man's arm and drove one nail through his wrist and another through the forearm just below the elbow. He repeated the procedure on the opposite arm. When finished he carefully replaced the tools in the backpack. He searched in the bag again without looking and removed a small scalpel. He removed the protective plastic cover from the ultra-sharp surgical instrument and went to work carefully removing the man's eyelids. Blood ran from the wounds. He removed a medical swab from the bag and cleaned the lesions, quickly stemming the blood flow.

When he was finished, he pulled back and, like an artist reviewing a canvas, he studied his work. He stood and looked around the room, to ensure that everything was placed as he intended. Satisfied, he let his hand fish in the bag again. He removed a small bottle, opened it, and held it beneath the man's nose. The man woke, startled, in shock and completely paralysed. He tried to move but his body would not respond. His eyes bulged in their sockets as he tried desperately to blink.

'Hello,' the stranger said, staring into the man's wide, terrified eyes. 'I have been looking forward to spending a little quality time with you and your family.'

Kobec knew that he had taken a risk talking to Palmer, much as O'Connor had. He recognised that he was acting too quickly. He was being driven to exploit the precarious situation resultant from the murder of Jack Barker's brother. It was a risk, but not an entirely blind gamble. Frank Palmer was an open book. There was no doubt that the detective's career was about to reach a dishonourable end. There was also a reasonable possibility that he would succumb to Jack Barker's grief-fuelled rage. For now, Kobec knew that Palmer could be very useful to him. He had the access to Jack Barker that few had. He knew the man and his organisation better than most. Palmer was now caught between a rock and a very hard place.

Roman Kobec was a man whose life had been driven by an insatiable lust for wealth and power. In London, Jack Barker wielded the power. It was inevitable that he would eventually encounter the gangster. He had been provided with reams of information about Barker and his criminal empire. The villain was old school. He was ruthless and violent. In another life they might have been allies. He would be no easy target, but he had weaknesses. The death of his brother had wounded Barker. It had unhinged the already unstable man. It had created an opportunity, one that Kobec was being urged to capitalise on, against his better judgement. Barker had turned against friends and foe alike in pursuit of his brother's killer. People were no longer prepared to sit by and wait for him to annihilate them. A rebellion was imminent. Roman Kobec had been nominated to lead it. Barker had alienated a lot of people in the London underworld and its periphery. He had added to an already long list of enemies. He had no adversary formidable enough to challenge him. Many in the London underworld would band together to support someone that they believed could.

Kobec had spent months making inroads into the London underworld. His endeavours had been guided by a powerful hand. He had had many contacts in the city before his arrival. Men like Charles O'Connor, whom he had supplied heroin to for more than a decade. O'Connor had introduced him to others. His reputation had brought people to his table. He was no fool. When Barker was gone, he would share the spoils with those he needed. He would deal ruthlessly with those who refused to accept change. It was not the life that he had wanted or chosen, but he would make the best of it.

He had the support that he needed to tackle Barker. The people responsible for his permanent relocation to London had intended him to embed himself in the city's underworld. It was part of their perverse plan. The Russian had prospered for many years. It had made him indulgent and vulnerable. He had paid the price. Now he was glad to be getting his hands dirty again.

Roman Kobec was a hard man. He had been raised near the town of Luhansk in the harsh eastern reaches of the Ukraine. His father, Vladimir Kobec, had been a renowned smuggler. He had developed extensive trafficking routes from Afghanistan, north through Kazakhstan and the Rostov region of Russia, and into the Ukraine. Vladimir Kobec had worked for years with the Sicilian underworld, supplying the secretive criminal organisation with large quantities of the heroin, which had then been smuggled across the Atlantic to America. When Roman Kobec was sixteen, his father had been assassinated after a dispute with a rival trafficking syndicate. He and his mother had been forced to flee. Three years later, Kobec had tracked down the men responsible for his father's murder, after which he had gone to work rebuilding the family business. By the age of twenty-five he had been moving more than two tonnes of heroin a month.

Later he had diversified into arms trading. Kobec had found it infinitely more profitable to pay for heroin shipments with weapons rather than cash. Following the collapse of the Soviet Union, cheap weapons had flooded the black market, offered for sale by disenfranchised ex-Soviet military officers. Kobec had prospered, supplying weapons to a myriad of despotic regimes. He had accumulated vast wealth selling arms to diamond-rich East African nations, and warring Balkan states embroiled in bloody civil wars. When the Taliban regime took control of Afghanistan, he had supplied weapons to both the religious zealots and the Mujahedeen warlords who opposed them. Before Nine Eleven, he had been known to supply weapons to al-Qaeda insurgents in Afghanistan and Africa. It was the war of terror that had driven Kobec's wealth to heights. His organisation had expanded and thrived during the never-ending conflict that had seen the rise and fall of ISIL and other terror groups whose immense finances had made them key customers.

His success had continued until a British agent, posing as a Syrian arms dealer, had infiltrated his organisation. It had taken three years for the deep-cover agent to gather sufficient information and evidence to bring down Kobec and his vast network. His terrorist links had ensured that several agencies had taken a keen interest in the Russian. In November 2019 he had been covertly abducted from an exclusive Athens hotel. He had been flown to an airbase in Cyprus, where American and British intelligence agencies had interrogated him. There had been no need for any questionable techniques.

Kobec had been smart enough to know that his days of freedom were over. He had also been smart enough to know that he possessed knowledge that those questioning him would find invaluable. He had known of a major terrorist attack planned by GICM, a Moroccan-based terrorist organisation aligned with al-Qaeda. They had intended to strike London. He had known the details of the attack. He had possessed sufficient information to force his captors to make a deal with him. Three days after his arrest, a British anti-terror unit had raided a house in the North London suburb of Haringey. Four terrorist suspects had been killed during the raid. A sophisticated dirty bomb, manufactured from home-made explosives and radioactive materials extracted from an array of industrial and medical devices had been recovered in a nearby lock-up garage. Details of the thwarted attack had never been made public.

Kobec had proved his worth. The allied agencies saw him as an asset. What the Russian had been unaware of at the time, was that the American and British authorities had been planning a complete and rapid withdrawal from Afghanistan. Despite the positive reports emanating from Afghanistan for years, the war there had been lost to the Taliban. The allies had known that after their withdrawal, the war-torn country would become a potential haven for terror groups like ISIS-K and al-Qaeda. Kobec's connections with the Islamic extremist groups in Afghanistan were extensive. His network of contacts was vast and reliable. A deal had been struck.

CHAPTER SIX
Red Mist

Palmer had a few hours of fitful sleep. In a dream, Roman Kobec's eyes had bored into him. The Russian was a dangerous man, there was no mistaking it. It remained to be seen whether he was as dangerous and ruthless a man as Jack Barker. That question now seemed certain to be answered. The detective woke with a feeling of deep foreboding. His apprehension would prove well founded.

The task force was settling down for their morning briefing when the call came through. Claire Hunter received the news first. The blood drained from her face as she listened to the caller. When the call ended, she stood robotically, and walked to where Palmer stood talking sternly to DI Williams.

'Guv,' she interrupted.

'Give us a minute,' Palmer growled, in his usual morning temper.

'It's important, guv, I don't think it can wait,' Hunter insisted.

Palmer swung around and barked, 'What?'

'I just got a call from Southwark CID. There have been more murders, same MO as the Barkers.' Palmer stared at the constable until she was forced to ask, 'Are you okay, guv?'

Palmer nodded his head slowly.

'What's the address?' he asked feebly.

'I'm not sure, guv,' Hunter replied. 'somewhere south-east.'

Palmer faced the murder wall. He stood with his hands on his hips, concentrating his thoughts, before he turned to Hunter and ordered, 'Get me the address. DI Williams, Doctor Moore, Mullin, with me now.' As they hurriedly left the room, Palmer pulled Porter aside.

'Make sure you have that report ready when I get back,' he said in a low, stern voice.

'On it, guv,' Porter replied.

The passengers sat silently gripping their seats throughout the high speed charge to Southwark. Palmer punished the three-litre engine of the unmarked Ford. The ride was frightening. They skimmed past cars, buses and pedestrians. They raced west through Whitechapel, the notorious hunting ground of Jack the Ripper, then south toward the river, crossing over the ornate Tower Bridge. There was a lot of activity at the destination when they arrived.

The house was a large four-storey building, which had served as a local pub for more than a hundred years until Paul Morton had purchased the building. He had refurbished the structure into a stylish home. His renovations had included soundproofing the old cellar to create an indoor shooting range. The area around the house had been cordoned off. Uniformed officers held back a swelling crowd. The first media vans had arrived – vultures attracted by the scent of death. Palmer blasted his horn to move people aside. Impatient, he left the car in the middle of the road near the barricade. He was obviously expected. A young detective approached him as he exited the car, her face covered by a Metropolitan Police issued face mask.

'DCI Palmer?' she queried. He nodded and ignored her outstretched hand.

'I'm DC Beckett. DCI Holland is inside, sir. He said to bring you and your team through.'

They went through the procedure of fitting white disposable suits, shoe protectors and latex gloves and entered the house. The large entrance hall and front room were clean and undisturbed. The home had been tastefully decorated.

'It's upstairs, guv,' their escort advised. Palmer and his team followed her up the narrow stairs that were clearly a feature of the original structure. Scenes-of-crime officers were already at work in the large second floor bedroom, which had once formed part of the pub's function room. Palmer saw Pat Casey bent down on one knee in front of a body, which hung, crucified, against the far wall of the room, just as Billy Barker had been. The blood drained from Palmer's face. The scene looked familiar. There was no doubt that it was the same assailant who had dispatched the Barker family. Apart from the man nailed to the wall crucifixion-style, there was a woman lying next to the bed just as

Barker's wife had. Palmer saw that she had clearly sustained a head wound. He guessed incorrectly that the damage had been caused by a single gunshot. He would learn later that the husband and wife had each been killed by two bullets to the head. A man lay next to her, face down, with no discernible injury. It was the young boy lying naked across the bed that caused Palmer to freeze. He looked much as young Lucy Barker had. He had been savaged.

'How are you doing, Pat?' Palmer asked, turning to face the home office pathologist.

'You're a little far from your manor.'

'I was asked to attend by the powers that be, lucky me,' Casey replied, turning from examining the crucified victim.

'Like I don't have enough on my plate already, I have to deal with this horror show.' His description of the scene was fitting.

'Frank,' another voice greeted. Palmer recognised DCI Paul Holland despite the mask.

'How're you doing?' he greeted, stretching out his hand before awkwardly revising the greeting to a fist pump. Holland was a tall man with a pockmarked face and slicked back grey hair. It made him appear harder than he was. He headed a Major Investigation Team based in Southwark. He had been a tough customer in his day, but his day had passed. He was gliding along the path to retirement, counting down every second. He and Palmer had met several times over the years, both on various cases and at Met socials.

Palmer shook his hand firmly.

'I've been better, mate,' he replied.

'What do you think, same unsub, the crap from your manor spilling over to mine?' Holland asked.

Palmer smiled. Unsub. People watched too many Hollywood productions.

'No doubt,' Palmer confirmed. Then asked, 'Who are the victims?'

DI Mullins answered before Holland could.

'That's Morton, Paul Morton. He used to be a face around South London. I nicked him a few years ago for GBH,' Mullins stated. Then added, 'He got a walk.'

Palmer nodded. He knew Morton, but he still did not recognise the pallid, lifeless face of the hideous creature that hung from the wall.

DCI Holland looked at Mullins, nodded agreement.

'Quite right you are.' Then he asked, 'And who are you?'

'DI Mullins, guv,' she answered, letting her eyes flirt a little. It never hurt to impress a DCI.

'Well, the rest of our victims are all relatives, all lived in the house.' Holland led them to the double bed.

'That poor little bastard was Morton's youngest son. He had him with some crack whore from North London. Mother's been on the missing list for years. He was raising the boy on his own, a good father by all accounts. These two,' Holland said looking down, 'that's his eldest boy and his wife, newlyweds. The boy was said to have been following in Daddy's footsteps; he is already a suspect in more than one contract killing,' the detective advised. 'A real model family, good fucking riddance to them.'

Palmer sniffed and wiped a hand over his face. He needed to get out of the house. The room was large, but suffocating. It was overcrowded with officers and scenes-of-crime technicians. He looked at Tara Moore, who was scanning the room from top to bottom with a distant look on her face.

'You saw the carving on Morton's chest?' Holland asked.

Palmer shook his head and walked over to the remains of Paul Morton. The profiler followed.

'Can you open the shirt a little more for us, Pat?' Palmer asked the pathologist, who was still processing the body. Casey complied. A six-inch letter E had been clearly and neatly carved onto the lifeless chest, defiling the intricate, spread eagle tattoo.

'Done post-mortem, same as with Barker,' Casey verified.

'E, P – E, what the fuck does it mean?' Palmer wondered out loud, turning away from the wall. 'What do you think, Doctor?'

The psychologist didn't seem to hear.

'Doctor Moore!' Palmer said louder and she snapped out of her daze. 'Are you okay?'

'Yes, Inspector, sorry,' she replied, embarrassed. 'I was just trying to take in everything.' Palmer nodded, unconvinced. The profiler was visibly shaken by the scene inside the house, but the detective needed her to see it first-hand.

'Right, Williams, you stick around here, see what comes up, and keep me posted. Mullins, you stay with the DI,' Palmer instructed. Then he turned to DCI Holland and asked, 'Can we fast-track the forensics on this one, Paul?'

The DCI nodded,

'Already in motion, Frank, Borough Command has given this A one priority.'

Back in the car heading north toward the station, Palmer asked Tara Moore, 'So what do you think now, Doctor?' He hesitated and then added,

'I am sorry that you had to see that.'

'You can call me Tara, Chief Inspector,' the profiler replied, turning to look at the detective. Palmer briefly met her gaze and quickly looked away. The slightest smile played on his lips.

'I am not quite as delicate as I appear,' she retorted.

The psychologist had unstiffened since their first abrasive meeting. Now seeing how the scene in the house had affected her, Palmer's opinion of the woman had improved.

'I think it's evident that the father was the principal target here again, as was Billy Barker,' the profiler said. Hesitating briefly, she appended, 'Which means that there is likely something that links him to Billy Barker and whatever that is, links both to our killer.'

Palmer nodded. He was beginning to understand the profiler's view that the murders were personal rather than "business" related.

'Well then, *Tara*,' Palmer said, emphasising the psychologist's name, 'we need to find the common denominator that links them, and we need find it quickly.'

Glancing across at Palmer again, the profiler said, 'This Paul Morton was a known criminal, so was Billy Barker; I don't believe that's a coincidence. That is where we need to begin.'

Palmer agreed. He remembered Morton. He was the violent type, used to be muscle for hire and, if rumour was to be believed, a talented hitman: a freelancer. Like Macfarlane, he had also had some success as a boxer.

'And the letters P – E, my guess is they're initials,' Palmer suggested, thinking out loud.

'Unless they are the start of a word and our killer intends to kill more people in order to finish spelling it out,' Dr Moore responded.

'Homicidal hangman,' Palmer said. 'We'd better hope it's a short bloody word then.' He picked up his phone and was about to dial a number when it rang.

'Frank, is that you?' He recognised Pat Casey's voice.

'Pat,' Palmer confirmed. 'What've you got?'

'Look,' the pathologist started then fell silent for a moment. 'I couldn't talk earlier,' he said, then stalled. Palmer sensed that something was wrong.

'I thought I'd let you know the lab had a result on that foreign hair from the Barker girl. It's not good,' Casey said. Palmer did not understand the message.

'Meaning what?' he asked too abruptly, then apologised. Casey brushed it off. He was about to give the detective unwelcome news.

'Well, they got a positive match on the DNA,' the pathologist advised. 'It was yours, Frank.'

Palmer frowned and his foot unconsciously hit the brake, causing the car behind him to swerve wildly to avoid ramming into his rear end.

'I don't understand,' he voiced once the car was stopped. 'It was mine?'

'Aye,' the pathologist replied. 'It must have been contamination, Frank, from when you were at the house.'

Palmer shook his head, ignoring the angry shouts of motorists who were edging past his vehicle. He ended the call, deep ridges forming across his forehead. He had a bad feeling. Something was not right. He could sense it. Years as an investigator and a well-developed survival instinct told him there was more to this than was evident.

'Everything okay?' Tara Moore asked, startling the detective.

Palmer nodded absently and replied, unconvincingly, 'Yeah, it's nothing.' He thought for a minute before saying, 'I'd like you to do me a favour when we get back to the nick; I want you to take a look at a man I believe may have some involvement in this.'

The detective was hesitant, but he had an overwhelming sense that time was running out.

'DS Porter is putting together a file on him,' Palmer explained. 'He's a known Russian businessman, recently relocated to London.'

The doctor nodded.

'Sure,' she replied. 'Have you got any solid reason to believe this man is implicated?'

Palmer didn't answer at first. He just nodded, sucked in his bottom lip, looked into his rear-view mirror, and drove on.

'Could be,' he finally replied. 'But let's just have a poke at him for now, strictly between us and the four walls, okay? We can't afford to jump on the wrong bandwagon.'

The psychologist looked sideways at him and nodded her agreement. The sky had cleared. The bright morning sun reflected off the dew-covered surfaces and blinded Palmer as he headed back east. When they arrived at the station, the detective waited in the car, inviting the psychologist to go on ahead. He dialled Jack Barker's number.

The gangster answered on the second ring.

'Barker.'

'Jack, it's Frank.' Barker remained silent and Palmer continued.

'Do you remember a face named Paul Morton?' The question was rhetorical. Palmer was aware that Barker knew Morton.

'What about him?' Barker parried.

'He was done in last night, along with his whole family. It was the same person who killed Billy, no doubt.'

Barker was silent again, but after a while he said, 'I've haven't seen or heard of Morton in years, never liked him to begin with,. The gangster paused then said, 'I heard what happened to him, same as with Billy.' Palmer was not surprised.

'Did he have anything going on with Billy?' the detective asked.

'Not that I know of, and I would know,' Barker replied.

There was a short silence again, before Palmer said, 'Well if you think of anything…'

After the call Palmer sat thinking. Barker, Morton. They needed to go back to the street again, find out whether Billy had anything going on behind his brother's back. It wasn't impossible. Jack was overbearing when it came to Billy, always had been. Palmer knew Billy had felt suffocated by his older brother.

The taskforce, minus Williams and Mullins, were gathered in the incident room again. Palmer stood beside the murder wall speaking with Dylan Porter. When everyone had settled in, he turned to the board and said, 'Listen up, this is the situation. We have four more victims, at this stage there's strong reason to suspect they're linked with our case. The murders are almost certainly the work of the same killer.'

Palmer went over the details of the latest murders. Every head in the room shook as he recounted the scene inside Paul Morton's house, especially when he described the injuries to Morton's nine-year-old son. So, they were now looking for a link between Paul Morton and Billy Barker. If the same killer had murdered them at such a close interval, there must be a connection between the two. Palmer barked orders. They were to check the national crime database and go out onto the streets again, speak to sources, maybe someone could tell them what the link was. They now had two letters, P and E. The killer was marking his victims for a reason; they needed to find out what it meant.

Palmer had been informed shortly before the team had assembled that the CPS wanted Bryan Smith released. He apprised the team. Given the latest events, none had any real notion that Smith had anything to do with their cases. When they finished Palmer asked DS Porter and Tara Moore to meet him in his office in five. It was enough time for him to down a glass of vodka. Porter arrived with the profiler and an iPad.

'Right, what have you got?' Palmer asked, once the detective was seated.

Porter cleared his throat, looking nervously at the profiler, until Palmer nodded for him to continue.

'Roman Kobec is an elusive character, guv,' Porter began. 'He is originally from East Ukraine but is a Russian national. There is a lot of rumour and speculation surrounding him, but not a lot is actually known about him. There are suggestions that he was involved in weapons trafficking, and Interpol had him in the frame for the murder of a Lithuanian national in Paris in 2008.'

Palmer considered the information. It was not much. He nodded toward Porter again, his cue to continue.

'Kobec has had business interests in London going back a long way, but he appears to have relocated to London with his family permanently in early 2020.' Porter paused, pushing his finger across the screen in his hand.

'He has since invested seriously in property here. The Police Intelligence boys have kept an eye on him because of the weapons trafficking allegations, but it doesn't look like he's put a foot wrong since he arrived here, guv.'

It made no sense to Palmer. London was a big pond but was it a big enough pond for the likes of Kobec. If Kobec intended to make London his permanent home, it made little sense for him to instigate such a hostile takeover of the biggest criminal organisation in the city. It would focus the entire Metropolitan Police force and the intelligence services on his activities.

'Should I go on, guv,' Porter asked, noting that Palmer was lost in thought. Palmer nodded.

'What most people know about Kobec is that he tried to buy Millwall last year.' Porter ran his finger across his screen. 'The FA blocked the sale, which raised questions in the press about why Kobec had been allowed residence in the UK if they had such reservations about his character.' Porter looked up from the screen. 'The story never really gained traction, looks as if it was quickly forgotten.' Porter shrugged. 'Since then there has been little word about Kobec.'

Palmer looked intently at Tara Moore when Porter was done. None of what Porter divulged indicated that Kobec may somehow be responsible for the murders of the Barker and Morton families. Perhaps Morton he had been dealing with Kobec and had put a foot wrong. It was all just speculation.

'How *was* a man with his reputation able to gain residence?' Tara Moore asked.

It was a worthwhile question, how indeed.

'He and his family were granted "indefinite leave to remain" a month before arriving in London,' Porter said. Looking down at the screen in his hand, he added, 'There is something odd about that, guv, there was no application date or any details related to his visa application on file.'

Something about that was not right. Palmer had had a lot of dealings with the immigration services over the years. East London had the largest population of illegal immigrants in the country, many of whom became involved in criminal activities. An immigrant visa application was a long and arduous process that took months, if not years, to complete. Applications invariably resulted in an extensive volume of personal information related to each applicant. It was something that needed checking.

'So,' Palmer said after some thought, slapping his palms onto his desk. 'Could this man be interested in staking a claim to the throne of the London underworld?' The question was directed at the profiler. He already knew the answer, he had heard it from the horse's mouth, but he was keen to hear Tara Moore's insights into Roman Kobec. She remained silent and thought for a moment her hands held together as if in prayer.

'Do you mean could this man's ambitions somehow implicate him in the murders of both families?'

Palmer nodded.

'It seems that Mr Kobec's involvement in any criminal activity is supposition, so unless you have information that indicates otherwise, I'm afraid I think not, Chief Inspector,' the profiler answered.

'If Mr Kobec is some Machiavellian mastermind, there is still a personal motivation behind the crimes that do not fit with contract killings,' Tara Moore rationalised. She turned to look at Porter and then back to Palmer and continued.

'If this Kobec had planned a foray into Barker's world, why not just kill Barker himself, why kill his brother first and warn Barker that he was coming?'

Palmer nodded. The psychologist had a point. Kobec did not appear to be a man who would beat around the bush. He appeared to be far more direct.

'Okay, Dylan, I need you to check further into this, see whether anything matching the MO of these murders has ever come up against Kobec,' Palmer ordered. Clicking his fingers he added, 'Find out how he managed to get those visas and locate the immigration records.' Porter stood to leave.

'Dylan,' Palmer spoke solemnly. 'Keep this quiet. If Jack Barker finds out we're even sniffing around Kobec, he could go off on one, and that,' the detective expressed prophetically, 'would mean a fucking bloodbath.'

DS Porter and the psychologist left Palmer's office. He sat staring at the open file on his desk. His mind searched for a solution, something he had missed. He was startled when the phone on his desk rang. The station receptionist advised him that his ex-wife was on the line. He reluctantly agreed to take the call. Patricia Palmer was a fierce woman in the traditional East End sense. She and Palmer had suffered a stormy eight-year marriage, which had ended in a bitter divorce. His wife had won full custody of their young daughter and ownership of their house. Palmer had not contested either. He had just been glad to be rid of the woman.

'Well, I hope you're happy!' Patricia Palmer spat venomously when she was put through.

'What the hell are you on about now, woman?' he retorted, not bothering to be polite.

'It's your daughter, she's in hospital, Frank, *hospital!*' the woman yelled.

Palmer's eyes closed. He did not have the strength left to deal with this. He said nothing and waited for his ex-wife to continue, as he knew she would.

'And you don't give a rat's backside, do you, Frank? She could be dead in a ditch for all you care, you're pathetic, Frank, pathetic!'

Palmer continued his silence. Years of experience had taught him that silence was the best way of dealing with Patricia.

When he said nothing, the ever-angrier woman continued.

'She had a drug overdose. It's lucky her flatmate came home when she did, or our daughter would be *dead.*'

Palmer's head dropped, and he asked dolefully, 'Which hospital is she in?'

He drove through the old stone arch and into the parking lot of St Bartholomew's Hospital. He found a parking space and headed for the

George V building. He found the ward he was looking for and stopped a blue-uniformed nurse who was passing the unmanned station. The polite woman explained his daughter's condition in a sincere voice, surprisingly to Palmer without any outward hint of judgement. When finished, the efficient nurse showed him onto the ward and pointed to a bed at the far corner. The blue vinyl flooring was polished to a shine. It gave the ward an air of cleanliness. Neat, patterned curtains hung from the windows.

The disconsolate detective stopped next to the bed and looked down at his sleeping daughter. A white plaster held a needle in position on her arm. A line ran from the needle to a clear plastic bag hanging from a steel hook above the bed. Palmer reached down and touched his daughter's arm. He felt overwhelmed. The strain of the past days was suddenly exacerbated by the sight of his daughter. She stirred and opened her eyes slowly. She looked directly at her father but seemed unable to recognise him. She was a pretty girl with an angelic face that was now as white as the pillow that her head rested on. Dark rings underlined her bloodshot eyes. Her cheeks were hollow and sunken. She closed her eyes for a minute and then slowly opened them again.

'Daddy,' she said weakly.

A lump formed in Palmer's throat.

'It's okay, sweetie,' he replied, trying not to sound like he felt. 'You just rest now, angel, don't try to talk.'

Tears formed in the corners of the girl's eyes and ran slowly down her cheeks. Palmer leaned over and kissed her forehead, then fell into the chair beside the bed.

'I'm sorry, Daddy,' the girl managed to say before falling back to sleep.

Palmer wiped his hands across his face, then let his head rest in his hands for a moment. He looked up to find a young Asian doctor standing at the foot of the bed.

'You her father?' the doctor asked, tersely. Palmer nodded.

'She had a narrow escape,' the doctor explained. 'This could have been a lot worse.'

Palmer sighed, looked down as his feet, then back at the white coated figure and asked, 'What was it?'

'Heroin,' the doctor replied. 'Must have been from a bad batch, probably laced with something like fentanyl. It caused a severe reaction, but she'll be okay this time.'

Palmer was at a loss for words. He had known for a while that his daughter was using drugs. He had spoken to her about it before. But he had had no idea that she was using heroin.

'How long will she be in here for?' he asked.

'We'll keep her in for a few days and monitor her condition,' the doctor confirmed in a slightly comical Asian accent. Then added, 'We'll have a counsellor come and see her too.'

Palmer nodded again. It was all he could do.

'You look as if you could use some rest yourself,' the doctor expressed, observing Palmer. He gave the doctor a defeated smile. The coronavirus pandemic had taken the world by surprise. The United Kingdom had been slow to react. That delay had resulted in apocalyptic scenes and national lockdowns. The youth may have been spared the worse of the virus, but they had suffered, nonetheless. Mental illness amongst teenagers was at an all-time high, while access to drugs was easier than ever. It was a recipe than had dire consequences.

Every pew in the church was filled. Three black, flower-covered coffins dominated the front of the church. Those unable to find a seat stood along the rear wall. Most of the men in attendance wore black suits. Many, including Jack Barker, still wore their sunglasses. Barker sat in the front row next to his estranged wife. His dark glasses hid his swollen eyes. Palmer edged his way through the crowd at the rear of the church until he found a place to stand. The service was almost over. He listened as the priest, dressed in coloured vestments, ensured all present that the deceased were already enjoying eternal happiness in heaven. Palmer's eyes fixed on the crucified figure behind the altar. He shuddered. Thankfully there were few present who knew the full horror of Billy's demise. After a recitation of the Lords Prayer, he concluded, '*In nomine Patris, et filii et Spiritus Sancti.*'

The pallbearers stepped forward. The organist began to play. All eyes were fixed on the coffins as they were raised onto the shoulders of black suited men. The disproportionate size of Lucy Barker's coffin was notable.

Palmer made the decision not to follow the procession to the graveyard. He walked slowly back to his car observing the row of waiting horse-drawn funeral carriages as he crossed the road. A pair of Belgian black horses stood motionless in front of each carriage seemingly aware of the sorrowfulness of the occasion. Plumes of white feathers decorated their heads. Palmer caught sight of Collin Grey loitering on the pavement as he neared his car. Grey was a known criminal who controlled a vast territory in North London, from Highbury to the Holloway Road. Drugs, prostitution, robbery – he was into it all. King's Cross was the capital of his domain. Grey had started out working for Jack Barker years before. With Barker's help he had forged his own territory. Originally from Bethnal Green, the villain still had a broad cockney accent and still supported West Ham United. He was a short, stocky man with a rapidly developing midsection and an even more rapidly receding hairline.

'Collin, you look fucking lost mate,' Palmer called as he approached. Grey looked around nervously. He was clearly not comfortable wearing a suit. The one that he wore hung awkwardly from his body as if it were melting.

'How you doing, Frankie?' he asked, his flat tone betraying his disinterest in the detective's well-being.

'Peachy,' Palmer answered sarcastically.

'Is there something I can help you with?'

Grey looked around again and asked conspiratorially, 'Look, can we go somewhere and have a sit down?'

Palmer was suddenly more interested in Collin.

'You know the boozer in Shoreditch, The Feathers? I'll be there in fifteen,' Palmer replied, indicating the direction of the pub with his head as he unlocked the door to his car.

The pub was quiet. It was one of the few remaining traditional pubs in the area. Most others had been remodelled into trendy wine bars. There were a few old-timers sat the bar bent over a betting sheet. A drunken woman, who looked older than her years, was trying to balance on a stool in front of a defunct television set. She was using the blank screen to guide the red lipstick she was smearing across her lips. Palmer ordered a large scotch and found a corner seat. It had been a while since he had spoken to Collin Grey. He was interested to hear what the man had to say. There were no faces that frequented the pub. They could speak privately.

The detective didn't have to wait long. The nervous-looking Grey walked into the pub just as he took a seat. He saw Palmer, looked around the pub, then hastily made his way to the table. He sat quickly and started speaking immediately.

'Look, Frank, I don't want to be seen here so I'll get straight to the point. Jack is hurting a lot of people, people who are friends. He needs to stop or it's all going to go tits up.'

Palmer nodded. It was the same desperate line that he had heard from Charles O'Connor. Collin and Charlie were well acquainted. The pair had several common business interests.

'What do you want me to do?' the detective asked. It seemed certain that Grey must have had contact with Roman Kobec. What was less certain was whether Kobec had requested that he speak with Palmer.

'Have a word, Frank. There's a lot of talk on the street. What does Jack expect us to do? We can't all sit by and wait for him to top us.' The argument was difficult to challenge.

'I've had a word, Collin. But you know Jack, he's not easy to talk to, especially now.' Palmer stalled, choosing his words. 'This thing with Billy.' Palmer stopped again, shaking his head. 'He has taken it hard,' he continued. He quickly added, 'Who wouldn't?'

Grey remained silent. Palmer could tell that the man was seriously on edge. He had obviously had a few grams of gear up his nose.

'What have you heard about Billy?' Palmer eventually asked.

Grey shook his head.

'That's the thing, Frank, no one knows anything, no one's heard a fucking thing, but Jack is just not having it.' He paused and looked directly at Palmer,

'I was hoping that you had something Frank, because out there,' he gesticulated toward the street, 'no one has a clue and if the filth has no idea…' He held his hand up to Palmer to excuse his use of the terminology. 'Then this is not going away any time soon Frank.'

The men sat in silence again for a while, Palmer spinning his half-empty glass on the wooden table, thinking.

'Have you heard of Roman Kobec?' he eventually asked. The look on Grey's face gave him his answer. The man paled but said nothing.

'He's approached you?' Palmer probed.

'Christ, Frank, what do you know about that?' Grey was suddenly more nervous, his eyes wide, flitting. He turned around, scanning the pub again for any known faces.

'Be careful, Collin, is all I'm saying. Things are falling apart. If you hear anything, you let me know.'

Grey nodded. He had heard enough. He stood and extended his fist.

'You won't mention our meeting?' he asked.

Palmer bumped his fist with his and shook his head. The fist pump had been a common gangland greeting in London from long before COVID 19.

He sat thinking after Grey left. The man had seemed genuinely surprised when Palmer had mentioned Kobec. So, what was Grey looking for, reassurance? Was he testing the waters before he dived in with the Russian? Had Barker had found out about Kobec and sent Grey to test him? Paranoia, it was a pestilence once it started. Maybe he was becoming paranoid, but just because he was paranoid did not mean that someone was not out to get him. He remembered reading that somewhere. He had mentioned Kobec, not Grey. He shook his head and said in a whisper, 'Get a grip, Palmer.'

The question that Collin Grey had been trying to answer, was whether there was any end to the matter in sight. He was no doubt being tempted to join the Kobec rebellion. He wanted to know whether he had a choice. He had gotten his answer. Palmer knew that Barker would not stop looking until he found the man responsible for his brother's murder. His violent quest may be his undoing, but even knowing that would not stop his rampage. Roman Kobec was correct.

Barker was an unsophisticated bull. Bulls could be very dangerous animals, especially when provoked and wounded. One thing Palmer was certain of was that Kobec would have no shortage of support if he decided to act against Barker.

There was no telling whom the raging Barker would act against next – it may even be him. He drained his glass. As Palmer left the pub, he took little notice of the man seated at the table close to where he had sat. He had been there since Palmer had arrived, nursing the same beer. Roddy McBride turned and stared after Palmer. He knew who Palmer was, and he knew who Collin Grey was. However, he didn't know who Roman Kobec was. He was sure that the name would be worth a few quid. He smiled and pulled a battered old phone from his pocket.

Palmer returned to his office deflated. It had been a long day, from a horrific crime scene to a hospital, to a funeral. He collapsed into the chair behind his desk and stared absently at the files in front of him. Then he looked up at a blinking icon on his computer screen. He moved the mouse and clicked it. He had four new messages. The first was from Pat Casey. The second took the air from his lungs. He read it again and then dialled a number on his phone. DI Mullins answered almost immediately.

'Get Doctor Moore and meet me in my office,' he ordered.

Minutes later, having read the message on Palmer's computer screen, Mullins said, 'Well, I think we have to treat it as genuine, guv. Only a limited number of people know all of this information.'

Dr Moore nodded in agreement. There was a lot of information about the recent crimes that had not been released to the press. Whoever had sent the message had included enough to get Palmer's attention. He moved the small white arrow on his screen to the print icon and clicked the mouse. When the message had printed, Mullins picked it from the printer tray and handed it to Palmer. It read:

Dear Frank,

The Lord is slow to anger and abundant in lovingkindness, forgiving iniquity and transgression; but He will by no means clear the guilty, visiting the iniquity of the fathers on the children. The children suffer for the sins of their fathers. The fathers must see their pain. The children will not speak to God of what I did, nor will you or Jack.

P.E.

'Get someone up here and let's see if we can find out where this came from,' Palmer ordered. Mullins turned and left.

'What do you think, Tara, do you think this is genuine?' he asked the profiler.

The psychologist was silent, thinking. Eventually, she responded.

'I think that it could be, and it indicates that we've definitely not heard the last from our killer.'

Palmer gritted his teeth. They needed a break.

'I need a drink,' he eventually pronounced, standing. 'Care to join me?' he asked before thinking.

Surprisingly Tara Moore replied, 'After today, it is hard to say no, Chief Inspector.' It wasn't the answer he had expected. He had merely asked the question out of politeness and habit. Taken aback he said, 'I thought we were past titles, *Tara*.'

Having decamped to the local pub, they sat in a comfortable silence in a quiet corner. Palmer was still thinking about the message.

'A penny for them,' Tara eventually probed.

Palmer smiled.

'I was just trying to make sense of that message,' he said.

'Hmmm, you've had prior involvement with the Barkers, Frank?'

Palmer was unsure if it was a question or a statement, but either way, it made him feel awkward. He adjusted his position before nodding.

'Oh yes,' he answered, exhaling heavily. 'We go back a long, long way, me and the Barker boys. We grew up together. For me it was either get in or get out. I decided to get out while I could,' he explained.

'Well, could this be related to something that happened when you were still more acquainted with the Barkers?' the psychologist speculated.

The question hit Palmer hard and was followed with a second blow.

'That message infers that you're somehow involved in what's going on, Chief Inspector, sorry, Frank.' The psychologist smiled briefly, after correcting herself, and then added, 'We can't ignore that.' She sipped her drink and continued.

'So, if this relates to the Barkers and you, I think we need to go back to the time when you were more closely acquainted with them.'

Palmer thought for a minute. It made sense. But then he had been involved with the Barkers for a long time. To find a specific event, which may or may not relate to the killings, would be near impossible. Still, something sparked. It made sense and it explained the gnawing feeling that he had had that the case somehow involved him. He could not disclose his more recent association with the Barkers. That was not an option. He could not place himself and his relationship with Jack Barker at the heart of their investigations.

'There's nothing I can think of that would lead some animal to kill all of those people,' Palmer mused. He appended, 'And besides, where does Morton fit in? I never really knew him.'

They sat quietly again until Palmer drained the last of his glass and asked Tara if she would like another drink. She nodded. He stood and walked to the crowded bar. When he returned, the psychologist asked, 'So how long have you been with the Met, Frank?' Palmer smiled. He was relieved that she had changed the subject.

They chatted easily for the next two hours, Palmer getting up at regular intervals to refill their glasses. By the time the bell rang for last orders, they both felt unsteady on their feet. They walked out of the pub, the fresh air jarring them as they stepped into the night.

'So where do you stay?' Palmer asked. The question sounded less innocent than he had intended, but he was pleased to see the doctor smile.

'Why is that, Frank, would you care for a nightcap?' the profiler teased.

Palmer blushed slightly.

'Well, I'm not sure. We've got an early start and...' Palmer began, but the doctor raised her hand and placed a finger gently against his lips. Then she turned toward the street and raised her hand. They got a cab almost immediately and made the short trip to Farringdon mostly in silence.

Tara Moore lived in a newly converted warehouse adjacent to the Smithfield market. It was a part of the city where old and new collided to form urban quarters, which consisted of regenerated brick buildings interspersed with new office towers of steel and glass.

'Very nice,' Palmer commented, as he walked into the apartment. He had just enough time to close the door when the doctor set upon him.

She pushed him against the wall. Palmer's first thought was that she was a great deal stronger than she appeared to be. She tore at his clothing, her lips moved across his chest. He let his hand run down to her buttocks and pulled her tightly against him. With well-practiced ease, he slid a hand around, undid the button of her trousers and pulled down the zipper. He slipped his hand between her legs. She winced as his fingers rubbed against her wet panties. Then his fingers were inside her. She arched backwards pushing her pelvis forward. Palmer pumped his fingers.

The doctor called out his name. He removed his hand and swung her around, pulling down her trousers as he did. He pushed her head forward and she held onto the half round console table to steady herself. In an instant, he was inside her. They moved roughly backwards and forwards together, faster, until the profiler let out a loud, 'Yeeeesss'. And Palmer exploded inside her.

They stayed like that for a few minutes, the doctor standing and pushing herself backward into the breathless detective. They eventually made it into the lounge. The flushed psychologist disappeared into an adjacent room. She returned wearing a loose-fitting robe with a floral pattern running the length of one side. Her feet tapped out a beat on the old timber floorboards as she walked.

'Can I get you a drink?' she asked casually. Palmer nodded. There was a stirring in his loins again when he caught a glimpse of a pert, white breast beneath her robe.

CHAPTER SEVEN
Bring Out Your Dead

'We've got the IP address, that's the number,' the baby-faced officer from the Cyber Crime Unit announced, smugly. He was proud of his abilities.

'Well, run it,' DI Mullins said, playfully smacking the younger office on the back of his head. 'Let's see whose number it is.'

It was another few minutes before the officer asked, 'Isn't your DCI, Frank Palmer?'

'Yeah, has that got to do with anything?' Mullins replied, irately.

'Well, everything actually,' the cyber officer replied, staring at the screen in front of him.

'That message was sent from a Wi-Fi router attached to the phoneline in his house.'

'What the hell?' Mullins reacted, disbelieving.

'That can't be, check it again,' she said, now genuinely annoyed.

'The digital record does not tell lies, ma'am, that's what the record says,' the young officer confirmed, shifting his body to allow Mullins closer access to the screen.

DI Mullins moved around and looked at the screen. It confirmed what the Cyber Crimes officer had told her. She glanced across the room at Dylan Porter, who was focused intently at the screen in front of him, and called, 'Dylan, come over here a minute.'

The detective stood and walked over.

'What's up?' he asked.

'We've traced the message—the one DCI Palmer received. It was sent from a computer connected to the phoneline in his house.'

'Are you sure?' he asked, just as Mullins had.

There was no mistake. The message had been relayed through a third party server and it had taken a while to trace its origin, but there was no mistaking it, the message had been sent from device that was connected to the Wi-Fi in DCI Frank Palmer's house.

DS Porter looked at the screen and said, 'Go and get a coffee,' to the young officer who had conducted the trace. He obeyed. When he stood DS Porter added, 'And keep this to yourself.' The young man nodded and left the room.

'So,' Porter said, turning to Mullins. 'What does this mean?'

Mullins shook her head. It was difficult to say. Did the killer gain access to Palmer's house and use his computer to send the message, or did Palmer send the message. Those seemed to be the only two viable options.

'It couldn't be the DCI, but why would the killer break into his home to use his computer to send this message and then go to such extremes to make the message untraceable?' Mullins asked.

Dylan Porter said nothing. He stood staring at the screen. Whatever the answer, it now seemed certain that Frank Palmer was more involved in the case than they had realised. It was not lost on Mullins or Porter that his DNA had been found on Lucy Barker's mutilated body.

'You wouldn't need to access the house, you would just need the password to access the Wi-Fi,' Porter voiced, absently, then added, 'Look, there has to be an explanation. It's ludicrous to think that the DCI is somehow involved in all this. I think whoever's responsible is playing with us.' The detective sergeant failed to sound completely convincing.

'So, what do we do?' Mullins asked.

'We have to tell the DCI, but let's keep it between us until we do. It's late, why don't we finish up and take a fresh look at this in the morning.' Mullins reluctantly agreed.

Early Sunday morning Palmer slipped quietly out of Tara Moore's bed, dressed hurriedly, and made his way out onto the street in search of a cab. He didn't need one. A sleek black Bentley crept up to the kerb behind Palmer as he headed toward City Road. He stopped and turned to face the oversized vehicle. He was in no mood for Roman Kobec and had no idea how the man knew where to find him. The car pulled alongside him, a rear window descended with a whirring sound, and the menacing face of Roman Kobec appeared.

'Detective Chief Inspector Palmer, how nice to see you,' he greeted politely. 'Please allow me to offer you a ride.'

Palmer wanted to refuse, but he knew it would be pointless. Roman Kobec was not the kind of man who took no for an answer. The door opened and Palmer climbed in. He sank back into the luxurious leather seat and took the glass of Glenfiddich Forty-Year-Old from Kobec's outstretched hand. He did not bother asking Kobec how he knew where to find him at such an unsociable hour, or why he would choose to meet in such circumstances. It bothered Palmer that the Russian elected to do business from the back seat of a luxury car. Instead, he thanked him for the drink as the limousine pulled away from the kerb.

After a short silence, Kobec asked, 'So, Chief Inspector, how is your investigation progressing?'

Palmer took a big sip from the crystal glass before answering.

'I'm sure you're aware there have been some developments since we last spoke,' he answered in a manner that made it clear he was too tired to answer any questions.

Kobec ignored him and asked, 'And your Mr Barker, how is he?'

Palmer sipped again, draining his glass.

'He was still breathing fine last time I saw him,' the detective replied sarcastically.

'Well, I am sure that is only a temporary state of being for your friend,' Kobec responded in a menacing tone. 'So, have you satisfied yourself as to my credentials, Chief Inspector?'

Palmer smiled. It was no surprise the gangster knew he had checked him out thoroughly.

'You have quite a reputation, for someone people know so little about,' Palmer retorted.

It was Kobec's turn to smile.

'Well then, let's not procrastinate,' the Russian said, leaning toward Palmer and tapping the detective's knee. 'This is my offer,' he began, suddenly all business, 'I will give you one hundred thousand pounds as a show of, how do say, good faith, yes.' Kobec fingers danced across the package on the seat next to him.

'For this, I will require certain information from you concerning Jack Barker's organisation, as a reciprocal gesture,' Kobec hesitated.

'After Jack Barker is, ah, let's say, put aside,' the Russian used another sweeping hand movement, 'and once all of this unpleasantness has passed, then we shall continue our association, for which you shall be very well rewarded.'

Kobec laid the deal out in plain, unambiguous terms. It was obvious that he planned to eliminate Jack. His success was still, in Palmer's opinion, far from guaranteed. Palmer was sure Kobec had already struck deals with many former associates of Barker's. There was no honour among thieves. That was a fallacy. In the land of the blind the one-eyed man was king. In the land of the gangster the man with the most guns, and the least conscience, was king.

Kobec sat patiently and waited for the detective to respond. Palmer stared out of the window. He was trapped with no easy way out. After a while he looked at Kobec and nodded. It seemed to be the only decision he could make at the time. Jack Barker was out of control. Someone was going to stop him one way or another. Kobec smiled broadly, picked up the package, and handed it to Palmer. Palmer did not take it.

'I want one assurance first,' he stated. 'There will be no bloodbath. This needs to be done clinically.' Palmer met Kobec's gaze. 'With Jack gone there will be no reason for his people to resist you if you deal them into your game.'

Kobec nodded and replied, 'Those are my thoughts exactly, Detective Chief Inspector.'

Palmer took the package. The car stopped and he stepped out, knowing that his soul had been traded, from one demon to another.

As he watched the car's rear lights disappear along the empty street, he had a crushing feeling that he had just made the worst mistake of his life. Things had moved too quickly. Jack Barker had made his own bed. It was a soaked with the blood of many people but was he weak enough. It was inevitable that his enemies would get to a point where they would no longer tolerate his actions. He had killed their brothers, their sons, and their friends. He had made it simple for a man like Roman Kobec to find allies in places where he may have struggled to find any before.

So why shouldn't I benefit from his demise? Palmer thought, trying to shake the foreboding from his mind. But that was the point; he wasn't convinced Kobec could deal with Barker. He couldn't imagine anyone dealing with Barker. If that was the case, then Kobec may soon be out of the picture, and he would still be a hundred thousand to the good. Always a silver lining. He managed a wry smile, but the knot in his stomach tightened. It concerned Palmer as to why Roman Kobec was in London. He could live anywhere, so why had he suddenly decided on London?

'We need to talk, guv, in private,' Mullins urged as she entered Palmer's office.

'I'll see you in the incident room then,' Dr Moore said, standing to leave. Mullins waited awkwardly for the profiler to leave before closing the door. The detective sensed a change in the temper between Palmer and the psychologist. She had interrupted an uncomfortable exchange of pleasantries between the DCI and the profiler. Palmer had been unsure whether their intimate encounter had been purely alcohol induced, or whether the Tara Moore had any genuine feelings toward him. They had only been acquainted for days, but it seemed far longer. He had been surprised to find her in his office when he had arrived. He had been as surprised to realise that her presence had not been unwelcomed by him. He had leaned over and kissed the seated profiler casually before moving around the desk to his chair. Mullins had arrived shortly after.

'What is it?' Palmer asked Mullins testily when they were alone.

The DI hesitated and then replied, 'It's the email you received, guv, the one we believe is from our suspect.'

Palmer nodded and mumbled, 'Yes,'

'Well, guv, the message was sent from a device connected to the Wi-Fi at your house, it was your IP address, guv.'

Palmer said nothing. He stared at Mullins as if he had not heard what she said. Finally, he barked, 'What?'

'They traced it last night, guv, there's no mistake, they checked it and checked it again,' Mullins confirmed.

Palmer shook his head. This could not be happening.

'How?' he questioned incredulously.

'We don't know, guv. We have no idea.'

Palmer shook his head.

'What is going on?' he muttered disbelievingly. He sank deeper into his chair, then asked, 'Who else knows about this?'

'Just Dylan and me, guv, and the officer from Cyber who did the trace, but he was told to keep it to himself,' Mullins replied.

'We can get a forensics team over to your place, see whether there's any sign of forced entry or whether they can get anything off your router.'

Palmer didn't answer. Someone was messing with him, trying to put him in the frame. He had only recently installed Wi-Fi at his house. It had been more for his daughter than for him. He had since discovered online poker, so made regular use of the service.

'Fuck!' he yelled and slammed his hand down on his desk startling DI Mullins. He knew that the situation was serious. If he did not send a team to his house, he would be asked why he had not. If he did, then the entire task force would be aware of the reason. He would have to answer their questions. In the end there was only one choice.

'Get a team over there,' he ordered, throwing his keys on the desk.

'What do you think, boss?' Paul Burrows asked. He sat on a stool in Jack Barker's kitchen. Barker stood over the stove, a pan in one hand, and a spoon in the other. He didn't answer Burrows. He focused on gently stirring the eggs. Scrambled eggs were one of his favourite meals. They reminded him of his mother who, no matter how hungover or how badly beaten, had always been out of bed every morning to prepare breakfast for her boys. It was the only time they had had any peace in their house. When his father was passed out in a drunken slumber, they could pretend they were a normal family. They would laugh and talk like normal families did. By the time Jack and Billy returned from school, their father would be awake and drunk. He would sit slouched in his old chair and shout orders to his terrified wife. No one was permitted to make a sound in the house, not a whisper. When they inevitably did, the blows rained down. The man had been a twisted bully.

That was his life, until Jack had grown stronger, and his father had grown weaker. One day Jack had arrived home to find his father beating Billy with the buckle end of a heavy leather belt. He had lost his temper and attacked his father in a blind rage.

The man had sustained severe head injuries. He lived out the rest of his days in a psychiatric hospital. Jack and Billy had claimed that an intruder had attacked their father. He had never regained enough of his faculties to contradict their version of events. No one had cared either way.

Barker lifted the pan off the stove and placed it on a glass board. Then he turned to face Burrows.

'What can it mean?' he asked, shrugging. 'There's one person who can tell us and that is Detective Chief Inspector Frank Palmer himself.'

Burrows nodded and asked, 'Do you want me to pick him up?'

Barker sighed. His head moved faintly.

Burrows stood to leave, then turned to look at his boss.

'This Kobec, Jack, he's a piece of work. We need to watch him.'

There was no need for Burrows' warning. Barker already knew who Roman Kobec was. He was aware of the foreigner's growing presence in London. He had been surprised when Harry Black had informed him that he had seen Palmer getting into a flashy motor in the early hours of Sunday morning. Black had been leaving a Farringdon nightclub when he had seen Palmer get into the vehicle. Thinking it odd, the villain had taken down the vehicle's registration number. Barker had found it curious enough to have the car's ownership traced. It was owned by a front company linked to Kobec. That had peaked Jack's interest. Later that day, one of his boys had called to advise Jack about information he had received from a grass named Roddy McBride. Barker had intuitively put the pieces together. London was a big city, but their world was small.

Jack had been aware that Roman Kobec had been acquiring interests in London. He had fully expected that he would meet the man soon enough. Now, Palmer and a known face, Collin Grey, had been overheard discussing his brother, when the Russian's name had been mentioned. Later, Palmer had been seen meeting with an unknown person in an expensive motor that was found to be linked to Kobec. Barker's instinct told him that these events were connected. It was not likely to be a coincidence that the things were occurring while Palmer was investigating Billy's murder. Kobec had the reputation of being ruthless and direct. If the Russian had wanted to get to him, it would not likely have been through his brother, it would have been through his front door. Despite his recent actions, Barker was a man who had learned not to jump to conclusions, or to make rash judgements. Nevertheless, there were questions that needed answering.

'So, how's the investigation going, Frank?'

It was a question that he was growing weary of addressing. This time it was Superintendent Jane Fletcher asking. As usual, her faithful lapdog, DCI Young, sat across from her.

The heat in the office was stifling. It made it barely habitable. Palmer coughed to clear his throat and then answered, 'We're following up on several leads, ma'am.'

The superintendent nodded.

'What about this message, Frank, the one that was sent from your house?' DCI Young asked.

Palmer was startled and angered by the question.

'We're working on it. I have forensics at my house now,' he replied in a terse tone that made clear his annoyance at being asked the question. 'We'll have to wait and see whether anything comes of it,' he added sharply.

The two officers nodded.

'You are aware, Frank, that this investigation is high profile. We cannot afford to be embarrassed,' Superintendent Fletcher voiced her concern.

It was Palmer's turn to nod.

'I'm well aware of that, ma'am,' he responded. 'But I think whoever is responsible is trying to taunt us, either to demonstrate that they are in control, or to side-track the investigation.' Palmer paused for breath. 'That's why the message was sent and why it was sent from my IP address.'

The superintendent did not look convinced.

'Well, if the press get a hold of this, they'll have a field day, especially if they discover your DNA was found on the Barker girl.' Palmer reeled.

'We need some results, Frank. We need something solid before all of this spirals out of control.'

Palmer detected the hint of a threat. He was growing angry, even more so when Young added, 'DCS Sloane is looking closely at all of this, Frank, all eyes are on you. You need to bring us something.'

Us? You little prick, I ought to reach over and ring your scrawny little neck, you fucking toerag. The thought flashed through Palmer's mind, and he had to restrain himself from lashing out.

Palmer stormed into his office, slammed the door behind him, and sat down heavily. The meeting with Fletcher and her chihuahua, Young, had left him simmering. He put his head in his hands, trying to think clearly. Someone was playing games with him. What was happening was linked not only to Jack Barker, but to him too. He had to focus. They had certainly had their share of scraps and run-ins in the old days. Nothing that could have left a lasting legacy of hatred, enough to make someone kill seven people. After joining the Met he had helped Barker out on occasion by feeding him information, helping to stitch up a rival now and again, and keeping him informed of investigations he should be aware of. He had not gone out with Jack and murdered anyone.

Palmer lashed out and swept the pile of documents off his desk just as Tara Moore knocked.

'Need to talk about it?' she asked as she walked into the office.

Palmer shook his head.

'Someone is screwing with me, but I can't think of anything to tie all of this together. It makes no bastard sense at all.'

Dr Moore smiled and moved around his desk. She sat pushed against the edge and ran her hand gently through his hair.

'It will be all right Frank,' she soothed.

'You and I both know that the DCI and Jack Barker were as thick as thieves in the past, Dylan,' DI Mullins said. She and DS Porter were standing out in the station car park, smoking.

'I know that, but his association with Barker is old news. No internal investigation has ever uncovered any evidence of wrongdoing against him,' Porter defended,

'From what I hear the DPS has tried throwing the book at him and they've never come up with a single charge against the DCI.' He hesitated while a uniform officer passed.

'They grew up on the same estate, him and Barker.' Porter dropped his cigarette end and stomped out the remaining ember. 'And if he has an association with Barker, then why would he be involved in killing his brother?' he added.

Mullins drew on her cigarette and exhaled a cloud of smoke. Like millions of others, she had been trying to kick the habit for years. It had proved all but impossible.

'Look,' she replied. 'I like Palmer, I'm not suggesting that he was involved in the killings directly, but he is linked to this mess in some way, Dylan. We have to be open to that or we might just get ourselves sucked in and fucked over by this situation.'

Dylan Porter shook his head again.

'Look, I've spoken to my governor in confidence. He's going to do some poking around. In the meantime, we need to find a link between Barker and Morton.'

Mullins nodded, and after some thought, said, 'What if we included the DCI,' she paused. 'I mean what if we tried to find something linking the Barkers, Morton and the DCI?'

Porter looked at Mullins. He was not happy at the thought, but it did make sense. It made a lot of sense. He reluctantly nodded his head, knowing in any other case it would be a good line of enquiry.

'Okay, quieten down,' Palmer called. Those present sensed his mood. The room was soon silent.

'It is day five and we're exactly where we started, which is fucking nowhere,' Palmer announced, his hands placed on his hips and he looked menacingly from face to face.

'Have we found a link between Barker and Morton yet? No. Have we got any intelligence from the street? No. Any witnesses who saw our killer coming or going? No. Any clue at all? No!' He paused allowing his words to sink in.

'Now, each of you here has something to be getting on with and I want a lead from one of you today.' His eyes bored into the team; his face was fixed in a grimace as he looked around the room. The instigators diverted their eyes.

Eventually Palmer turned to DI Williams and said, 'We need to get back on the street. Someone out there knows something. You need to go and find that person. Porter, Campbell and Watts are with you. I don't care how many doors you have to kick in, how many heads you have to bang, someone knows something.'

Williams nodded and Palmer continued, 'Bright, I want you to trawl through Jack and Billy Barker's files again, from scratch, and go through Morton's file. There has to be a link there. Find it. Use Hunter and Miller to assist.'

Bright nodded and looked across at Hunter. He had no complaints about working with the young DC. She was smart and intuitive.

'Mullins,' Palmer barked. 'You and Galloway go back to see DCI Holland in Southwark, see if anything new has come up. When you're done there, go back to Victoria Park. Speak to the neighbours again and see whether anyone's memory has improved.' The room fell silent, until Palmer yelled, 'Right, get to it!'

DI Williams was keen to get back out to the streets. He had a new name to throw about, a name he had never heard before. A name that his informant Roddy McBride had given him: Roman Kobec.

The sky had cleared, and the temperature was expected to jump. Palmer was alone, heading to see Anthony Stanford. The career criminal had not replied to several messages the detective had left for him. The old man was no friend of his, but Palmer hoped to convince him that it was in his best interest to cooperate. He had a reputation for knowing things that most did not.

Stanford ran his firm from a snooker hall on the Hackney Road. Like Jack, he was an old school villain who had survived for as long as he had because he generally kept to himself. He employed two fiercely loyal minders who were always by his side. He was feared because he was cold-blooded. According to a gangland legend, Stanford had once submerged a man in a vat of sulphuric acid for parking his car in front of Stanford's garage door. It was an unlikely story, but the people who knew him believed that it *could* be true.

Palmer pulled his car into a parking space opposite the snooker club's entrance. He noticed the bulking form of John Dunnigan standing at the entrance, which meant that Stanford was inside. His main line of business was vice. He controlled a large part of the city's sex trade. There was a joke on the street that Soho was named after Stanford's constant wandering around the historic red light district asking, 'So, ho', where's my money?'

He was well liked among his peers. Like most London villains, he and Jack Barker had done business together for many years. But Anthony Stanford was his own man; no one refuted that, not even Jack Barker.

'Chief Inspector Palmer,' John Dunnigan greeted, as Palmer approached the entrance. His eyes narrowed looking directly at Dunnigan. The big man had fallen out of the ugly tree and hit every branch on the way down – twice.

'I'm here to see Anthony,' Palmer said, stopping a few feet in front of Stanford's stooge.

'Well, the boss ain't here. What a pity, and you came all this way to see him,' he replied gesturing with his thick arms, 'I'll let 'im know you called by.' The big man's tone was mocking.

Palmer was not a small man, but he was quicker than he looked. He often used it to his advantage, as he did now with John Dunnigan. He moved forward and struck the man a crushing blow in the solar plexus. Dunnigan didn't see it coming. He dropped to his knees, fighting for breath. Without saying another word, Palmer stepped over him and climbed the old wooden stairs leading up to the snooker club.

The interior was cavernous, poorly lit, and uninhabited. Neat triangles of red balls stood in place on green, felt-covered tables. Palmer walked to the office located at the far end of the hall. The carpet beneath his feet was tacky. He didn't bother to knock. He opened the door, causing the young girl who had Anthony Stanford's embarrassingly small penis in her mouth, to jump in fright. Luckily for Stanford, her jaw had slammed shut after its cargo had been discharged.

Anthony was not pleased at the intrusion.

'What are you playing at, Palmer!' he shouted, seeing the detective. His hair was grey and combed back. He was overweight and had a Bond villain look about him.

Palmer was unfazed.

'Get out!' he said to the young girl, whom he doubted was older than sixteen.

'Zip yourself up, Anthony, we need to talk,' the detective said. Before Stanford could protest further, the office door burst open, and John Dunnigan stormed in.

'You wanker, Palmer,' he yelled. 'I'll fucking have you.'

Dunnigan looked to lunge at the detective, but Stanford ordered him to stop. Calm now, the villain was intrigued by Palmer's visit.

'It's okay, John,' Stanford said, raising one hand up as if ordering a dog to heel. 'I am sure the chief inspector has a good reason for being here.'

Dunnigan reluctantly obeyed and backed out of the office, not taking his eyes off Palmer.

'Someone ought to put some manners on you, Palmer,' he said before leaving.

'Please take a seat, Frank,' Stanford invited. His anger had subsided, replaced by a false cordiality.

'So, what's this all about?' he asked calmly, opening a desk drawer and withdrawing a bottle of scotch and two glasses. He poured a heavy shot into each glass and pushed one toward Palmer.

'I think you know, Anthony. I don't think that even you've been untouched by what's been going on. It's chaos out there,' Palmer replied.

Stanford smiled but said nothing.

'I think it would be in everyone's best interest to get things back to normal, get back to the status quo, so if there's anything that you can tell me, anything at all?' Palmer studied Stanford, while lifting the glass to his lips.

'Don't you think that if I knew what was going on, Frank, it would have been sorted by now?'' Stanford retorted. 'Jack and Billy are friends of mine. If I knew who'd topped Billy, I'd have dealt with him myself.' He raised the bottle and refilled Palmer's glass.

'Someone has to know something. Your ears are always close to the ground; your slags are the eyes and ears of the city. How can this happen without anyone knowing a thing?' Palmer's voice was strained.

'All I can give you, Frank, is my opinion, that's all,' Stanford replied.

Palmer gulped down his scotch again before asking, 'And what's that?'

'I don't think what happened was from the street, it was…' The grey-haired villain paused, sipping his drink. 'It was something else,' he finished, twisting his free hand in the air.

Palmer looked down into his empty glass and sighed heavily, then stood to leave. As he pulled the office door open, he turned and asked Stanford, 'Do the initials PE mean anything to you?'

'PE? Not that I can think of. No, hang on, physical education, my worst fucking class at school,' the overweight man answered, and bellowed with laughter. Everyone was a comedian nowadays, Palmer thought, unamused.

The brightness outside blinded him as he left the club. He could feel Dunnigan's menacing gaze follow him as he crossed the road. Squinting in the sun, he made out the unmistakable, muscular physique of Paul Burrows leaning against his car, talking on a phone. He ignored Palmer as he approached. The detective was forced to wait while the big man finished his call.

When he did, Palmer asked, 'What can I do for you, Burrows?'

The big man smiled and said politely, 'Hello, Frank, mate, Jack was hoping to have a word with you.'

'Well, Jack will have to wait. I'm busy right now,' Palmer replied.

Burrows smiled again.

'I'm sure you are, mate, but this really can't wait. I'm afraid I'm going to have to insist.' It was a thinly veiled threat.

Palmer hesitated, then conceded, knowing that it was an argument he would not win.

'Where is he?'

'He's at home, Frank. I'll drive you. We won't be long; I can drop you back after.'

Palmer knew there was no point in protesting. As big as Palmer was, he was no match for Paul Burrows. Few men were. If Barker had ordered his henchman to fetch Palmer, then that was what he would do, one way or another. They drove to Barker's house listening to an old David Gray album. Burrows, whose voice sounded like an injured mule falling off a high cliff, and landing on a hornet nest, insisted on singing along to the music. It was a harrowing experience. Palmer spent much of the journey gritting his teeth.

He was glad to be out of the car when they arrived at Barker's Essex mansion. The detective felt suddenly anxious as he followed Burrows along a tree-lined footpath. He also felt the familiar pangs of jealousy and regret as he looked up at the two ornate columns, which guarded the house's entrance like enormous stone warriors. The house was a testament to criminal success. Like hell crime doesn't pay. He could have shared in all of it. He could have had what Jack had. But you had to be born like Jack Barker – it was genetic – and despite his faults, Palmer did not carry those same genes.

When he saw Barker, all of those thoughts were swept from his mind and his apprehension grew. The gangster was casually dressed in a sports jacket and chinos, clean shaven, and sober. He greeted Palmer politely and told him to take a seat in the lounge while he spoke to Burrows. The detective obeyed.

'So, Frankie, how are things?' Barker asked as he walked into the lounge to join Palmer. He was alone. There was no sign of his adjutant.

He took a seat on the luxurious chair opposite and spread his arms over the bulky, leather-covered arms. He looked directly at Palmer.

'Things are all right, Jack, but I have a lot to be getting on with. What was so urgent that it couldn't wait?' Palmer asked edgily, fighting to keep his voice even. Barker nodded, smiling pleasantly. It was unnerving and he knew it.

'Well, this won't take long, Frank,' he replied. He then asked, 'Where does Anthony Stanford fit into your investigation?'

Palmer thought for a moment then answered, 'I just wanted to find out if he'd heard any word on the street. You know, he's always well-informed, those whores of his have ears like radars.'

Barker laughed softly.

'Yeah, I guess he is usually a fountain of information,' he agreed. Then stalled, before asking casually, 'And Roman Kobec, where does he fit into your investigation?'

Palmer tried too late not to register any surprise at the question. He had no idea how Barker knew about Kobec, or how much the gangster knew about the Russian. The detective felt himself sink into his seat. He knew that the next five minutes may dictate whether he lived or died.

'Kobec's someone we're looking at,' he replied matter-of-factly. 'He's a Russian.' Palmer paused, wiping his hand across his forehead. 'There are rumours he used to be involved in criminal activity. He relocated to London a year or so ago with a healthy bank balance, claims to be retiring,' Palmer finished.

Barker smiled again and asked sarcastically, 'Do you think that I wouldn't know that much?' His eyes still fixed on Palmer. Jack said, 'I know who Kobec is, but what I want to know is why you were getting into his motor at six o'clock on Sunday morning. Is he a friend of yours, Frank?'

Palmer paled visibly. Had Barker been following him? How did he know about his meetings with Kobec? It had surprised him that Kobec had known where to find him. How the hell did Jack Barker know about it?

'Friend,' Palmer smirked. 'No, Jack, he's no friend,' the detective replied honestly. 'I put the word out that I wanted to speak to him, and next thing I know he pulls up beside me when I'm heading home and offers me a lift. I had a word with him, that's it.'

Barker pursed his lips and nodded.

'You wanted to speak with Roman Kobec, Frank, about what exactly?'

Palmer's mind raced. He knew a wrong word could mean his life.

'There are rumours that he is making inroads in London, Jack. It was plausible he had knowledge that could be useful,' Palmer answered weakly.

Barker nodded and then pointed to the enormous television screen fixed against the far wall of the lavish room.

'I fucking love this bloke,' he said. 'He's as funny as fuck.'

Palmer looked at the television. He did not recognise the stand up comedian on the screen. Barker laughed and then asked, 'What did Mr Kobec have to say?'

The detective shuffled anxiously. The padded sofa was suddenly uncomfortable.

'He said that he is retired, he lives here with his family, has a legit property business, and he wanted to quash any rumours before they got started.' Palmer managed to keep his voice even. 'He has heard of you

Jack, and he wants no part of any trouble with you.' Palmer hoped that he had managed to sound convincing, knowing that stroking Barker's ego was the right move.

'He had to tell you this so urgently he couldn't wait until the sun was up,' Barker questioned doubtfully. 'He had to pick you up at six in the morning, what is he, a fucking vampire. Got sharp teeth has he?' Palmer sensed a change in Barker's tone.

'He is Russian, Jack, who knows how they think,' Palmer answered. He felt his control slipping.

Barker sat forward in his seat and asked, 'Explain it to me again, Frank, why were you looking at Kobec?'

Palmer thought carefully again before answering. He looked down at the expensive Persian carpet that covered much of the floor in the room, then looked back into Barker's eyes.

'We're looking at anyone who might benefit if you and Billy were taken out of the picture, Jack. It's procedure. Kobec was a person of interest, we wanted to take a look at him, make sure we could eliminate him from our enquiries.' The detective was clutching at straws.

Barker nodded his head slowly.

'You don't think that Mr Kobec has any plans to take advantage of the situation as it is now, maybe try to get a foot in my door?' he asked. The menace was now palpable. Barker was no fool. He was fully aware that his rampage in pursuit of his brother's killer had made him vulnerable. He had made new enemies of old friends.

Bollocks, Palmer thought, if Barker believed for a second that was a possible scenario, then things were about to get a whole lot worse.

'There's no way, Jack. It'd be suicide, and he knows it. I don't think he's a stupid man, he knows well enough that it would be stupid for him to fuck with you.' More ego massage and a hint of desperation.

They sat in tense silence for a while. *How long would it be before Kobec tried to move against Barker,* Palmer thought and had the sudden realisation that he may not be around to find out.

After what seemed an eternity Barker calmly and politely said, 'Okay, Frank, thank you for coming, please keep me informed.' As if by telepathic request, Paul Burrows walked into the lounge. 'Paul will take you back to your car, Frank.'

An icy chill ran down Palmer's spine. Barker knew. Palmer was all too aware that the gangster had an acute sixth sense that enabled him to perceive any threat long before it became apparent to others. It was that ability that had enabled him to reach the pinnacle of the criminal ladder, unscathed.

Palmer half-expected Burrows to take the Canning Town turn-off from the A13 and drive him out to Barker's yard, but to his relief they continued and returned him to his car as promised. The journey was not without torture though, as Palmer was subjected to further torturous renditions of David Gray.

When he was safely back in his car, he sank into the seat and closed his eyes. His heart pounded in his chest. He was not a man given easily to fear, but now his world was filled with too many dangerous men. His life had turned into a living nightmare in just five short days. He needed a clear head. He needed to think, but he had time for neither. His main concern was that Jack Barker had now made Roman Kobec the central focus of his attention. Kobec had lost the element of surprise and that meant that the odds of him ousting Barker had fallen considerably. Barker would bring in all the people he could trust, people like Anthony Stanford, who were hardcore and faithful. If a war exploded on the streets, it would be long and bloody.

He had backed Kobec too soon. It had been naïve to think Jack Barker would be easy to oust. He considered whether he should inform Kobec. If he didn't and Kobec acted now, he wouldn't know that Barker had been forewarned. That could spell disaster. If Palmer warned Kobec, he could rethink his strategy. He was an intelligent man. He would think twice about making a move against Barker, knowing the gangster was expecting it. There seemed little option.

Palmer took the phone from his pocket and dialled Kobec's number. Voice mail answered. He hung up. As he started the car the phone rang.

'Chief Inspector, can I be of assistance?' an accented voice enquired.

'Who is this?' Palmer asked.

'I am an associate of the man you were calling.'

Palmer smiled. Kobec took no chances. He wouldn't talk on the phone; phone calls could be recorded.

'Tell your boss I need to speak with him urgently, and I mean urgently,' Palmer said and hung up. Less than a minute later, the phone rang again. It was an unknown caller.

'Yes,' Palmer said harshly into the phone.

'Frank, is that you?' a familiar voice said.

'Pat, Christ, sorry, I was expecting another call. How are things, any news?' the detective corrected.

There was a short silence before Casey spoke.

'Where are you now, Frank?'

Palmer frowned and answered, 'I'm leaving Hackney, heading back to the nick. What's up, mate?'

'I need to speak to you, urgently, in private.' Casey's tone was ominous.

The foot pressed harder on the detective's chest. It was the same message he had just left for Kobec.

'Okay, mate, where do want to meet?' he asked in response.

Casey cleared his throat and then said, 'How about The King's Head?'

Palmer liked the idea. God knew he could do with a drink.

'Okay, mate, half an hour,' he suggested.

Casey agreed and hung up. Before Palmer could put the phone down, it rang again.

'Chief Inspector Palmer,' the accented voice said.

'Underground parking, Canary Wharf, level one. Enter via Westferry Circus, parking bay one forty-eight, three o'clock.'

The phone went dead. Palmer threw it down on the passenger seat. He headed south to meet the pathologist.

Jack Barker sat alone, thinking. He accepted that he had reacted irrationally and unprofessionally to his brother's murder. He had not only made enemies of old friends, but he had angered old enemies. To a man like Kobec, who was far from retiring and fast establishing himself in the London underworld, the chaos might seem like too good an opportunity to pass up. Barker knew that the Russian now controlled several manors south of the river. He was looking to expand north. He may have concluded that Barker had been weakened and exposed by the loss of his brother. Intuition told Barker that Kobec had not created the situation. Kobec would have seen Barker as an asset and a potential ally. Not a threat. Jack doubted Palmer's explanation that the Russian was merely ticking a routine box in their investigation. He would have heard about it from his sources at the Met had that been the case.

That meant that the likelihood was that Kobec had approached Palmer. He would not have approached the detective now unless he was looking to take advantage of current circumstances. That was the most likely magnitude of the Russian's involvement. In the fading light, Barker's head slowly nodded. A terse smile played on his face. War was coming. Palmer's loyalty had wavered. If Kobec was speaking to Palmer, then he must be speaking to others too. No one had come forward and reported the Russian's advances, which meant that the men Kobec had been talking to had been listening. While Barker had been blinded by grief and rage, the predatory Kobec had slipped from the shadows, silently and unseen. He had left his attack too late. He had given up the advantage.

'Paul, get all of the boys together and meet me back at the house,' he ordered when Burrows answered his call.

'Trouble, boss?'

'Yes, Paul, trouble.' Burrows was excited. They had had many years of peace and prosperity. The past week had ended that. Burrows had no complaints. He was a warrior and warriors needed wars. To reach Valhalla they needed to die in battle, not rotting from age.

The King's Head was getting busy with the lunchtime rush. COVID 19 had changed the atmosphere is many public places. People were relearning how to socialise. Casey was already there, sitting at a table near the rear door. Palmer walked through the melee, colliding with several patrons and a cute waitress before reaching the table. He stretched his hand out and greeted Casey,

'Hello, mate, what are you having?'

Casey lifted a half-empty glass, and replied, 'Why not, I'll have another, Bells, make it a large.'

Palmer returned a short while later with their drinks and took a seat across from the pathologist.

'So, what's this about, Pat?' he asked intently.

Casey drained his glass and took a sip from the fresh drink that Palmer had bought before he answered. Palmer sensed that the man was tense.

'Scenes-of-crime recovered a hair and fibres on the bed at the Morton house; they got a DNA match from the hair. We also recovered microscopic skin fragments from beneath the son's fingernails, enough to extract a viable DNA profile – not a complete profile, but sufficient to make a positive match.'

Palmer nodded. His stomach tightened. He knew what was coming next. He shook his head vigorously. Before Casey had time to continue Palmer said, 'It can't be.'

The pathologist stared directly at him and nodded.

'I'm afraid so, Frank, both samples were a match to you.' Palmer paled noticeably and Casey added, 'The hair was found under the boy's body, so there's no chance it was contamination at the scene.'

There was no doubt now. He was being set up. His chest felt heavy. His breathing became laboured.

'Look, Pat,' he managed to say. 'You and I go back a long way. You know me, you know there's no way I was involved in this. You know that,' the detective implored. 'Someone is trying very hard to put me in the frame.'

Palmer's face dropped into his hands.

'Someone's been in my house. They could've collected whatever they needed to stitch me up.'

Casey stared into his empty glass and shrugged. Palmer could guess what his friend was thinking. He had known Palmer for a long time and his gut feeling was that Palmer was not involved in the killings. But he also knew Palmer was no saint. He could have been involved in whatever had sparked these killings. No one went to such lengths to frame someone for a crime without very good cause. Not crimes like these.

'Who else knows about this?' Palmer asked.

'At the moment, it's just me and the lab techs that carried out the tests,' Casey replied. Then added, 'You understand, Frank, this is too serious to keep to under wraps, it could mean my career.'

Palmer nodded. Casey was traditional and loyal. He was also straight down the line. He knew that Palmer crossed the line occasionally. He accepted it, but he would not risk his career for the detective.

'I know that Pat, but I need time. I'm begging you, mate, just a couple of days.' Palmer sounded desperate. He *was* desperate. If this latest evidence came to light, he would be off the case for certain. He could even be arrested and charged.

Casey was silent for a while, but he eventually conceded.

'Okay, Frank, I can't promise you anything, but I'm owed a few favours. If I can, I'll get you twenty-four hours. That's the best I can do, then we have to release the results.'

Palmer was visibly shaken. He drove slowly back to the station in a state of incomprehension. He walked on autopilot to the incident room. The initial forensic reports for the Morton case had arrived. Several of the team were gathered, pouring over the results. DI Mullins briefed Palmer. The killings matched the Barker slayings in almost every way. The same implements, chemicals, and techniques had been used. Palmer left the incident room dejected and went to his office, where Tara Moore sat studying a copy of the autopsy reports.

'Frank,' she greeted, as he walked into the office. 'You look like crap.'

Palmer smiled. He walked around the desk and collapsed into his chair.

'Rough day?' the profiler asked, gently reaching across the desk, and placing her hand on his. Her touch felt electric. Palmer noticed an immediate stirring in his trousers.

He reluctantly pulled his hand back and rubbed his brow. The day had been worse than rough. He still had the meeting with Roman Kobec to attend.

'We have nothing, not a thing. How can that be?' he asked rhetorically.

The psychologist did not attempt an answer. She looked at Palmer. Dark rings had formed beneath his eyes. His skin looked sallow and drawn. He seemed to have aged ten years in five days. There was a tap on the door. It swung open just as the profiler said, 'Listen Frank, about the other night—'

'Not disturbing anything, am I?' DI Williams asked, walking into the office uninvited. DS Galloway followed behind.

'No,' Palmer responded, looking at Tara Moore whose cheeks had reddened slightly. 'We were just discussing the sum total of our investigations. It was a short conversation,' he mused sardonically.

Williams smiled, ignoring Palmer's cynicism, and said, 'Don't worry, guv, we'll solve this case. You can be sure of it.'

Palmer thought he detected a hint of disparagement directed at him. He shrugged it off. More paranoia.

'What about this Roman Kobec?' Williams asked. 'You've been looking at him.'

Well, so much for paranoia and DS Porter keeping his mouth shut, Palmer thought, not knowing that it was the grass Roddy McBride who had passed Kobec's name to Williams, as he had to Barker.

'Yeah, we've looked at him,' Palmer answered. 'He's a wealthy Russian businessman, if he wanted to eliminate Barker, he had the resources to do it quickly and cleanly. He would not likely have broadcast his intentions to Barker and acquired the focus of the entire Met, by killing his brother,' Palmer said quickly and convincingly.

DI Williams nodded and insisted, 'I don't think we can discount him completely, but we've come up with another possible from the files.' He had Palmer's full attention.

'Do you know Horace McFadden, Frank?'

Palmer shook his head. The name did ring a bell, but he could not place it.

'He was a loan shark, worked out of the West End,' Galloway interjected.

Palmer nodded. He vaguely remembered Horace McFadden. He used to run a strip club in Soho. Lending money at extortionate rates was his primary business. He had clashed heads with Jack Barker and had come off second best, as far as Palmer could remember. Barker still owned his club.

'Yeah, I remember Horace,' Palmer replied. 'Big cunt, no neck, disappeared in the late nineties.'

144

'That's right,' Williams replied. 'Right after his brother, Arthur, was gunned down by an unknown assailant. He was with his wife and son at the time he was killed, bled out in his wife's arms with his nine-year-old kid looking on. Barker was put in the frame for it back then.'

Palmer thought about it. Barker had never mentioned it. It seemed like a long shot.

'Does anyone know where McFadden is now?' he asked.

'We're working on it,' Williams replied.

'Okay, keep me posted and locate Arthur McFadden's wife and son too,' Palmer said in a tone that indicated the meeting was over.

When he and the profiler where alone again, Palmer asked, 'You don't mind if we pick up that conversation a later, I have to rush.' Before he left, he leaned over and kissed the woman's soft lips. Her scent was intoxicating.

'Not at all,' she replied.

In the privacy of his car, Palmer dialled Barker's number. Paul Burrows answered it on the fifth ring and passed the phone to Barker.

'What is it, Frank?' he asked in a baleful tone.

'What can you tell me about Horace McFadden?' the detective asked.

'Horace, what about Horace?' Barker answered with a question.

'Well, one of my team has come up with his name as another possible line of enquiry,' Palmer explained.

Barker laughed on the other end of the phone.

'Well, I'm sure I wouldn't know, Frank, but I think they're wasting their time. The last I heard, old Horace had gone into construction. Concrete, if I remember correctly,' he said and hung up.

Palmer understood Barker's veiled meaning. Horace McFadden's body was buried in a concrete structure somewhere and probably had been since his disappearance thirteen years earlier. It was good news in a way for Palmer. It would give Williams and the team something to bite on while he tried to figure out what was really going on.

He drove to the car park, leaned out of the window, and withdrew the small ticket protruding like a tongue from the ticket machine. As soon as he did the boom swung up. He drove into the underground parking, under the scrutiny of the estate guards. The tyres of his car squealed on the smooth concrete surface. He looked out for Kobec's car but found parking bay one forty-eight vacant. He pulled into it. Less than a minute after he stopped, his passenger door opened and Roman Kobec settled himself in the passenger seat.

'Chief Inspector, how pleasant to see you once again,' the Russian said. He was wearing sunglasses despite the dim light in the parking garage. 'So, what is it that you must so urgently tell me?' he queried.

Palmer looked around nervously.

'Don't worry,' Kobec assured. 'I have people watching, we will not be unduly disturbed.'

It did little to ease Palmer's nervousness.

'It's Jack Barker,' he said. 'He's on to you, and I think he's on to us.'

If the news concerned Kobec, it did not show. He said nothing. His face remained unchanged. He just nodded slightly and pursed his lips.

'Is that so?' he asked calmly. 'And how did that come about?'

'I wish I knew,' Palmer replied honestly.

Kobec studied the detective's face. He was an expert at reading people and discerning truth from lies.

'Very well, I will have to take this into consideration, Chief Inspector,' he responded. Then asked, 'Do you have anything else for me?'

Palmer nodded.

'Yeah, our investigation is now looking at you too,' he advised the Russian.

Kobec smiled and Palmer realised he already knew this. He had been testing Palmer. Without another word, Kobec opened the door and was gone. As the door closed Palmer's phone rang.

CHAPTER EIGHT
Understanding

You must recognise opportunities, not try to create them.
Chapter Four, Sun Tzu - *The Art of War*

It was early evening. He stood motionless on the damp grass, hidden from view by the overgrown shrubs that filled the small garden of the otherwise neat, terraced house. He could see into the kitchen where an old lady busied herself preparing dinner. From time to time, an old man joined her, pottering about doing nothing. He knew that the rear door to the kitchen leading into the garden would be unlocked. It always was until the couple retired for the night. It was the last part of the old man's nightly ritual. He had no intention of waiting that long.

When the meal was ready, the woman carried the bowls of food into the adjoining dining room and placed them on the neatly laid table. Once he was sure that they were seated for dinner, as they always were at seven p.m., he made his way to the kitchen door. He turned the handle slowly and pushed the door open. The first time he that had entered the house, the door had squeaked. He had applied an oil spray to the rusted hinges to ensure that it made no sound when he returned.

He slipped silently into the kitchen. He could hear the couple talking. A television was on in the background with a familiar theme tune playing. As usual, the woman had left the teacups and teapot neatly laid out on the kitchen counter. When they had finished their meals, she would carry the empty dishes to the kitchen before preparing the tea. He lifted the lid of the tea pot, withdrew a small vial from his pocket, and emptied the contents into the vessel. Then he slipped silently from the house again.

An hour later he returned. The old lady had done exactly as she had done every night for many years, except that that evening after sitting down to enjoy a cup of after-dinner tea, her eyes had become heavy, and she had fallen into a deep sleep next to her motionless husband. He carried the aged couple into their bedroom. They had relocated their bedroom to the ground floor after the old man's hip replacement surgery. In the room, he laid the old woman on the bed and seated the old man on a chair, securing him with duct tape, and tying a gag around his mouth. Then he waited.

After half an hour the man began to stir. The intruder stood and removed a small bottle from his bag and placed it beneath the man's nose. He woke suddenly, tried to speak but choked on the gag. Smiling, the black-clad figure moved to the bed and placed the bottle beneath the woman's nose. She was also gagged and restrained. Her wrists were bound together behind her back. She stared up in terror, then turned her head and saw her husband tied to the chair. The intruder smiled down at her, pleased with the old lady's reaction. Then he produced a long, thin, metal object. He held the woman's head steady with one strong hand, and with a swift movement, used the sharp object in his other hand to remove her left eye from its socket. The old man's eyes bulged in horror. He shouted incoherently through his gag and shook his head violently from side to side, pulling against his restraints.

The killer turned his head and looked at the old man, smiling.

'So how have you been keeping, Senior Officer Breen?' he asked. His voice was even and calm, with no hint of excitement or fear.

He sat quietly when he was done. The last of the fading light filtered through the curtains. They may understand now why he had killed them. They would know that vengeance had come. Then he heard a noise, the distinct sound of a key turning in a lock. He did not panic, instead, he stood silently, moved to the door of the bedroom, opened it slightly, and listened.

'Mum, Dad,' a voice called. It was a female. He smiled; this could be an added bonus.

'Mum,' the voice called again.

He walked slowly to the bed and reached into the bag beside it. He withdrew a black ski mask and pulled it over his head, then turned and headed for the door again. Before he reached it, the door opened and there stood an overweight, middle-aged woman.

'What the…' the woman began but was cut off by a well-placed punch to her throat. She stumbled and fell forward onto her knees, grasping at her crushed larynx. Her eyes bulged. He looked down at her coldly. She would be dead in minutes.

He saw the man too late. He had entered the house while he had focused his attention on the dying woman. The man caught a glimpse of the scene inside the room and bolted, frantically keying nine-nine-nine into his phone as he ran. He exited the house screaming for help like a terrified child and ran along the street.

The killer decided not to pursue the man. Instead, he calmly lifted his bag, gave the room a quick examination, and headed out the back door.

The patrol car had been in the vicinity when the call had come in. The vehicle screeched to a halt outside the house, its flashing lights lighting up the surrounding houses. The officers quickly exited the vehicle. Curious neighbours had joined the man on the street as he pointed to the open door of the house.

'He's in there,' he shouted. 'He's killed them all!'

An officer radioed for backup as he cautiously made his way toward the door. He removed a telescopic baton from his belt, and with a well-practiced swing extended it fully. He lifted it over his shoulder and pushed the front door open with his hand.

'Hello?' he called into the dark of the house. 'This is the police. Is there anybody inside the house?'

Silence.

He edged through the door cautiously, his breathing heavy, his heart racing. The house seemed in good order; there was nothing out of place that he could see in the torchlight. He called out again and got the same response, silence. His partner followed close behind as they edged along the cluttered passage. Ahead a door was open, and a light was on. The officer came to the door and moved quickly to face into the room. He was unprepared for what assaulted his senses.

'Jesus Christ!' he said, then called urgently into the mouthpiece of his radio. He did not have to wait for backup; it had already arrived.

'Check the house, but be careful,' he called when he saw that more officers had entered behind him. He moved into the room and checked for a pulse on all three victims. There was none.

'Serge,' a uniformed officer called out to him from the door. 'The back door is open.'

'Get outside and get a description of the suspect from the guy who phoned this in,' he ordered. 'I want every available car in the area now. Check for anyone or anything suspicious,' the uniformed sergeant added.

The killer had moved quickly from the house, over the back fence, retrieving his helmet as he went. He had picked out an emergency escape route in case of just such an occurrence. He left nothing to chance. The motorcycle was parked in the alley running behind the terraced houses. As he entered the alley, he saw them. Two youths were at work on his motorcycle, clearly attempting to steal it. He called out and ran toward them. They looked up at the approaching figure, turned, and ran.

The killer mounted the motorcycle and tried to insert the key into the ignition. Something was blocking the key slot. Calmly, he removed the bag from his back and withdrew torch. The louts had inserted a screwdriver into the keyhole. Its tip had broken off and was jammed in the lock. He turned the bag in his hands and reached into a side pocket to retrieve a small multi-tool. Working carefully, without any hint of panic, he removed the obstructing tip. When he finished, he slung his bag over his shoulders, secured it, and pushed his helmet onto his head. He started the bike and accelerated out of the alley, arriving at the adjacent road at the same time as a patrol car.

The officer in the passenger seat held up a strong, handheld spotlight and shone it directly at the figure on the bike. He was blinded by the light, but manoeuvred around the car easily, and accelerated up the road, north toward the Angel. The patrol car turned and gave chase, the officers calling in the pursuit as they did. Within minutes there were three cars, blue lights flashing, sirens wailing, in pursuit of the motorbike.

The powerful motorcycle accelerated, pulling away from the pursuers. Suddenly a bright beam of light burst from the sky and lit up the street in front of the patrol cars. A helicopter had joined the hunt. The motorcycle headed toward the Old Street roundabout at a hundred miles an hour. The lead pursuit car tried in vain to keep up. Its experienced driver did not see the small Ford Fiesta turn onto the road ahead. The patrol car slammed into the back of the small vehicle and turned onto its side. It careened into the oncoming traffic, impacting with two cars before coming to a halt. The driver was unconscious. The officer in the passenger seat struggled to release her safety belt. The smell of petrol quickly focused her mind. She fought to free herself from the wreckage as the first flames licked at the car's engine. Adrenaline coursing through her body, the young officer escaped the remains of the patrol, and rushed to the aid of her colleague. She forced the door open and struggled to untangle the lifeless driver from his restraint. Once she had released the belt, she pulled at anything that she could grip, dragging the unconscious man onto the street. The ruptured fuel line ignited, acting like a fuse, it sent flames rushing toward the fuel tank. The car was engulfed in an orange-red blaze which lit up the facades of the surrounding buildings and climbed high into the night sky. Rescuers quickly located the two injured officers, who had escaped the vehicle with seconds to spare.

From above, the police observer tried to keep his focus on the motorcycle. It had crossed the roundabout and was heading into the Square Mile. The City of London police had been alerted and waited at their checkpoints for any sign of the offending motorcycle. The helicopter circled above, its beam turning the darkness to daylight. They had lost sight of the suspect. He had turned into a side street or an alley. He was gone.

'Bugger!' the observer yelled into his headset. The pilot shook his head and made another turn above the area where they had last seen the bike.

Palmer's phone rang as he stepped into the shower. He turned the water off, stepped out of the cubicle, and picked up the lit handset. He listened intently. When he finished, he dialled Mullins, Williams and Porter. They met forty minutes later. The street was filled with flashing lights and crowds of curious onlookers. A scenes-of-crime team was already inside the house and a mobile command unit was being set up. DS Galloway had arrived with DI Williams.

'It looks like we may have a break at last,' Palmer said, unable to disguise the excitement in his voice.

'Our boy has struck again, only this time he was disturbed. Mullins, I want you to find out who lives here. Who they are, what they are, who their families are, and what their dog's name is, everything.' Mullins nodded, hiding her disappointment at not being taken into the house.

'Mike, Dylan, let's get suited and booted and go take a look. Galloway, give Mullins a hand,' Palmer finished.

The scene in the room was familiar: a bloodied body on the bed and another frozen in position facing the bed. In this case the body had been fixed to a chair rather than crucified to the wall. The room itself was a monument to seventies' fashion: bright colours and floral print. Scenes-of-crime were already carefully working their way through the room, searching for evidence invisible to the naked eye. One of the technicians turned to Palmer as he entered, and said, 'Frank, I didn't know this was yours.'

Palmer smiled.

'How're you doing, Ben? They've not sacked your incompetent arse yet?' he joked.

'Not yet. They still haven't figured out how useless we are, have they, Frank?' the man responded.

Palmer smiled and nodded. Many a true word is said in jest.

'What have we got?' Palmer asked more seriously.

'Well, I've read about those cases over at your manor and this seems pretty similar. I think these two,' he pointed to the bloodied mess on the bed and the man still secured to the chair, 'were the targets. He was tied to the chair; she had her hands secured behind her back.' The man paused, walking over to stand beside the bed.

'She died a nasty death, but she was old, so I don't think she would've held out for very long. Both eyes were removed, there are burns, cuts, bruises.'

The forensic examiner turned to look at the old man, still seated in the chair, facing the bed. His face and the front of his shirt were completely blood-soaked. 'The old boy had his carotid artery severed, the time of death around three hours ago, four at the most. Both died around the same time. Their body temps are pretty much of a muchness.'

The examiner paced across the room and looked down at the woman slumped on the carpet near the door,

'This one, it appears that she walked in on our suspect getting his jolly on with this lot. She was struck in the throat, one bloody powerful blow, crushed her larynx, and killed her within minutes. Her husband arrived shortly afterward. He made it out alive, called nine-nine-nine.'

The examiner paused and turned back to the old man in the char,

'Oh, and this,' the examiner added. 'The sick bastard carved up the old boy's chest, looks like a G to me.'

Palmer walked over and stared down at the seated man's mutilated body. The examiner pulled his nightshirt open and the letter was clearly carved on the man's lifeless chest: G. Now they had three letters, PEG.

'PEG, what does that mean?' Palmer said out loud. 'Make sure we get some clear photographs of that,' he ordered.

Palmer looked around the room once more and then walked out into the passage and out of the front door. The three detectives stood outside in the cold wind, listening to the uniformed officer who had been first on the scene as he relayed the events to them. No one interrupted him. When he finished Palmer asked, 'Were you aware of the suspect being in the house at any time after you entered?'

'No, guv,' the officer answered.

'Hmm,' Palmer mumbled. 'Are you absolutely sure?'

'Yes, guv, positive,' the officer replied.

Palmer thanked him and instructed him to submit a full report before finishing his shift.

'This is the most important case you've ever been involved in, Sergeant,' Palmer informed him. 'I need every detail, no matter how small.' The uniformed officer nodded and left.

Seeing that something was on Palmer's mind, Williams asked, 'What are you thinking, guv?'

Palmer waited a while before answering.

'Well,' he began. 'From the time that the first officers entered the house to the time the car spotted the bike coming out of the alley was about eight minutes, give or take.'

Williams and Porter nodded in agreement. It was what the first officers on the scene had reported.

'This guy is good; we know that. He would've been long gone within eight minutes. So, what delayed him?'

The detectives nodded, understanding what Palmer was saying. They would need to go over every inch of the yard and the adjacent alley. There was a chance the killer had dropped something and spent time looking for it in the dark, or he had needed to clean or remove an item of evidence before making good his escape. This could be the break they had been desperately waiting for.

'I want every officer involved here tonight interviewed by our team, Mike. Can you take care of that?' Palmer asked.

DI Williams nodded.

'Dylan, get onto traffic. I want every CCTV from every camera on every route to and from this area and from the route the bike followed when it was chased.'

DI Mullins called to Palmer before he could continue. She walked up to the small group, still talking on her mobile. When she finished, she turned to Palmer.

'Right, guv, the house belongs to Dennis Breen, seventy-two. Lived here with his wife, Lilly. He's a retired prison officer, worked at the Scrubs nick for thirty-three years, retired seven years ago. Two kids: daughter Jane, thirty-nine; son David, thirty-five; must've been late starters.'

Palmer shook his head. A retired prison officer. How did this tie into Billy Barker and Paul Morton?

'I want you to check all records. I want to know if and when Barker and Morton were ever in the Scrubs together, then...' Palmer stopped talking. Something in his memory jarred. Barker, Morton and Wormwood Scrubs Prison.

'Are you okay, guv?' Mullins asked.

'Yeah, I'm fine,' Palmer muttered. 'Get moving with that search. I think we've just been given the link that ties all of this together. Oh, and one more thing, include the word peg and the initials P-E-G in your search.'

'Peg?' Mullins asked, confused.

'Yeah, the old man had a G carved onto his chest.' Mullins looked at Palmer, her forehead creasing.

'Get a move on, I'll see you all back at the station,' Palmer hurried.

He turned and headed for his car, then drove back toward East London. His mind was searching for the common denominator that linked Billy Barker, Paul Morton and Wormwood Scrubs Prison. PEG. It struck Palmer that he was forgetting something. He had excluded two vital elements from the equation: himself and Jack Barker. A memory stirred, fighting its way into his conscious thought. The name slammed into his head like a freight train into a rusted Volkswagen. He almost lost control of his car.

CHAPTER NINE
Sins of the Fathers

Palmer had left London at the age of twenty. His friend, Jack Barker, had been on an unrelenting quest to scale the ladder leading to the upper echelons of the city's criminal fraternity. The climb would be long, dangerous, and difficult to survive. Palmer had known that. He had also known that he did not have the stomach for it. He wasn't a coward, but his deepest fears included ending up in twenty-hour-a-day lock-up, on a life stretch. That was where he had imagined Jack Barker would end up, if not in West Ham cemetery or, more likely, in a shallow grave in an Essex Forest. Palmer had not been prepared to risk all in the pursuit of wealth and power.

He had relocated to Belfast at the invitation of his mother's family. The pitiful woman had left Northern Ireland years before, having elected to marry a Catholic man. The choice had left her shunned by her family, alone in a strange city with an abusive husband and a newborn child. She had taken her own life when Palmer was twelve.

Not long after his arrival in Belfast, Frank had been dragged into service in the Royal Ulster Constabulary by an uncle who had refused to take no for an answer. He realised later that it was an attempt by the Unionist to exorcise the Catholic from him.

'It's the right thing for you, Frank, boy,' his Uncle Derrick assured him. 'It'll do you the world of good.' The man had not been wrong. Despite his chequered youth, Palmer had taken to policing almost instantly. His career had started with early promise. He had been well liked and tenacious, with an instinct that had served him well. After eventually joining a homicide unit, Palmer had found that the excitement of working as a homicide investigator had faded sooner than he had expected. Nonetheless, he was a good investigator. Although his career had been adversely affected by his association with a hard-line UFV faction, he had been respected for his abilities. When the tedium of life as a detective and the frustration of the constant political interference had eventually become too much, he had decided to return to London.

His chosen vocation had been met with incredulity and disbelief when he had transferred to London and joined the Metropolitan Police. It had been seen as a betrayal by Jack Barker. Barker had been serving a four-year sentence when Palmer had returned to London. By the time of the gangster's release, Palmer had been settled in the city again. Their re-acquaintance had been inevitable. Palmer had found his old friend to be far more genial than he had expected.

The detective had become a regular at Barker's clubs. Ecstasy and cocaine had been sweeping across Europe. Barker had controlled a large portion of their import and distribution in London and the UK. He had been amassing a fortune. Palmer had been swept up in the flood of easy money and good times. As payment for his indulgences, Palmer had fed Barker details of cases that were of interest to him. The villain had fed Palmer information about his competitors. It had been a mutually beneficial arrangement. While Palmer had been making arrests it had been difficult for anyone to point a finger at his friendship with 'Big Jack' Barker. The arrangement had given Frank Palmer the best of both worlds. He had managed to convince himself he was doing no wrong.

In the spring of 2007, Jack Barker had introduced Palmer to Judy Grace. She had been the wife of a wealthy businessman who had grown bored and disdainful of her tedious life. She had fallen in lust with the gangster after meeting him in a West End nightclub. Judy had been attractive, but Barker had not been interested in her or her looks. Jack's eyes, as always, had been on one thing and one thing only, money.

In this case, it had been her husband's money that had caught the gangster's eye. He had wined and dined Judy, feeding her cocaine in generous quantities to make her more malleable and doing things to her in the bedroom she had only ever dared imagine in her wildest fantasies.

By the time she had been firmly enough in his clutches, Barker had conceived a diabolical plan to separate her husband from his money. The Graces had a young daughter who the husband had doted on, to the extent that the needy Judy Grace had become jealous of the relationship between father and daughter. Barker had used the woman's growing resentment of her daughter to poison the woman against her family. Barker had always been very adept at mind games. When he had decided that she was ready, he had disclosed his despicable plan to her. It was, he had told the obsessed woman, the only way they could be together forever.

On a warm July evening, Judy Grace, at Barker's instruction, had drugged her daughter and had used a sex toy to sexually assault the incapacitated girl. Instead of being reviled by the task, she had revelled in it. Such was the effect that Jack Barker had on those who became ensnared in his dark and twisted world. The following morning, the woman had visited the station and had made an allegation against her husband, claiming that he had been sexually abusing their daughter.

Barker had made Palmer aware that the complaint would be made. He had assured the detective that the charge had been genuine. The man was nonce. He had been sexually abusing his daughter. In their world, that made the man fair game. Palmer had known that the pieces did not fit, but he had ignored that and had focused instead on Peter Grace's guilt. Grace had been arrested. After a gruelling interrogation by the then CID Detective Sergeant Palmer, Grace had been charged. He had been refused bail, had been remanded in custody at Wormwood Scrubs prison. Two days after his arrival on the prison's remand wing, his badly beaten body had been found in his cell. Despite the horrific injuries that he had sustained, the prison authorities had insisted that his death had been by his own hand. Because of the nature of his crime, the police had been reluctant to pursue the matter. Judy Grace had inherited half of her husband's estate. Jack Barker had begun the task of relieving her of her newfound wealth.

Palmer had put the pieces together. He had understood what Barker had done. He had known that an innocent man had died in prison. It had been sobering for him, especially as he had watched Barker systematically stripping Judy Grace of all she had. He had realised that there was no boundary that Jack Barker would not cross. He would destroy anyone to get what he wanted. Palmer's friendship with him had cooled after the affair. Barker had never relinquished the hold that he had over Palmer. When Barker had taken all that he had wanted from Judy

Grace, he had cast the used and broken woman aside, disposing of her like an unwanted animal.

At the time that Peter Grace had purportedly committed suicide, Billy Barker had been serving the last year of a three-year stretch at the Scrubs. Paul Morton had been serving time on remand, awaiting trial for robbery charges that had been eventually dropped.

P-E-G. It wasn't a word. They were initials, just as he had first thought. Peter Edward Grace. It tied all of them together. Palmer was certain that the investigation would show that Breen had been an officer on the remand wing when Peter Grace had been found dead in his cell. The case had played on Palmer's conscience after Peter Grace had died. As far as Palmer could recall, Peter Grace had had no family except for his wife and daughter. That is what had made him a mark for Barker. A gnawing feeling told the detective that he was right. The killings were somehow linked to Peter Grace. They had nothing to with Roman Kobec or any other underworld figure. It was information that he keep to himself for the time being. He did not want the Grace matter being investigated. He needed time to figure out how to deal with it.

He headed back to the station, going over and over the Grace case in his mind. He decided that the first step was to track down Judy Grace. He went to his office and logged onto the police network. He keyed the name Judy Grace into the search bar and hit enter. It took less than a minute to complete the search. The list included seventeen Judy Graces. He narrowed the search to south-east England. He still had three hits. He looked through each record, assessing the age of each. There was only one name that fitted. It was her. It was the Judy Grace he was looking for. Her last known address was listed as having been Strood, Kent. There was no record of her past 2008. She had died on August fourth of that year. There were no details about her cause of death on file. Palmer printed the page, folded it, slid it into his pocket, and then he sat, staring at nothing.

Not far from the police station, in a small, rented garage, Deacon Brown was hard at work. He sat at a workbench, lit by a small but powerful lamp. In his right hand he held a soldering iron. He touched it to wires running to an electronic board. His left hand held nothing. His arm was missing from below the elbow. He had lost it when one of his creations had prematurely detonated. It had been a parcel bomb destined for the rival of a businessman. It had put him out of action for a while, but he had recovered soon enough. Having only one hand was a disability. It took him slightly longer to complete a project. Brown had used his creations to rid Jack Barker of several rivals. Harry Greer, a cocaine importer, and general lowlife, expired in his Porsche 911. Tony Baxter died in his Range Rover. Now the boss was targeting a man called Roman Kobec. He was to perish in a piece of high-end English engineering. It was a challenge for Deacon Brown. He liked a challenge. The trick was to ensure that all of the occupants of the vehicle died. It was an art form. He was an artist.

Deacon Brown's latest creation was a masterpiece. It had directional-shape charges, which would ensure that the blast destroyed the entire vehicle. It was packed with enough C4 to destroy two vans. He was taking no chances, as Jack had ordered. It had a remote detonator that could be activated up to five miles away with a phone call.

'Got anything?' Porter asked.

'Nothing yet, but I know there's something the DCI's not telling us. I could see it in his face, Dylan, so could you,' Mullins replied.

'I'll speak to my DCI again, but let's keep this tight. Let me know if anything comes up,' Porter said and hung up the phone.

'Everything okay?' Palmer asked, startling Mullins.

She was momentarily thrown. Had Palmer heard her talking to Porter? She had to assume not.

'Yes, guv, everything's fine.'

Four detectives were in the incident room. DI Mullins was seated before a twenty-three-inch screen. Others were paging through files. It was almost seven a.m. None had slept. They were all tired, but they felt that they were close to a breakthrough.

'I'll be out for a few hours,' Palmer advised his second in command 'But I want a full report on Breen when I get back, everything,' he ordered.

Mullins nodded.

'Sorry, yes, guv, I'll have it ready,' she stammered guiltily.

The drive south to Strood in the Medway towns took an hour. Palmer was familiar with the area. His ex-wife's family were from Rochester. He had spent a lot of time there in the past. His SatNav led him to the last address listed for Judy Grace. It was a terraced workman's house on a street of mostly poorly kept buildings, punctuated by the occasional refurbished house. The area had been up and coming before the 2008 crunch. It would still be some time before it shook off its benefits-class grime. Palmer walked up a short path and knocked on the door. No one answered and he knocked again. After a while he heard loud grumblings and a heavyset man in a vest and boxer shorts answered the door.

'Do you know what the time is?' the man asked.

Palmer held up his badge. It stopped the man's protests, but he still had a face like a smacked arse.

'What can I do for you?' he asked grouchily.

Behind him, a nails-on-blackboard voice shouted, 'Who is it, Gal?'

'Do you know a Mrs Judy Grace?' Palmer asked he man.

The man did not answer but Palmer saw recognition in his face.

'What's this about?' he asked. 'What has she done now, killed someone?'

Palmer smiled. The man wasn't far wrong.

'So, you know her?' Palmer asked again.

The man hesitated and then stepped aside from the door and said, 'Why don't you come in?'

Palmer walked past him, not bothering to wipe his feet. The man showed him through to a cluttered, tobacco-stained room. Palmer refused a cup of coffee and the man disappeared for a minute. He heard muffled voices and then the man returned. He sat opposite Palmer and said, 'So, Judy Grace, it's been a while since I heard that name.'

'How did you know her?' Palmer questioned.

'We used to live next door, she lived here, in this 'ouse, her and that poor kid of hers,' the man explained.

'Her daughter, Anne,' the detective confirmed. The man nodded.

'Do you know where the daughter is now?' Palmer asked.

The man shook his head,

''Fraid not,' he answered. 'The council evicted her, and we got the house. It was bigger than ours next door,' the man advised, then fumbled. 'That was in two thousand…' He hesitated and then called out,

'Brenda, when did we move into this 'ouse?'

Palmer heard a shuffling noise and an overweight woman in a dirty housedress walked into the front room.

''Allo,' she greeted. Palmer nodded. 'Now, let's see.' She used fingers to calculate the years.

'Hmm, it was 2007. No,' she said, then concluded, 'yes, 2008, I'm sure, I think.'

Palmer smiled and thanked the woman who blushed and sat down next to her husband.

'This is about Judy then?' she asked.

Palmer nodded.

'Do you have any idea where she went when she left here?' he asked the woman.

'No, I haven't a clue, I'm afraid. If I could help you I would,' she quickly added.

'What can you tell me about her?' Palmer asked the wife. Years as a detective had taught him that women always knew more about their neighbours than men did.

'Well, I'm not one to talk ill of another, you understand,' the woman began with the seasoned gossiper's opener. 'But she was a handful. Drank a lot, you understand; she was drunk by ten o'clock most mornings, swearing and carrying on at that poor girl. What she went through…' The woman's voice trailed off and Palmer sensed genuine sadness in her words.

'What do you mean?' he queried.

'Well…' The woman seemed reluctant to talk about it. Palmer waited patiently, not hurrying her, and eventually she looked at her husband, who nodded slightly.

'She used to beat the girl something awful,' she explained. 'She treated her no better than an animal.'

Her husband interjected.

'One day,' he began. 'Well, that woman was in a terrible rage and the little one climbed over our back fence to get away from 'er. We could 'ear 'er screaming and swearing, and we found little Anne cowering in the back yard. She couldn't 'ave been more than thirteen or fourteen, and she were small for her age. She was in a state, as thin as a weed. Brenda brought her inside, and we called the Old Bill.' The man paused. He seemed embarrassed and looked nervously at his wife.

'We could see that she had bruises,' he said. Palmer saw the woman's face had turned grey and tears had formed in the corners of her eyes.

'It wasn't long after that 'appened that they left,' the husband finished.

'And the police came to fetch the girl?' he asked.

They both nodded.

'Like they 'ad before, but they always brought her back again.'

Palmer was glad to escape the suffocating house. He was heading for Medway police station when his phone rang. It was DS Porter. They had found a clear image of the motorcycle from three cameras, but the registration number on the bike had been copied. It didn't exist. They had enhanced the image of the rider and the techs were busy building a computer image of him. They could not see his face, but they may be able to give a better physical description.

There was one other thing of interest. Forensics found a screwdriver with a broken tip in the alley. They also found the broken off piece of the tip. It seemed as if the killer might have lost the keys to the bike when he was forced to rush from the house. He had used a screwdriver to force the lock and start the motorcycle. They were scouring the area now for the keys. It supported what Palmer had speculated. The killer had been held up fleeing the scene.

Palmer navigated across the River Medway and headed south through Rochester. He continued along winding roads, past the Chatham dockyards. Medway police station was housed in a modern brick and glass building, several miles away in the town of Gillingham. When he arrived, Palmer showed the desk sergeant his badge and explained what he needed.

'You're a bit far from home, guv,' the sergeant said, showing Palmer through to the busy station canteen. 'Get yourself a cuppa. It may take a while to find the file.'

Palmer took the uniformed sergeant's advice and ordered a cup of coffee. It wasn't as bad as he expected. He was thankful for that since he had to order a second cup before the sergeant returned and led him to a small room with a single desk and two chairs. On the desk was a manila file. Palmer thanked the man and pulled out a chair.

'You can take copies if you need, guv, the copier is down the hall to the left, but you can't remove any original documents,' the sergeant advised, before pulling the door closed.

Palmer sat and paged through the file. It seemed that Judy Grace had relocated to Strood shortly after Barker had cast her aside. It was unclear why she had chosen to move there, but she had been in trouble with the police within months of her arrival. She seemed to have been a thorn in their side from that time on. Her neighbours had been correct. Grace had been charged on two occasions for physically abusing her daughter. A catalogue of errors by the police and overworked, underfunded social services agents had seen the child returned to her mother after both cases had collapsed. It was a story that Palmer had heard many times before. On one occasion it had been suspected that Grace had kept her daughter chained up in the damp cellar of their house for weeks. The list of offences against the young girl that the mother had been charged with were staggering.

On the last page Palmer found what he was looking for. Judy Grace had been relocated by social services to a council estate in High Wycombe, Buckinghamshire. He folded the page that included the address and put it in his pocket. He thanked the desk sergeant on the way out and headed north, back to London. The catalogue of abuse perpetrated by Judy Grace against her own daughter had shocked Palmer. He spent much of the return journey thinking about his daughter. He knew that he could have done better by her, should have done better. He loved the girl. He was aware at times over the years that his love for her was all that had kept him functional, kept him from falling over the edge and into the abyss. His daughter made him want to be a better man, even when he was unable to be.

It was afternoon when Palmer passed through the Blackwall Tunnel. The day was warm. A perfect summer's day. He emerged from the north side and turned west. He felt agitated and dejected. He would have to fight a battle on two fronts now. On one side there was Jack Barker, Roman Kobec, and the looming conflict between them. Maybe there was time to cool things down. He could prove to Jack that Kobec had no hand in Billy's death. On the other front, someone related to Peter Grace was exacting vengeance for the man's untimely demise in Wormwood Scrubs prison.

He was heading for the station, but the urgent need to quell the demons that invaded his mind sent him to Stepney instead. He smelled the familiar odour of stale urine as he climbed the stairs to the second floor of the council block. He banged on the door. After a minute, Sharon Collins, his on/off partner, answered the door.

'Well, fuck me, look what the cat dragged over,' she said when she saw Palmer.

Palmer said nothing and brushed past her into the smoky interior. A girl, who Palmer didn't recognise, was spread out on a dirty double sofa, a large hash joint in her hand. He collapsed into a faded single chair without taking off his coat.

'Well, I'm fine, thank you for asking,' Sharon voiced sarcastically, walking into the room.

'Sod off, Shaz, and make me a fucking hit,' Palmer replied.

'You little whore, you poisoned me! That's all you ever did! I should have strangled you at birth.'

The young girl shook violently, staring up at her mother with wide, terrified eyes.

'You're just like your father, pathetic. You know what they did to him.' She stumbled toward the girl and bent over. 'They killed him, they killed him because he was weak.' Her breath was foul, acrid.

'Please, Mummy, don't,' the girl pleaded weakly.

'Please, Mummy, don't,' the woman mimicked. 'Don't what? Don't do this?'

She stepped forward and kicked the young girl, who fell backward and lay motionless on the filthy carpet. She knew if she moved her mother would strike her again. The same thing happened repeatedly. Sometimes she was lucky, and her mother would stay sober for a month, maybe two, but it always started again. Her mother would tell her the same story repetitively, beating her, kicking her. Her father had been weak. If he had been stronger, he could have protected them, protected them from the likes of Jack Barker and Frank Palmer.

The girl lay still on the floor until she heard her mother's laboured breathing fall into a regular pattern. As usual she had passed out on the lice-infected sofa. The girl sat up. Her face was swelling from the imprint of her mother's foot. Then she heard the voice and her hands stopped shaking. It was him; it was David. He would protect her.

Anne Grace sat up in her sweat-soaked bed. She shook her head to extricate the last remnants of the nightmare as her breathing steadied. She was used to bad dreams; they had plagued her for years. She swung her feet off the bed and stood unsteadily. She hesitated, waiting for her head to settle, and then she walked into the bathroom. She let the cold water run and splashed it onto her face, over and over.

Palmer had wasted precious time that he did not have with Sharon Collins. The intensity and stress of the past week had demanded a release before he could continue. He had needed to satisfy the demons that clung to his back and leered constantly over his shoulders. He knew that it had been a mistake. The assortment of substances he had inhaled and ingested had done little to soothe his anxiety. He had slept for less than three hours. His mind had persistently returned to the interview room where he had interrogated Peter Grace years before. He could picture the man's face clearly. He had been a proud and gentle man, horrified by the accusation that he had abused his daughter. Palmer had known that he was innocent. He had tried to convince himself afterwards that Grace had been guilty, but he knew that he had been innocent. The man had feared for his life, feared for his daughter's safety. He had begged Palmer for his help once he had realised that his own wife had been responsible for his situation.

Now it seemed that the devil himself had come to set things right. It was time for recompense. The only currency that would be accepted was blood. Palmer tried to call Barker but was unable to reach the villain. That was not a good omen. It was disconcerting. Jack was up to something. Palmer was certain that whatever it was, it included Roman Kobec.

'There were two occasions when Billy Barker and Paul Morton were at the Scrubs at the same time. Breen was there on both occasions,' Mullins informed her audience.

'First in 1998, Billy Barker was on remand for a blag in Lewisham, Morton was doing a two stretch for GBH.' Mullins paused, looking at the whiteboard. She tapped the board with a marker.

'The second time was in 2007, Morton was back on remand for a contract killing; Billy Barker was finishing a stretch,' Mullins reported. Then added, 'Incidentally, Morton walked on the charge. This seems to be the last contact we can find between these two, in or out of prison.'

Heads nodded.

'Okay then,' Palmer instructed. 'We need to find people who were acquainted with either one of these two, and who were in the Scrubs during those periods. Bright and Miller, you two are on it. Work with Hunter, bring in anyone who comes up and is still around for an interview.' The detectives nodded.

It was DI Williams' chance to brief the taskforce. He stood and walked to the front of the room, apprehensively. Like many, public speaking was high on his list of fears. Unknown to any but himself, and despite being a routine part of his job, it still made him uncomfortable.

'We've interviewed all of the officers involved in last night's incident, as well as the husband who escaped the house. We don't have a clear facial description of the suspect, but we do have a better physical description,' he informed the team.

'The suspect was wearing leather riding gear, and a full-face helmet. Our tech wonder boys have given us this.' The DI used the tablet in his hand to put the image of a black-leather-clad figure on the screen behind him. There were murmurs across the room.

'I know, it is not a lot,' he hesitated looking up at the large screen. '*But* we now know that the suspect is Caucasian, five feet nine of slight build, and strong,' Williams rotated to face his audience. 'He killed the woman who surprised him last night with a *single* blow, so he must be well trained.' He waited to make sure everyone in the room had absorbed the information.

'Now that we have a better idea of what our suspect looks like and we know that he rides a motorcycle, we can go back to the previous scenes, question the neighbours again, see whether this new information jogs any memories.'

He looked at Palmer who nodded.

'Good thinking,' the senior officer agreed. 'Galloway can take Watts and Campbell and get some uniforms to assist. Get back out to Barker's house, badger the neighbours again, then Morton's.'

Palmer dismissed the team and called Porter. He did not see the quick glance that Porter gave Mullins as he approached the DCI.

'Have they found any keys yet, at the last scene?' Palmer asked.

'Nothing, guv, they've looked everywhere. It looks like the screwdriver wasn't related to our case. It's gone for prints, I'll keep you posted,' Porter advised.

Palmer nodded. Then he had a thought.

'Hang on,' he said to Porter. 'What if the screwdriver didn't belong to our suspect, what if someone else was using it to try to start the bike?' The area had a reasonably high crime rate. An expensive motorcycle in a dark alley might be too tempting an opportunity to turn down. Porter nodded. There was no need for Palmer to explain. He was annoyed that he had not thought of it.

'Get onto Islington nick and get a list of active car or bike thieves on their manor, tell them we want them turned over. I want to know if anyone tried to nick that bike. And tell forensics I want the screwdriver tested for prints as a priority.'

DI Williams stood by listening and nodding in agreement. It was a feasible scenario and a good call by Palmer. They may have a witness that interacted with their suspect. Palmer left the incident room and headed for the car park. He drove toward east along City Road, through King's Cross, along Euston Road and onto the A40 heading west. The road elevated for a brief stretch as he headed west allowing a transient view across city. The bright sun reflected off hundreds of windows, making the buildings appear alive. The motorway was busier that Palmer had expected. The A40 became the M40 motorway and he continued for fifteen miles before he exited at High Wycombe. His on-board navigator found the estate on the outskirts of the old town. The ageing housing development was in a rundown state. Almost every part of it was in need of urgent maintenance. It took a while to locate the flat that the detective was looking for. He knocked on the door and was startled when it was answered almost immediately.

'Who are you?' a small boy no older than five asked.

'Is your mummy home?' Palmer asked in the comic voice that adults used when addressing young children.

'Who are you? What's your name?' the little boy asked again.

Before Palmer could speak again, a young, heavily pregnant woman came to the door. She opened it fully and ordered the boy inside.

'What you want?' she asked rudely. 'You're not from the social, are you?'

Palmer flashed his badge.

'Oh great, filth. What's 'e done now?' the young woman asked.

'Nothing as far as I know, whoever he is,' Palmer answered. 'I'm looking for Anne Grace.'

The woman stared at Palmer blankly and asked, 'Who the fuck is she?'

'She used to live here at this address,' Palmer replied.

'When?' the woman asked abrasively.

'About fifteen years ago,' Palmer replied. The woman's eyes widened.

'Well, 'ow the 'ell am I 'sposed to know everyone who ever lived here? I don't know, do I. Fifteen years, you 'aving a laugh, mate, was only six years old then, wasn't I,' the young woman advised the detective in a whining voice.

'You've never heard the name before?' Palmer ignored her outburst and pressed.

'Look,' the woman replied. 'I only moved in here two months ago. Why don't you ask that nosey old cow next door, she knows everyone's fuckin' business and she's older than Margret Thatcher.' With that the young woman slammed the door in Palmer's face.

Palmer's anger rose, but he took the young woman's advice and knocked on the neighbour's door. It opened as quickly as the first door had.

'Can I help you?' an old woman asked before descending into a coughing fit.

Palmer waited for her to regain her breath before answering. The pregnant woman wasn't far off. The old girl was probably older than Margret Thatcher would be, were she still alive. When the woman finally stopped, he said, 'I'm looking for Anne Grace, she used to live next door, with her mother, Judy Grace,' Palmer pointed to his right. 'Did you know her at all?'

The woman was perceptibly taken aback.

'Who are you?' she asked, suddenly alert and suspicious.

'Sorry,' Palmer apologised, and withdrew his badge. 'I'm Detective Chief Inspector Frank Palmer.'

The woman squinted to inspect the badge.

'Well,' she said, 'you'd have a hard time finding Judy Grace.'

'You knew her, then?' Palmer asked. The old lady nodded,

'She's dead a long time now,' she replied.

Palmer breathed out. He was aware of that.

'Do you know how she died?' he asked. The woman flinched.

'You're not a policeman from around here, are you?' she queried. The question was obviously rhetorical.

Palmer shook his head and confirmed, 'No, ma'am, I'm with the Met, London.'

The woman snorted her disapproval.

'Well, her daughter killed her,' the woman explained. 'Beat her to death right there, next door, where that horrible little tramp lives now.'

Palmer went cold.

His navigation system failed him in his search for the local police station, but he found his way there after a brief detour. He found a young constable manning the front desk. The clearly inexperienced uniformed officer was unsure how to assist him and went in search someone who could.

'Frank bloody Palmer, as I live and breathe,' a female voice called from behind him as he stood waiting.

He turned quickly, surprised at hearing his name. At first, he did not recognise the woman who had spoken, but recognition came quickly.

She was still a looker. She had a sultry dominatrix appearance. She was tall with athletic shoulders.

'Debbie, Debbie Stanley,' he greeted. 'Well, blow me over with a feather, it *is* you,' he added, spreading his arms.

'In the flesh, hell, it's been what, eight, ten years at least, how are you?' the woman asked. Then appended, 'What are you doing slumming it out here in the boondocks?'

'Working on a case,' Palmer answered. 'You still on the force?'

'Yeah,' the woman confirmed. 'DI, this is my nick.'

Palmer smiled.

'So, you survived the apocalypse then?' he asked. He and Debbie Stanley had worked together for several years when he had first joined the Met.

They spent the next fifteen minutes in her office catching up and sipping coffee. Palmer fed Stanley half-truths to explain why he was looking for information about Judy Grace.

'It was before my time,' she said. After they finished their coffee, she went off in search of the case file relating to the murder. She returned to her office a short while later with a file in hand and another officer in tow. The man was tall, deathly thin, and grey.

'Frank, this is DS Hanson, he worked this case way back when.'

Palmer stood and shook the detective's hand.

'Why does the Met have interest in the case, after all this time?' the older detective questioned.

'We believe that it may some bearing on another case we're working on. I'm just tying up loose ends really,' Palmer lied.

The DS looked sceptical. A DCI travelling all the way from London to tie up a loose end didn't sound right.

Debbie Stanley handed Palmer the file.

'I've got to see to something quickly, Frank,' she said. 'Feel free to use my office, and Jeremy here will help you with anything you need. I'll see you before you go.'

Palmer thanked her and hurriedly opened the file. DS Hanson stood awkwardly for a while, and then decided to take a seat opposite Palmer as the detective skimmed the statements in the file. After a while he looked up and asked, 'So, what can you tell me about this, Serge?'

The DS, still unsure of Palmer, told him all that he could remember. Neighbours had called the police after a disturbance at Judy Grace's council flat. When they had arrived, it was all quiet. They had knocked but had gotten no answer. They had decided to forcibly open the door. Once inside they had found Anne Grace huddled in a corner of the kitchen. She was covered in blood from head to toe. In the lounge they had found the battered body of her mother lying on the sofa. The young girl, who had been known to police because she was on an at-risk register, had used the heavy brass base of a lamp to beat her mother to death. They estimated that she had struck the woman at least fifty times. The daughter had been charged with murder, but the CPS had declared her unfit to stand trial. She had been committed to a secure psychiatric facility. Palmer was impressed by the detective's recall.

'Did she say why she did it?' Palmer asked when he had finished. The older man looked into his eyes and nodded slowly.

'Yes, and no,' he answered cryptically. Palmer waited for him to continue. 'The girl claimed that she had not killed her mother, she always claimed that it was her brother that did it.' Palmer frowned.

'Thing was, she never had a brother,' the detective explained.

Palmer did not see Debbie Stanley before he left. He asked DS Hanson to thank her and left the station with the address of the institute that Anne Grace had been committed to.

CHAPTER TEN
War

The dangers of direct conflict and how to win those confrontations
when they are forced upon you.
Chapter Seven, Sun Tzu, -*The Art of War*

Paul Burrows and Harry Black sat in the front of the white van. In the rear, Deacon Brown held his latest creation on his lap. The eyes were fixed across the open green on the closed gates of Roman Kobec's home. It was a substantial three-level building, which had been recently renovated. Two heavyset men in dark suits stood inside the ornate gate. The tell-tale bulges in their suit jackets, evident through the binoculars, indicated that they were armed.

There was no chance of gaining access to the property without being detected. That is why Paul Burrows had devised another plan. They had cut a hole through the chassis of the van, big enough for Harry Black to fit through. They had a second car waiting along the road from Kobec's house. When the Russian's car emerged, they would follow. The second car would be positioned in front of the sleek Bentley. They would sandwich the car until the lead vehicle stopped at a set of traffic lights. Burrows would pull the car alongside Kobec's. Harry Black would drop through the hole in the rear of the van, slip beneath the limousine, and attach Deacon Brown's package.

The lead vehicle would ensure that Kobec's driver did not pull away while Harry was still beneath the car. Black was delighted with the plan. It was old school, proper gangster.

'How are you feeling, sweetie?' Patricia Palmer asked her daughter. Beatrice Palmer sat on the bed. The girl was dressed, but still looked pale and drained.

'I'm okay, Mum, please don't fuss,' she pleaded.

The older woman fought to keep her thoughts to herself. There was so much she wanted to say to her daughter. She wanted to take her by her shoulders and shake her until she swore that she would never touch another drug again. She knew to give her daughter space. She was afraid of chasing her away. So, she fought to keep silent. They had spent more time together in the past fifteen months than since her daughter was a baby. It had strained their relationship. She had noted that her daughter's behaviour had changed during the endless days of isolation. She had spent more and more time in her room alone, her eyes fixed on the screen of her iPhone. Lockdown had been difficult for them all. The nurse eventually arrived with her medication and signed her release form.

'We don't want to see you back here again, young lady,' she gently scolded, then stood back; a signal it was time for mother and daughter to leave. They drove in silence back to the house Patricia Palmer shared with her boyfriend. He was five years younger than she was, but the couple were genuinely in love. Beatrice was glad when her mother had found someone. She got on well enough with Patrick. He was funny and made her laugh. He seemed the opposite of her mother, but then they did say that opposites attract.

Jack Barker sat back in a sumptuous leather armchair in the expansive lounge. The room had a high, ornately decorated ceiling. There was no television in the room. The main feature of the decor was the artwork that adorned the walls. Two Picassos were affixed side-by-side. On the wall opposite hung a modestly bordered Monet. It was Jack's opinion that the art should not have to compete with the frame. He looked relaxed. On the sofa opposite, Bradley Carter and Bennie "The Leg" Jensen, sat anxiously. Collin Grey and "Irish Charlie" O'Connor shared a sofa to the right of Carter and Jenson. Barker had summoned them. None had thought to refuse the invitation. They all had two things in common. They were wicked men who controlled the gangland activities in their respective parts of the city, and they had each recently become acquainted with one Mr Roman Kobec.

'Those mackerels couldn't win a game if their lives depended on it,' Carter goaded Collin Grey, referring to West Ham United's recent loss. Barker laughed along with the men, keeping the mood light.

'Right, let's get down to business, gentlemen,' he eventually said. The room chilled.

'There's a move being made on my operations, someone's trying to get me out, to get me dead,' he announced.

'Who would be that stupid?' Collin Grey responded too quickly, professing disbelief.

Barker smiled.

'Any of you lot heard of a man named Roman Kobec?' he asked.

The men looked at each other and all, except Bennie "The Leg", shook their heads and feigned ignorance.

'Yeah, I 'ave,' Bennie replied. He leaned forward and continued speaking in his usual hurried and unpunctuated style.

'Strange cocksucker, 'e rocked up at my gaff at one o'clock in the morning, Saturday, I 'ad a game on with Mickey Dunn and 'is mob, next thing Big Larry comes in and says there's some fucker outside in a plush motor asking to see me, like a limousine or 'summin, I shit you not, 'ese fuckers watch too many movies, anyways, I go outside and there's this geezer, larger than fucking life 'e was, in the back of this motor the size of a fuckin' football pitch.' He shook his head and he laughed.

The men in the room fixed their eyes on him. Their smiles were humourless.

'What did he want?' Barker asked calmly. Bennie did not answer immediately.

'You know 'e didn't really want anything, he just introduced himself,' Bennie said after a while, his forehead creasing.

'I can't remember exactly what 'e said, I was fuckin' rat-arsed, no jokes, out of my fuckin' skull, I 'ad been on a three-day bender with Davie 'Two-heads' – you know Davie eh, Jack – and I wanted to get back to the game, that fuckin' Mickey was cleanin' me out.'

Barker smiled again. Bennie could not prevent beads of sweat from rolling down his cheeks. He was unnerved.

'So, you spoke with him, Bennie?' Barker asked, keeping his voice light.

'Only to tell 'im to sling 'is fuckin' 'ook is all,' Bennie replied.

'Why didn't I hear about this?' Barker questioned, raising his hands to accentuate the question.

'I'd forgotten about it, Jack, honest. I didn't remember the geezer's name 'til you said it now, I was wasted,' Bennie explained. Benjamin Jensen was a career criminal who was descended from a long line of criminals. When he was twenty-two, he had been accidently shot in the leg by an accomplice while robbing a high street bank. He had walked with a limp ever since. The incident had earned him the nickname, Bennie the Leg.

'I am right up my own arsehole looking for the cunt that offed my brother and you didn't think to remember that a man like Roman Kobec visited you at your gaff at one o'clock in the morning.' It wasn't a question, just confirmation.

Bennie shrugged but remained silent. Jack had a point. He had messed up, but he had also been less than honest about his meeting with Kobec.

'Well, this Kobec is planning a move against me, so we have to watch for him. He's a player; do *not* underestimate him. I want to know if he comes knocking, is that understood?'

The men nodded in unison. Barker looked directly at Bennie.

'Yes, okay, Jack,' Bennie conceded after a short silence.

'Right then,' Barker exclaimed. 'Who's for a refill and some lunch?'

The men looked physically relieved and nodded eagerly. A plainly dressed woman arrived with fresh drinks. The men chatted easily among themselves, discussing various means of dealing with the Kobec threat. They drank and ate the snacks that had arrived with their drinks.

Collin Grey was the first to show signs of distress. His face reddened and his hands flew up to his throat. He dropped his drink as he grasped at his thick neck. Bradley Carter, who ran London's most prolific car theft syndicate, had the same sudden affliction, as did Charles O'Connor, the notorious drug baron. They writhed in their seats, fighting for breath that never came. Their eyes bulged and their mouths frothed until one by one darkness overtook them.

Bennie stared in horror. Barker sipped his drink calmly, unmoved. When the three men stopped twitching, he looked at Bennie and said, 'Now, you will let me know if Kobec calls on you again, Bennie?' The white-faced man nodded. He understood what had happened. He also knew that he had narrowly escaped the same fate. His meeting with

176

Roman Kobec had been far more substantial that he had conveyed to Barker. As he often did, Bennie had used his quick thinking and his perceived lack of intelligence to overcome a dangerous situation. He knew that if he had chosen to say nothing, as his associates had, he would have suffered the same end as them. His story had been half true. Bennie was not sure if Barker had totally believed him. The gangster may have intended to leave a witness to broadcast the warning to others that may be thinking of crossing him.

Across the city, Roman Kobec's sleek limousine exited through the gates of his luxurious home. Harry Black quickly climbed between the seats and into the rear of the vehicle. Paul Burrows pulled out, speaking into the two-way radio in his hand as he did. The midday traffic was relatively light. Burrows pulled the van in behind the Bentley. They travelled west, passing through two sets of traffic lights, before arriving at a set of lights just as they were changing from amber to red. The timing was perfect. There was one car ahead of the Kobec's. Burrows waited for a taxi to pass him before pulling out and stopping alongside the luxury vehicle.

'Go!' he ordered.

Black disappeared out of the van. He hesitated for a second and then shimmied quickly under the Bentley. He gently raised the device in his hand and pushed it onto the undercarriage of the car. When it was firmly pressed against the chassis, he pressed a small button, which activated the electromagnet. The device silently fixed itself to the vehicle. He heard a horn blare. The lights had changed. The driver of the Bentley was hooting for the car in front to move. Black quickly shifted out from beneath the car and climbed up into the van. Deacon Brown used his one good arm to help Black up. Burrows pulled off, leaving the limousine behind.

Inside the luxury car, two children played, oblivious to the danger they were in. Their mother sat on the rear seat reading a magazine. Their father was supposed to have joined them. He had promised, but as usual something had come up. He had given them each a hug and a kiss and had patted them gently on their heads as they had left.

'I think the DCI was right, guv. We got the results back off the screwdriver. They found a partial print, enough to get a match. Rodney Cox, a small time no-good from Highbury, been done twice for nicking motors,' Porter said.

Williams stood and walked over to where he sat.

'Do we have an address for him?' he asked. Porter nodded.

'Right, let's pick him up then, make it a priority,' Williams ordered.

The detective inspector had a grudging respect for Palmer. Despite his extensive list of character flaws, he was a good detective. It had not surprised him though, when Porter had approached him about his and DI Mullins' suspicions that Palmer was somehow more involved in the case than was evident. They thought he was holding something back from the investigation team – something pivotal. Palmer's erratic behaviour since the Breen murders seemed to lend weight to Porter's claim. It placed DI Williams and the rest of the team in a compromising position. One they could not ignore. No officer ever liked to investigate their own. There was always an element of betrayal and disloyalty associated to any such investigation, irrespective of the guilt of the offending officer.

CHAPTER ELEVEN
For Love or Money

The luxury Bentley Mulsanne made its way through the streets of London, its occupants hidden behind the dark tinted windows. The driver had to make a wide turn to access the narrow roadway leading to the McDonald's drive-through. It was perfect. There was a thirty-yard road leading to the fast-food restaurant.

Burrows slowed the van and pulled over. A momentary thought passed through his mind: *do Russian gangsters eat burgers?* When the car was halfway along the narrow road, he said, 'Now!' The elegant black car exploded into flames. The van rocked as the blast wave hit it. Pieces of black metal rained down around the destroyed limousine. Burrows pulled away from the kerb, a broad smile on his face, behind him Deacon Brown howled, unable to contain the joy of seeing the destruction his creation had wreaked.

Burrows dialled a number on his phone and when it was answered he said, 'It's done.'

It was late when Palmer arrived in front of the ornate wrought-iron gates of the Granger Institute. The Granger family had donated the seventeenth-century mansion, which had been converted into an institute for the care of the mentally ill. The facility included a secure unit, which housed dangerous patients committed by the Crown. The Granger Trust also provided funds, supplemented by government funding, which enabled the institute to operate. Several well known mental health specialists used the facility to conduct research. One such specialist was Dr Henry Farnsworth. Palmer had managed to speak with the psychiatrist on the phone. He had persuaded him to wait at the facility until he arrived. Palmer had assured him that it was a matter of life and death.

The gates swung open, and Palmer steered his car up the driveway. Immaculately kept gardens lined the entrance on both sides. Palmer parked and headed toward the entrance of the main building where a stern nurse waited for him.

'You're the detective from the Metropolitan Police, the doctor is expecting you,' she informed him icily as he approached. 'He has been waiting for some time, and he has an engagement this evening. I do hope this visit is important,' she muttered.

Palmer was tired. He had covered a lot of miles since the morning. He held back from accosting the nurse, smiled, and said, 'It is a matter of life or death.'

He had discovered from the case files on Judy Grace's murder that Anne Grace had been sent to a secure government facility in Hampshire. He had called there and after a heated argument with a receptionist had finally been connected to the institute's director. She had informed Palmer that Anne Grace had been transferred to the Granger Institute many years before, at the urging of Dr Farnsworth. She had agreed to the transfer and that was the last that she knew of the young girl.

Palmer was shown into Dr Farnsworth's spacious office. Because he often held sessions there, several chairs were neatly arranged in a circular pattern. The adjacent walls were lined with shelves that held a staggering array of books on the human condition. Behind an enormous desk at the far end of the room sat the unimposing figure of Henry Farnsworth.

Palmer approached and the psychiatrist stood. He didn't look particularly pleased to see the detective.

'Chief Inspector Palmer,' he greeted.

'That's correct,' Palmer confirmed unnecessarily and stretched out his hand toward the doctor.

His hand was ignored and the psychiatrist took a seat, indicating for Palmer to do the same.

'Now, how can I help you?' he asked, closing an open file on his desk.

'As I said on the phone, I believe you treated a patient named Anne Grace,' Palmer advised.

The doctor nodded and replied, 'As I informed you, Chief Inspector, I did, but her records are confidential, I am not at liberty discuss her case with you.'

'Can you tell me whether she's still here?' Palmer queried.

The psychiatrist remained silent.

'Doctor, this really is a matter of life or death.' Palmer inhaled audibly, his patience strained. His eyes narrowed and fixed on the man opposite.

'Fine.' The man relented. 'She was released several years ago, Chief Inspector,' he reluctantly disclosed.

Palmer was surprised.

'After killing her mother?' he asked, sceptically.

'She had made a full recovery, Chief Inspector. She passed several stringent tests, and we found that with the correct medication she was no longer a threat to society.'

Palmer smiled. Well, she was somehow involved in hurting a great many people, he thought.

'Does she receive any outpatient treatment, do you still treat her at all, Doctor?' the detective asked.

'Look,' Farnsworth responded, adjusting himself in his chair. 'As I've said to you, Chief Inspector, I can't discuss these matters with you, they're confidential.'

Palmer nodded and said, 'Let me be a little more divulging, Doctor.' His tone was more belligerent. 'I believe that Anne Grace is somehow involved in a series of brutal murders in London, nine to be precise, including young children.' He let the facts sink in, then continued.

'If I must, I will get a warrant to have all of her records released to us. If we find she's in fact involved in these crimes, which is highly probable, we will look for accountability, Doctor.' The words were delivered with menace.

'You can choose to help me now or you can hinder me, but choose the latter, Doctor, and I'll turn your fucking life upside down.' Palmer raised himself out of his seat and planted his hands on the desk. 'I will rain shit all over you for so long you'll be forced to change your name to Doctor Brown.' Palmer's face was drawn, malicious. 'Do I make myself clear?' he finished.

The physiatrist was clearly shaken by Palmer's outburst.

'You can't threaten me, Chief Inspector,' he managed to retort, unconvincingly.

Palmer laughed, a hint of madness in his eyes.

'I'm not threatening you, Doctor,' he replied, his eyes narrowing. 'I am making you a bloody promise.'

The detective's eyes burnt. The psychiatrist surrendered and began speaking.

Back in his car, Palmer picked his mobile phone off the passenger seat. The handset had been set to silent. It showed eleven missed calls. Mullins, Williams, unknown, Mullins, Porter. The list of unanswered calls went on. Palmer had informed Mullins earlier that he was working on a new line of enquiry. It was a sensitive issue that could finally shed some light on the case. For now he needed time more to think. He ignored the calls and tossed the phone back onto the passenger seat.

Driving east along the M4, back to London, he rolled the car window down, hoping that the air would clear his head. He was overloaded with information. He knew that he was on the right track. The killings were related to Peter Grace. Judy Grace was dead, murdered by her daughter. That left Anne Grace, already a killer. She had been released from the Granger Institute the week after her nineteenth birthday.

Dr Farnsworth had first met Anne Grace at the bequest of a colleague. She had been completely withdrawn and had not spoken a single word since being found covered in blood, on the kitchen floor of her home, having bludgeoned her mother to death. Farnsworth had begun treating her. When she had responded favourably, he had requested that she be transferred to the Granger Institute. Her progress had been remarkable. She had shown herself to be a young lady of considerable intelligence.

Farnsworth's initial diagnosis had been that she was suffering from a dissociative identity disorder, the result of years of unimaginable abuse at the hands of her mother. She had forged an alternate identity deep in her mind. A personality that could deal with her tormentor when she could not. This personality was fearless where she had been weak. In her mind, she had conceived this character as being a brother, her protector. A boy named David.

'He would have appeared as real to her as you or I,' Farnsworth had explained. 'He was strong and confident, and he had destroyed her mother in order to save her.'

She had been damaged goods, but certainly treatable. Shortly after Anne Grace's nineteenth birthday, Farnsworth had triumphantly declared her treatment complete and entirely successful. He had submitted a request for her release. She had gone before a panel whose members had concurred with the psychiatrist. Anne Grace had been released, unconditionally. Her solicitors had arranged for temporary accommodation for the young Anne. That had been the last time that Doctor Farnsworth had seen or heard of her. He had no address for her, but he did, ungrudgingly, provide Palmer with the name of her solicitors.

There was another notable fact that interested Palmer. Half of Peter Grace's money had been placed in trust for his daughter. Those funds were to be paid to his daughter on her twenty-first birthday, by which time they would have amounted to almost four million pounds. It may have been that Peter Grace had been concerned about his wife, but the trust funds had been locked behind an impenetrable legal barrier that would have prevented Judy Grace from accessing her daughter's inheritance. *Four million pounds*, Palmer had thought. *You could buy a professional and a lot of revenge for four million pounds.* It seemed to be a likely answer. Anne Grace had hired a ruthless assassin to exact revenge on those involved in her father's murder. It was unclear how much the girl would have known about what had happened to her father. She had been a young child when he had been murdered.

Palmer had asked the psychiatrist if he thought that she was capable of being involved in multiple homicides. His answer had been cryptic, avoiding any direct inference that she may well be.

'The majority of people with asocial personalities are not given to violence, but if given a reason and cause, and especially when an asocial personality suffers from schizoid tendencies and is generally aggressive, their propensity for violence can be extraordinary.'

Farnsworth's words echoed in Palmer's mind. He opened the window wider to allow more air in. It was possible that Peter Grace's daughter could possess such hatred that she could be responsible for such horrendous acts of violence. The evidence was mounting, but Palmer still had misgivings. It was difficult to accept. If Anne Grace was somehow responsible, it was unclear what her end game was. She intended to drag him down, that much was evident. Palmer sighed heavily.

The emergency services were on the scene within minutes. The entire area had been cordoned off. An Explosive Ordnance Disposal unit had been dispatched by the Counter Terrorism Command. It was apparent that no one inside the vehicle had survived the blast. In addition to the limousine's occupants, a nineteen-year-old boy who had been passing nearby had been killed. Seven others had been seriously injured.

The police had managed to get the vehicle's registration from footage recorded by the McDonald's CCTV cameras. They had traced the registered keeper's address. Two uniformed officers had been dispatched from the police station nearest to that address. They arrived at the warehouse within an hour of the blast. The building was situated off the Woolwich Road, along the river. A sign hung above a large roller-shutter door on the side of the structure facing the road. It read "RUSCO Export/Import". It provided no other details. A glass-aluminium door adjacent to the roller-shutter was painted with the word "OFFICE". There were several private off-street parking bays for use by the building's occupiers. They held two black Mercedes SUVs and a Mercedes S320 sedan. The rest were vacant.

An officer pressed the intercom fixed to the side of the glass door. No answer. He tried for a second time. Still no answer. An alley ran between the warehouse and a neighbouring building. The second officer followed it and arrived at a private dock area which serviced the buildings. There was an open door leading into the warehouse. The officer heard voices inside. He knocked on the open door and called out. A man quickly appeared in the narrow passageway. He looked at the officer with some suspicion, then glanced back down the passage, as if he were intending to run the way he had come.

'I can help,' he asked, his accent strong.

'I'm Constable Matthews,' the officer explained. 'I am looking for the owner of a vehicle registered to this address.' The man appeared not to understand.

The officer explained in greater detail, until the man nodded slowly, raised his hand, and said, 'You wait here.' He disappeared back into the building. A short while later another man appeared. He was smartly dressed in an expensive suit. His English was considerably better.

'How may I help you, Officer?' he asked in accented, but clear English. The officer explained what had happened and the man's face changed. It contorted and his skin tightened. When the officer had finished, the man advised coldly, 'I will inform the parties involved.'

The young constable reached forward with a card in his hand.

'We will need someone from your company call this number urgently,' he instructed. 'We need to identify the occupants of the vehicle and notify their next of kin.' There was a brief, awkward moment when neither man moved. The accented man finally snapped out his hand and took the card.

Roman Kobec was speaking on the phone, when Tura Arynov, one of his closest lieutenants, stepped into the office. The men had left Kobec's residence less than two minutes after his wife and children had. They had arrived at the warehouse shortly before the patrol car had. Kobec saw the look on Arynov's face. He knew that Arynov was a man not easily unsettled. Something had notably shaken the man. Kobec placed his hand over the phone's microphone and asked, 'What's wrong?' The question made the man's appearance worsen.

'You'd better hang up,' his lieutenant said. Kobec spoke hurriedly into the phone and placed the handset back in the cradle. His face remained stony as Arynov delivered the devastating news.

Roman Kobec was a man who had been born into an underworld where extreme violence and a black heart had been prerequisites for survival. If business required that you kill your best friend in cold blood, then that was what you did. It was their world. He was not an entirely cold hearted man. Eight years earlier he had met and fallen in love with Adriana. They had had two children, a son and a daughter. He thought that they would be safer in London. Now he knew differently. Now he knew without a doubt that he had sorely underestimated Jack Barker. He had been forced into a confrontation with the man. It would now be a war. The Russian had no doubt that Barker was responsible.

Kobec had never been a man to shed tears. He did not know how. He suddenly felt vulnerable and exposed. He gave Arynov orders to immediately increase their security. They needed to bring in people from abroad to bolster their forces in the city. When he had finished giving orders, he sent his lieutenant out of the room, not wanting him to witness his momentary weakness. The Russian had elected to establish an office at the warehouse, rather than choose an office in some sought after location. It was an environment that he was comfortable in. As a smuggler and trafficker, he had spent much of his life in waterside buildings, like the one he stood in now. He looked out across the river, closed his eyes and allowed his head to drop.

The old manor house was set far back from the road, surrounded by ancient woods. Its exterior was rundown and looked in need of repair. It was purposely kept that way. The interior was luxurious, decorated in the style of a nineteenth-century bordello. The Black School, as it was aptly named, was accessed via a private, gated road, which was permanently guarded and under constant remote surveillance. Despite being in operation for more than nine years, the house was a well-guarded secret. Only a select few knew about it. Those with money or power whose sexual appetites included deviance and debauchery.

Detective Chief Superintendent Sloane stopped at the gate and waited for the guard to open the double leaf wrought-iron gates. When he did, the policeman raised his hand in thanks and drove through the narrow entrance. He was a regular at the house and was expected by its owner.

Once inside the expansive Victorian manor house, a scantily dressed young girl showed Sloane through to a private area. Jack Barker was seated at a decorative bar, waiting for the senior detective.

'Jack.' Sloane greeted him, crossing the room beneath the elaborate crystal chandelier with his hand extended.

Barker briefly shook the outstretched hand and said, 'Take a seat, Steven,' Sloane obliged. Barker filled an empty crystal glass from the bottle in his hand.

'So,' Barker said. 'This thing has got all bent out of shape. We need to get some control.'

Sloane knew Barker had enough on him to sink his career and to ensure that he spent the rest of his years behind bars. He only had one choice and that was to do whatever Barker asked.

'I think we need to bring in another team to take over, Jack,' the senior detective replied. 'Your friend Palmer may be working on his own agenda here.' He paused to gauge Barker's reaction. Barker gave nothing away and Sloane continued.

'I can't justify keeping him on as SIO, it has become apparent he may have some involvement in this entire debacle Jack; he has to go.'

Barker thought for a minute. He knew Sloane was right. Palmer was up to something, though no one, himself included, seemed entirely sure what that was. He eventually nodded and said, 'Okay, but leave Palmer to me, I'll find out what he's playing at.'

Sloane sipped his drink.

'Look, Jack, we're going to have to arrest you, to make it look good. If we don't, eyebrows are going to be raised. They've nothing concrete on you, it's all circumstantial, but even the commissioner is getting involved now. Next it will be Number Ten.' The senior officer again gauged the gangster reaction, before adding, 'I have a meeting with Piers Hall this evening, we'll find a way to get things under control.'

Barker had expected that his arrest was imminent. It did not concern him. Sporadic arrests were part of his life.

'Well, it can't be helped,' he responded more affably than Sloane had expected. 'But I want everything you have on Kobec, everything. He's gone to ground; I need to find him before he finds me.'

Sloane paled.

'I know how you're feeling, Jack, but there's a lot of surveillance on Kobec's premises. It may not be the right time to have a go at him. Give it a few days. Let me get you some useable intel.'

Barker laughed, shaking his head.

'I don't think Roman Kobec plans on giving me a few days,' he responded amusedly.

Sloane knew it was the truth. Kobec had just lost his family. He was not about to walk away from this fight.

'Let's leave Kobec to me,' Barker stated, patting Sloane's back. 'Now, while you're here, Sandra has a new girl, she's just your type. Why don't you stay a while and enjoy yourself?' Sloane protested feebly and looked down at his watch. He had some time before the meeting was scheduled to begin.

Palmer arrived home past nine. He was exhausted. He realised as he stepped from the car that he had left his phone on silent for the entire journey. It still lay screen down on the passenger seat. He reached across to pick it up and it lit up as he did. He looked at the screen in dismay. Something had happened. Something very bad had happened. He found Mullins' number and touched the green button. She picked up as he pushed his key into the front door lock. When the call ended, the detective felt a wave of nausea rush over him. He bent over and dry heaved, making a horrid choking sound. The world had come crashing down. He had been summoned to a late meeting. He withdrew the key from the door and turned back toward his car. His phone rang again before he reached it.

At Borough Command, an efficient-looking receptionist manning a modern looking desk, and obviously expecting Palmer's arrival, advised him to go straight up the adjacent stairs to the borough commander's office. He knocked once on the heavy wooden door and entered. The office of Chief Superintendent Piers Hall was spacious, well decorated, and modestly furnished. Superintendent Fletcher sat in one of four chairs situated in front of the borough commander's sizeable desk. Beside Fletcher, Detective Chief Superintendent Sloane sat hunched in a chair, looking distressed. Beside him sat two men who Palmer did not recognise. All turned to face him as he walked into the office. He closed the door behind him and greeted them.

'Guv, ma'am,' he said, acknowledging the senior officers.

'DCI Palmer, where the hell have you been? You're meant to be running the biggest murder investigation in the city and no one has been able to contact you for hours!' Sloane immediately remonstrated.

'Apologies, sir, I've been following up a lead relevant to the investigation. It's important,' Palmer replied with an undisguised hint of dissent in his voice.

'It is called a mobile phone for a reason detective,' Sloane said curtly waving the handset in his hand. 'And are you no doubt aware by now of the latest developments involving Roman Kobec?'

Palmer nodded.

'What does it mean, Frank?' Fletcher question Palmer. 'Was this the work of Jack Barker? Does Barker know something we don't? Is Kobec responsible for these series of murders?' The superintendent bombarded Palmer.

He didn't answer. *Time*, he thought, *I just need some time*. The eyes of all present bored into him.

'I don't know, but we can't assume anything,' he eventually managed to reply.

'If this is the start of a war, we need to know, Chief Inspector. It has the potential to be the worst crime-related violence this city has seen since the 1930s, and by some bloody margin,' the borough commander interjected, fixing Palmer with his icy stare. 'The commissioner is looking for answers and we'd better have something for him soon,' he warned.

Palmer looked at the uniformed man behind the desk but remained silent. What did they expect him to say?

When no one spoke, DCS Sloane said, 'This is Kevin Beck, he's from Special Operations and this is Commander Goodchild from MI5.' Palmer frowned.

'What has this got to do with MI5?' he asked reactively, without thinking.

'Bombs exploding on British soil are always of interest to MI5, Chief Inspector, especially in the current climate,' Goodchild replied. His private school accent sharpened Palmer's annoyance. 'And if there are going to be more, we'd like to know, before rather than after the event.' The intelligence officer let his words hang for a moment before continuing. 'We would also like to find out who supplied the device that was used today.'

Palmer nodded. He had little interest in what Scotland Yard and MI5 wanted. He had to find Anne Grace. She was the key. He knew that the situation was critical. Kobec was going to react. He doubted that Jack Barker had intended to kill Kobec's family. More than likely he had been targeting Kobec himself. Barker was smart and efficient. He would not concern himself with an eye for an eye. He would eliminate the target first and satisfy his thirst for revenge after.

'We can't be certain that this incident is the work of Jack Barker,' Palmer offered, standing awkwardly and out of place in the office. 'We were looking at Kobec as a possible in the Billy Barker case, but that's all,' the detective added. To Palmer's surprise the MI5 agent supported him.

'What do we have to link Barker to this?' Commander Goodchild asked no one in particular. 'Kobec is a man with many enemies.'

The question went unanswered. There was another momentary and excruciating silence, until the Special Operations officer, asked, 'Detective Palmer, I take it you're familiar with Collin Grey, Bradley Carter and Charles O'Connor?'

Palmer nodded wearily. They were known faces, heavyweights, two of whom he had met with in the past two days.

'They all worked under Jack Barker's protection, that's common knowledge, and word on the street is they were all about to get into bed with Roman Kobec,' Beck advised.

Palmer looked at Beck menacingly.

'We don't know that,' the detective snapped. 'It's that kind of speculation that probably ignited this thing.'

'*We* don't know, *I* do, Chief Inspector. That is what Special Ops does. We know what's going on, that is our business: information.' The reply was derisive. Palmer sensed a hidden meaning in Beck's words.

'We've kept it on a need to know basis, but their bodies were discovered earlier today, dumped on wasteland near Tilbury Docks,' Beck continued.

Palmer closed his eyes and stretched his chin up. There was no doubt that Jack Barker was responsible. He was one of the few men who really knew what Jack Barker was capable of.

'This investigation has outgrown you, Detective Chief Inspector,' Sloane advised before anyone else spoke. 'It is being handed over to a new special task force. Detective Superintendent Dunne will head it up, you are acquainted with him I believe, you will need to debrief him fully in the morning.'

Palmer did not protest. He was relieved in part, to relinquish the responsibility.

'In the meantime,' Sloane continued, 'we've issued a warrant for Jack Barker's arrest. There's a team out looking for him now. What we need to know is how he'll react given the current...' He stalled, then finished, 'circumstances.'

All eyes were on Palmer again. He looked around the room and couldn't keep himself from smiling.

'I don't have a crystal ball, sir,' he answered insolently. 'There's no way for me to know how he'll react. Barker is unstable right now, that I know for certain. Anything else would be speculation.'

'Do you think Kobec was involved in the murders of the Barker, Morton, and Breen families?' the MI5 agent asked. It was a pertinent question and one that Palmer now thought he had a positive answer to. *No.*

Instead, he replied, 'I have no idea. He didn't fit the profile, and our forensic psychologist seems convinced the murders were of a personal rather than business nature. I tend to agree with her, but it's impossible to be one hundred per cent sure until we catch whoever's responsible.'

The interrogation lasted a further five agonising minutes, after which Palmer was left with no illusions: the axe was coming down. He had one avenue of escape. Find Anne Grace and find the killer.

Roman Kobec stood looking out of the window into the darkness. Below, lights played on the water as the River Thames snaked its way through the endless sprawl of brick and concrete. His head had cleared, but he still fought to keep his composure. That was the problem with death. It was so final. Dead was dead. No amount of regret or grief could undo it.

The Russian had been raised in a world where extreme violence was commonplace. When you had seen death so often and on such a magnitude as Roman Kobec had, you viewed mortality less circumspectly. Much like his adversary, no amount of wealth had been sufficient to vanquish his demons. His psyche had been forged in the fires of the collapsing Soviet Union. He was a man of war. His weapons had brought destruction on an epic scale. It seemed hypocritical that he should now lament the obliteration of his own family at the hands of a man no different from himself. He had dealt in death his entire life. It was his knowledge of the destruction that Vladimir Putin intended to unleash on Europe that had resulted in his relocation to London rather than to a remote CIA black site. It had been many years since the threat of a global conflict had been so real, so close, and yet much of the world remained oblivious to it. He would be tasked with supplying weapons to Ukraine while gathering intelligence on Russians troop deployments.

Despite his lifelong acquaintance with war, the violent death of his family had shaken him. Jack Barker had been profoundly misjudged and his family had paid the price. He did not believe that the gangster had purposely targeted his family – they were collateral damage – it was him that Barker had been after. There was no doubting that it was Barker. Three of his new associates had turned up dead shortly after his car had exploded. Barker was letting everyone know that he was still the lord of his manor.

No one could explain how the bomb had been planted. As always, the car had been thoroughly checked before it had left the house. It had been a last minute decision to allow his wife to use the limousine. It was cumbersome on busy roads. The Mercedes was better suited to the longer journeys in heavier traffic. It was unlikely, but not impossible, that one of his men had betrayed him. Everyone had their price. Kobec knew that better than most. He also knew that he had to decide, fight or flight. Barker obviously was willing and able to fight. He remembered the words of Friedrich Nietzsche that his father had often quoted: *That which does not kill us makes us stronger*.

His muscles tensed and his mind focused. The Russian gazed into the night.

'If Jack Barker wants war, then so be it,' he decided.

Palmer was glad to be out of the borough commander's office. It had been suffocating. Everyone was aware that the events were spiralling out of control. No one knew precisely what action to take to stop it. He welcomed the fresh breeze as he walked to his car. His phone rang as he climbed behind the wheel. It was Tara Moore. As tired as he was, he was glad to hear her voice and pleased when she agreed to meet him at his house. He could do with a friendly face. He also wanted to hear her thoughts on the possibility that Anne Grace was somehow involved in the murders. He gave her the address and headed home.

By the time he arrived, the profiler was already waiting for him. They went into the house and were naked from the waist down within minutes. The sex was rough, just what Palmer needed. He was surprised by the doctor's passion. She did not hold back. She called out and moaned loud enough to wake the neighbours. They climaxed together, the doctor straddling Palmer on the worn sofa.

There was the usual awkward moment after sex that newly acquainted couples have, but they soon talked freely. The conversation quickly turned to the investigation. They discussed the horrific actions that had annihilated much of the Kobec family. The incident had made headline news across the UK and beyond. CNN had featured the bombing as their lead story of the day. They had focused on Roman Kobec's links to al-Qaeda and other extremist groups, especially in Afghanistan.

Palmer informed the profiler that a detective superintendent would be taking over as the senior investigation officer on the case. They continued their conversation in the kitchen. Palmer prepared microwave meals as they each sipped a bottle of beer. The detective was seeking an opportunity to bring Anne Grace into the discussion without alerting the profiler to the link with the Grace case. He ducked and skirted around the topic until the perceptive Tara Moore queried, 'Is there something you're not telling me, Frank?'

He wanted to confide in her, but he couldn't bring himself to trust her enough.

'It's nothing,' he lied. 'Just a possible new line of inquiry.' He felt suddenly exhausted. He needed rest.

Palmer was peripatetic once more. He was heading out again in search of answers. He had met with the replacement SIO, Detective Superintendent Dunne early, after which they had attended a briefing in the crowded incident room. The news of the day was that Jack Barker and his henchmen, Paul Burrows and Harry Black, were in custody. Palmer was unmoved by the news. It had been expected. Jack would be taking it in his stride, stretched out on the bunk in his cell calmly reading the morning papers as if he were at home. The man that Palmer needed to speak to today was not in a cell. He was in a hospice in Wandsworth awaiting the inevitable. Palmer needed to convince himself that he was not chasing a phantom. He needed to know whether he was right about Anne Grace.

He knew where the hospice was located. He had passed it many times and wondered if he might end up in a place like it one day. In the post-COVID morning traffic, it took an hour to make the journey. The detective was frustrated by the time he arrived at the facility. He strode impatiently to the reception desk and was annoyed to find it unmanned. When a heavyset nurse finally arrived, Palmer was forced to mask his irritation with despair. He asked for Mathew Taylor, explaining to the nurse that he was a beloved family member. Taylor was a favourite uncle on his mother's side he affirmed. It was a lie, but had he informed the nurse that he was a police officer seeking to question a dying patient, the response would have been far less favourable. Palmer did know Matt Taylor. He had been a renowned blagger in his day who had spent more than half his life behind bars. Palmer was shown into a small, tidy room where a frail old man lay on a bed. A clear mask covered his nose and mouth. It was an image that the recent pandemic had made all too common. A clean blanket and sheet were neatly folded down and the patient's arms rested on either side. Palmer could hear the man's laboured breathing. That's what fifty years of smoking did to you.

'I'll leave you to sit with your uncle, Mr Taylor,' the nurse said politely and left.

Palmer went to the side of the bed and shook the old man's arm. Matt Taylor was a shadow of the man he had once been. He woke, startled, and looked up at Palmer. He tried to speak, but only succeeded in drooling down his chin.

'Been a long time, Matt, remember me, Palmer, Frank Palmer?' the detective asked.

The man's face showed recognition. He blinked and replied softly, 'Have I died and gone to hell?' Palmer smiled.

'Still the smart arse, Taylor,' he responded.

The dying man managed a weak smile.

'I need some information, Matt.'

The man moved his head slowly from one side to another.

'What could I know?' he whispered. 'What I do know, I'll take to the grave.' He began to cough.

'If you don't tell me what I want to know you'll be heading to the grave in about two fucking seconds, mate,' Palmer snarled.

Despite the nearness of his death the thought of rushing into it still brought fear to Taylor's face.

'Now listen carefully,' Palmer explained. 'I want you to think back to 2007. You were banged up on remand in the Scrubs, you shared a cell with Paul Morton. Do you remember?' The old man remained silent, but Palmer could tell that he remembered. It was clear that despite his ill-health, his mental faculties were still in good working order.

'There was an incident in the prison, a man was done in, a nonce.' Palmer studied the old man, looking for signs of recollection. 'They said it was suicide. His name was Grace, Peter Grace,' the detective added, trying to spur his memory.

The dying man's eyes flickered. He stared back at Palmer and nodded.

'Did Morton kill Grace?'

Nothing.

'He's dead, you know, Paul Morton. Someone killed him, his sons, and his daughter-in-law. Tortured his youngest son to death while he watched,' Palmer informed the man. Taylor's eyes opened wide. He was no friend of Paul Morton's, but he feared the man. Morton was a psychopath, a killer.

Palmer repeated the question, 'Did Morton kill Peter Grace?'

Taylor was motionless but then his head nodded again, an almost imperceptible nod.

'Are you sure?' Palmer asked.

Taylor nodded and closed his eyes.

'Stay with me, mate, we're nearly there, one more question. How did Morton get out of the cell?'

Nothing. Palmer shook the dying man. A few garbled words escaped his mouth before he fell back to sleep.

'The screw, Breen,' he muttered.

It was all that Palmer needed. Now, he was certain that he had the answer. If Paul Morton had killed Peter Grace that tied all of the pieces together. It proved that he was right. The killings had nothing to do with Roman Kobec. This was about Peter Grace and his daughter. If he found her, he would find the killer. Someone the insane bitch had hired to exact revenge.

CHAPTER TWELVE
Battleground

How to understand the economy of war and how success requires making the winning play, which, in turn, requires limiting the cost of competition and conflict
Chapter Two, Sun Tzu -*The Art of War*

'Do we know what Palmer's been working on?' Detective Superintendent Dunne asked.

Williams shook his head and replied, What I've told you is all we know, guv, but it seems possible he's up to his neck in all this.' The two men were sat at a table in the almost deserted café.

'We need to be careful here. We need to be sure. It'll rock the Met if a senior detective turns out to be involved in this mess, so there can be no doubt, are we clear?' Dunne reinforced.

Williams nodded.

'Okay, then let DI Mullins and DS Porter carry on digging, let's thicken up the file before we act,' the new head of the task force said, heaping another sugar into his coffee.

The Eden Club was quiet. Business would pick up around lunchtime, as it always did. Businessmen, bored with the routine sex lives, reinvigorated by Viagra and cocaine would come in to play. They would ask to be spanked and whipped, to have their toes sucked and their backsides penetrated with strap-on dildos. No request could shock an experienced working girl in Soho.

Stuart Bagley ran the club. It was registered in his name, as was the five-storey building that housed it. The true owner was Jack Barker. The upstairs levels had been converted into a quasi-prison, where girls trafficked from Eastern Europe, Asia and Africa were forced to live until they had paid off their 'debt' for having been smuggled into the UK. Twenty-two girls worked at the club. The business could turn over fifty grand on a busy day. Each girl could turn ten to twelve tricks a day for which they would have roughly five pounds deducted from their debt. In reality there was no escape for the girls. They had been force-fed heroin to make them more malleable when they had first been captured. Before their spirits had been broken. It quickly became the only means by which they could escape the horribleness of their existence. Most of them just learned to accept their predicament, growing emotional scar tissue to protect themselves from the endless violations. Troublemakers ended up at the Black School, servicing doctors, solicitors, judges, and high-ranking police officials with more unusual tastes. Most people would be shocked to learn how many of their peers participated in violent, deviant sex. Strategically placed cameras in several rooms of the Black School ensured that Jack Barker had many influential people to call on in times of need.

While the girls sat around in their lingerie, waiting for the first punters to arrive, Stuart Bagley sat in his office arguing with Neil Thurrock, his six-foot-six Dominican doorman. When they heard the first screams, Bagley assumed two of the girls must be going at it. It wasn't uncommon. They often got into catfights. Bagley usually enjoyed watching and only stopped the girls when weapons were drawn, or a beating got nasty.

'Go and see what the fuck's going on, Neil,' he instructed.

The big man stood, opened the door, and immediately fell backward, stiff as a board, crashing onto the office floor. A neat red circle had appeared on his forehead. Bagley was too shocked to react. His mouth formed an O. Movement at the door tore his gaze from his fallen colleague. He looked up in time to see a black-clothed, balaclava-wearing assailant step into the office. The intruder raised his hand and pulled the trigger of the specialist .22-millimetre automatic pistol. The weapon was silenced. The rounds used were designed to fragment when they entered the body, which meant there were no exit wounds. The kills were more clinical. There were also no spent bullets to recover. Less ballistics to trace. Bagley had raised his hand in a futile attempt to protect himself. The first round tore through it and struck his cheek, the second smashed into his skull.

The attacker looked around the office and quickly located the picture he was looking for. He tore it from the wall, exposing the safe that he had been told would be there.

'Dainus,' he called into a mouthpiece connected to a narrow arm running from beneath his balaclava. Another man appeared at the office door. He carried a small black bag. He went immediately to the safe and began to work. Eleven minutes later six men exited the club and climbed into a black minivan with tinted windows. They had left with more than a million pounds of Jack Barker's money. Nothing moved inside the Eden Club. The only person not dead or injured remained frozen in fear beneath her bed on the third floor. Kobec knew people like Barker. He knew best how to hurt them.

At the same time that his associates had entered the Eden Club, another man, dressed in black combat trousers and a thin black military style shirt, carrying a tight-fitting rucksack on his back, scaled the north wall surrounding Essex Scrap Metals. He landed inside the fence without a sound and immediately fell to his stomach. His heartbeat was steady, not betraying the excitement that he felt.

He enjoyed these missions. It had been a while since the boss had allowed such action. It was long overdue. When Roman Kobec had married he had also softened, there was no denying it. Kopjov had assumed that that had been the reason that they had relocated to London. When the assassin had learned of the death of Kobec's wife and children, he knew that it would mean a call to arms. The Roman Kobec of old had retuned.

Andrzej Kopjov was ex-Russian Special Forces. He was fifty-four years old with the physique and stamina of a much younger man. He had been raised on the streets of communist Moscow. The soldier had killed his first man when he had been just fourteen. His father had sent him away to escape retribution for the killing and had himself been killed in his stead. Three years later the body of the man responsible for his father's murder had been discovered in the woods outside of the city. While in the military, Kopjov had been selected for search and destroy missions in Afghanistan. He had been captured and tortured by the Mujahedeen and had been released during a prisoner exchange. A month after his release he had been back in the desolate mountain reaches of the war-torn country, hunting the elusive enemy.

After the fall of communism, Kopjov had, like many ex-Russian Special Forces, gone into the private sector. He had met Roman Kobec in Kazakhstan in 1996. Kobec and a group of men had travelled to a remote region of the country, near the Russian border, to locate and punish a heroin smuggler who had double-crossed him. In the ensuing fight, Kopjov had killed seven of Kobec's men. Eventually, he had been wounded. The smuggler that he had been protecting had been bound, doused in petrol, and set alight. Kobec had admired Kopjov's courage and loyalty. Even while watching his paymaster burn, he had been defiant and unflinching. Instead of killing him, Kobec had offered him a job. He had been with him ever since. Loyal until his death. He had grown wealthy in Kobec's employ, but he missed the mind-bending adrenaline rush of battle. He had kept himself in marathon-ready condition. He was always able and willing to fight. His wait was over. In his backpack he carried two claymore mines, one of his preferred weapons. His arsenal also included the silenced Heckler &Koch MP5SD in his hands, four hand grenades, and a 9mm Glock automatic. His mission was simple. Search and destroy. Leave nothing alive.

He crept forward, keeping low. He could hear the dogs barking up ahead. He knew that they were kept in a cage during daylight hours. In front of him a huge pile of buckled and rusting metal rose like a grotesque sculpture. He edged around it. Another heap of metal appeared. To the left sat an enormous crane, its giant claw hanging lifelessly. Next to the crane was the crusher, beyond which he could see the low, flat-roofed building that housed the yard's office. There were no signs of life.

As he neared the building, he saw movement. A man in his early twenties holding a pump-action shotgun walked between two rows of decaying metal carcasses. He silently raised the muzzle of the silenced Heckler & Koch. He pulled the stock into his shoulder and aimed at the young man's head. Thirty yards, it would be a simple shot. He waited until the man stopped to light a cigarette, then squeezed the trigger. The round hit his target in the back of the head. The dead man silently dropped to his knees and fell facedown. Kopjov quickly moved forward, weapon in hand, and stood over the fallen guard. To be sure, he fired another two rounds into the lifeless body.

'You're telling me these reports were purposely withheld?' Porter asked.

The young lab technician nodded his head and looked down at the tiled floor.

'And it was Mr Fleming who asked you to do that?' Mullins included.

The technician nodded again.

'I just work here, mate. I get told to hold the reports, I hold the reports.'

The two detectives walked out of the building in silence. They were seated in their unmarked car before Porter spoke. He looked across at Mullins and said, 'What does this all mean?'

Mullins raised her eyebrows, and shook her head, replying, 'Buggered if I know, let's go and see Fleming and find out.'

They made the short journey to Fleming's office. They were asked to wait while the receptionist went in search of the forensic examiner. They both stood when they saw the man approaching.

'Detectives, how can I help you?' he asked.

'Can we talk in your office?' said Mullins.

'Sounds ominous,' Fleming replied leading the way into his office. When they were all seated, he asked, 'So, what's this about?'

'It's about these,' Porter responded, throwing a file onto the desk. Fleming opened it and read the first page, nodding as he did.

Before he finished reading, Mullins asked, 'Why were these reports withheld?'

Fleming leaned back and ran his hands through his hair.

'Look,' he shrugged. 'I was asked to keep these reports back for a day as a favour.'

'A favour?' Mullins asked incredulously.

'Do you have any idea of the scale of the investigation these relate to?'

Fleming nodded.

'Who asked you for the favour? Frank Palmer?'

Fleming shook his head.

'No, it was Pat Casey,' he replied honestly.

Detective Superintendent Dominic Dunne sat across the table from Jack Barker. DI Williams sat beside him. Hector North, Jack Barker's solicitor, sat beside his client. Dunne went through the mandatory introduction for the purposes of the recording. Now he looked directly at Barker.

'Do you know a man named Roman Kobec?' Dunne asked.

'No comment.'

'Are you aware that Mr Kobec's wife and two children were killed in a car bomb explosion yesterday?'

'No comment.'

The interview lasted an hour and never got the senior detectives a response of more than a "no comment".

They repeated the performance with Paul Burrows and then with Harry Black. Except for a "Go fuck yourself" from Burrows and a request for a Big Mac from Black, they got no useful responses.

'Inspector Palmer,' Kobec greeted when Palmer answered.

The detective had been expecting the call.

'Mr Kobec, I was sorry to hear about your family,' Palmer said, trying to sound as genuine and empathetic as possible.

'It was unfortunate,' Kobec replied coldly. A shiver ran down Palmer's spine.

'But now it's time to finish what has been started,' the Russian stated calmly.

'Look, I don't think that's a good idea right now, this thing is out of control. I think it's time to show restraint,' Palmer pleaded, sounding like a politician.

Kobec laughed.

'Restraint?' he mocked. 'That is an interesting perspective, Chief Inspector, but unfortunately it is not the perspective of a man about to bury his entire family.'

Palmer had no choice but to agree to meet Kobec. The man's calmness was terrifying and menacing. Palmer did not need the distraction but ignoring the man could clearly have severe consequences.

He turned left and headed for the Blackwall Tunnel. He emerged into the light in Greenwich and made his way to the address Kobec had given him. He found the unimpressive building, close to the water and parked across from it. He put his police parking permit on the car's dashboard in clear view. The last thing he needed was to be clamped. He looked up at the warehouse. There seemed to be no life inside. Palmer noticed the high-end CCTV cameras fixed to the building's facade.

He heard the sound of a lock unbolting and the glass and aluminium door, marked office, opened. A big man waved Palmer into the building and then closed and locked the door. Without speaking, the guard gestured for the detective to raise his hands and then patted his legs, body, and arms. When he was done, he nodded to another man who stood along the hallway. The man said, 'Come,' and disappeared into a doorway. Palmer followed.

The man led him along a corridor and up a flight of stairs. They emerged into a narrow back lane. They crossed it and entered the building opposite. Another black suited guard stood at the entrance of the building, making no effort to conceal the AK-47 in his hands. He ignored Palmer as he squeezed past. They headed along a hallway and then climbed another flight of steel stairs. Palmer was out of breath by the time he reached the second level and was shown into a sparsely furnished room.

'Wait,' his guide instructed and left. It was a few minutes before Roman Kobec entered. He was immaculately dressed as always.

'Chief Inspector Palmer, thank you for taking the time to see me,' he welcomed, as if Palmer had a chosen to pay him a social visit.

Palmer remained silent. He was unsure of what he should say to the man.

'I won't waste your time, Detective, I want Jack Barker,' Kobec stated, getting straight to the point. He placed his hands behind his back and paced around Palmer.

'He's in custody right now, there's no way of getting to him,' Palmer replied nervously.

Kobec smiled.

'If history has taught us anything, Chief Inspector, it is that anyone can be gotten to, anywhere,' he responded.

Kobec did not sound like a man in mourning. He sounded very much in control. Palmer noted the contrast between Jack Barker and Roman Kobec. How differently they had reacted to the loss of someone close. Listening to Kobec now, there was no doubt in Palmer's mind who would win the war between them.

'Valek!' Kobec called loudly, startling Palmer. The bulky minder opened the door. A neatly dressed young man in rimless glasses, entered behind him, carrying round paper tube. He silently removed a document from the holder, and unrolled the A1 sheet on the table, placing a weight neatly on each corner. Palmer recognised as the design layout of a building. The young man removed two pencils from his pocket and placed them neatly together on the displayed plan. The two men retreated from the room and once again it was just Palmer and Kobec.

'I want to know about the security at this station, I want to know every detail.' His tone made it clear that he wasn't asking.

As he headed through the traffic, making his way slowly toward the West End, Palmer convinced himself that there would be no way for Kobec to get to Barker inside the station. He had told the Russian it would be foolhardy to try. Palmer had given him what had he asked for, nonetheless. Now, he put Kobec out of his mind. He had more pressing matters to attend to. Doctor Farnsworth had given him the name and Westminster address of Anne Grace's solicitors, Smith, Lacey, Green and Associates. An hour later Palmer walked into their reception. A very polite and well-spoken woman greeted him as he entered. He walked over to the desk and removed his warrant card.

'I'm Detective Chief Inspector Frank Palmer,' he advised. 'I need to find out some information about one of your clients; it's a matter of some urgency.'

The woman eyed him suspiciously. The welcoming smile quickly faded, and she replied, 'Wait here, please.' She disappeared and returned a few minutes later. 'Someone will be with you shortly, Detective,' she advised and busied herself with paperwork.

Palmer did not take a seat but paced around the room. After ten minutes a short, balding man in an ill-fitting pink shirt walked into the reception and enquired, 'Chief Inspector Palmer?' The detective nodded.

'I'm Basil Green, would you like to come this way?' the man said extending his arm.

Palmer walked along a narrow passage lined with a series of naval prints in matching frames. He passed several doors before the man said, 'In there, Chief Inspector.' Palmer walked into a neat and modestly furnished office. The balding man walked around the desk and indicated for Palmer to take a seat.

'Can I get you anything, tea, coffee perhaps?' he asked before they began.

'No, thank you,' Palmer answered, keen to get to the reason for his visit.

'Well,' the solicitor said awkwardly. 'What exactly can I do for you, Detective?'

Palmer explained how he had obtained the firm's address and gave the solicitor a diluted explanation as to why he needed to trace Anne Grace's whereabouts urgently.

'I apologise, Detective,' the solicitor replied when Palmer had finished. 'But I'm afraid I still don't quite understand how Ms Grace is involved in these crimes?'

Palmer nodded.

'There are facts that I'm not at liberty to divulge, Mr Green,' he explained. 'As I've said, her involvement relates to an incident which occurred some time ago.'

'And that could assist you with your investigation?' the solicitor asked.

Green had read about the murders in the papers. Palmer initially didn't want to disclose which case he was working on, but he knew that any solicitor would stonewall him about a client's details. He had hoped that the severity of the case would be sufficient to ensure the solicitor's assistance. It wasn't. He could apply for a warrant and force the solicitor to give him the information, but he could not do that without alerting the investigation team. It would also require time that he clearly did not have.

'It would be of great assistance to us,' Palmer affirmed. Then added, 'It could help us solve the case,' to reinforce his point.

But it was no use. The solicitor, sensing that Palmer was not being entirely straightforward, said, 'Well, I'm afraid I can't disclose any client details. I'm sure you're aware of the privilege that exists been us and our clients, Chief Inspector.'

Palmer reached into the inside pocket of his jacket and withdrew an envelope. He opened it and spilled the contents onto the desk. Three high quality colour prints were of Lucy Barker and three were of Paul Morton's son. Palmer laid them out so that the solicitor could see them. He tapped a photograph showing the brutalised body of the young girl lying on a stainless-steel autopsy table.

'She was eight years old,' Palmer said. 'She was tortured for hours before she died. Her father was forced to watch before his throat was cut.' Palmer could see that the solicitor was visibly shaken.

'Now more people are going to die in this very same manner, Mr Green, if I don't find whoever did this. All I'm asking is for an address, nothing more,' the detective pressed.

The solicitor sighed and then, without speaking, he stood and left the office. He returned a short while later carrying a file. He sat back down and placed the file in front him. He stood again, quickly and asked, 'My apologies, was that a tea you wanted?' He left the office again, leaving the file on the desk.

Palmer smiled and reached for the folder. He skimmed through the papers, getting a quick understanding of how Smith, Lacey, Green and Associates had acted for Anne Grace. As far as he could tell, it had been years since they last had any dealings with her, but he found an address.

When the solicitor returned, Palmer was standing, ready to leave.

'I'll be off then,' he said when the solicitor entered the office.

'Well, Inspector, I am sorry that I was unable to be of any assistance to you,' the solicitor apologised.

'How bad is it?' Dunne asked Detective Sergeant Blake. Blake was from West End Central. He had just stepped out of the Eden Club in Soho.

'It's bad, guv,' he replied. 'Worst scene I've ever attended.' The detectives stood on the pavement outside the club, all dressed in familiar protective gear.

'Well, shall we,' Dunne said resignedly to Jason Bright, gesturing to the door.

'Welcome to Soho, mind the gap, stand clear of the whores please,' Bright muttered as they entered the club. There was little doubt that the attack on the club had been retaliation by Roman Kobec. The war, which they had anticipated and feared, had begun. The entrance hall of the club led into a gaudily decorated space, filled with two-seater sofas and concealed LED lighting. The carpet was clean but worn. A steel lattice frame fitted with an array of lighting hung from the centre of the roof, above a square podium. At the far end of the lounge there was a mirror clad bar. There were three doors that led from the room to unseen parts of the building. One led to the office, a second accessed the staircase leading to the upper floors. A third door gave entry to the fire escape. There were eight bodies in the room. All were young women who had been dressed to excite. Each had sustained at least two gunshot injuries. Red stains fanned out on the floor and parts of the walls. The scenes-of-crime officers were taping, photographing, scraping, and dusting every inch of the room in search of evidence, however microscopic. Dunne knew that they would find little, if any, clues by which to identify the perpetrators. Whoever had been responsible for the carnage had been professional. They would have left no trace.

Sergeant Blake had followed the MIT officers back into the building.

'There are two more in the office,' he advised, pointing to a door adjacent to the bar. 'And eleven more upstairs, guv.' He pointed to a double door, that was wedged open. 'All gunshots,' he confirmed. Then added, 'Oh, and the safe in the office has been cleaned out.'

'Hit him where it hurts,' Dunne said. No doubt this was the work of Roman Kobec.

As Dunne crossed the room his phone rang. The senior office paled as he listened. When the call ended, Dunne stood frozen momentarily, then turned slowly to Bright.

'They hit Barker's scrap yard out east too, seven dead,' he revealed, not bothering to conceal the trepidation in his voice.

'We can hold them for another twenty-four hours,' Dunne advised. 'After that it will be difficult.' His eyes moved from object to object in Detective Chief Superintendent Sloane's office as he spoke.

'Does Barker know about the attack on his yard yet?' the senior officer asked.

Even though Dunne had taken over as senior investigating officer, Sloane had insisted on being kept apprised of the investigation. Dunne had no objection. If it all went wrong, and it seemed likely that it would, he did not want to be the lone sacrificial lamb. He needed senior officers to help him carry the burden if need be.

'Not yet, sir, but he's waiting to see his brief again. We've tried everything to delay the meeting, but we can't hold him off for much longer,' Dunne explained.

Sloane nodded.

'And Kobec, do we know where he is?'

'I am afraid not, sir, we have teams watching his premises and watching most of Barker's businesses, but we're dealing with highly organised groups. I'm afraid that it is not going to be that easy to stem the tide,' the detective said honestly. 'We are likely going to see a lot more blood spilled before we get it all under control, sir,' he predicted.

His foresight was well founded given the carnage at the Eden Club in Soho and at Barker's scrap yard. It was undoubtedly one of the worst days of organised violence in the city's history. There was little doubt that Barker would use every available resource at his disposal to retaliate.

'We can't simply sit about and wait for the city to be turned into a battlefield. This is not 1920s Chicago, Dominic, there must be something that we can do,' Sloane implored, his desperation boiling over.

'We're having an emergency meeting at the Yard in an hour, the commissioner will be chairing the meeting personally,' the Chief Superintendent notified his subordinate,

'What do I tell him?' Dunne was not sure if an answer was expected. Either way, he had no answer to give. The senior officers were aware that there was an obvious solution. Keep Barker and his firm in custody, arrest Kobec and his closest henchmen. Lock them all up indefinitely. Democratic society was not well equipped to deal with a situation like this. It was why Al Capone had been able to run riot for so many years and had eventually been jailed for tax evasion and not murder.

'There's another development, sir, that you should be apprised of,' Dunne said. Sloane groaned. He did not have the capacity for any more unwelcome news. Dunne's tone told him that was exactly what he was about to hear. The detective took a deep breath before he spoke.

'It seems that DNA evidence recovered from the Morton house was purposely withheld by the forensics lab,' he advised. Sloane grimaced.

'It is evidence that incriminates Chief Inspector Palmer,' Dunne added. Sloane's jaw dropped.

'How?' he asked disbelievingly.

'It appears that Pat Casey, the pathologist, asked the forensics team to withhold the evidence, at Palmer's behest. Casey has been around for a long time, his request wasn't really questioned,' Dunne explained.

'Christ,' Sloane exclaimed. 'If the press finds out about this, we'll be bloody crucified. I will be crucified,' he animatedly pointed his thumb at his chest.

They sat in silence for a while until Sloane asked, 'Does this mean that Palmer was directly involved in this?'

'I'm not sure, but I'm certain he knows a lot more than he's telling us. I'm afraid it doesn't look good for him,' Dunne answered honestly. Both officers had been aware of Palmer's connection to Barker, but the series of events that he appeared to be directly linked to did not fit with what they knew of the detective.

It was not what Sloane wanted to hear. He knew that if evidence proved that Palmer had been involved in the murders, it would reflect directly on him. It would irreparably damage his career. He sank deeper into his chair.

'How do you intend to handle this?' he asked Dunne.

'He's now part of the ongoing investigation, but I'll inform you before we take any direct action against him, sir.'

Sloane nodded weakly.

CHAPTER THIRTEEN
Killer Instinct

Andrzej Kopjov had memorised the layout of the police station. He was dressed in a Metropolitan Police uniform and seated in a car at the rear of the station watching the automatic gate. He had noted that a small light flashed on the right hand side of the gate before it opened. He had timed how long it took for the gate to open once the light began to flash. He did not wait long for it to begin blinking again. He could see no car on the street near the gate, which meant that a vehicle would be exiting the secure car park. He opened his door and stepped out onto the pavement. The gate was halfway open. He could see the bright livery of a patrol car, its roof lights flashing, waiting to leave the station. He pulled his hat down low and crossed the street. Eager to respond to whatever emergency had initiated the rush from the station, the driver waited until there was just enough room to clear the gate before accelerating out. The gate was fully open for twenty seconds before it began to close again.

Kopjov walked toward the gate confidently and slipped through it a second before it closed. Experience and training had taught him that guards who monitored the security cameras at secure entrances almost always, having watched the screen for two minutes or so, diverted their attention as the entrance was being secured. It was the study of such intricate details that made him such an efficient killing machine.

He strode across the station car park with purpose, as if he belonged there. It helped that they lived in an age when wearing a mask was normal. Even though no longer mandatory, many still wore them. His English was good enough, but accented, so he avoided direct contact until it was necessary. He opened the door and walked into the station, making straight for the toilets. Once safely inside a toilet cubicle, he removed two identical weapons from the small bag he carried with him. The.22 magnum semiautomatics were designed to be carried as concealed weapons. The weapons had high quality silencers. They were ideal for the job at hand. He slid one pistol beneath his vest and placed the other back in the bag. He checked the other items in the bag. Two smoke grenades, two stun grenades, and two Czech-made hand grenades. It was a small but deadly arsenal. Finally, he removed a thin spray canister and pushed it into his pocket. The highly pressurised military grade compound 2-chlorobenzalmalononitrile based contents would floor any man in an instant. The mask that he wore had been manufactured to filter the gas. The boss had insisted that there be no police casualties. This was not Russia. Like America, Britain took the killing of its police officers very seriously.

He stood quietly for a moment, concentrating, focusing. He went over every detail of the mission, step-by-step in his mind. When he was ready, he exited the toilet. He turned left and headed for the custody suite. He went unchallenged, blending in flawlessly. He got to the custody suite quickly and looked through one of the glass panels of the double swing doors leading into the restricted area. It was quiet. There was one uniformed officer behind the desk and a female officer leaning against the front of the desk talking to him. Kopjov entered quickly and raised the canister in his hand. Before the officers could react, he released two jets of the pressurised contents. Both officers went down instantly. He moved with feline, fluid motion and struck the female officer, then stepped behind the desk and hit the second officer as he was reaching for the alarm button. His actions were deliberate, practiced. The punches were precise. The targets would be unconscious for long enough to enable him to complete his task. He effortlessly reached down and lifted the female officer, dragging her behind the custody desk, out of immediate sight.

He calmly opened the blue covered book, which he had retrieved from a shelf behind the desk. It was just where Palmer had said it would be. He quickly scanned through the latest entries. *J. Barker: Cell 8. Paul Burrows: Cell 3. Harold Black: Cell 4.* He reached down and loosened the key chain from the custody sergeant's belt. He walked at a steady pace toward the cells. He looked down at the keys. Each was stamped with a number. He found the master key marked as Palmer had advised.

When he arrived at cell eight, he opened the narrow rectangular hatch on the door and looked inside. The cell was empty. He cursed under his breath, then moved to cell three. Paul Burrows was there. He could make the shot through the hatch, but he needed to be sure. He inserted the key, turned the brass handle on the blue steel door, and pulled it open.

Burrows was lying on a concrete bench fitted with a thin mattress. He appeared relaxed as if he was lying on a sofa in his front room. He saw the gun too late. It spat out four rounds in quick succession, three more than were necessary. Kopjov closed the door and moved to the adjacent cell. He cursed again. Black's cell was also vacant. He heard the sounds coming from the corridor outside. There was no time and nowhere to hide. The doors swung open and Jack Barker stepped into the custody suite. His hands were cuffed in front of him and he was accompanied by two plain-clothed officers. The survival instinct that had kept Barker alive in a dangerous world for a long time, told him immediately that something was wrong. He saw the gun before DI Williams did and spun around as Kopjov fired. The round caught Williams in the neck. The detective dropped immediately, pulling Barker down with him. Barker scrambled backward through the door, propelling himself with his feet. Detective Sergeant Bright looked down at his senior officer, too shocked to react. Kopjov fired again. The policeman fell backward against the door.

The assassin ran forward and jumped over the body of Williams to get through the swing doors. Barker was not in the corridor. Kopjov's mind worked quickly. He had to decide whether to hunt down Barker and risk killing more police officers, or should he quit and leave. He wanted Barker.

He walked along the corridor, looking into each room that opened off it as he went. Then the siren sounded. Bright, bleeding heavily, had managed to crawl behind the custody desk and activate the emergency alarm. Kopjov hesitated, quickly considering his escape routes. Barker would have to wait.

He took the bag from his shoulder and removed a smoke grenade. He pulled the pin and rolled the canister along the corridor. Thick yellow smoke escaped from it as a group of officers turned into the corridor. He ran to an adjacent passage, which according to memory would lead him to the station's front desk. The alarm blared.

At the reception, a uniformed officer was anxiously talking on a phone. Several civilians were seated in the waiting area behind him. The officer saw Kopjov enter the reception. He had no time to react before the man was past him and had exited the building through the public entrance. The assassin ran from the station and made it to his car before any officers followed. He saw that the light was flashing on the gate. It was about to open. He threw his bag onto the front seat of his car, reached into it, and withdrew a white canister. He pulled the small pin from it and hurled the grenade toward the gate. Then he quickly climbed into his car.

He drove off, not speeding to draw attention, observing the scene behind in the rear-view mirror. As the gate had opened enough to allow the patrol car to exit, a flash of brilliant white light had exploded in front of it, blinding both officers in the vehicle. The sound of the discharging stun grenade reverberated through the surrounding buildings. Then all was quiet.

Kopjov wound his way through the narrow back streets, taking a route he had mapped out earlier, one that was mostly devoid of CCTV cameras. He turned into a narrow side road, which led to a row of derelict-looking garages constructed from the brick arches of a redundant railway line. He parked and looked around to ensure that he was alone. He reached backward to retrieve a jacket from the back seat of the car, then carefully observed his surroundings again. The narrow road was deserted. He stepped out of the vehicle, then quickly opened the back door and flicked a switch on the red canister that was sat on the floor space behind the driver's seat. He closed the door, straightened his jacket and walked off. Six minutes later he was on a D6 bus heading east. He heard the faint echo of the explosion as the car went up in flames.

Islington, like many of London's boroughs, included a mix of lower income areas, where many lived on poorly maintained council estates, middle class areas, in which property was no longer affordable to the middle classes, and pockets of high cost housing. The extraordinary rise in the cost of housing in London had seen large swathes of the borough rejuvenated under various urban renewal schemes. Palmer made his way through one such area, along Upper Street, Angel. The road was lined with restaurants, pubs and wine bars. He headed north, past Islington Green, then turned left onto a narrow side road and then quickly right onto an even narrower lane. He slowed and looked intently out of the passenger window at the row of white terraced houses to his left. He found the address that he was looking for just as the navigator advised the detective that he had arrived at his destination. He pulled into a vacant residents-only parking space.

His phone rang as he stepped out of the car. The conversation lasted five minutes. When the call ended Palmer leaned back against the car. The blood had drained from his face. He was pale and unsteady on his feet. His chest felt as if it was it the grip of an iron fist. His head reeled. Mullins had called to inform him about the attack at the station. Williams was dead. Bright had been seriously injured. Paul Burrows had been killed in custody. Jack Barker was screaming blue murder. Everyone had been shaken by the event. Palmer wondered when it would all end. He was suddenly sure that he would not be around long enough to find out.

He shuddered and took a minute to compose himself, then walked to the front door of the address he had found in the solicitor's file. He knocked on the door. No one answered. He could hear music coming from inside the house. He pushed open the letterbox and peered in. He could see a sparsely furnished entrance hall, nothing else. He called through the slot.

'Hello?' Nothing. He reached over and tapped hard on the glass of the bay window adjacent to the door. The music quietened. He knocked again and heard someone approaching the door, the steps echoing on wooden floors.

The door opened and an annoyed young woman stood in the entrance. 'What!' she asked abruptly.

Palmer grimaced. He held up his warrant card.

The woman was unfazed. The past two years had done little to improve the public's perceptions of the police. The result had been a sharp decline in the respect that people had normally afforded officers of the law.

'Well, what do you want?' she asked aggressively.

214

'I'm DCI Palmer. I'm looking for someone who used to live at this address or may still live here.'

The woman opened her eyes wider and raised her hands palms up.

'Well, who is it you're looking for?' she asked.

'Anne Grace,' Palmer answered, now becoming irritated by the woman's attitude.

'Never heard of her,' she answered quickly.

'Do you own this house?'

'Do I have to answer your questions?'

Palmer shook his head and fought to keep calm. He pursed his lips and looked directly at the offensive woman.

'I could go away and come back with a search warrant,' he replied warningly. 'Then I could tear your house apart piece by piece. Those polished timber floorboards would have to come up and we may have to open holes in a few walls. Of course, you could claim for any damages, but the process is slow, and it'd probably take about five years before you saw a penny.' Palmer smiled. 'Even then, it'd only be a fraction of what you claimed.'

The woman's face quickly lost its arrogant facade. She loved her house. 'Yes, I own this house,' she answered, swallowing hard.

'I bought it three years ago, well, my father bought it three years ago, at an auction.'

'Do you know who he bought it from?'

The woman thought for a while, but eventually shook her head and replied, 'I'm afraid not.' Before Palmer could ask another question, she added, 'But I can give you the name and address of the auctioneers.'

CHAPTER FOURTEEN
Point of No Return

In war, the general receives his commands
from the sovereign, collects his army
and concentrates his forces. -
Chapter Eight, Sun Tzu - *The Art of War*.

Jack Barker sat calmly in his cell. His rage had passed. He knew that his survival depended on clear thinking. He was at war. He had lost too many people already. Kobec was showing himself to be equally ruthless, perhaps even more so. It had been close. He had almost been taken out. Only his razor-sharp instinct had saved him. When he had seen the assailant walking toward him from the cells, his brain had surveyed and assessed the scene in an instant. There had been no one behind the custody desk. The officer walking toward them had one hand behind his back and carried a small bag slung over his shoulder. His facial expression had not altered when he had seen Barker and the officers enter the custody suite. Barker had recognised that look. The look of a professional about to do his job. He had had a split second to react.

Now he sat quietly, thinking. There were only two ways to resolve this conflict. The first – reaching a compromise with Kobec – was not a viable option. He had eradicated the man's family in a single blast. The Russian was not about to make any deals with their killer. The second option was to take out Kobec. That was not going to be easy. London was still his city. He backed himself to defeat the Russian. In truth he relished the challenge.

He could only think of one way to get to Kobec. Detective Chief Inspector Frank Palmer. He knew that his old friend had made a deal with Kobec. He did not blame him for it entirely. Had their roles had been reversed he would probably have done the same thing. It was the innate instinct to survive. Barker still doubted that Kobec was responsible for his brother's murder. He had cunningly used the ensuing chaos to gain support for a hostile takeover. Either way, Palmer had assessed the situation and had backed Kobec as the eventual victor. He understood now why the detective had made that decision. Things had not worked out. Frank Palmer was caught in no man's land. Barker knew the detective a lot better than Kobec did. He knew how to get to him.

A short while later the cell door swung open. Barker smiled up at the two officers standing in the entrance. Behind them he saw the CO19 officer, his weapon held across his chest. Despite the strongest urging of DS Dunne, Barker had refused to remain in the safety of the station. His solicitor had applied pressure in the right places to get him released. After all, it had been demonstrated that the police station was not as secure as would have been expected.

A media frenzy waited for him as he left the station. The reporters had been tipped off about the gangster's imminent release by sources in the Met. Four black vehicles and sixteen men also waited outside the station for Jack Barker to appear. As he exited the station, television cameras began to roll.

'Mr Barker, Mr Barker,' reporters called, but he ignored the calls and headed straight for the closest of the four vehicles.

Norris Jones sat beside Barker. Harry Black, who had also been released on bail, was driving. His survival had, like Barker's, been due to fortunate timing. He had been in an interview room meeting with his brief when the attack had occurred.

'Right, give it to me,' Barker ordered.

Jones filled him in on the Eden Club massacre and the scrap yard attack. Barker's face was steely, showing no emotion. Not even his secretary had been spared. Rather than trepidation, Barker felt a jolt of excitement. It was a lion fighting a lion.

'He's got some real talent working for him, Jack, we can't afford to underestimate him again,' Jones advised earnestly. Norris Jones had been Paul Burrows' closest friend. They had served in the SAS together. Burrows had brought Norris to work for Barker when he had left the forces. They had been a formidable pair. Jones was from Cardiff. He had grown up in the rough dock area of the city. He was known for his sense

217

of humour and love of practical jokes, but when it was time to work, the big Welshman was all business. He knew his trade well. He was a tier one operator. Jones was a weapons and explosives expert. He had no misgivings about killing. Now it was time to work. There was a battle to be fought and vengeance to be had.

Barker nodded. He knew Jones was right. Sending someone into a police station to kill a man in custody took balls, skill and organisation.

It also demonstrated that, as Barker did, Kobec had loyal soldiers who were prepared to put themselves on the line for him. The convoy headed for an industrial estate in Creekmouth. Jack Barker owned the estate. The warehouses at the riverside business park that were rented to outside firms had been closed. The tenants had not questioned the move. Jack Barker intended to use the estate as his base of operations for the coming weeks. It had been designed for such an eventuality, although the intensity of what they were now dealing with had never been contemplated. The largest warehouse sat at the far end of the estate, its back facade bordered the river. It housed Gulliver's Transport Limited, a freight company owned by Jack Barker. In readiness of Barker's release, his goons had turned the building into a fortress. Barker saw the silhouettes of two men standing on the roof of the warehouse as they approached. What he was not aware of, was that his adversary was held up in a similar building, across the water on the south side of the Thames, only a short distance away.

'It's time we speak to Frank Palmer,' Dunne said. DS Porter nodded slowly. He had nothing against Palmer and hoped there was some explanation. When taken together, the evidence against the detective was damming.

'I want to speak with Doctor Moore before I speak to Palmer,' Dunne instructed. 'See if you can locate her. Tell her I want to her here when I get back from the Yard,' Dunne ordered.

Porter nodded and left.

Dunne had drafted in four more MIT officers. They were waiting for him outside the office. The case, it seemed, was spiralling out of control. The commissioner had made it the Met's highest priority. There was talk of a chief superintendent being brought in to take over. Dunne knew that it was unlikely. There was no positive outcome in the case. Even if they caught every person responsible for the mayhem of the past week and bought them to book, the damage had already been done. A lot of people wanted answers. There was little incentive for a more senior officer to get involved in running the investigation and risk tarnishing his or her reputation.

It now appeared likely that Barker's brother had been killed on the orders of Roman Kobec. There seemed little doubt that he was behind the killings. The Russian had introduced a new level of violence to the streets of London. It seemed that one of their own had been working with Kobec. For now, they needed to stem the tide.

The large and lavishly furnished boardroom was on the fourth floor of New Scotland Yard. Sir Duncan West, the commissioner of the Metropolitan Police Service, was seated at the head of the polished oak table. To his left was Assistant Commissioner Henry Wilson-Bailey. To his right were Commander Goodchild of MI5 and Jeffrey Paine, Goodchild's MI5 section head. He was the man many tipped to be the next head of the GCHQ.

Kevin Beck of Special Operations sat next to the MI5 operatives. Seated across from them were Detective Superintendent Dunne, Detective Chief Superintendent Sloane, Chief Superintendent Piers Hall, and Superintendent Terry Willows of the Serious and Organised Crime Group. There was an uneasy silence in the room, disturbed for a short while by Gladys Meadows who delivered a large tray of tea and biscuits. She left the tray in the centre of the table and retreated.

'Right, gentlemen,' the commissioner began, his accent practiced and perfected. 'We all know why we're here. We have a dire and intolerable situation on our hands. Car bombs, mass killings. These are things associated more with Baghdad and Kabul than London, and yet we're experiencing an unprecedented series of these crimes.' He paused and looked from face to face. 'Detective Superintendent Dunne, as most of you are aware, is now heading the investigation into the serial murders, which appear to have sparked this deluge of violence. Superintendent Dunne, would you be kind enough to give us an update on the status of the investigation,' the commissioner finished.

Dunne coughed and lifted the cover of the laptop in front of him. He had connected the device to the boardroom's audio-visual system via a secure wireless connection.

'This is Jack Barker, the centre of our current investigation,' Dunne began, as a police mug shot appeared on the large screen fixed to the rear wall of the room. The detective did not feel the need to explain who Barker was.

'This was his brother Billy Barker.' The screen changed.

'It was his murder, which I'm sure you're all familiar with, that was the catalyst for the...' He did not want to use term war. 'The current conflict between Barker and this man.' Dunne pressed the arrow key again and the face of Roman Kobec showed on the screen.

'This is Roman Kobec, a high net worth Russian national with right of abode in the United Kingdom. He is rumoured to be a trafficker, arms, narcotics, people.' Dunne stalled, he wished that he had had more time to prepare for the meeting. 'We now believe that he was responsible for the series of murders that commenced with the Barker murders.' No one in the room said a word; all eyes were fixed on the face of Roman Kobec. His menacing eyes were unsettling.

'Kobec recently relocated to London.' Heads shook, that was a separate matter to be investigated. 'And we now believe that his motive for the murders was to cause a rift between rival criminal gangs and to use the ensuing unrest to mount a takeover of Jack Barker's interests, as well as the interests of several of Barker's associates.'

Heads nodded, but no one spoke.

'It appears that Barker became aware of the threat posed by Kobec and tried to eliminate him,' Dunne continued. 'Whether by intention or accident, he eliminated the wife and two children of Roman Kobec.' Dunne had changed the screen to show an image of the annihilated Bentley.

'Kobec's retaliation for these murders was swift and brutal, including sending an assailant into one of our police stations in an attempt to assassinate Barker.' As Dunne spoke, the screen changed. It showed images from inside the damaged police station.

Dunne was about to continue when Goodchild asked, 'What concrete evidence do you have against Roman Kobec, this all seems like speculation to me?' Every head turned to face the intelligence officer.

'It sounds like bloody well founded speculation, Commander,' Assistant Commissioner Henry Wilson-Bailey retorted harshly, looking coldly across the table at Goodchild. Dunne ignored the exchange and continued.

'We believe Kobec has had a MIT DCI assisting him: Frank Palmer. We have evidence that they've been meeting covertly, and we have DNA and other forensic evidence directly linking Palmer to several murders, including that of the Barkers.'

The commissioner grunted. When all of this became news, the Met's reputation would take another severe blow. One of their own, a senior detective, acting as an assassin for a Russian drug lord. It did not get any worse than that. Fact had surpassed fiction.

'That's all very well, but from covert meetings to mass murder, that's quite a leap of the imagination, and certainly, Palmer's guilt doesn't prove Kobec's. He could've been acting on his own,' Goodchild insisted. Then quickly added, 'And why, with all of this evidence, has Detective Chief Inspector Palmer not been arrested and charged yet?' The intelligence officer's defence of Roman Kobec did not go unnoticed.

'It appears that some forensic evidence implicating Palmer was purposely withheld from our investigators,' Dunne replied indirectly. He shuffled nervously before continuing.

'As you will be aware, DCI Palmer was heading the initial investigation.'

The room fell silent.

'How is it that this man Kobec was allowed residence in the United Kingdom,' the assistant commissioner asked. 'His record, proven or not, would have prevented his entry into the country.' Wilson-Bailey looked at Goodchild as he spoke. It was a question that two men present could answer, but they remained silent.

'What's your plan of action from here?' Goodchild asked Dunne, evading the assistant commissioner's question.

'We believe it's premature to arrest Palmer at this time. It may cause Kobec to run before we can act against him, but we will be talking to all parties in the very near future.' Dunne paused again and looked directly at Goodchild.

'As far as Kobec's involvement, we are confident that we can link him to several of these crimes.' Goodchild looked unimpressed. The atmosphere in the room was tense, tangible.

'Well, we need to do more than just talk to these men; we need to put an end to this, Detective Superintendent,' the commissioner interjected.

'You will have all of the assistance that you require, Detective Superintendent, all of the Met's resources are at your disposal, but we need results, we need them soon.' The commissioner's voice was strained.

Dunne nodded and looked down at the keyboard in front of him.

'What about Barker, do you have enough on him to put him away?' Jeffrey Paine, the MI5 section head, who had remained silent, questioned.

'Surely the sooner we can get these people off the streets, the better. I can't understand why this man Barker has had the run of this city for so long.' It was a lie. Paine knew the answer to that question.

'We've arrested Barker and questioned him. We don't have enough to satisfy the CPS that the charges will stand up in court, but we're close to putting him away for a very long time,' Dunne replied.

The senior detective withstood the barrage of questions for a further twenty minutes. After each of the senior officers had given their input and offered their assistance, the commissioner called an end to the meeting. It was not lost on Dunne that none of the senior officers, except for DCS Sloane, wanted to be directly linked with the investigation. If Palmer was, in fact, guilty, it would be a huge blow to the Met. Police corruption was one thing, but a senior detective involved in crimes of this magnitude was unprecedented. Everyone associated with the case would be tainted.

As the officers filed out of the room, Jeffrey Paine approached the commissioner and said, 'May I have a word in private, sir?'

They waited until all the other officers were making their way down the corridor toward the lift foyer before walking back into the boardroom.

'What can I do for you, Jeffrey?' the commissioner asked warily.

'Well, sir, I'm afraid that this is a rather delicate matter, it relates to Roman Kobec. I think you'd prefer to be seated, sir.' Paine gestured to the nearest seat.

The commissioner said nothing. He nodded slightly and took a seat. He was suddenly sure he would need to be sitting when he heard what the intelligence agent had to say.

'Well, sir, we first came across Roman Kobec four years ago.' The commissioner paled. Paine continued.

'He had been supplying weapons to the Taliban in Afghanistan in exchange for heroin, which he was then smuggling into the EU and the United States.' It was not lost on the commissioner that four years was before the Russian had relocated to London.

'The CIA had known of Kobec for some time but could not get close to him, he was a phantom.' Paine coughed to clear his throat.

'Six managed to get a deep-cover agent to successfully infiltrate his organisation.' Paine stalled. He was unable to hold the commissioner's gaze.

'Kobec was quietly arrested in Athens in August 2019 and taken to Cyprus for interrogation,' the senior intelligence officer advised. The man sat before him was ashen but remained wordless. Paine continued.

'Before we could get anything out of him, Kobec revealed that he had information regarding an imminent and very credible terrorist threat.' A brief pause. 'We were forced to listen,' he finished.

The commissioner remained stoic, avoiding Paine's stare, until the intelligence officer added, 'London was the target for the planned attack.' The commissioner's eyes quickly locked with his guest's. Paine explained further.

'Kobec knew who, he knew how, and he knew when, we had little choice but to make a deal with him.' The commissioner's head sank again for a moment, then he slowly looked up at the MI5 section head in disbelief. He raised his palm to face the intelligence officer, indicating for him to stop speaking.

'Do you mean to tell me that Roman Kobec is working for you?' the commissioner asked incredulously, 'That he is an MI5 asset?'

Paine remained motionless. The senior policeman's eyes bored into him, until eventually he nodded slowly. The commissioner struggled to process the information. He could not hide the tremors that shook his hands.

'Jesus Christ, Jeffrey!' he blurted in a whispered scream. 'What the bloody hell were you lot thinking?' The commissioner's normally ironclad composure was wavering. His accent was quickly returning to the north where it had originated.

'The man is a bloody monster and you brought him into my city.' It wasn't a question. It was confirmation of something that the commissioner found inconceivable.

'You lot are meant to be intelligence, how was that intelligent?' He looked directly into Paine's eyes again. The intelligence officer's defiance quickly returned.

'These are dangerous times we live in, Duncan,' Paine began his weak justification. 'We have had to make unsavoury bed partners. It's the way things are, I'm afraid, sir,' he replied remorselessly.

'The way things are is no justification for this,' the commissioner responded.

The intelligence agent lowered his eyes. He understood the commissioner's opinion, but he believed that there had been more than sufficient justification for their decision. He responded, with more detail,

'In October 2019, after we successfully prevented the attack that Kobec had warned us of, we recovered a viable explosive device, a dirty bomb, a big one.' He used his hands to illustrate.

'Had the device been successfully detonated, the Square Mile would be uninhabitable today. Hundreds, maybe thousands, of lives would have been lost.'

The commissioner looked down at his interlaced hands. This is what the world had come to. If what Paine was telling him was the truth, it would be difficult to argue.

'So how did Kobec end up in London?' the senior officer asked, then quickly raised his hand again,

'No, no don't tell me, you brought him here,' the commissioner asked and answered, staring up at Paine. There was no simple way to tell the man charged with protecting the citizens of London that they had purposely relocated one of the most dangerous criminals in Europe to his city. Paine breathed in heavily.

'It was part of the deal we made with him,' he replied. 'By establishing him here we created an invaluable intelligence asset to assist us in preventing any future attacks. He had never been compromised, not even his closest allies had been aware of his arrest.'

'So, what does this mean, we can't touch Kobec?'

'We're absolutely certain that Roman Kobec had nothing to with the murders of Billy Barker or the other families, sir.'

'How can you be sure?' the police chief questioned.

Paine sighed. The commissioner was not going to appreciate his answer. 'The Barker murders stirred up a hornets' nest, we still have no idea who was responsible for that horror show, but it made Jack Barker vulnerable.' The intelligence officer leaned forward, before continuing.

'He was lashing out, upsetting a lot of people. We suggested that Kobec use the disruption to deal with an unwanted situation.'

'You advised what?' the commissioner asked disbelievingly.

'We wanted Kobec to be established in London, it was taking time, and this seemed like a viable opportunity to get him a leg up on the ladder,' Paine explained.

Listening to his own words, the intelligence officer was all too aware of the severity of the mistake that his agency had made. They had attempted to employ tactics akin to those used during the troubles in Northern Ireland. In Belfast, British intelligence had set up paramilitary organisations to gather evidence and to attack IRA targets. It had proved successful in that campaign.

Paine continued with less conviction, treading carefully.

'We have been aware for some time that Jack Barker has compromised several prominent individuals, politicians, civic leaders, police officers.' Paine paused, allowing his words to linger,

'The situation with Barker has become untenable, if left unchecked the man may soon compromise Number Ten.' The commissioner knew that what Paine had said was not an exaggeration. 'The opportunity to deal with him appeared to present itself when his brother was murdered.'

Paine watched as the policeman's eyes closed briefly. The commissioner had visited Jack Barker's rural establishment on many occasions. He had voracious desires, as video evidence in Barker's possession could prove. Sadomasochistic sex with young men was his particular poison of choice. He realised that the senior intelligence officer seated opposite had some knowledge of his acquaintance with Barker.

'We planned to remove Barker and to install Kobec in his place. We would have solved many problems,' Paine was saying. 'And we would have had an intelligence asset as never before, to assist us with domestic and outside threats,' he disclosed. He needed the senior policeman on side. Seeing the commissioner's defeated expression, he advised cautiously, 'What I am about to tell you, sir, is top secret.' The commissioner's eyes narrowed. He indicated his understanding.

'We are leaving Afghanistan, us, the Americans, every western force, there is no more delay. We have lost the war there. Despite what the news tells the public, the reality of the ground is that we got our backsides handed to us by the Taliban.' He hesitated, then finished, 'They will seize power within weeks of our departure, maybe even days.'

The commissioner did not respond to the information.

'In Kobec we saw an asset who could provide the kind of intelligence that we need to keep our country safe.' Paine repeatedly drove his finger into the table to reinforce his statement. 'Afghanistan will pose a danger to UK interests once again,' Paine rationalised. He leaned forward and made a pyramid with his hands. The commissioner looked pale. He wanted the meeting to end.

'That will not be our biggest threat,' the intelligence office supplemented. He hesitated, looking directly into the senior officer's eyes. In a low voice he explained, 'A key reason that NATO wants out of Afghanistan in such a hurry is to turn their focus back to the real problem: Russia. Our intelligence tells us that Putin intends to launch a full scale invasion of Ukraine soon, and he does not intend to stop there.'

He let his words hang in the air. He could tell that the commissioner was disbelieving.

'These are not delusions Duncan, the threat of another war on European soil is all too real, we need every asset available to us,' Paine emphasised, pausing to ensure that the man sat before him was paying attention. 'Kobec knows Russia, he knows Putin, and a lot of his dirty little secrets, we needed him,'.'

Duncan West's face creased. It was not lost on him that Paine had used the past tense when referring to Kobec's usefulness. His eyes fell shut for a moment and then opened slowly. The senior police officer nodded almost imperceptibly.

'So, what do you expect me to do?' he managed to ask weakly, crestfallen.

'Nothing for now, just let the investigation take its course,' Paine replied. 'But we will need your assistance later. We felt you needed to be apprised of the situation.'

The commissioner agreed. He had no choice and Paine knew it.

'I want Kobec reeled in,' the commissioner insisted. 'I *cannot* have police officers killed on my watch while I sit by and do nothing. This situation needs to be resolved, and I don't care what you have to do to resolve it,' he reinforced.

'I understand,' Paine confirmed. 'We'll ensure that there'll be no more incidents initiated by Mr Kobec.' The men stood, readying to leave.

'We intend to ensure a rapid and permanent solution to the problem, sir,' Paine said shuffling uncomfortably. 'Your Special Operations have a team watching Kobec and Barker; we need that surveillance removed,' he requested.

The commissioner looked at Paine and nodded again. He understood what was being inferred. Kobec was no longer an asset. He had become a liability. When Paine left the room, the commissioner collapsed back into a chair and sat alone, staring out the window at the city. The coronavirus pandemic had been hard on the city. It had highlighted many flaws in the social structure and had pushed the health services to breaking point. The only positive had been that it had facilitated a sharp drop in serious crime. Now it seemed that it had only served to create a pent-up turmoil that had now exploded across his domain.

The offices of Taylor James Auctioneers were situated in a converted warehouse in Wapping. The area, once the haunt of pirates, was now mostly a trendy residential district close to financial heart of the city. Hints as to its past could still be seen on the facades of the old buildings and the cobbled streets. Palmer found a parking space and walked across the narrow road. The reception area he entered was neat, modern and unmanned.

'Hello!' he called out. He heard muffled sounds from the rear partitioned section of the office and a petite young blonde dressed in a neat business suit appeared.

'Can I help you?' she asked politely.

Palmer flashed his badge.

'Is your manager in?' he asked.

'No, he ain't,' she replied in a squeaky East End accent. 'Can I help you?'

'I'm looking for some information regarding a property your company auctioned some time ago. It's very important,' Palmer explained.

The young woman looked uncertain as to how she should respond.

'I think you'll have to wait for one of the managers to get back. They'll be back in about an hour,' she replied, deciding on safety first. The decision to give information to a police officer was not one she was going to make.

'Look,' Palmer pressed. 'You keep files here of all your transactions. All I need to know is who the property was auctioned for, who owned it.'

The girl was not convinced. Palmer persisted, explaining the urgency and hinting at the seriousness of the matter. Time was of the essence he affirmed.

'I need you to help me saves lives,' the detective pleaded dramatically. The receptionist finally relented. She had complete access to the electronic files. The woman found Palmer's presence unnerving. She wanted rid of him. He gave her the address, the name of the buyer, and the year that the property had been auctioned. The woman keyed the details into the system. It took a few seconds to complete the search. There was only one result. She opened the file, which contained the details relating to the transaction. Another click and Palmer heard the familiar sound of a printer awakening. The woman reached beneath the reception desk, retrieved the printed page, and handed it to the detective. Palmer clutched the paper. The feisty woman refused to release it until he had sworn never to tell anyone that she had given him the information.

The record was not what he had hoped for. The seller was listed as the Grace Family Trust. The trust had a registered address in Guernsey. Palmer shook his head. He was chasing a ghost. Once in his car he slammed his hand against the steering wheel. On the passenger seat of the car, his phone rang. It was Dunne. He had been ordered back to the station. He had a sinking feeling. This was not good. The sword was finally about to fall.

It was well past midday by the time he reached the station. It had already been a long day. He picked his way through the forensic examiners who were still scouring the area outside the station and braced himself for a difficult conversation.

CHAPTER FIFTEEN
Burning Bright

Palmer found Dunne in DCI Young's office.

'Close the door, Frank,' he said as Palmer walked in. When Palmer was seated, he went on.

'I won't beat around the bush, Frank. In the past few days several things have come to light which we need to address.'

Dunne hesitated, looking for a reaction. There was none. Palmer appeared apathetic, dead still and looked directly at the senior officer.

'As you're aware, your DNA was found on the Barker girl, and a message apparently sent from our killer was later determined to have originated from your home IP address.' Dunne hesitated again, but Palmer was not about to bite. He wanted to hear everything the senior officer had first.

'And now,' he continued, 'it's come to light that DNA evidence recovered from the Morton house was purposely withheld from the investigation.' Dunne looked at Palmer, no longer trying to conceal his antipathy,

'Evidence that implicates you, Frank,' Dunne asserted harshly. Palmer remained silent, sensing that the senior office had not finished.
'Apart from that, I have learned that you've been meeting covertly with our chief suspect, Roman Kobec.'

That got a reaction. Palmer's eyes betrayed his otherwise composed exterior.

'Now, you can see how this looks, Frank, can't you?' Dunne asked.

Palmer remained reticent. The atmosphere in the small office was tense. He began to nod slowly. He was not sure how far Dunne would go. Would he be arrested or was this just the first salvo.

'I know how it looks, guv, but that's because it's been made to look that way,' Palmer finally responded. Dunne slammed his hands down on the table.

'Well, tell me how it is, Frank,' he shouted. 'Tell me what the fuck is going on here, because unless you do, I can only see things from one side.' He paused to compose himself. 'You of all people should understand that,' he continued in a more amenable tone. 'This whole mess is out of control, we need to put a stop to it, a lot of people are dead, and a lot more are going to die.' Dunne's animosity had been quickly replaced by desperation. The senior detective pushed his hands back through his hair and sighed. He resumed in a steadier voice.

'If you can help us, Frank, then help us for Christ's sake. Help us and help yourself at the same time.' He leaned forward as he spoke, his bulky body causing the desk to creak.

'I'm being stitched up, guv,' Palmer responded, suddenly exhausted. 'I don't know why or how, but I'm being stitched up.' He looked into Dunne's eyes and could tell that he wasn't buying it.

'To what end and by whom, Frank? Give me something to believe in because I'll tell you exactly what people are thinking.' He pointed to Palmer's chest. 'They think that you killed Billy Barker and Paul Morton and their families to initiate a gang war. You did this because Roman Kobec paid you to, because he intends taking over Jack Barker's operations. The evidence is going that way, Frank, it's simple and it fits. I need something concrete to keep the wolves from your door.' Sweat ran down Palmer's back. Should he tell Dunne about Anne Grace?

'Look, guv, I don't think that the murders of Barker, Morton and Breen had anything to do with Roman Kobec. He saw the shit storm following Billy's murder and he jumped at the chance to gain some ground in the city,' Palmer explained. 'He made one big mistake, he underestimated Jack Barker. But these things aren't linked.' Palmer looked directly at Dunne. 'What's happening between Jack Barker and Roman Kobec had nothing to do with those murders,' he avowed firmly. Dunne studied Palmer carefully.

'Then who killed them?' he asked.

Palmer wavered. He looked down at the desk. Shaking his head slowly, he stated, 'I think it has something to do with Wormwood Scrubs nick.' 'It's the common denominator that ties Barker, Morton and Breen together. They were all at the Scrubs at the same time on two separate occasions. I think that's the key to finding the killer.'

'And what links you to this?' Dunne probed. 'Why would the perpetrator of these crimes want to stitch you up?'

Palmer shrugged.

'That's what I've been trying to figure out. I've been looking through old cases,' he lied. 'Trying to find a link to someone I may have sent down around the time Barker and Morton were at the Scrubs. I just need more time. I'll find the answer.' Dunne thought about it. It did not sound impossible or entirely implausible. Also, no one had come up with a feasible motive for the Breen murders yet. Dunne was also aware that his investigators had found a solid alibi for Palmer for the night of the Barker murders. He had kept that information from the detective.

They sat in uncomfortable silence again until Dunne advised, 'Okay, Frank, I'll give you twenty-four hours to convince me, or I'll be left with no choice.' He did not have to explain what he meant.

Palmer left the office shaken. He needed a drink to steady himself. He needed something stronger to help him focus, to keep him in control.

'Frank?'

Palmer was startled. He looked up to see Tara Moore standing in front of him.

'Are you okay?' she asked. 'You seem a little on edge.' She hesitated, looking directly at the detective and added, 'Actually you look a lot on edge.'

Palmer smiled. He was pleased to see the psychologist.

'It's been one of those days. Do you want to get a drink?' he asked.

'I'm just finishing up something for the superintendent, then I'll be free,' the profiler replied, reaching out to touch the detective's arm. Their eyes locked for a moment. Palmer nodded.

'Give me a call,' he said and headed for the stairs.

He sat in the car and picked the sheet of folded white paper off the dashboard. The Grace Family Trust. The trust had its registered address listed as Guernsey. He needed to find out more. He knew of one person that could answer his questions.

He headed west, but he didn't get far. The three cars came from nowhere. One stopped in front of him, one behind, and a third beside him. Before he had time to react, he was dragged from the car and pushed into the backseat of a SUV.

'Frank, I'm glad you could pop by,' Jack Barker greeted him jovially. He looked a lot better than in he had in recent days, much like his old self. Palmer's eyes took a minute to adjust to the harsh light.

'I've had quite a day, Frank,' Barker said, smiling. 'Quite a day, I'll tell you.' He laughed and indicated with his head for the two men holding Palmer to release him.

'How's your day been, how is your friend Mr Kobec? Missing his family, is he?' The two men who had stepped a few feet back from Palmer laughed.

'Frankie, you and me we go back a long way, mate, a long way. You remember old Rhubarb? Rhubarb Crumble we used to call him. Mr Grumble his name was, taught us woodwork, right fucking nutter he was, used to carry that thick cane around. You remember he hit you on the hand one day 'cause you were holding a tool the wrong way or some shit. You remember what I did, Frank...' Barker circled the detective.

Palmer remembered the incident clearly. Harold Grumble had been a mean old man who had taken pleasure in tormenting young boys. He had hit Palmer one day, a heavy blow across the knuckles of his right hand. The detective absently rubbed his hand just thinking about it. It had been more than Jack Barker had been prepared or willing to tolerate. He had lifted a heavy wooden mallet and had struck Grumble on the back of the head. The teacher had gone down hard. Barker had rained blow after blow on him, screaming like a boy possessed. Both he and Palmer had been suspended from the school for a month. After the incident Harold Grumble had taken early retirement. They had never seen him again.

'It seems like another lifetime, but I was there for you, Frankie, I was there. Even after you joined the filth, I still helped you. Remember those times, Frank, all those good times?' Barker stretched his arms wide. 'And now, Frank, it has come to this – you trying to help some foreign mackerel to take me out.'

Palmer was too tired to be scared. He shook his head.

'I didn't try to do anything, Jack,' he defended.

Barker smiled.

'Now it's time for you to do the right thing, Frank, the right thing. I want to know where Roman Kobec is, and I want to know what your involvement is with him.' Barker stood still in front of Palmer,

'How is it that you have you become the prime suspect in your own fucking investigation?' He spoke harshly, spittle spraying from his mouth.

Palmer shook his head again, and a blow landed before he saw it coming. It dropped him instantly. Barker drove a boot into his side. He stayed down, expecting an onslaught that never came. He pulled himself to his knees and looked up at Barker.

'Kobec had nothing to do with Billy, Jack,' he spat. 'Nor Morton or Breen.'

Barker sniggered.

'Is that a fact?' Barker questioned sarcastically. 'Who exactly did have something to do with my brother's murder, Frank? You?'

Barker had not expected an answer. The one he got silenced him.

'Peter Grace.'

Barker recognised the name instantly. He looked at Palmer, who was wiping blood from his lip.

'What are you talking about?' he asked angrily. 'Grace, is dead, a long time dead,'

Palmer slowly lifted himself off his knees and stood on shaky legs.

'You remember Peter Grace, don't you, Jack, his wife stitched him up because you told her to,' Palmer responded cynically. He tapped his chest. 'I made sure her old man was sent down, Billy arranged for Paul Morton to kill him in the Scrubs, and Breen was the fucking screw you paid to open his cell door and look the other way.'

Barker's mouth hung open. He looked confused.

'That's what this is all about, Jack. That's why Billy was murdered. It had nothing do with Kobec, he was just trying to weigh in while you looked weak.'

Barker turned away from Palmer and walked to the desk, which looked out of place in the building's cavernous interior. Palmer followed. Barker collapsed into the chair. Palmer took a seat. They sat looking at each other. The Grace affair was what had driven a wedge between them. It had been a step too far for Palmer. Barker had known it at the time.

'When did you figure this out?' Barker eventually asked. He was far from convinced, but he wanted to hear what Palmer had to say.

'After Breen was killed,' the detective replied. 'It's the only thing that links us all together,' he explained. 'And the initials PEG.'

'PEG, does that mean, for Christ's sake?' Barker growled.

'Peter Edward Grace, his initials, Jack, the same three letters carved into the chests of three victims, it's not a coincidence, it all fits.'

Barker was reluctant to agree,

'Fits how, Frank, maybe in your mind?' the gangster retorted. 'Grace had no family, and why now, after all this time?' Barker was not persuaded, but his instinct recognised some truth in what Palmer told said. He moved his head slowly staring across at the detective, thinking.

'He had a daughter,' Palmer corrected. 'The girl killed her mother in 2007.' He was sure that Barker was unaware of the facts. 'Beat her to death, Jack. She ended up in an asylum and was released years ago.' Barker's eyes remained fixed on the detective. He let his words sink in.

'That's not all,' he continued. He had kept the fact that he thought may convince Barker for last.

'She had money, Jack, a lot of money – money her father had left in trust, money you couldn't touch. She had more than enough money to buy the talent needed to come looking for us.' Palmer was relieved to finally have it all out in the open. Barker remained quiet. He closed his eyes. It made sense. There was no doubting it. But even if it was true, and he was still far from convinced that it was, it did not change the fact that Roman Kobec had tried to kill him. Kobec had instigated the trouble between them. Kobec had to be dealt with first. He was the greater threat now. Palmer's phantom could wait.

'Okay, Frank,' the villain finally conceded. 'Maybe this is true, but it makes little difference right now.' He raised his hands like a priest giving a blessing. 'Kobec tried to take me out, this thing between us isn't going to go away until one of us is gone,' he said. He paused, then added menacingly, 'So, I need to know where Kobec is.'

Palmer bent his neck back and looked up at the corrugated iron roof. Then he looked back at Barker and nodded. What did he have to lose, he was screwed either way.

'After I've dealt with Kobec,' Barker added confidently, 'we'll deal with the other problem. If this phantom of yours exists, then we'll find her, and we'll kill her.' He pushed a small notepad across the desk as he spoke.

Palmer reached forward, picked up a pen from the desk, and wrote an address on the pad.

'As far as I know, that's where Kobec was last known to be,' he informed Barker, and pushed the pad back toward him.

'Your car is outside,' Barker responded. Palmer stood to leave. When he was a few steps from the desk, Barker called out, 'Frank, let's keep this to ourselves.'

Palmer walked into the pub, which was more crowded than he preferred. He looked around, trying to pick out the face of Tara Moore in the throng. He found her standing at the far end of the bar.

'Should we get out of here and find somewhere quieter?' he asked once he got to her.

'You read my mind,' she replied. They made their way out into the warn evening and found a small restaurant a few doors down from the pub. Palmer was hungry. He realised that he had barely eaten for days. They were shown to a table. Palmer ordered a large scotch and soda for himself and a gin and tonic for the profiler. They each took a menu from the masked waitress who went off to get their drinks.

'Tough day?' the psychologist asked when they were alone.

Palmer nodded.

'Were you at the station when the attack happened?' he asked.

The profiler nodded. Palmer felt a tinge of guilt.

'It was frightening, kind of surreal,' she explained.

'I can imagine. It could have been a lot worse, though.' His shoulders sagged. 'This whole thing has gotten way out of control.'

'You know, I had a conversation with Superintendent Dunne today,' Tara said. 'He asked an awful lot of questions about you. Is there something going on?'

Palmer sniggered.

'Yeah, someone's trying to put me in the frame for the murders at Barker's and Morton's,' he answered hesitantly.

'What! Are you kidding?' the profiler replied, astonished.

'I wish I was,' Palmer responded truthfully.

'But why?' the profiler asked the obvious question.

'God only knows, we're dealing with a sick mind, who knows what's going on in his head?' Palmer replied too loudly. A few heads turned to look at him. 'I'm sorry,' he apologised. 'This is just getting to me a little.'

'It's okay,' Tara comforted. She reached across and put her hand on his. 'Things will work out,' she assured him.

The meal was good. They managed to avoid the subject of the case for most of it. They spoke about sport and other trivial things, but eventually the conversation came full circle.

'What did Dunne want to know about me?' Palmer asked.

The psychologist hesitated. Palmer sensed she was not keen to talk about it. He didn't rush her.

'Well, he wanted to know if I thought you were capable of murder or being involved in murder,' the psychologist answered.

Palmer gave a humourless smile.

'What was your answer?' he asked.

She grinned and slowly shook her head.

'Now you know I cannot divulge that information Detective,' she replied seductively. 'Unless you are willing to force it out of me.'

They left the restaurant hurriedly. The lovemaking was frenetic and rough. Palmer had doubted that he had the strength for it, but once his hands ran over her naked body, he found new reserves of energy. When they finished, he fell into a deep sleep.

The incident room was silent. The four officers were momentarily lost in their own thoughts. Dunne broke the silence.

'No one outside these walls hears about this. We will handle the surveillance and the internal investigation until such time as I say otherwise.'

Porter, Mullins, and Galloway nodded. It was an unpleasant situation. One of their own, the man who had been their senior officer, was implicated in the very crimes they had been investigating. There seemed no doubt that Palmer's hands had blood on them. When the press got hold of the story it would be seriously damaging to the service, and it would taint everyone associated with the detective.

CHAPTER SIXTEEN
Blinded by the Light

He woke in the early hours of the morning and left the apartment silently. It was close to freezing outside and he pulled his collar up against the cold wind. It took a few minutes to heat the car, and then he headed for Surrey Quays.

Noel Latham was a fraudster and a hacker of exceptional talent. He had made a small fortune during his relatively short career. He could fool any experienced banker into believing he was one of theirs. He dressed correctly, spoke correctly, and knew everything that there was to know about banking systems. He predicted the crash before most and made a lot of money shorting stocks in 2008. Palmer had met him while investigating an online scam years before. The man had been intelligent, charming, and completely guilty, although proof of his guilt had proved elusive. In the end Palmer had given up and let Latham walk with the understanding that if he ever needed information in the future, the fraudster would provide his services. Since then, the man had helped Palmer on a few cases. He was not pleased to see the detective at his door at four thirty in the morning.

'What are you doing here, Palmer?' he demanded as he opened the door.

'Nice to see you too, Noel,' Palmer replied, brushing past the man into the well-furnished, upmarket apartment.

'It's the middle of the night, Frank. You're taking the piss,' the angry man insisted. A young woman walked into the front room. She was stark naked and unfazed when she saw Palmer.

'Are you coming back to bed, sweetie?' she asked Latham in a singsong voice.

'In a minute,' Latham replied, annoyed.

Then another girl appeared, as naked as the first.

'Look, you two go back to bed. I'll be there in a minute.'

'Am I disturbing something?' Palmer asked, smiling.

'As a matter of fact, you are,' Latham replied. 'So tell me what you want and make it quick.'

'I need some information and I need it now,' Palmer explained.

'The sooner you help me, the sooner I'll be out of your way, and you can get back to whatever it was you were doing.'

'Okay, okay, what is it?' Latham conceded, knowing the only way to get rid of Palmer was to give the detective what he needed.

'I need all of the information you can get me about this trust.' He handed the hacker the sheet of paper that the secretary at the auctioneer company had printed for him.

'How do you think I'm going to get that information now, suck it out of my thumb, it's the middle of the bloody night, Frank,' he complained.

'Can't you get it online?' Palmer asked.

'Everyone's a tech wizard nowadays,' grumbled Latham. 'Follow me,' he said, resigned.

They went into a room that was being used as an office. It was, like the rest of the flat, neat, with everything perfectly aligned and stacked.

'Try not to touch anything,' the obsessive Latham said. He sat down behind the desk and switched on the computer. Within minutes he was attacking the keyboard with fervour. After a half an hour he stopped.

'Well, whoever controls this trust doesn't want guests. Most of the funds from the transactions of the trust go into a numbered account, impossible to trace, but there are several transfers to an account in the Turks and Caicos Islands, a tax haven with very strong privacy laws,' Latham explained.

'Can you dig some more? I need something, a contact number, an address, anything…' Palmer pleaded.

'It's not going to happen in a few minutes, Frank. It'll take time.' He looked at the detective. 'Honestly,' he added.

'This is important, Noel. You do this for me and we're square, for good. I mean it, you have my word,' Palmer replied.

'For good?'

'For good.'

'Okay, I'll let you know when I have something,' Noel agreed.

Palmer arrived home just as the first hints of daylight appeared. He could see faint strips of orange and flecks of pink on the distant clouds. *Pink sky in the morning, shepherd's warning*, Palmer thought. *Pink sky at night, the city's alight.*

He showered and dressed, then sat on his sofa and thought about what he needed to do to get himself out of the mess he was in. He needed to find Anne Grace. That was a priority. He needed to get Dunne off his back. He needed to get Jack Barker off his back. He needed to get Roman Kobec off his back.

He stood and walked over to the side cabinet and took out a bottle of single malt. He poured himself a triple shot and downed it in one, then repeated the motion. He returned to the sofa. Daylight was coming fast. He sat down and tried to think clearly.

'You ask too much of me, Mr Goodchild,' Roman Kobec said. His voice was emotionless.

'It was you who urged me to act against your Mr Barker, and how sorely you underestimated him,' Kobec's eyes burnt into the MI5 agent. 'Only it's me who paid the price for your misjudgement, and a high price it was.' The Russian's voice was steady but filled with venom. 'And how can I blame Jack Barker? He acted exactly as I would have acted.' He turned his back of the intelligence officer and returned to the seat behind the desk. Goodchild followed and dropped into a seat opposite. He had no response for the Russian.

'No,' Kobec resumed. 'It's you and your agency with my family's blood on your hands.' Goodchild was silent. He was all too aware what an enormous mistake they had made in charging after Barker. They had seen the opportunity and made the decision to act. Regret was a wasted emotion. Barker had been tearing the London underworld apart trying to find his brother's killer. People had been afraid. Fear made people more pliable, more willing to listen, to negotiate. The service saw an opportunity to deeply entrench Roman Kobec in the London underworld, a shortcut that could eliminate years of legwork.

Now their impatience had put them in a precarious position and put paid to Kobec's usefulness. Jack Barker had proven to be more intelligent and organised than they had given him credit for. The primary reason that they had underestimated Barker was because they had had so little information about him. That had led to a fundamental error. Assumptions had been made about him and his firm, assumptions based on flawed intelligence.

'I know that we made mistakes, Roman,' Goodchild replied eventually. 'But we have to show restraint now. This is London, not Kabul. You can't go around killing police officers in their stations.'

'That was a regrettable, but an unavoidable error. It was not meant to happen,' Kobec interjected.

'Look, we'll finish this, we'll get Barker, you have my word, but for now, you need to lay low, let things quieten down, we'll smoke Barker out and deal with him.'

Kobec smiled.

'*We* will deal with Barker,' he repeated. 'You are not going to get your hands dirty, are you, Commander?' he asked mockingly.

Goodchild's face reddened.

'We will do what we feel best serves the interests of our country and the safety of its people,' the officer responded.

Kobec smiled, pleased to have rattled the man.

'That sounds very patriotic and romantic, Mr Goodchild. Tell me, does that interest extend to terminating me?'

Goodchild shook his head.

'We have no intention of doing that, I can assure you. You are of great value to us, Roman, you are aware that changes are coming in Afghanistan, we can't be left blind, we need your network,' the commander assured.

Kobec smiled again. The English were so full of self-importance.
'Very well then, Mr Goodchild, I shall for now desist in any actions against Mr Barker, but I will not wait for long.' He paused, staring directly into the agent's eyes. 'And should your Mr Barker take any further action against me, my hand will be forced.'

Goodchild nodded.

CHAPTER SEVENTEEN
Lessons in Blood

The use of intelligence focuses on the importance of developing good
information sources.
Chapter Thirteen, Sun Tzu - *The Art of War*

'What do you think?' Barker asked.

The table in front of him resembled a military operations room. A large aerial photograph showed a large portion of south-east London and incorporated all of Greenwich. A section of the photograph had been outlined with a red marker. It demarcated the buildings owned by Roman Kobec. A trace of the address Palmer had given them had shown that it belonged to New Eastern Property Development Limited. The company also owned four adjacent buildings. They were post-war constructions that had replaced warehouses destroyed by the Luftwaffe. In all there were a lot of square feet to cover. It would be difficult to get in and search all of the buildings without their presence being detected. A quick reconnaissance of the buildings had shown that none of them appeared to be occupied. There was a new sign above one, but apart from security cameras, there were no other signs of occupancy. Two of the buildings had been boarded up.

'It'll be difficult unless we can narrow down what sections of the buildings are being used,' Norris Jones said.

'What about doing a recce of the buildings?' Tom Baxter, another ex-services member on Barker's firm, asked. 'One man in, exterior lookouts, check the layout, and find out which parts of the building they're using.'

Barker shook his head.

'Too risky, we don't want them to know we're coming.'

'We could use a diversion,' Norris Jones responded.

'What kind of diversion?' Barker queried.

The big Welshman looked down at the photograph.

'This building is old, a lot of timber in the structure. If we started a fire in that building, alert the fire brigade, they'd be all over it. We could access this building here, dressed as emergency services, and work our way through it. Another team could enter here and a third team, here. The fire would drive anyone in these building out of either the front or rear exits, here or here,' he tapped the paper. 'If they use the rear exits, it'll bring them out onto the dock. If we put a fourth team covering the entrances, here, from this building, we'd catch anyone exiting any of these buildings.'

Barker frowned. It was an elaborate plan. He didn't like it. They needed something low-key.

'It's too over the top, Jonesy,' Barker expressed. 'We need something a little more subtle, a little more James Bond and little less Arnold fucking Schwarzenegger.' Everyone around the table laughed.

'We could blow the whole lot up,' Deacon Brown suggested. Everyone looked at him.

'How is that being subtle?' Barker asked and slapped the back of the bomb maker's head.

'We could cut the power,' Jones offered. 'Go in at night, using night vision goggles, a small team.'

Barker nodded. It was more along the lines that he was thinking of.

'But it's still too big an area to cover. We'd need to narrow down the exact location Kobec's using. Keep thinking,' he ordered. 'I've got some calls to make.'

He turned and headed across the warehouse to his makeshift office.

'What do you think?' Roman Kobec asked.

'It'll be more difficult now, boss,' Kopjov replied. 'They're aware of us tactically and their security's good. They're using a warehouse complex across the river as a base, it's well manned. We can't know exactly where Barker will be.'

Kobec nodded.

'You don't intend to wait as Goodchild requested, Roman?' Viktor Mihalik asked. He was one of a few people who addressed Kobec by his first name. Kobec looked at his deputy.

'Do you know the story of the old lady and the snake, Viktor?'

Mihalik shrugged.

'An old lady was out walking in the woods in winter when she came across a snake frozen in the snow. She took it home and nursed it back to health.' Kobec paused for effect.

'When the snake was well, the old lady went into the woods again to release the creature, and as she did so, it bit her.' Mihalik and the other men listened intently. It was seldom the boss said something that wasn't worth hearing.

'As she lay in the snow dying, the old lady asked the snake why he had bitten her after she helped him, and the snake answered, "You stupid woman, you knew that I was a snake".' Kobec saw the blank expression on Mihalik's face. He had not understood what his boss was trying to convey. Kobec smiled and explained.

'Commander Goodchild is a snake. I know that he is going to bite. We need to beware and take care of our own business, then we shall take care of him, before he has the chance to sink his teeth in.'

His aide nodded. Kobec turned to Kopjov again.

'What do you suggest, Andrzej?' he asked. Kopjov smiled narrowly.

'We wait and watch, ready to react rather than act. I think this Jack Barker is like a bull. He will come for us, and when he does, that is when he will be weakest, and we will have our chance.'

Kobec thought about it. The assassin was right. Barker was not likely to wait this out. He would act and they would be ready to react.

'Be ready,' Kobec ordered.

There was no need to tell Kopjov.

Palmer was standing on a cliff overlooking a red sea spread out in front of him. In the crashing waves below, he could see people struggling and crying out for help. He felt no pity for them. A breeze blew against his face, and he felt the warm sun on his skin. Then something grabbed his leg. He looked down and saw hands coming from the ground and clutching him. They were pulling him down, and there was a ringing in his ears, a loud ringing. He awoke, startled.

'Christ!' he cursed. He rubbed his face and then realised his phone was ringing. He picked it up.

'Guv, are you okay?' It was Mullins.

Palmer coughed and replied, 'Yeah, what's up, what time is it?'

'It's ten thirty, guv. Detective Superintendent Dunne is looking for you. We've had a break.'

Palmer sat up realising that exhaustion had finally bested him. He had fallen into a deep sleep.

'What break?' he asked. A minute later he hurriedly dressed and headed out the door. Before he made it to his car, the phone rang again.

'Frank,' the voice was like a bullet to the head.

'Jack,' Palmer greeted wearily. 'What's going on?'

'I need you to set up a meet with Kobec,' Barker replied.

'He won't go for it, Jack. He's smarter than that,' Palmer countered.

'Well, there's a way to get him out, Frank. I need to see you.'

'Look, Jack, something's come up. I can't get away now.'

There was silence on the phone, but eventually Barker asked, 'Is this about that Grace crap?'

Palmer ignored the question.

'Jack, I need to do something *right now*.' His tone was harsher than he meant it to be. He expected a reaction from Barker.

Instead, the gangster said calmly, 'Call me when you're done, I'll be waiting.'

When Palmer walked into the station, he felt like an outsider. The place that had been a second home to him for so many years now felt strange and hostile. He felt eyes burning into him. Rumours had spread of his involvement in the recent cases which had inexplicably led to an attack on the station. Palmer ignored everyone and made his way to the incident room. Dunne was there with Mullins and Porter. They all turned to face him as he entered the room.

'Guv,' Mullins greeted.

Dunne stood and gave Palmer a slight nod.

'Where is he?' Palmer asked without greeting the officers.

'Where's who, Frank?' Dunne asked.

'The kid they picked up from the Breen scene,' Palmer replied.

'He's in custody, waiting for his brief,' Dunne confirmed.

'I need to speak to him,' Palmer said.

'I don't think that would be a good idea, Frank, considering,' Dunne replied.

'Considering what, Detective Superintendent?' Palmer spat. 'Considering that I'm being stitched up and my fellow officers would rather believe I'm guilty of multiple murders than assist me, is that what I need to consider?' Palmer boomed.

'Look, Frank, we don't want to get into all that now, it's not the place,' Dunne urged.

Palmer laughed and looked past Dunne at Mullins.

'What did the boy say?' he asked her. Mullins was silent. 'What did he say?' Palmer demanded. Mullins shifted uncomfortably on her feet. She looked at Dunne, who gave a slight nod.

'He was in the alley the night the Breens were killed. There was a motorcycle parked there. They were just looking at it, according to him, and this person came from nowhere, all dressed in black.'

'Person?' Palmer asked. Mullins hesitated, before continuing.

'He said the person was wearing a helmet and dressed in black leather.' She stalled. 'He couldn't be completely certain, but he believes that it was a woman.'

Palmer's head reeled. It couldn't be.

'Mullins, Porter, give me and the DCI a minute,' Dunne instructed.

They obeyed and left the room.

When they were gone Dunne said, 'Okay, Frank, now it's time to come clean. You know more about what's going on than you're telling us. I want to know what you know *now*.' Palmer looked at the man. He wanted to tell Dunne everything, but he couldn't bring himself to do it. He shook his head slowly.

'Look, guv, you agreed to give me until this evening, let me deal with this. I can find the person responsible. I just need time.'

Dunne looked at Palmer like a cat gazing at a cornered mouse.

The senior detective reluctantly agreed. 'Have it your way, Frank, but it's your life on the line here. If I were you, I'd try to put some trust in someone.'

CHAPTER EIGHTEEN
The Second Hand

The source of strength is unity, not size, and the five ingredients you need to succeed in any war, in order of importance are, attack, strategy, alliances, army, and cities. - Chapter Three, Sun Tzu - *The Art of War*

Palmer left the station and headed to Noel Latham's apartment. He needed information. His phone rang and he answered without taking his eyes off the road in front of him.

'Daddy!' a desperate voice called. It took a few seconds to register his daughter's voice on the phone.

'Honey?' he replied. 'Is that you?'

'Sorry, Frank, your little honey is a little tied up right now,' a monotone voice interrupted. The voice was clearly the result of an electronic masking device.

'Who is this?' Palmer yelled.

'Why, Frank, don't you know, it's me,' the voice replied.

Palmer narrowly avoided an oncoming vehicle as he jerked the steering wheel. He got the vehicle under control again and pulled to the side of the road.

'Is this some kind of joke?' Palmer barked, sensing that it wasn't.

'A joke, no, it's no joke, Frank. It's time for us to meet. You, me and Jack.'

Palmer's mind was racing.

'What are you doing with my daughter?' he asked, panicked.

'Oh, we're having a great time, Frank. I've been telling her about how we met,' the voice teased. 'Now, Frank, I want you to listen to me carefully. You can save your daughter, I'll trade her for Jack Barker.'

There was silence until Palmer agreed. 'Okay.'

He listened as the caller continued with the directives. When the call ended, he made sure that the road was clear and then swung the car around.

'How do we resolve this without embarrassing ourselves?' Sir John Gelding asked.

'It's a bloody mess. It should never have been allowed to get this far.' The two men seated in front of their boss, the head of MI5, remained silent. They knew that they had made a grave error in judgement regarding Roman Kobec. The rational had been sound, the execution had been disastrous.

'I don't believe that we can still consider keeping Kobec as an asset, sir. Things have gone too far; a police officer has been killed. We can't risk the truth of this matter ever becoming known,' Jeremy Paine stated. He had approved the operation. He knew that his head and his career were on the cutting block. It was time to pull the plug and consolidate their losses. He could still save himself and those of his team embroiled in the mess.

'I agree, sir, we have little option. We have to consider Kobec a liability and deal with him as such,' James Goodchild added. The intelligence service head made a pyramid with his fingers. He knew what was being implied. He had to authorise the action without putting his own neck too far out. The home secretary had already called regarding Kobec. If the plan backfired, they would all be gone. It was a serious situation.

'Does Kobec still trust us?' he queried.

'For now, I'd say yes,' Goodchild replied. 'But we want to act before he has too much time to think.'

Jeremy Paine nodded his agreement.

'And what do we do with Jack Barker?' Gelding asked.

The men looked at each other.

'I think that we can leave him for the Met to deal with,' Paine replied. 'They have several cases pending against him, he'll go down, we're confident of that.'

The room was silent, the atmosphere tense. They didn't have a lot of options. John Gelding knew it.

'Very well,' he consented reluctantly. 'But if this goes wrong, gentlemen, heads will roll and mine won't be one of them.'

Both men nodded in unison.

'Listen to yourself, you've lost the plot!' Barker shouted. He shook his head viciously.

'Some bitch killed my brother because of what I did to her tart mother and her pathetic father years ago, they were nothing, less than nothing, I don't buy it,' Barker insisted.

'Jack, this woman killed your brother, she killed Lucy, and now she has Beatrice,' Palmer pressed.

'So, what is Roman Kobec, a figment of my imagination?'

'Yes, Kobec moved against you, Jack, after you eliminated his entire goddammed family, his children, for Christ's sake, but he had nothing to do with Billy.'

The men stood motionless, staring at each other.

'I don't know, Frank,' Jack imparted. 'Maybe you believe this bollocks that Judy Grace's daughter turned into some kind of psycho vigilante assassin.'

'We destroyed her family, Jack, in the worst way imaginable. She set out to destroy us. It's not a big leap of the imagination. You can't believe it because what, she's beneath you? Well, I think Billy would disagree with you, Jack,' Palmer barked.

Barker's head moved forward in a fluid, well-practiced motion. It struck Palmer before he had time to react and sent him reeling backward, blood spurting from a cut on his forehead.

'Don't you talk about my brother!' Barker raged, moving forward, and laying a boot into Palmer's side. Several men came from the shadows of the warehouse, but Barker quickly motioned for them to stay back. Palmer rolled onto his stomach and lifted himself onto his knees. The gangster stood next to him, looking down with fire in his eyes. Palmer swung up with his right fist and connected with Barker's ribs. The gangster cried out, more in surprise than pain. Palmer swept his leg around and took Barker's legs out from under him. He slammed down heavily on his back. Before Palmer could strike again, two men pulled his arms painfully backward. Barker sat up and reached around to rub his back. He looked up at Palmer and pursed his lips.

'Well, Frankie, still got a little of the old fire left in you after all,' he mocked. He took the hand that was extended to help him up.

'Leave him,' he ordered as he stood. The men obeyed instantly. As soon as Palmer was released, Barker landed a straight right to his stomach. The detective fell to his knees. He fought to raise himself onto his feet again. The fight was gone from him. The two men stared into each other's eyes again.

'It's the truth, Jack. It doesn't matter what you think, it's the truth. You have no idea what Judy Grace put her daughter through, it would make a monster out of anyone. She has my daughter, Jack.'

Barker turned away and walked back to his desk. He lifted a bottle of scotch and poured himself a hefty drink. He downed it in one, refilled the glass, and then turned and walked back to where Palmer stood, bent over. He handed him the glass and said, 'Well then, let's go and kill the bitch.'

The floor of the hanger was clean and polished. A Cessna CJ4 filled half of the space. Behind the sleek jet, eight men stood before a portable command board, which displayed a series of maps, street plans, and photographs. The men had two things in common. They were all professional killers and they had all, at some time, served in Her Majesty's forces. Paine had decided to make use of freelance agents rather than serving personnel. It would give them at least a vestige of plausible deniability if it all went wrong. Commander Goodchild was the only operative in the room still officially employed by Her Majesty's government. He stood before the men, pointer in hand.

'We know that Kobec is using this building as his headquarters,' the pointer tapped to an aerial photograph. They were going old school; no electronic traces would be left. The A2 sized photograph was identical to the one that Jack Barker's team had used. It wasn't a coincidence.

'He also owns the properties adjacent to it here and here, and uses them too,' Goodchild continued his brief. 'We don't know what corner we'll find him in,' he advised. 'We'll have a thermal imaging drone on the target, it may give us a better location, but,' Goodchild paused, looking at the warriors before him, his wagging index finger raised, 'he is at war, his alert status is high, so be prepared for anything. This man is tough, we won't go down without a fight.'

The men all nodded. Fighting was their trade. It was not something they feared. The eight mercenaries would form two kill teams, which would be supported by a backup team and air surveillance. This was a vital operation. When the briefing was over, the men headed to the rear of the hanger. An array of weapons and equipment had been placed on the long work bench that was fitted along the rear wall. The men went through the process of selecting weapons and equipment. They would use compact, silenced weapons that were easily concealed and would allow them to launch an attack anywhere, at any time. Three identical black Range Rovers were parked beside the tables. Their drivers sat patiently, waiting for the men to complete their preparations, the last part of which was a check of their communications. They had been assigned call signs, they carried out a final check of their equipment and climbed into the waiting SUVs.

Goodchild took a nervous glance around him and headed for the lead vehicle. He had tried unsuccessfully to contact Kobec. His messages had gone unanswered. It meant only one thing. The Russian had guessed that they would come after him, which in turn meant that he would be expecting them. A wounded tiger was a perilous animal to hunt, especially when it could see you coming in the jungle. Kobec was overexposed, albeit through no fault of his own. Goodchild knew that he had made an irreparable mistake, a mistake Roman Kobec would have to pay for with his life.

The instructions that the mechanical voice had given Palmer had been clear. He and Barker were to go alone to St Mary's underground station in East London. The long-abandoned District Line station had been in disuse since the thirtieth of April 1938. It was situated on Whitechapel Road between Whitechapel and Aldgate. During the Blitz, the disused station had been converted into a bomb shelter, until the above ground station building had been destroyed during a Luftwaffe raid. Since then, the station had remained as a time capsule, used from time to time by London Underground as a storage facility. The lines passing through the station were still operated occasionally, to transfer rolling stock between the District and the Metropolitan lines. The station's decay below ground had been surprisingly slow.

The only direct entrance to the station from ground level was via its redundant emergency staircase. These stairs could be accessed through the yard of the adjacent hotel. They had had little time to prepare or to conduct any reconnaissance of the site. Norris Jones had sent one man ahead to investigate the hidden entrance. He had found that construction works were being undertaken in the yard area. It had been hoarded off, with temporary timber boarding. It appeared that the building works had been suspended. A makeshift access had been included in the hoarding. The operative had quickly breached the poorly secured entrance and had located the door leading to the redundant station. He had reported back to Jones.

The big Welshman had been unhappy with the situation. He had implored Barker to rethink going into the abandoned space with Palmer. The gangster had listened. He was not convinced that Palmer was being on the level, but his instinct told him that he was. Barker felt compelled to follow through.

He had armed himself with a Glock 19 and had given instructions for a select team of men to follow behind them into the station after he and Palmer had entered. Jack drove the BMW X5, with the detective sat opposite him. His mood was light. It unnerved Palmer. As they wound their way west the gangster reminisced about past days. Better days. He talked about his brother, Billy. About others that had passed at one time or another.

'There are more ghosts in my life than people,' Barker mused.

They left turned onto the Whitechapel Road and found parking opposite the hotel as Norris had suggested. Palmer's heart thundered in his chest. He felt unsteady. Barker looked across at the detective and sniggered.

'Come on Frankie boy, your bottle gone?' he teased. 'This is your show mate, so let's do this.' Once out of the SUV, Palmer felt better. He thought of his daughter's voice pleading for him to help. Anger overtook all other emotions. Both men looked south across the busy road. There was no sign that an underground station had ever existed there. Directly across from them was fifty feet of blue painted hoarding strewn with brightly coloured graffiti. There was a hotel to the right of the temporary timber wall, and a decaying Victorian building to the left.

They crossed the busy street, accessed the yard and followed the directions that Norris had provided. They found the steel door standing ajar, as the Welshman had advised. Behind it the redundant stairs led downward.

'Boss, Frank Palmer and Jack Barker just left the warehouse together, alone,' Kopjov said into the phone. He pronounced Palmer as Pulemar and Barker as Bulkar.

Kobec was doubtful. It had to be a trap or a decoy.

'Are you sure it was them, Andrzej?' he questioned.

'It was them, boss,' the assassin confirmed. 'I am following them now, Danius is watching the warehouse,' he added before his boss could ask.

'Okay,' Kobec replied. 'Follow them, but keep your eyes open, remember these are snakes.'

Kobec ended the call. He was certain that they were being baited. A few minutes later Kobec's phone rang again. He was smiling when he finished the brief conversation. He called Kopjov.

'Keep with Barker,' he ordered. 'I am on my way to meet you. Do nothing until I arrive,' he added.

'But how do you know where we are going?' Kopjov asked, confused.

'I know, it is not important how. I will meet you there,' Kobec replied cryptically. 'Valek!' he called.

His aide arrived within seconds. He barked orders. Kobec had bought a man in Barker's organisation. It had cost him, but the investment may have just proved worth it. Barker had apparently discovered who had been responsible for his brother's murder. He and Palmer were now on their way to a potential showdown with the killer. It presented an opportunity for Kobec to deal with him.

'Romeo one, Romeo one, alpha four, target is exiting the building at location echo one. It looks like target is on the move, repeat, target on the move.'

'Roger, alpha four. Alpha team, prepare to move out. Keep your distance. Bravo team, hold your positions, over.'

'Romeo two, Romeo two, Romeo one, require airborne at location echo one. Target is on the move, over.'

'Roger, Romeo one. Romeo two, airborne is en route.'

'Alpha four, Romeo one, status, over.'

'Romeo one, alpha four, target is in black Mercedes GLK registration bravo, delta, six, zero, sierra, tango, delta, followed by a second unit, Mercedes S320 black, registration bravo, delta, one, zero, golf, foxtrot, alpha. Confirm target plus two subjects in lead vehicle, three subjects in second vehicle, over.'

'Roger alpha four, Romeo one has eyes on the target and is mobile. Alpha team, follow, over.'

Goodchild felt a familiar rush. The hunt was on. His phone rang, unknown number. The call surprised him. He had no idea what was going on. Jack Barker was likewise on the move.

'Like old times, hey, Frankie,' Barker joked. 'Remember the time we turned over that Paki shop near the green and that old cunt came at us in the dark,' he laughed harder. 'You nearly shat yourself,' the gangster recalled. He peered over the worn wooden balustrade into the darkness below. Palmer was anxious.

'Come on then Frank, let's go hunting,' Barker called, clearly enjoying the thrill of the moment.

Palmer's heart pounded in his chest as they made their way down the decaying brick lined stairs. The first flight was short. It led to a larger landing from which the stairs continued further down into the dim light. Exposed bulbs hung from corroded wires, casting shadows on the walls. The ancient electrics hummed a dull tune. They reached the bottom of the stairs without incident and emerged into a derelict ticket hall scattered with debris from collapsed sections of the vaulted roof above. A worn wooden sign read "Booking Office". Adjacent, another sign showed the direction to the trains. The followed that direction along a tube-like passage with tiled walls. They arrived at a junction. To the left a passage led to the old eastbound platform; to the right another led to the westbound platform. Rusted old signs showed the way.

'Which way then, Frankie, eastbound or westbound, I fancy a bit of the West End,' Barker joked.

Palmer didn't answer. He wished that Barker would be silent.

'Eastbound,' Palmer finally whispered. 'They said eastbound.' It made sense. The westbound platform appeared to be in total darkness.

Sensing Palmer's fear, Barker called out, 'Hello?' His voice echoed through the station.

'Jack, for Christ's sake!' Palmer pleaded.

Barker laughed and said mockingly, 'You insisted I join you for this party, Frankie.' The dim light cast a shadow across Barker's smiling face and Palmer could see it clearly. Madness. Complete madness. Above them Norris Jones led a team of Barker's men into the entrance chamber. They moved quickly and silently.

'I don't know what's going on, boss,' Andrej Kopjov said truthfully. 'Palmer and Barker went into the building site, four of Barker's men followed after them. They're armed, it looks as if they're expecting trouble,' Kopjov explained. Then he added, 'I don't know what this place is, it looks like nothing.' The assassin was stopped adjacent to the forecourt of a service station. He had a clear line of sight to the wooden hoarding through which Barker and his men had disappeared. To the left was a hotel, to the right was an Islamic book shop. A little way along the road he could see the minarets of a mosque. His view was sporadically interrupted by red buses and other passing traffic, but his eyes remained fixed on the door.

'I'll be there soon. Wait for me,' Kobec instructed again.

'Alpha team from Romeo one, target is stopping. Keep back and await orders. Let's see where they're headed, over.' Four men reacted as one.

'What do you think, guv?' Mullins asked.

'I knew that Palmer was up to his neck in this,' Dunne replied. 'We need to call for backup. Call it in, we need SO19,' Dunne ordered.

'Dylan, come with me. Let's go and look,' the senior officer instructed, glancing at Mullins anxiously. Porter nodded.

'Get us that backup,' he pressed.

They had followed Palmer and Barker from the warehouse across the East End and onto Whitechapel Road. Another black SUV had stealthily followed behind Barker's X5. The destination appeared to be a nondescript building site along the Whitechapel Road. They had watched as Barker and Palmer had made their way across the busy road and had disappeared through what appeared to be a door in the poster and graffiti covered timber hoarding. They had been followed a short while later by a team of Barker's men, who had exited the shadowing SUV. Neither party had detected the unremarkable white Polo. It had a single occupant who was now stopped at the service station and observing the target address.

The two officers crossed the street quickly. DI Mullins and the unknown observer monitored their movements. The officers stepped through the unsecured door into the cluttered courtyard. To their left a short makeshift passage led to a single rusted metal door that stood partly ajar. They were exposed. If anyone stepped back out of the doorway they would be seen immediately. Despite the risk, they approached the entrance. Dunne looked through the gap into the murky entrance chamber.

'What is it?' Porter asked.

'No idea,' Dunne replied. 'There's only one way to find out.'

Porter was hesitant, but he knew there was no turning back.

'Should we wait for backup, guv?' he asked weakly, trying not to sound as afraid as he felt.

Dunne thought for a minute. Something was about to happen; he was sure of it. They did not have time to wait.

'No,' he replied. Porter nodded. He had tried.

Dunne went through the door first, and the junior detective followed closely behind. Despite the dust and debris, they both recognised the unmistakable architecture of an underground station.

'It looks like part of an underground station,' Dunne whispered.

'There are no stations near here,' Porter replied in a low voice.

'Not now there aren't,' the senior detective responded, quietly. 'But there used to be. I think this is part of the old station that was bombed out during the war.'

Porter frowned. It was long before his time. He looked down over the railing. Nothing was visible, but they could clearly make out the fresh prints in the thick dust. The place reeked of danger. The officers began the descent, stepping carefully down the time-worn stairs. The sound of pigeons, disturbed from their roosts, echoed from below. They were less that fifty metres from a major thoroughfare but headed into the abyss.

'What has happened?' Kobec asked, once in the passenger seat of Kopjov's nondescript car. Valek climbed into the back seat.

'First Palmer and Barker go in, boss, through that door in the wood fence,' the Russian pointed across the busy road to blue hoarded construction site opposite.

'Then four of Barker's men go after, now two more men,' Kopjov explained. 'Policemen I think.'

From where the car was parked, they still had a clear view. Kobec's contact had told him that Barker was heading for a disused underground station. It did not look like the entrance to an underground station.

'It could be an opportunity, boss, we have the element of surprise,' Kopjov urged.

'What if it is a trap?' the pragmatic Valek asked.

Kopjov shook his head.

'No, this is something else, not a trap,' Kobec replied. 'Let's go, and keep sharp, boys.'

'Boss, I do not think you should risk yourself, it is not necessary,' Kopjov protested with genuine concern. Kobec smiled at his loyal assassin.

'This is for me to decide, Andrzej,' he responded. 'And besides,' he added, 'I have you with me, what can go wrong?' He patted the man's rock-hard shoulder.

'It will be my hand that finishes Jack Barker,' Kobec added.

Andrzej smirked. Today he would be at his best. He did not like the fact that they had no clear idea what they were walking into. His senses were already heightened.

'Alpha one, alpha three, targets are on foot, do we follow? Over.'

Goodchild thought for a minute. It could be Kobec luring them into a trap. Either way, he was satisfied that he had a superior team. Trap or not, they would finish this now.

'Alpha team, alpha one, converge on my position, over.'

Goodchild was on foot and making his way along the busy walkway past the hotel, toward the makeshift entrance that several men had now passed through.

It was not known what had attracted them to this place, but it appeared certain that a showdown was about to take place between Jack Barker and Roman Kobec. They would be there to mop up, to ensure that neither man escaped. Like the men that had gone through the entrance before them, they soon discovered the station access. The tech support officer seated in a windowless room at GCHQ head office, quickly assessed the location and provided the team with a summary of the below ground structure. As they descended into the bowels of the station, Goodchild, instructed, 'Weapons free.'

CHAPTER NINETEEN
The End Game

Mullins was anxious. She had noticed the man sitting alone in the vehicle. She had watched as two men had arrived and had gotten into the car shortly after Dunne and Porter had stepped through the temporary barrier. The men had tried and failed to appear inconspicuous. Mullins had recognised one of the men as Roman Kobec.

'Bugger,' she cursed out loud as Kobec and two men exited the car. As they crossed the street, they were joined by three more men, who had appeared seemingly from nowhere. Their meagre efforts did little to conceal the fact that they were heavily armed. They quickly disappeared through the hoarded entrance, as her colleagues had.

Mullins dialled Dunne's number. It went to voicemail. They needed their backup. The detective inspector watched in complete astonishment as another group of men appeared from two different directions and congregated on the pavement directly in front of the timber hoarding. There were five in all. The men were clothed in black-clad fatigues. They had an obvious military appearance. Even at a distance they had the unmistakable bearing of hunters tracking prey. They spoke hurriedly before, one by one, they vanished.

'XX Four, this is XX Two hundred, please confirm ETA of backup to Whitechapel Road,' Mullins called into the radio in her hand.

'XX Two hundred they are en route, ETA five minutes,' the responder advised.

Far below, Palmer and Jack Barker inched their way along the derelict platform. The roof above was held on heavy evenly spaced steel pillars which supported thick riveted steel beams. The platform was strewn with debris and covered in a thick layer of dust which had accumulated over decades. The structure vibrated with the movement of trains passing through nearby tunnels. Barker had drawn his weapon and held the Glock in his hand.

A scream startled them.

'Daddy!' echoed through the old station. Ahead, about thirty yards into the disused tunnel, they saw a light.

'You should have taken me up on the offer of a gun,' Barker mocked wryly. Palmer said nothing.

They reached the end of the platform and walked down the narrow ramp, which led onto the disused tracks. They could make out a light emanating from a brick lined doorway. Ahead, the tracks curved left. They moved slowly toward the light. As they moved, Barker glanced back the way they had come. He caught sight of Norris Jones' head peering from the passageway that led onto the platform. He felt emboldened knowing that his men were behind him. Adrenaline coursed through his veins. He felt alive. Palmer had activated the torch on the smart phone.

They stepped carefully along the tunnel, until they came to the arch which the light was emanating from. It led into a short access passage, at the end of which a heavy steel door, which normally kept the passage sealed from the tracks, stood ajar.

Barker turned again to look toward the platform, then stepped into the passage and through the open door. The door accessed an archaic maintenance storage space. The room was narrow but ran to where the single bulb allowed them to see. Palmer lifted his phone and shone the torch beam along the row of disused steel racks. As he did, the heavy door slammed shut behind him. Barker sprang backward and threw himself against it. The door did not budge. They only had one way left to go. They moved deeper into the room. Isolated from his men, the gangster had an unfamiliar feeling. Apprehension.

Dunne and Porter reached the bottom of stairs and cautiously stepped into the dimly narrow passage leading to the platform. At the junction where the passage separated, Porter asked in a whisper, 'Which way, guv?'

Dunne pointed to the right. The area to the left was dark. There were clear prints in the dust leading to the eastbound platform.

Jones peered along the tracks into the darkness. He did not want to use his torch. He heard a sound behind him, whispering voices echoing off walls. He looked backward. The man closest to him moved and signalled silently that there was someone coming up behind them.

Jones made a sweeping gesture, indicating for his men to get off the platform. With fluid movement they dropped over the platform edge onto the tracks. Jones backed down the ramp and into the darkness of the tunnel and pushed himself tight up against the tunnel wall, his assault rifle aimed toward the platform.

Dunne and Porter heard the slamming door. They froze and listened and then they heard more noise, coming from the stairs above them. It was hopefully their backup. They stepped quietly along the passage leading to the platform.

On the landing above them Andrzej Kopjov cursed under his breath. Anyone below would have heard the sound as he stumbled on the steps. He waited, listening for any signs of people below. He could see the base of the stairs. There was no movement.

Jones saw DS Dunne step from the passage and onto the platform. He recognised him and the man who followed closely behind. Filth. What was this, a set up? He waited, expecting to see more officers emerge from the passage, but none did.

Dunne and Porter walked a short way along the platform and then stood looking from side to side. Porter looked down at the thick layer of dust covering the platform surface, trying to decipher the recently made marks in the thick layer of dust.

'I don't like this, guv,' Porter whispered. Dunne nodded slowly. The senior officer had the sudden realisation that they had made a grave error not waiting for their support.

Kopjov pushed his back against the wall and crouched down. Keeping his position, he edged his way along the passage. When he reached the end, he signalled for the rest to follow. They quickly and silently lined up along the wall beside him, Roman Kobec among them. Above them on the stairs, the mercenary unit led by James Goodchild descended slowly.

The Russian extended a thin telescopic tube with a small camera fixed to its end. He looked at the screen in his hand as he guided the camera. The equipment was designed to operate in poor light. He could make out the two policemen standing motionless on the platform. There was no sign of Barker or his men. He assumed that they had moved along the tunnel. It seemed the most obvious direction. Then his trained eyes noticed the marks in the thick dust on the platform floor. He quickly assessed the situation. Barker's men had been on the platform, had heard the policemen arriving, and had dropped down onto the tracks. They had not all made it as far as the tunnel.

DS Dunne had drawn the same conclusion. His blood froze as he realised, that they were standing in the open. Barker's men were only feet away on the tracks. Someone had come down the stairs behind them. He touched Porter's arm and signalled to the tracks. Porter frowned but quickly realised what the senior office was trying to convey. They began to retreat, slowly, back the way they had come.

Kopjov watched them. He had to decide. There was only one option. He spoke hurriedly, his message communicated to the earpieces of the men next to him. He removed a grenade from his battle jacket and pulled the pin. Those beside him braced themselves, preparing for action. Kopjov nodded and turned to face the platform. With a trained motion he flung the grenade onto the abandoned tracks.

Barker edged forward ahead of Palmer. He was not afraid, just angry. He didn't like games. He had no time for games. If some bitch wanted to mess with him, he was up for it. They reached the back of the store and noticed a doorway door leading to an adjacent room. Barker looked back at Palmer, raised his pistol and moved into the room. The smell of damp and disuse was suffocating. Rusting shelves filled with decaying tins of unknown substances lined the walls. Rotting wooden cable drums crowded one corner. The smell of rat infestation was distinctive and overwhelming. A single unprotected bulb hung from an old cable casting shadows on the brick walls. Barker looked around. Except for scurrying rats, the room appeared deserted. It wasn't.

Palmer was behind the gangster as they entered the second room. He was startled by a sudden loud hiss. Without warning, Barker fell to the ground. He lay unmoving. Palmer was monetarily paralysed by the shock. His eyes searched the shadows. He focused on a silhouette in the darkness. The figure hesitated for a moment, then stepped into the dim light just as the blast wave from Kopjov's grenade caused fragments of brick and plaster to rain down from the frail roof and sent decaying shelves crashing onto the damp floor. The tremor added to the detective's alarm.

'Hello, Frank,' the assailant greeted, seemingly undeterred by the surrounding chaos. She spoke in an unnaturally deep voice. Her eyes appeared sunken and hollow in a face that Palmer was seeing for the first time devoid of make-up. Her hair was tied back tightly. It made her face appear harsher. She was dressed in black leather riding suit. Though it was undoubtedly the woman whose bed he had been sharing, her posture and gait were different. She appeared taller, more masculine.

Palmer was stunned. His mind fought to make sense of the situation. He had to abandon rationality and reason.

'Tara, I, I don't understand,' was all that he managed to stutter.

'Oh, it's not so difficult to grasp, Frank,' the psychologist replied. 'Just take a minute to think.'

He didn't need any more time. It was obvious who Tara Moore was. It was obvious that she had played him. He exhaled a defeated laugh. She had been there all along. She had been in control.

'Anne Grace, I presume,' Palmer stated, his voice stronger.

'My, my, you really are a hopeless detective,' the woman responded in a mocking voice, stepping further into the light.

'I am *David*, Inspector.'

Palmer shook his head and laughed disconsolately.

'All of this, all of those people, you killed them, children, you did those things to children,' Palmer spat. His eyes bored into her. 'You think you change your voice, use a different name and you're a different person,' Palmer probed incredulously. 'It is you who did those things, Tara.' His anger was growing.

'Oh, come now, Frank,' Anne Grace said. 'Let's not pretend that you have a heart.' His mind had cleared enough that the reason for his excursion into the abandoned section of the underground, struck him.

'Where is my daughter,' he snarled.

Norris Jones saw the object thrown onto the tracks. He knew immediately what it was and called, 'Get off the tracks now!' His men obeyed immediately and sprung onto the platform. One man reacted a second too late. Fragments of steel tore into his body as he attempted to pull himself onto the platform. The blast rocked the station. Large chunks of plaster and loose brickwork rained down from the roof.

The two detectives had been taken by surprise. They unwittingly shielded Barker's men as Kopjov and his team emerged from the passage onto the platform. Their weapons spraying hot, copper-jacketed projectiles. Jones raised his weapon and fired. He hit Andrzej Kopjov with his first round. The big Russian tumbled backward.

Kobec and his remaining men had their attention fully focused on Barker's backup team on the platform. They had left their six o'clock position exposed. Goodchild ordered his men into the fray. They picked off two of Kobec's crew instantly. To avoid the attack, the Russian darted from the passage and threw himself onto the tracks below, joining Barker's wounded soldier who still lay writhing in agony.

Jones thought quickly, assessing the situation. He had recognised Kopjov as he and two others had burst onto the platform firing. The two detectives had been cut down in the crossfire. Soon after, someone had attacked the Russians from their rear. A firefight was ensuing with his remaining men, the Russians and an unknown force fighting a pitched battle. The air had filled with a think dust that limited visibility in the dim light. Jones had noted a second passage along the platform, which joined the east and westbound platforms. Staying in the shadows, close to the wall, he edged quickly onto the platform and found the tube-like passageway linking the platforms. He had been trained to fight in pitch blackness, but he turned on the torch fixed to his HK416. Time was limited if he was to save any of his men. He moved quickly through the tunnel and found the westbound platform in total darkness. He doubled back, levelling his weapon. He was soon at the main access to the platform. He headed into the passage. At the junction he could either head to the ticket office or the eastbound platform. He moved stealthily along the route marked to the rains. The pedestrian tunnel curved to the left. As he rounded the corner, he saw three heavily armed men crouching at the end on the passage and firing their weapons. Two more operatives were on their haunches leaning with their backs against the tiled wall of the passage. Jones recognised one of the men. They had served together in Iraq. The recognition came too late. His finger had already squeezed the trigger of his weapon.

'You've never had a heart, the only person that you ever cared for is Frank Palmer,' Anne Grace said to the stupefied detective.

'Look, Tara,' Palmer responded. 'We can sort this out, what could I do, your father, he…' Anne Grace exploded. Her face contorted as she screeched.

'My father, what Detective, loved me, was a good man, was an innocent man.' Her eyes burnt. 'You knew he was innocent Frank; you knew he never touched her, never touched Anne, you knew what they were doing to him, but even when he begged, you did nothing.'

Palmer looked at the woman standing in front of him. It was as if he was seeing her for the very first time. She was frightening in the way only pure evil can be. He could tell that she was fighting for self-control. She breathed in deeply and steadied herself.

'Do you know what they did to him, Frank, that slut told Anne, told her everything, every detail about you and Jack, what you did to him.' Her control was wavering. 'They said he abused her, his own daughter, so they took everything from him, they tortured him, and they killed him, Frank.' Her words echoed in the cavernous room, interspersed with the sounds of the gun battle raging in the station.

'Look, I'm sorry for what happened,' Palmer apologised. 'But it's got nothing to do with my daughter. Now, where is she?' His voice was desperate.

'Sweet little Beatrice, she's a nice girl, she deserved better than you; what kind of a father are you, Frank, you're pathetic,' Anne provoked him.

'I'll do anything, anything,' Palmer entreated.

'You can't do anything, Detective, you can't give her, her life back, the one you stole.'

'It was a long time ago. It was a mistake, I know,' Palmer pleaded desperately.

'A mistake, oh, Frank, why didn't you just say that in the first place,' Anne Grace mocked. 'That makes everything okay then, it was just a mistake.' She laughed loudly. It was a haunting, insane cackle.

Palmer noticed the gun in her hand. It had been concealed behind her back, but now it hung at her side. The shape of the silencer on the end was distinct. The detective guessed correctly that it was the weapon that had been used in the previous murders. She walked forward and Palmer backed away. When she reached Barker, she leaned down and picked up his Glock.

'It's taken me a long time to get here, Frank,' she stated flatly, as she stood and pushed Barker's weapon into her jacket. 'A long time indeed,' she mused. 'This is what her life became, Detective, hate and death.' She smiled, her eyes still fixed on Palmer.

'You destroyed her, Frank, you destroyed her father, her family, and this is all that was left.' She spread her arms wide. 'Me and her vengeance.'

'Tara, Anne, please…' Palmer pleaded.

'I am David!' she roared. Looking into her eyes the detective could see that the woman was possessed by another personality. On the filthy floor, Jack Barker began to stir. He tried to push himself but his hand slipped on the greasy surface and he fell forward. Anne Grace laughed. Barker lifted himself into a seated position, turned and looked up at the woman.

'This must be the little bitch?' he asked rhetorically. The woman scowled, then smiled.

'The great and powerful Jack,' she said theatrically. 'Lord of all London.' Barker looked around assessing his surroundings. Then he looked down at the floor.

'Looks like you were right after all, Frankie,' the gangster voiced calmly. Then he turned his head and faced the woman again.

'Little Annie, the fruit of the loins of that pathetic loser Peter Grace,' he laughed. 'Your father was nonce, a fucking wrong'un, I saved you from him you ungrateful little tart,' the villain spat. That was his version of reality. He pushed down and lifted himself onto his unsteady legs.

'Jack, she has my daughter,' Palmer interjected weakly.

'Her,' Barker replied pointing to Anne Grace. 'Don't worry Frank, I'm going to…' The sentence went unfinished.

Anne Grace raised the weapon and, without warning, pulled the trigger. A dull pop sounded in the room. Then another. That was all that it took to dispatch the mighty Jack Barker.

The man who many had seen as invincible, larger than life. The man feared by all who knew him, was gone in an instant. Palmer gasped. For a split second he thought of jumping forward and tackling the insane woman, but he stayed frozen in place. Sounds of gunfire echoed around the room. There was a war raging in the old station.

Anne ignored the melee. Her focus was entirely fixed on her prey. She had waited for so long for this day.

'Do you want to see your daughter, Frank?' she asked, looking up from the lifeless body of Jack Barker. A faint smile still played on her lips. Palmer nodded slowly. She turned in an easy, leisurely way walked back into the shadows. She returned, dragging something behind her. Something alive that writhed as it was being pulled.

Oh, please, God, no, Palmer thought as his daughter was pulled into the light. Her hands were bound behind her back. Her mouth had been taped shut. She was drenched. The smell of gasoline fumes quickly filled the room. Palmer took a step toward his daughter. Anne raised the gun in her hand.

'Stay put, Frank, or this'll end sooner than you want it to,' she warned, grinning.

'You see, what Jack did to my family,' she voiced calmly. 'That was his nature, he was an animal.' Her eyes shone with hatred. 'What you did was worse,' she appended, looking down at the terrified Beatrice.

'It was worse because you were meant to be there to stop things like that from happening, instead, you aided in their lies and dishonesty,' the incensed woman explained. 'You were corrupt, a dirty cop, rotten to the core, Frank, you have the stench of decay all about you.'

'I'm begging you, please don't do this, please,' Palmer implored. His eyes were fixed on his daughter. She looked up at him, her silent eyes begging for him to help her.

'This is what my father felt like,' Anne taunted. 'He needed help, he begged you.'

'Please, please,' was all Palmer could utter. The gun unexpectedly landed at his feet in the dirt.

'You have a choice now Frank,' his tormentor explained. 'There is one round left in that gun.' Palmer stared at the weapon on the filthy floor. 'You can use it to try to kill me, or you can use it to end your daughter's suffering, you decide.'

With that, she struck the flint on the brass Zippo lighter and dropped it.

The screams of wounded men were amplified the confined space. The air was thick with the acrid remnants of burnt gunpower and dust. Norris Jones walked cautiously along the passage and back onto the platform, stepping over the bodies of the men that he had slain. He was the only one to have survived unscathed. He stood on the platform edge and stared down at the tracks. Roman Kobec looked back at him from where he lay on the tracks. He managed a weak smile. The spirit was strong, but the body was no longer capable. The ex-SAS man raised his weapon and pulled the trigger. Toward the end of the platform Andrzej Kopjov was crawling toward the darkness of the tunnel. A section of his skull was missing. He was already dead, his body just refused to accept it. Jones heard loud voices echoing from the stairs above. He was in no mood for any more confrontations. He looked around again, then headed down the platform and into the darkness. In the distance he could hear a tube train punching air through the tunnels.

Flames engulfed his daughter as Palmer stared in horror. She was unable to scream, but her eyes remained fixed on her father as she thrashed around on the floor, trying to extinguish the fire. Palmer looked frantically around for something to douse the flames. He stripped off his jacket and tried in vain to extinguish the flames. There was nothing he could do. It was too late to save his daughter.

Though his hands were burnt, he reached down and picked up the gun. Through the smoke he saw the smiling face of Anne Grace. He knew that he had no choice. He raised the weapon and fired a single shot. His daughter went still. He stayed there looking down at her. The rancid smell of her burning flesh overwhelmed his senses as tears filled his eyes. Fury rose inside him. He looked up, but he was alone. The criminal profiler, the insane homicidal maniac, Tara, Anne, David, was gone.

CHAPTER TWENTY
Tears for the Living

When the first armed officers arrived on the scene it resembled a battle zone. The bodies of dead and dying men littered the old station. Only one man was taken to the surface alive. He died in the ambulance en route to the Royal London Hospital, only minutes away. As the investigation team spread out, they discovered the bodies of Jack Barker and the charred remains of an unknown female in a disused storeroom a short way along the eastbound tunnel.

The British Transport Police, meanwhile, were dealing with an incident at nearby bank station. A man had staggered from the tunnel of the eastbound platform. He was disorientated and covered in dirt and grime. His hands were burnt. His grime covered face was tracked with the lines of tears. He struggled incoherently with the two uniformed officers as they tried to question him and eventually took him into custody.

'Are you sure you don't want a drink, Frank?' Detective Chief Superintendent Sloane asked.

Palmer shook his head.

'Right, so then let's start at the beginning again. Let's go over this case, the Grace case, you say.' Palmer nodded vigorously.

'Look, why are you asking me this all again, I've told you, pick up Tara Moore, she's the killer, she's responsible.'

'Yes, we've spoken to Doctor Moore, Frank, and we'll speak to her again. But for now, let's go over this again.'

'What do you think happened?' Jane Fletcher asked DCI Young. Young shook his head.

'I don't know, ma'am, but it's a bloody mess. It's going to leave us all covered in the proverbial you know what,' he replied.

Jane Fletcher was aware of what the repercussions of this disaster were going to be. She had little doubt that it would cost her, her job, or at best a considerable demotion. Most of the blood was shed on her manor, even in her own station.

'Personally,' Young added, 'I think Palmer was working with Kobec all along, in the end, he tried to set Barker up so that Kobec could take him out.' He had a satisfied smirk on his face and added, 'You know they found fifty thousand pounds in cash in his house, and his prints were on the gun that killed Barker.'

'How did Palmer's daughter become involved?' Fletcher asked.

The DCI had given the question some thought. The conceited man was certain that he had the answer.

'I think Barker knew that Palmer was going to set him up and took out some insurance,' he offered. 'They argued, things got out of hand, Barker killed the daughter, they fought, Palmer shot him, then he made his way along the tunnels.'

Fletcher nodded. It was certainly plausible.

'I think that Frank Palmer helped to create a situation that they simply could not contain,' Young suggested. The senior officer nodded.

'We need to consolidate our position here, try to limit the damage and get things back to normal as soon as possible,' Superintendent Fletcher responded.

'It's a mess, sir. The Yard knows that one of ours was involved, they just don't know in what capacity,' Paine explained.

'Well, right now we need to carry out damage limitation. I'll go and speak to the commissioner personally. I think that it'll be in everyone's best interest to put this whole matter to bed as soon as possible,' John Gelding responded.

'So Frank, one more time. You're telling us that Roman Kobec had nothing to do with the earlier killings?'

Palmer nodded. Dark rings had formed beneath his eyes. His skin was ashen.

'It was actually Tara Moore who was responsible for the Barker and the Morton murders?' the interviewer asked disbelievingly.

'And the Breen murders,' Palmer added.

'Yes, sorry, and the Breen murders, and she killed all of those people because she thinks you stitched up her father fifteen years ago.'

Palmer nodded again. He had little energy left for confrontation.

'Okay, Frank, that will be all for now. We're going to carry out a few inquiries and then we'll speak again.'

Palmer's head fell into his bandaged hands.

The two officers watching the interview through the one way mirror stepped from the small viewing room and into the corridor.

'What do you think?' Sloane asked the police psychologist who had carried out the interview with him as he stepped out of the room.

'I think he's delusional, maybe clinically so, but we'll need more time.'

Sloane nodded.

'Well, he's being charged and remanded in custody, we'll have time to get to the bottom of this.'

Word had spread like wildfire that Detective Chief Inspector Frank Palmer would be arriving on the wing. A hundred eyes peered out from the barred windows, watching the pathway that led from the reception block to the remand wing. When they saw the officers making their way along the walkway, with half a dozen new arrivals, the waiting inmates called out. Their threats and curses echoed across the prison wing.

Palmer ignored them. He looked up at the windows without acknowledging the occupants looking down at him. The small group waited for the lead officer to find a key to fit the gate that led into the remand wing's yard. They passed through the gate into the fenced area, then waited for the screw to find the key to fit the gate leading onto the wing. The officer stood aside and allowed the men to file past before slamming the heavy gate shut.

At the small, guarded cage at the entrance, called the box, the prisoners waited for their papers to be processed. Palmer had wisely chosen to be segregated from the main population. That meant being locked up in the segregation unit, the section of the prison occupied predominantly by sex offenders. Eyes bore into him as he stood waiting for the officer in the box to process his papers.

In his cell, he sat on the thin mattress and hung his head in his hands. His mind was a battlefield. As Frank Palmer became lost in his thoughts, Anne Grace was being offered a glass of chilled champagne. She accepted the drink from the stewardess, leaned back in her spacious first-class seat, and sipped the bubbly beverage. In a distant corner of her mind, David rested. She was sure that she would not hear from him again. He had been her protector. Her avenger. He would always be there if she ever needed him. Now it was time to put the pain behind her and to begin a new chapter. She was looking forward to arriving in Australia.

The sound was unmistakable. A key was turning in the lock. Palmer sat up in the darkness and heard the heavy metal thud as the lock was disengaged. The thick, blue metal door opened slowly. A figure stood silhouetted in the doorway. His voice was unmistakable.

'Chief Inspector Palmer, how pleasant to see you,' a cold voice said.

EPILOGUE

They had decided on a venue in the West End. There would be a lot of people around. Neither man was taking any chances. There had been a lot of blood spilled. Trust had become a rare commodity. Viktor Mihalik arrived first and took a seat at the rear of the restaurant. Jones arrived a short while after. It wasn't difficult for him to identify Mihalik. He walked across the restaurant as the Russian eyed him professionally, looking for any tell-tale signs of a concealed weapon. He stood as the big Welshman approached. There was an uneasy moment as the men came together. Jones finally stretched out his hand. 'Mr Mihalik,' he greeted. The men shook hands. They took a seat and a waiter approached to take their drink order. Jones ordered a lager and Mihalik a glass of red wine. It reflected the enormous cultural difference between the men.

'So,' Jones said. 'It's been quite a time lately.'

Mihalik nodded.

'Enough, I think,' he replied.

Their drinks arrived before they spoke again.

Jones took a long sip of his beer and looked at Viktor Mihalik.

'I think it's time we talked peace. I'm sure we can find a way of working together, a way that will benefit both of us.'

Mihalik smiled and nodded.

'That is precisely what I think, Mr Jones. I believe that if your Mr Barker and my Mr Kobec had met under better circumstances, they would have forged a good relationship. They were men with much in common.'

'Well, here's to them,' Jones said, raising his glass.

Across the city the message icon on Noel Latham's computer screen flashed. The email was from a contact in the Caribbean. It read:

One transfer traceable from account Grace Family Trust: Turks & Caicos to account Barclays Bank, London. Transfer 25 June 2019: £150,000.00 to account Tara Moore.

Latham read the message, smiled, and keyed delete.